The Forgotten One

Being the fourth part of
Lake of Dragons

E. Michael Mettille

TMR Books
PO Box 510886
Milwaukee, WI 53203
www.themikereynolds.com

All images provided provided by Deposit Photos

Cover Artwork – © 2022 L.J. Anderson of Mayhem Cover Creations – www.mayhemcovercreations

Published by TMR Books 12/1/2022

ISBN 978-0-9975571-6-9

DEDICATION

For Shelia…until the end of time.

CHAPTER 1
THE RESCUE

The fresh, mountain air was cool on Elbahor that night. It smelled like rain, but Glaadrian new the shower was far enough off to not be a hindrance. The old dwarf's knees weren't acting up at all. They would be giving him fits if a storm were imminent. Despite the overcast sky above blocking all the light of a full moon no one on the mountain could see that night, the grizzled dwarf soldier was confident he and his group would remain dry during their mission.

That overcast sky was a blessing. The mountaintop was nearly pitch outside of a small dome of flickering, orange torchlight occupied by two battle-hardened trogmortem and the object of Glaadrian's mission, a waif of a dwarf named Alenaat. Though his position offered no view of the tortured dwarf, he knew the latter was chained to the Sacred Pine, a custom that had ended when Maelich chopped the head off a giant and freed a city of dwarves from that monster's rule. Maomnosett Ahm had been a hard ruler, not a creature Glaadrian looked on with anything close to fondness. However, by all accounts he'd heard sneaking through the caves beneath Alhouim—he refused to call the city he loved Maomnosett regardless whose rump warmed the throne—Ott was a million times worse. At least Ahm had been relatively fair when not pushed to his limits. Ott was just a cruel, malicious tyrant. In his first act as king of his stolen city he reinstituted that horrid punishment for the crime of a loud mouth and a loose tongue.

Had adrenaline not been coursing wildly through Glaadrian's veins he may have taken a moment to reflect on how odd it was for him to be sitting in the dark and waiting to challenge a couple trogmortem for the life of a waste like Alenaat. It would be quite a trick to find any dwarf in the city with the slightest shred of love for the scruffy slacker. That was before the poor soul was chained to the most sacred spot on Mount Elbahor, the most sacred spot in all of Ouloos as far as the dwarves of Alhouim were concerned. Alenaat could have killed Glaadrian's own mother, and he would still save the oaf. He might kill him afterward, but he'd pull the young dwarf off that tree first. The thought sent Glaadrian's mind tumbling down another path he should have avoided while waiting in the dark in ambush, Bindaar.

Bindaar had been another waste. Most would suggest a more worthless dwarf had never existed. He was even worse than Alenaat. That was, until Ahm had strung him up to that tree. It changed him. They strung him up a useless waste of air, and he came down a dutiful dwarf ready to serve his city and friends. One tear managed to spill over Glaadrian's squinting eyelids. It was all he'd allow himself. He silently hoped Alenaat's time on the Sacred Pine would have a similar effect.

A chill breeze sent a shiver through Glaadrian as he sat there in darkness delving more deeply into bleak memories than he should have. He pulled his cloak tighter around his shoulders. The thing smelled like stale blood and rot. It was a blessing he couldn't see it in the darkness. Weeks of battle and days sneaking through the caverns beneath the city had it looking as bad as it smelled.

An out of place whistle that failed miserably at sounding like any sort of bird mercifully brought his mind back into the moment. Lentaak was in place. That whistle—which hadn't earned the slightest attention from either of the guards watching over Alenaat—meant the quietest dwarf in Alhouim was hiding right behind the Sacred Pine waiting to strike. Everyone was in place. Though he couldn't see any of them in the darkness, he knew Chialdaan the fair-haired monster who had earned the nickname grong's bane for his efforts at the battle at Fort Maomnosett crouched in the fairy weed across the trail from him, and Muljaak, a dark-haired brute of a dwarf who stood nearly as tall as a man, hid in the shrubs further up the trail. It was time.

Glaadrian gripped his axe tight, stood up, and casually strolled toward the dim glow of torchlight with a whistle in his cheek. It was a happy tune his father had taught him when he was much younger and far friendlier. The song got the attention of one of the trogmortem standing guard in the warm glow at the base of the Sacred Pine. The head that popped out from behind the tree to examine the sound looked like any of the vile beasts from across the Great Sea he'd ever seen—pointy ears, a big, swollen nose, a humongous mouth filled with more jagged fangs than could comfortably fit, and green eyes which seemed to glow from within—but Glaadrian recognized this one from descriptions he'd heard whispered while scouting for the mission. The scar beneath the beast's right eye gave him away. If the stories he'd heard were to be believed, the monster's size was only matched by his merciless cruelty in battle. That beast would wrestle anyone at any time to prove his might.

"Pray the gods you have business in this place, or I will decorate this mountaintop with your scattered limbs," Haram-Vi shouted while squinting and stretching his neck toward the darkness.

"Except your right leg," the other guard added as he stepped out into the light. "I'll be gnawing on that. I've got a thing for legs."

Glaadrian recognized this one too. He was Malek-Ta, smaller than Haram-Vi but equally brutal and cruel. The dwarf stopped whistling and chuckled through his response, "Ain't but two of you? Best be heading back to the city to get some friends. The bloody waste be littered with the battered bodies of your kin who fell to this axe in me hand."

"Is that so?" Malek-Ta growled

"Aye it is," Glaadrian growled right back. "Come on out and test if me words ain't the truest you ever heard. I'll be painting this trail with your vile blood."

"Step into the light then. Prove your boasts," Haram-Vi challenged.

"Afraid of the dark are ye?" Glaadrian shouted up the trail. As much as he liked to think of trogmortem as mindless beasts, he knew it wasn't true. They were wily, cunning, and smart, but they were also prideful and saw the likes of dwarves and men as being beneath them.

Haram-Vi took the bait first, jogging from the safety of the torchlight into the darkness. Malek-Ta followed closely behind, grunting, "Those are the last words that will ever leave your filthy, dwarf mouth."

Glaadrian had slowly been backing away as soon as he'd grabbed the attention of the two guards. Once they entered the blackness of the trail, he quickened his pace. He could faintly see the glow of their eyes in the darkness, that dim and eerie green, but he knew they couldn't see him at all. Their eyes were accustomed to the bright desert sun, useless on the dark trail.

"Coward," Haram-Vi called out as his pace quickened.

Glaadrian ceased his retreat, gripped his axe tighter, and replied, "Come on and test that claim then."

"It's a trap," Malek-Ta hollered a moment before Glaadrian heard the rock bounce off the trogmortem's head. Muljaak had delivered the first blow.

Dim silhouettes were all that Glaadrian could make out in the darkness, but the glorious sounds he heard assured him the massive dwarf was cutting the giant trogmortem down. A dwarf axe makes very distinct sounds whether it be slicing through still air, chopping meat, or severing bone. He heard all three of those as the larger of the two shapes fell toward the trail. Muljaak must have cut the beast down like a tree. It would take a thick bone to make a sound like that. Glaadrian grinned in the darkness as he heard Muljaak's axe connect over and over again. The dwarf must have moved on to the softer parts of the monster. The sounds of meat and guts slopping about and spilling onto the trail mingled with the trogmortem's cries sounding a symphony to Glaadrian's ears. If only he could see the macabre art his chum made on the trail that night. In the darkness, the sweet music of the dying trogmortem's cries and pleas for mercy would have to suffice as they remained unanswered. There would be no mercy and no forgiveness for the monsters who had stolen his city and killed so many of his kin.

"Thank the gods I blessed ye with a quick death, vermin," he heard Muljaak quietly sigh at the pile of slop he had made on the trail. "If I could, I'd be following your sorry soul to the Lake to be torturing ye until the end of time."

He had but a moment to chuckle at his good friend's proclamation before realizing he had allowed the excitement of battle and the adrenaline coursing through his veins to distract him from the plan. Muljaak had only felled one of the beasts on the trail with them, and Glaadrian had lost sight of the other. He saw the faint flicker of Haram-Vi's eyes a moment before the monster plowed into him.

Glaadrian's equilibrium fled the trail as he rolled end over end with the massive beast. By the time they settled, he was on top of the monster but had lost hold of his axe. Too much thought can be an enemy when locked in battle, so he gave the missing axe very little. He couldn't see his target in the darkness, but the first thing his right fist connected with was soft. It seemed too large to be a nose being bigger than his fist, but the splatter of blood the blow earned suggested it was the giant, bulbous thing that took up a good chunk of Haram-Vi's face. The sound the creature made in that instant gave Glaadrian the faintest glimmer of hope he might best the beast with fists alone. The first blow he delivered with his left hand chased that hope away.

He couldn't know where on the big monster's head he had connected, but it was like punching rock. He swung two more times earning a giggle from his opponent. The growl that followed invited fear in to mingle with the rage boiling in Glaadrian's belly. He reached for his dagger, but it was too late. His head bounced hard off the trail as the big trogmortem got hold of his ankle and dragged them both out of the dirt.

Then the fire came. At least, that's what it felt like when Haram-Vi's claws slashed through the meat of his right thigh. The sound might have been worse than the cut itself. He heard bone crack. A racing mind chased along by fear can sometimes conjure images much faster than logic can run, but the idea his leg was off flittered away quickly once it occurred to him that he hadn't dropped back to the trail. His leg couldn't be off. Before he could even taste one morsel of relief, the big bastard tasted his flesh. It might have been his imagination, but he was certain he felt each individual fang as it punctured his skin. The burning agony continued as the jaws clamped down and began grinding back and forth on the bone beneath.

"Help," he cried out in the darkness, "the big bastard's gotten a hold of me leg."

It seemed an eternity passed as he hung there screaming and flopping like a big, beached chooker while a smelly monster of a beast gnawed at his leg. All his limbs flailed helplessly until his left foot finally connected with something. It must have been Haram-Vi's thick skull. It felt like kicking a mountain.

"Whose blood paints this trail, you little worm?" Haram-Vi growled before biting into Glaadrian's other leg and grinding at the bone.

The world grew suddenly quiet for Glaadrian in that moment. He could tell he still screamed by the burning in his throat. He could still feel Haram-Vi's horrible fangs grinding mercilessly at his leg. But all the sound was somehow gone. He wondered if this might be the end. It seemed a safe bet. Even safer when he felt his shoulder pop out of joint.

The sound returned. Ripping flesh hits a horrible note. It's worse when you know it's your own skin stretched beyond its limits. Though he felt the arm rip from his body, it still felt like it was attached to his shoulder, even after that bastard trogmortem clubbed him in the head with it.

"Help," he cried out again.

"Be holding him steady," Chialdaan finally answered, "and I'll be chopping that beast down.

Glaadrian had no more words to share. His entire body burned like fire licked him from all directions. He hadn't seen his good friend assault the monster who'd been chewing on him, but he heard the axe connect. The sound Haram-Vi made when that glorious dwarf axe connected with his thigh would have brought him the greatest joy if his mind weren't absorbed by pain and the stark realization that his soul had precious few moments to remain in the broken sack he'd become. He barely even noticed how far the trogmortem had tossed him into the fairy weeds. He'd probably die there among the enchanted plants.

It was a sad thing when he realized the last bit of joy he would have in the waking world was listening to the glorious sounds of his chums cutting his killer down. He wished he could see the results of their vengeance, but Haram-Vi's agonizing cries did a fine job of telling the story. The beast growled like a wild mountain scarra threatening an amatilazo off her pups. Both Chialdaan and Muljaak sounded just as monstrous growling, howling, and threatening right back at that monster. Oozing over the top of the grotesque symphony were other more horrible notes. The whistling of sharpened dwarf axes slicing through the mountain air before chopping through meat and cracking bone sounded a fine rhythm worthy of a foot-stomping dance. The drip and slop of blood and fluids and organs and entrails made a melody soaring over the top of it. If he'd had the voice left to spare, he may have sung out some words to finish the beautiful ballad. Ode to a Pile of Slop Who Used to be the Vilest of Vermin had quite the ring to it. If only that vermin hadn't destroyed most of his limbs, it might be a song he'd get to sing someday.

Glaadrian's mind drifted as the song played on. The fire raging in his body still burned, but it slowly lost its grip on his awareness. He felt weak. It was an odd thought, a thankful distraction. His heart was pumping as strong as ever and pulsing the blood right out of his mangled limbs. He'd be dead soon. As he lay there barely clinging to consciousness, dying wasn't the thing filling him with sadness. He couldn't stand up, grab his axe, and help his friends. What if they failed? What if that beast was chomping at their limbs like he'd done to Glaadrian? That was the saddest thought in his mind in that moment. He was a goner anyway. He didn't want his friends to die too.

"Let's go," Chialdaan's voice in his ear was an even sweeter song.

"Did ye vicious dwarves chop that monster into stew?" there wasn't much force behind his words, but he managed to muster the slightest chuckle.

"Aye, we did," Muljaak whispered in his other ear. "We chopped him up good. Ye'd be proud."

"Good go ye then, lads," a smile danced about his whispered reply.

Lentaak crouched low in the fairy weed just outside the clearing surrounding the great pine hiding in shadow a mere breath from the edge of an orange dome of light cast by a torch haphazardly stuck in the ground. He kept his breaths shallow and quiet. It was a gift he'd learned from his father—Coeptus bless his soul—who was widely known as the best thief ever to snatch a trinket from Ahm's palace. Despite that sneaky dwarf's stealth, he'd gone to the well one too many times. The rusty spindle Lentaak stared at with the oily chains wound around it at the back of the Sacred Pine were the same ones that held his father fast while he slowly died sprawled out across that great tree. He didn't get to see him at all in the three days he'd hung there. Not that his mother would have allowed it anyway, but Ahm forbid anyone to remain at his side or say any prayers over him. Stealing from Ahm was about as bad a crime as a dwarf could commit when that tyrant was king. As vile as Maomnosett Ahm thought his father was, he saw him as nothing less than a hero brave enough to challenge a giant and take back things which rightfully belonged to dwarves. The sentiment meant very little. Lentaak was so young when his father died on that tree, he'd spent most of his life without him. At least he'd learned a thing or two about staying quiet in the short time he'd had with him. He counted it his greatest asset, and it was exactly the skill that would save another sorry dwarf soul from finding the same fate.

As quiet as Lentaak was, it was risky to move around so close to the two trogmortem he knew stood guard on the other side of the Sacred Pine, but he had to gain a better vantage point before calling out the signal to start the attack. Trogmortem didn't see very well in the dark, but their hearing was as keen as they come. He was surprised they hadn't smelled him yet. He spent enough time sneaking about the caves that wound deep into the mountain, even to the valley below, listening to whispered secrets passed from dwarf lips to dwarf ears that his odor hadn't been anything close to pleasant in longer than he could remember. However, after following Bindaar on his vengeful but failed tirade and bathing in the blood of his enemies and his kin, his stink had grown even more foul. He could barely stomach the horrid odors wafting up from his sweatier bits. Hopefully his foes wouldn't catch a whiff. He held his breath and stealthily crept along the shadows until he could see the two trogmortem.

They all looked the same to him, massive, beastly brutes with giant heads full of fangs and foul intent. If only fighting were a skill his father had taught him, he'd charge into that clearing and chop those monsters down. But that wasn't the plan, and he wasn't equipped to execute that part of the mission. His part was to save the poor waste who was hanging from that tree, Alenaat. He never really liked the dwarf, but the whispers he'd heard about the rant that raised Ott's ire and got the young fool strapped to the Sacred Pine earned the poor fool at least a bit of admiration.

It was time. He whistled something meant to sound like a nocturnal bird's call. The awkward chirp that flopped inelegantly from his mouth failed at sounding like any sound any animal he'd ever heard might make. As soon as the odd tweet left his lips, he tensed and braced for an attack. It never came. Instead, he heard a familiar tune whistle out from the darkness further down the trail. Glaadrian's part had begun.

It only took a bit of chest beating and banter to get the two monsters to take the bait. Once they'd left the dim, orange dome of light and sounds of battle filled the air, Lentaak slipped quietly out of the shadows and got to work. It wasn't anything he'd ever trained for, but no one in his group had the skills necessary. Since he was the quietest, not to mention the least experienced in battle, the task fell to him.

Alenaat looked like a corpse hanging from that tree, bound by his wrists and ankles, and stretched almost to the point of popping joints out of sockets. The flickering torchlight played madness with shadows upon his face. Lentaak couldn't look at it for very long. Instead, he pressed his ear against the unconscious dwarf's chest. The breaths were shallow, but the tortured soul yet lived.

Lentaak grabbed his waterskin and pressed it up to Alenaat's cracked and broken lips. The poor dwarf's tongue darted out to gather the moisture, but his eyes didn't open. "Slowly," Lentaak coached, "Ye been on this tree for enough days the Lake should have already called ye home if all them stories I been hearing are true."

Once Alenaat had finally managed to get a good, solid drink, he groaned something inaudible.

"Shh," Lentaak whispered. "Save your strength. I'll be getting ye off this tree."

Lentaak slipped quietly around the massive pine and grabbed hold of the spindle he'd been silently staring at from the darkness. The rusty thing stuck a bit and groaned when he released the brake, but it spun free enough with a bit of force. He only allowed it a couple of turns before setting the brake again. After two days stretched across the Sacred Pine, there was no way Alenaat had enough strength to hold himself up.

Alenaat had slipped into a fresh set of groans as metal cuffs cut deeper into his wrists and ankles. The poor dwarf might have said something like, "Hurts," but it mostly just sounded like a pain-soaked wail to Lentaak.

"Hold on, friend," Lentaak spoke as soothingly as he could as he slipped back around the tree and propped Alenaat's weight onto his shoulder. "This'll hurt a wee bit more than ye already be hurting, but we need to get ye off this tree. Ain't nobody else around to help."

The quiet dwarf had just started working on releasing the first cuff when he heard Chialdaan whisper, "Lentaak, help."

"What do ye mean, help?" Lentaak whispered back. "The three of ye are supposed to be deep in them mines by…"

The rest of the words remained trapped in his mouth as Chialdaan set the grizzly mass that used to be one of the stoutest dwarves he had ever met against the tree next to Alenaat. Both his legs were shredded and dangling, and his left arm was off at the shoulder. Lentaak only had a moment to take the horrid sight in before Muljaak flopped into the light beside him. He seemed to be all in one piece aside from a good bit of swelling and bruising on his cheek.

"Ye should have left me behind and stuck to the plan," Glaadrian groaned with as much voice as he could muster.

"We don't leave no dwarves behind," Chialdaan shook his head.

Lentaak was speechless for a moment as he scanned the carnage. There was so much blood, it seemed impossible Glaadrian's soul remained with that sack of meat instead of on its way to the Lake. When he finally found his voice, it wasn't more than a hoarse whisper. "Help me get this one down off this tree. Then we can be tending to Glaadrian."

Chialdaan held Alenaat's weight against his shoulder as Lentaak removed the rest of the cuffs from the wrists and ankles of one he sadly wouldn't consider friend. Bindaar had always had a soft spot for the scruffy waste, but Lentaak remained skeptical. None of that mattered anymore. Once that bastard, Ott ordered the poor oaf strung up to the Sacred Pine, Alenaat became something of a symbol. Even more than that, he became a friend of all dwarves.

The torchlight was fading fast, but there was still enough to see the only real damage Alenaat had received came from those rusty, old, merciless cuffs digging into his flesh and from a lack of food and water. The poor dwarf's lips were dry and cracked, and he hadn't the energy to do anything more than quietly groan.

Lentaak slipped a fairy weed bud in between Alenaat's teeth and lower lip. "That'll help ease the pain a bit," he whispered into the broken dwarf's ear. Then he handed two wet strips of cloth and a couple clumps of dragon blossom over to Chialdaan and said, "Here then, help wrap up these wounds on his ankles. Be sure to coat them well with this. That'll be helping the healing. We ain't got much time to be sitting in the open like this."

Once Alenaat's wounds had been bandaged up, Lentaak and Chialdaan helped him up against the tree. Lentaak handed his water skin over to Chialdaan and said, "Be getting him to drink as much as ye can. Don't be rushing nothing. It ain't no good if he vomits it all back up onto the trail."

Chialdaan did as instructed, and Lentaak turned his attention to the grizzly mass of bloody flesh that used to be Glaadrian. Blood pumped freely from too many parts of the broken dwarf's body. Those mangled legs and that shredded arm were too much for Lentaak to take, so he didn't look for very long. It would take more than a bit of fairy weed and dragon blossom to fix that mess. Even a proper healer wouldn't stand a chance. Glaadrian was bound for the Lake, and there wasn't a damn thing any of the dwarves huddled around the Sacred Pine could do about it.

Considering the shape he was in, Glaadrian should have been howling with pain. He wasn't. Instead, with his teeth clamped tight, and a deep scowl hiding beneath his beard, he was staring into the darkness outside the orange dome. Lentaak thought it looked as if the stout, old dwarf was trying to will his soul out of his body, past the edge of the light into darkness, and on to the sweet relief of the Lake.

"Looks like ye had a rough go of it with them brutes," Lentaak whispered as he slipped a fairy weed bud into Glaadrian's cheek.

"Aye," Glaadrian whispered back.

After a few moments of painful silence, Lentaak realized that was all his old friend had left to say and replied, "We'll be getting ye off this mountain and to a proper healer."

Glaadrian's chuckle was lost amid a low cough, "Ye and I both know I ain't leaving this place. Ye best be getting Alenaat to safety. It seems there ain't a better place for any dwarf to start a journey to the Lake than leaning right up against this big, beautiful pine." He slipped his dagger out of its scabbard with the only limb he had left, handed it to Lentaak, and looked earnestly into his old friend's eyes as he finished, "Be making it quick, old friend."

"Ye'll be doing no such thing," Muljaak complained, "We ain't leaving none behind."

"That idea be as noble as it be stupid," Glaadrian whispered, "I ain't making it through them mines, and I'll only be slowing ye down. Ain't no point in all of us dying just because one of us be." The he looked back to Lentaak, nodded, and said, "Go on now. Make it quick."

Lentaak gripped the dagger so tight his hand began to cramp as he stared at the spot on Glaadrian's chest where he would plunge the thing and end his friend's suffering. His vision blurred with tears as his eyes filled up. That wouldn't do. He quickly wiped them away, but more came just as fast.

"Come on then," Glaadrian complained, "Quit your sniveling and get it done. It ain't no easy thing to be sitting here like this just waiting to die. Every part of me body burns like fires be roasting me up right here. Have pity and do the deed."

Lentaak sniffled hard, shook his head, and pushed the sorrow down into his gut. He gave his eyes one more good wipe, and his target was clear. Glaadrian's heart pumped just beneath that spot. He gave his old friend one last weak smile and slipped the blade between his ribs.

Glaadrian gritted his teeth when the skin popped, but his last breath was saturated in sweet relief. "Thank ye," were the last words he'd ever speak in the waking world.

Lentaak let the tears come, holding his friend close to the last. Once Glaadrian's eyes grayed over, and there wasn't a twitch left in him, he laid him back on the soft ground. He felt Muljaak's massive mitt on his shoulder as he said a few words over his dead friend's body, "Ain't a stouter dwarf or a truer friend ever lived. Helias, sweet Mother, Great Mother, guide to us all, please be taking special care with this one. Guide him home to your sweet embrace and the peace of that Lake to which we all be wishing to return."

"Telos," Muljaak whispered.

"Aye," Chialdaan agreed, "Telos."

As far as prayers go, it probably wasn't the best, but the real meaning in those words was the emotion which drove them out of the sad dwarf's mouth. Before Ott spoke the command to string Alenaat up on the Sacred Pine, there wasn't a lick of love for him in Maomnosett. That didn't matter to Glaadrian. He gave his life just the same. Lentaak decided right there in the flickering and fading dome of torchlight beneath the Sacred Pine, Glaadrian's name would never be forgotten. He would tell the story of the stout dwarf facing down monsters from across the Great Sea to all who would listen until the very end of his days.

"Time to go," Chialdaan gently nudged Lentaak's shoulder.

"Aye," Lentaak quietly agreed, "I have a path planned out for us through the mines beneath the mountain, a secret path me father used back when he would thieve from the palace during Ahm's rule. Ain't nobody else who knows about it. It runs all the way down through the mountain to the valley below. She'll be dropping us right at the shores of Galgooth across from the castle at Havenstahl."

Muljaak rubbed his swollen head and said, "That sounds like a safe bet. Even still, the two of ye can be helping Alenaat through them caves, and I'll be guarding your backs."

No more words were spoken as Lentaak and Chialdaan hefted Alenaat onto their shoulders and shuffled off to a secret cave entrance just south of the big pine with Muljaak scanning the trail behind them.

CHAPTER 2
THE GOD IS DEAD

Cialia woke in disorienting darkness. She was drenched to the bone. The last thing she remembered was allowing weariness to overcome her after driving her will into Brerto's very cells and blasting the bastard to oblivion. Exhaustion made sense. She had killed a god after all. Of course, she knew a god couldn't be killed, simply scattered to the wind, trapped in limbo. The only sad part as far as she was concerned was the vile wretch would remain completely unaware of his demise. The fact a god couldn't be killed is precisely why she believed it had been Kallum she faced over Havenstahl's broken castle.

By now she realized the great eagle she battled was Ijilv, the great hawk, disguising himself to strike fear in the hearts of the men of that city. Kallum remained safely scattered and unaware of his condition, never again to trouble the living world. She hadn't recognized him while trapped in Brerto's spell, that dream of a life she would love to live if only she could, but he was there. He obviously had a plan far grander than forcing the worship of any of the creatures on Ouloos. If only she knew what that plan was. The gods thrive on worship. It is all that matters to them. Parading as another god who may earn worship in your stead seemed a farce too ridiculous for any of the gods. On top of that, he was hidden to her. She could sense the others, not their exact whereabouts, of course, but she was drawn to their power. It was a troubling mystery how he managed to remain outside of her awareness until he wanted his presence known.

As she lay there in darkness contemplating the power of gods, the cause of the darkness became apparent. With Brerto scattered, his illusion had died. She saw it fail when he fell, but that seemed so long ago. How much time had passed as she slept there beneath the snow? Once she'd dug her way out and got a good look at the mountaintop, it seemed about a foot of it had fallen while she slumbered. As fast as it was coming down, it could have been hours or days. It would be difficult to know for certain, but the sky around the mountaintop was a swirling mass of fat, wet flakes.

Her form drooped as the weariness returned, and her chin flopped to her chest. Her blonde hair looked dark and dingy as it hung limply about her face. It felt like she held all of Ouloos aloft above her head, and the weight was crushing her down, pushing her deeper into the snow. Brerto's illusion would be a blessing. She could kid herself into believing she gained nourishment from the food which pretended to grow wild there. It wouldn't help, of course, but the serene beauty of it would serve as a pleasant distraction. She could replicate it, wander the garden feasting on the intriguing variety of things which grew there. It wouldn't make a difference. She had work to do, and eventually reality would need to be dealt with. Three more gods awaited judgement for their wicked deeds against the creatures she protected.

She stared off into the swirling white sky surrounding the mountaintop trying to recall the last time she felt so tired. The weariness made sense after killing a god, but it took a surprisingly small amount of effort to kill him. At least, that is how it seemed. Her condition suggested otherwise, but once she had conquered Brerto's illusion, he was powerless to stop her. She crawled into his mind, invaded his thoughts, and burned him up from the inside. Perhaps he had some arcane curse waiting for her deep in his subconscious, but she would have sensed that. There was nothing but fear, hate, and furious rage haunting his thoughts. Regardless the reason, she needed rest.

Was it minutes or hours she stared off into the furious storm raging around her? Did it matter? Did anything matter? Of course, it did. The work she was doing—scattering those gods who tormented the creatures of Ouloos—mattered. There could be no real peace until it was complete.

She needed her sisters. In that moment, however long it was, she decided to visit the Lake. She would plunge her toes into the sand, lounge on it with her sisters, and let its lifegiving waters rejuvenate her before the next battle.

CHAPTER 3
CASUAL CONVERSATIONS

The trail didn't feel right. A trail should be hard, packed tight from the thousands upon thousands of feet and hooves compressing it until no air hides between the granules of dirt, or soft from a coating of decaying leaves. The surface Maelich walked upon felt like neither of those things. A thick fog covered the non-trail all the way up to his waist. The fact that his movement through it failed to disturb it in the least also failed to disturb him in the least. The trail was no mystery. Neither was the fog. Even the trees surrounding him with bark that was too smooth and too shiny weren't mysteries. He had seen it all before. Would it be the black horse or the white horse this time? What difference did it make?

There was no breeze blowing through the trees or down the trail, yet his long, blonde hair whipped a wild frenzy above his head. The long locks flopped down in front of his face and then blasted back behind him as if he'd stepped into a whirlwind. Somehow the oddity of his hair whipping around in the calm, still air of the forest seemed less odd than how clean it looked flashing past his eyes. He hadn't had a good wash in longer than he could remember.

As he strolled over the imaginary trail through imaginary fog, it occurred to him that Maulom hadn't visited his subconscious since they met in the waking world. That probably made sense. They spoke every day. What cause could the white horse have to invade his dreams?

It had to be the black horse who would come to bother him. The scenery was the same. He paused, listening hard. In every previous encounter he'd had with the creature Maulom had dubbed a witch—apparently forgetting she communicated with him in precisely the same fashion he had before they met—she drew him to a corpse on an altar with cries for help. Where were the cries?

"I have no dead friends to show you today, Maelich," the black horse answered the silent question from behind him before adding, "I just want to talk."

Maelich spun to face the beast or witch or whatever she was. "What on Ouloos could we possibly have to discuss? You invade my dreams with horrors, visions of death. To what end? What do you want with me?"

Fear danced about the horse's eyes as her reply sounded more like a plea, "I want you to wake. I want you to mourn. I want you to remember the people you love."

"Then speak plainly to me," he shouted as he walked toward her. "Stop speaking to me in riddles. You come to me in dreams and tell me to wake. I wake and nothing changes."

"You are not awake as you wander the desert with Maulom and the Shaiwah," her voice cracked with the slightest whimper.

"Fine," he sighed, "I am asleep when I'm asleep and asleep while I'm awake. Life is a dream over which I have no control. Maulom is deceiving me, and you are deceiving me. My conscious mind and subconscious mind are both ruled by a white horse and a black horse who refuse to tell me anything but meaningless vagaries." The ground shifted violently beneath them as he finished.

"Maelich, please calm down," she begged. "I seek only to help."

If a sigh had ever been so deep or drawn out so long it would be a miracle. His form deflated as his anger fled in favor of frustration or melancholy, or perhaps some mixture of the two. Perhaps it was hopelessness. The mixture of emotions he felt in that moment of defeat wasn't terribly important. He was tired of it all, the game those two damnable horses played with him, the riddles interwoven in all the words they spoke, and the lack of anything tangible in his fruitless encounters with them. Even life itself held no joy for him. "If you truly want to help me, let's start with your name," he finally said, quickly adding, "And please don't tell me you are only known as the black horse. Maulom gave me that lie when he came to intrude upon my dreams."

"My name is Moluam," she replied.

"See…" Maelich began, fully expecting some nonsense about her only being known as the black horse and not having any kind of name besides the vague description. The fact she didn't give him some kind of line like that was almost disappointing. His brows dipped as he finished with another question, "No tricks? No intrigue? Why would you tell me that?"

"Maulom enjoys games," she shrugged.

It was almost as unsettling as his first meeting with Maulom as the white horse. However, this wasn't the first time he'd seen a horse shrug. The fact made it no less strange. This was only the second horse he'd seen shrug. However, a shrug from a horse who is plainly speaking makes just about anything else the animal might do far less amazing.

Once he had finished troubling over the shrug, he replied, "Don't you though? Is it not a game when you call out to me for help only to show me the corpse of some stranger? It feels like a game to me, a game you play with me as a pawn."

"No, it is not a game, and they are not strangers I show you. You are no pawn," her reply was curt.

Maelich's head shook slowly back and forth as he said, "It grows increasingly difficult not to feel that way. Nothing which has happened to me since arriving in the cracked and barren place where my body lies sleeping was something I decided to do. The story has been written, the rules of the game spoken, and I am just to play through it like an actor in some macabre playhouse."

"I love plays," the black horse smiled—this was at least as troubling as the shrug had been.

"But this is my life," Maelich fired back. "This is not a reenactment of some event from long ago or something sprung from the darkest places of some storyteller's imagination. These things are happening to me. My dreams are not even safe from this game."

"You are correct," she replied flatly. "This is not theater. However, we do all have our roles to play."

Maelich's chin dropped to his chest in frustration. Right at that moment he realized the fog was gone. He could actually see his own feet. His boots were all wrong. The things on his feet were nice, but they weren't his boots. Come to think of it, he needed some new footwear. Perhaps his subconscious mind was further along the path of acquiring some than was his conscious mind. Hopefully, he'd remember that once he woke. Either way, he took the boot on his right foot—which was far nicer than his boots in the real world—and kicked a small pebble down the trail. Rather, he attempted to kick that perfectly smooth pebble down the trail. The beautiful, shiny, black boot went right through the damn thing. Dreams.

"What is my role?" he finally asked.

"You will lead the Shaiwah to the land promised them. Maulom will continue to serve as your guide on this quest, and I will continue to help you mourn the loss of those you love. There will be more. I will show them to you, you will struggle to remember, and, hopefully, you will eventually wake up," she finished with a sigh.

"That certainly sounds like a game," he complained. "You said it wasn't a game you were playing, yet the words you use to explain this *thing* you describe make it sound very much like a game to me."

"Life is a game, Maelich."

"What if I choose not to play?"

"Our world will die," the chuckle accompanying her reply seemed out of place.

"I find no humor in the idea of our world dying," he tried kicking the pebble again despite knowing the effort would be futile. It was.

"There is none," she smiled, "I am powerless to affect any of this. Only you can save us. If you decide not to, what more can I do but laugh? Laughing is far more enjoyable than crying, and they both make precisely the same amount of difference in the grand scheme of things."

Maelich thought about it for a moment before replying, "I'm not certain I believe the things you say, but I'll grant you tears are as effective as laughter. Honor me with an answer to one last question, and then I am done with you. What is your relationship with Maulom? Why does he hate you?" he paused before adding, "Make that two final questions."

The black horse sighed, "Maulom does not hate me. He completes me, and I him. Neither can exist without the other, and we work both with and against each other. That is our lot. It is how it has always been, and how it will always be."

"You fear him," he countered.

"I do not fear him," she contended. "I fear he may have left the path on which he must tread. I fear what it will mean for our world if he veers from his path and, in turn, causes you to veer from your path.

However, I do not fear him. I am his equal in every way, and he mine."

There were probably more words Maelich could have said, but he was finished with the conversation. Though it still seemed she had games to play, the black horse—or Moluam, or whatever she wanted to call herself—had at least spoken plainly enough to him for most of the conversation. That was more than Maulom had ever done for him. That was something.

"Good-bye, black horse. I am sure I will see you again," he finally said, his tone flat. As the words left his mouth, Moluam vanished, and he was alone on the trail with no voices to trouble him but the ones in his own head.

CHAPTER 4
THE SNOW BEAST

The thick brush did nothing to prevent the light rain from soaking Chagon's heavy, chain mail cloak, but the farm hand refused to complain. He could just see the smug look Tarantian would give him if he did. Of course, the grizzled soldier had been absolutely correct when he suggested something lighter would be a far better option for traversing thick brush while trying to avoid the trail, but Chagon had decided within the first half mile he wouldn't give him the satisfaction of knowing it. He held onto the hope they'd be tested in battle, and the ridiculously heavy armor would finally prove its worth.

As if he were in Chagon's head, Tarantian chuckled, "Do you still feel good about that silly cloak?"

"Aye," Chagon pretended not to care about the extra weight he dragged through the brush with him, or the thick, wet hair matted to his itchy skull beneath the hood of the horrible thing, "I ain't so good with a sword as ye. When the fighting starts, this heavy armor will be saving me throat."

"If only it covered your throat," the soldier frowned. "At least your heart is safe from any blades which might come its way."

Chagon unconsciously touched the smooth skin of his neck. His companion was correct. The heavy thing he wore left his throat wide open, fair game for any blades wishing to slip into it or tear through it. The thought sent his mind careening down a dangerous path for any novice swordsman. How would he fair in a real fight with someone who knew how to swing steel? Besting Brinzo had been far too difficult a task. That disgusting man was no warrior. How long would he last in a contest with a trained soldier?

"Best not go too far down that trail," Tarantian commented as if he were still inside Chagon's head. "You will not know until you know. Luckily, I'll be there with you."

"Would you take me?" he asked, almost sheepishly.

"Without hesitation," the answer was surprising.

"Why? I've seen mighty men schooled in the way of the blade expertly wield their instruments. It ain't feeling like that when I do it," the green recruit frowned.

Tarantian's smile nearly ran out of face to spread across as he patted Chagon's back, but there was no humor in his reply, "You have passion. We've only had these few days on the trail to train…"

"This ain't no trail," Chagon laughed.

"Quite right," Tarantian agreed. "However, as I was saying, regardless the scenery, you have proven a quick study. Your movements require refinement, but you have a natural talent of which many true experts I have known would be jealous. I had five solid summers of training under my belt before my boots tasted the dirt of their first battlefield, and I felt like a fool. Twice I had to be rescued, and I only counted one kill. No one said as much, but I knew many of my comrades would have preferred I missed that battle. I would march to war with you on this very day and know you would do better. Never doubt yourself, my friend. Doubt is the only enemy you cannot overcome."

Chagon's cheeks reddened a bit, "I ain't sure if ye believe all them nice words, but thank ye nonetheless."

"Hold," Tarantian whispered as he reached out his arm to stop Chagon's progress and nodded toward a clearing which could barely be seen through the thick brush.

"Are them bodies?" Chagon whispered back.

"Maybe, but…" Tarantian trailed off as both men squinted through the thicket.

A horse snorted and then neighed. Chagon didn't know much about the trail, but he knew that was a clue. Grizzly mongs weren't picky about meat. They'd eat anything. On top of that, though the bodies littered about the ground in front of the handful of huts that made up the small village in the clearing were difficult to see clearly, they did appear to have all the meat remaining on their bones. Those beasts from the north may not have picked the bones clean, but they would have feasted on those men before moving on down the trail.

As if to confirm Chagon's assumptions, Tarantian whispered, "Amatilazo."

It would be a relief if he were right. The sun was still high in the sky, and those nightmares only hunt during the darkest hours of night. If it truly were amatilazo that brought an end to the villagers scattered about the ground, the two travelers should have no trouble replenishing their meager supplies. Good news tends to be scarce on the trail. This would truly be a blessing.

After a few moments of quiet observation that seemed so much longer, Tarantian finally broke the silence, "We should be safe, but be cautious."

The first carcass they encountered was lying on its stomach and seemed a bit bloated. It would be difficult to know for sure without the benefit of having seen the person prior to their untimely demise. It looked to be a man. His clothes were covered in blood, but all his limbs seemed to be intact. This would align with Tarantian's suggestion amatilazo were the cause of all the carnage. When the soldier finally pushed the corpse onto its back with his boot, all the ideas in Chagon's head were confirmed.

He had never seen a woman sport a beard like that which decorated the man's pale chin. To be sure, he'd known a woman or two with more than their fair share of fuzz on their chins or above their lips, but he had never met one with anything he'd consider a proper beard. This man's was thick, probably luxurious prior to being caked with blood. That solved one puzzle. The next was solved with the pale condition of the man's skin and the gaping, ragged tear in his throat. There could be no doubt he breathed his last with the rough tongue of an amatilazo stealing his life's blood.

"Do you need a moment," the rich baritone of Tarantian's voice was nearly startling. Any need to whisper had long fled.

"No," Chagon shook his head, "plenty of dead I've seen since leaving me farm. Can't imagine I'll be wincing at the sight of a dead man ever again."

"You're right about that," the soldier agreed. "You become numb to it. Every dead set of eyes you look into will kill a little piece of your heart until nothing remains. Men die. Sometimes you're the reason. Sometimes you aren't. You need to be okay with that either way."

He didn't take his eyes off the dead man as he replied, "Aye."

Given more time, the two men would have built a proper pyre and burned the bodies with fitting ceremony. There wasn't time for anything so formal. Though grizzly mongs weren't the cause of all the death in the small village, they were still about somewhere. Wasting time on ceremony in the wide-open clearing was a terrible idea and nothing either man wanted to do just then. Instead, they each picked a horse—Tarantian found a mighty, black steed without a fleck of white on him, and Chagon found a bronze mare with a deep, brown mane—before pilfering through the three huts that made up the small village and filling horse sacks with all they could carry.

After saddling up his horse and tying down his horse sacks, Chagon glanced over at Tarantian and said, "Glory."

Tarantian raised an eyebrow and asked, "What's that?"

"This beauty of a mare ought be having a name," the farm hand smiled. "I'll be calling her Glory on account of this magnificent coat that be blazing like the early morning sky heralding the coming of the rising sun."

The soldier's laugh was probably a bit heartier than he intended, "I had no idea you were so sentimental. That is almost poetic."

"You jest," Chagon complained.

"Not at all," Tarantian smiled. "I hadn't even thought to give mine a name. Sometimes duty gets in the way of important things like a name for a friend who will accompany you on a challenging journey. Thank you for reminding me," he paused and cocked his head up toward the sky before adding, "Salvation, that is what I'll call mine. It is no exaggeration when I say this journey has been my most challenging. We have both witnessed things no man should ever see…"

"Like men who eat men," Chagon interjected.

"Indeed," the thoughtful soldier agreed, "like men who eat men. If I'm being completely honest with you, happening upon this village and finding these horses was the first moment I truly believed we'd survive this mission. This horse is my salvation."

Chagon offered a genuine smile at the thought as an odd sense of joy filled him to the point that a tear or two dribbling down his face seemed imminent. He couldn't let that happen in front of Tarantian, or maybe he could. Perhaps the fact he could do that was precisely the reason those tears threatened in the first place. In the short time he and Tarantian had spent together, the sturdy and sure soldier had become the best friend he'd ever had. Of course, the admiration he felt for the hero hadn't diminished in the slightest. However, in the days since the trail where those horrible snow beasts decimated their caravan, that hero slowly transformed from larger-than-life myth to something of a chum.

Tarantian glanced up from his horse in time to catch one tear slowly dribbling down Chagon's cheek before he could wipe it away. "Are you crying?" he asked.

"Oh, shut your filthy gob," Chagon sniffled slightly before laughing the heartiest laugh he'd had in longer than he could remember.

"You're enjoying this journey, aren't you?" Tarantian laughed right back at him.

"And what if I were?" Chagon shrugged. "I ain't never had a chum so close as we've become, and the freedom of the trail is nothing like I've ever known," he paused before adding, "That might be sounding silly to one who's seen so much."

Tarantian walked over and patted a heavy hand across Chagon's back. "That does not sound silly at all, and you aren't the only one who feels that way. You're a good man, and I am honored to share this journey with you."

Before Chagon could add any words to support the other damn tear that managed to wriggle past his eyelid, a growl from deep in the darkness of the trees behind the village snapped both men out of the moment. Being his first real journey more than ten miles in any direction from his farm, Chagon wasn't near experienced enough to pick out the various sounds of the trail like his companion probably could. However, the horrible sound rushing out from that dark place was one he knew.

Chagon grabbed his horse's reins. The beast was all in a tizzy, stomping about and whinnying something that sounded like a starving baby wailing in the night. Riding away from the danger was not an option. Both horses were too agitated.

"Draw your sword," Tarantian shouted through clenched teeth, as if to add validity to the thought.

The world slowed around Chagon as he followed the command. He could see Tarantian's lips kept moving, but all sound ceased as his vision closed in around the darkness where that horrible growl had originated. That one spot appeared as if it were on the other side of a tunnel he peered through. Nothing else in the world mattered in that moment.

Then the beast tore out of the brush, leaping over the fence along the far side of the small corral where three additional horses and a pony stamped nervously. They probably snorted and trumpeted, but Chagon could here none of those sounds. The only sound he could hear was the guttural growl of that horrible snow beast.

The thing's eyes grabbed Chagon's horrified gaze as it leapt onto a small, white pony crushing the poor creature into the muddy ground. They were almost amber and looked like a man's eyes. In fact, the thing's face would look just like a man's if not for the mouth jutting out like it did and the shaggy fur covering everything but its flattened, pushed-up nose and forehead…and those fangs. No man had teeth that size. They had to be at least three inches in length, yellow and dripping in anticipation of tearing into soft flesh.

"Grizzly mongs," Chagon heard Tarantian shout, his ears finally registering something other than the beast's horrible growl.

It seemed less than a blessing. He heard the pop when those horrible fangs ripped into the poor pony's neck. Then ripping, tendons tearing, muscles shredding, and finally the sound of that vicious threatening growl sinking to more of a satisfied groan. Somehow the latter was the worst.

Chagon's legs refused to respond as he helplessly watched Tarantian run at the beast. It seemed a lone attacker. As strange as the idea was, the pack was nowhere to be found. Was it strange? He couldn't be certain of that. The caravan to Druindahl had been his first experience. There were hundreds, maybe thousands, in that pack. That didn't necessarily mean they always travel that way. Wild horses typically traveled and lived in herds, but it wasn't that strange to find a lone animal in the prairie. Perhaps grizzly mongs were similar.

The world moved in slow motion before his eyes. By the time Tarantian had leapt up onto the low fence surrounding the corral, one of the other horses had reared back to kick the snow beast off the pony. It was a valiant, though wasted, effort. The pony had long left this world, its blood saturating the fur around the grizzly mong's maw leaving it pink and frothy. The thing barely moved when the horse's hooves connected with its shoulder. A moment later the steed's head flipped carelessly through the air. Stony claws had cut clean through it like tubberslat cooked just right.

It was that same moment when the beast noticed Tarantian

crouched deep and ready to pounce with his sword held high. The soldier had barely stretched an inch into his jump before the grizzly mong lunged toward him all fangs and claws. It was lucky, the soldier's trajectory. Not lucky enough to earn any flesh for his blade, but it placed his throat just beyond the reach of those black claws.

Tarantian's body looked broken when it crashed to the muddy ground of the corral after careening off a horse's flank. It had only been the beast's forearm that connected with his head, but the mighty swat sent the soldier about ten feet through the air. Chagon finally found his voice as the beast turned to follow up on the assault.

It wasn't a sound he had ever made before. It didn't even sound like something that should come from a man, but it roared past his lips and filled the clearing like the shout of an entire battalion of soldiers. He got the beast's attention. As the thing turned and lunged toward him, he wasn't sure he wanted it. Tarantian lay unconscious and helpless. Chagon wondered if he was any more useful awake and standing with sword in hand than his chum lying unconscious in the dirt.

His blade didn't hit anything when he swung it. He launched the attempted assault far too soon for it to be effective. Instead, the hungry blade gobbled up a bunch of air. The whistling sound it made as it sliced through nothing more than a light breeze was satisfying. If only he had a few moments to enjoy it. It certainly sounded like Tarantian's training was paying off. As it were, the valiant move only earned him claws against the side of his head.

He'd begun ducking before the swat came, so it didn't hit with as much force as it could have. As he tumbled, it occurred to him that his head was still firmly attached to his body. For all the teasing Tarantian had given him over the chain mail cloak he wore, the heavy, shiny thing was serving its purpose. Scrambling back to his feet once he'd finished rolling was a bit of chore. The armor did slow him down. However, he managed to get his sword up in front of his face in time to block the next blow.

The beast's massive and furry arm didn't come off with the cut, but it was deep. That much he could tell even with fear-drenched adrenaline coursing wildly through his veins. It was a brief victory as the monster used its other arm to push him to the ground and bite into him. The pop of sharp fangs puncturing soft flesh never came. The thing tried to bite into him several times. He felt the pressure. No doubt there was a bruise or two in his future, but the armor held up to the assault as the monster chomped and chomped.

He tried to crawl away, but the thing was too damned heavy. On top of that, his sword was useless pinned beneath him. Despite the fact his flesh was protected, he wouldn't be able to hold the monster off for long. It felt like a carriage loaded down with supplies was parked on his chest. The beast mauling him had to be at least eight feet tall and as wide as two stout men. Bearing down on his chest as it was, his wind was all but gone.

He couldn't tell if it was the excitement of battle—furiously fighting with everything he had to keep his soul inside his body—or the fact he couldn't catch a full breath of air, but the world before his eyes began swimming a bit, dipping this way and that. Stars shot about in front of his vision, blazing white. They would start on one side of the beast in front of him and get lost in its fur before shooting out the other side. Just when everything started getting purple, the weight left him.

By the time he scrambled back to his feet, Tarantian had the beast well in hand. The thing's right arm dangled beside it, flopping uselessly as the monster battled the fierce warrior. Chagon's admiration for his trail mate only grew. It was the first time he witnessed the swordsman's prowess when he was at full strength outside of an ambush. His movements were like art, some kind of macabre dance of glorious death. The monster was wily, and its hide tough. The fact his own thick arms and shoulders failed to drive his blade all the way through the beast's arm was a testament to the thing's durability. That durability didn't seem to matter in the least as Tarantian's blade whistled through the air and flashed in the light, hacking pieces of the grizzly mong off as blood loss slowly killed its momentum.

After a few moments of unbridled awe, Chagon managed to raise his chin from his chest and charge into battle. A furious roar belted out of him and echoed off the trees. He sounded far mightier in his ears than he felt in his heart. Trepidation suddenly mounted as he watched his hero stumble. It seemed the grizzly mong wasn't ready for a journey back to the Lake just yet. Instead of turning Chagon away, it only strengthened his resolve. That was his most bosom chum knocked to one knee before that horrible beast.

The razor-sharp blade in his right hand would have been a better choice, but it was his shoulder which hit the beast first. It pounded into the grizzly mong's side just below its ribs. The horrible war cry pouring from Chagon's mouth somehow gained more volume. If he survived the encounter, his voice probably wouldn't. The thought was brief, chased away by his swinging blade.

The thing's throat was his target, and his aim was true. Unfortunately, the damned beast was wily, and that target was a good six inches higher than it had been by the time the glinting, metal death bringer connected. It sunk deep into the monster's shoulder blade and stuck. One quick tug was all Chagon could manage before his boots were above him beneath a blue sky sailing by far too quickly. A solid ten feet of air had passed by his face before he pounded into the dirt and slid another fifteen. The idea of jumping to his feet barely had time to reach the conscious part of his mind before the beast had covered the same distance and loomed above him all fiery eyes and flashing fangs.

The grizzly mong attempted raising its clawed fists up high above its head while stretching its body as if to generate the maximum torque possible when finally launching the next attack. One of those fists dangled uselessly at its side. None of it mattered. The attack would never come. A quick spray of blood coated Chagon's face as he watched Tarantian's blade pop through the monster's chest. Stabbing an opponent in the back may have seemed cowardly to some, but, in that moment, Chagon thought it might just be the most heroic damned deed he had ever seen. He scrambled out of the way just in time to avoid being crushed by the shaggy corpse.

"You saved my skin," Tarantian boomed before losing himself to laughter.

Chagon's face twisted up like he'd just bit into something most sour, "Are ye having a go at me? It was ye who saved my skin, more than once in that battle."

The soldier shook his head, "Here is a lesson for you. You take the glory when you earn it. Twice I was down, and that beast would have had me. I'm still here speaking with you right now instead of on my way to the Lake because you stood tall against fear. You will make a fine soldier, my friend."

Chagon's cheeks reddened as he accepted the praise.

After a few moments, Tarantian draped his arm across the farm hand's shoulder and added, "And you best not ever think of giving up that ridiculous cloak." He chuckled before adding, "Come now. Let's gather up these horses and get to Havenstahl."

CHAPTER 5
SISTERS

Cialia materialized at the edge of the Lake. Her sisters, the Dragons, were all about, massive and majestic and glowing red like fire. Some soared to heights unimaginable while others lounged or lumbered among the greenery surrounding it all. The grace of their movements was matched only by the strength of their forms. One stood out from the glorious mass, Helias, the first, the great Mother, the oldest and wisest of all Cialia's sisters. There she sat upon her stony peak, beautiful against the blazing sky. That magnificent creature stood and stretched her wings earning one tear from Cialia's dampened eyes. Her glorious form was a beautiful reminder of what she could never be. Though she was a Dragon in her own right, and equal in all ways according to Helias, her soul still haunted the body of a simple woman. She wondered if she would ever truly be equal among her kin.

"Sweet sister," Helias spoke with her mind rather than her voice, "you are weary. Your soul is bent beneath the weight of your toils."

Helias was correct. Life was like a massive boulder sitting across Cialia's shoulders and pushing her down. She gave in and let it force her to her knees into the soft sand as she replied also with her mind, "Sweet sister, beautiful savior, Mother to us all, you are correct as always. The world grows heavier every day."

Lameah sauntered up and laid her head down next to Cialia. "We've missed you, my dear. Will you stay a bit longer this time?"

"If only I could, but…" Cialia began to deliver her usual excuse before losing herself in the majesty of Lameah's massive eye smoldering like the embers of blazing fire.

"But duty and destiny and protection and blah, blah, blah," Helias interrupted. Though her words seemed to mock, her tone never lost its loving sweetness.

"You know me as well as I know myself," Cialia sighed, "maybe better, but, yes, my task is far from complete. The road behind me was hard, fraught with challenges, but the road ahead promises to be more challenging still. I just need a moment surrounded by my glorious sisters and the peace of the Lake, your home…"

"Our home," the most perfect of Dragons interrupted once more.

Cialia's smile was genuine as she agreed, "Of course, our home. I needed the solace of your company and our home to strengthen my soul before continuing on my journey."

"You are always welcome here," Lameah smiled back. "We ache for you whenever you go."

"And I you," Cialia frowned as she gently stroked the smooth scales of Lameah's face. "If only I could remain until the end of time. Someday, I will return to live among you for the rest of my days. I promise."

Helias chuckled, "My sweet, sweet sister, please do not make promises you know you cannot keep. There is always a journey, a mission. Someone always needs the protection of our fierce warrior Dragon. When will you ever let that go and truly become a Dragon?"

Cialia quickly sat back up and replied with a hint of irritation, "I am the fiercest of Dragons. I may look like a woman, absent a Dragon's majesty, but my mother swam in the Lake and he, it, is my father."

Helias' smile never faltered as she replied, "A Dragon takes no umbrage with any truth or opinion, my dear, but you are that which you describe. Your appearance doesn't matter. However, you are as much a woman as you are a Dragon, and that is why you can never truly become a Dragon. The woman in you is too strong to let that happen. She will defend and fight and protect until the Lake calls her home. I say this with love, sweet sister, but when you return to us for good, it will only be your soul which makes the journey. You will sink into the Lake and return to Coeptus never to enjoy the peace of this place as one of us. On that day, my heart will cry. I will lament the loss of you like no sadness my heart as ever felt."

Cialia slumped back against the sand. A small part of her wanted to continue the debate, continue presenting her case and justifying her actions, but Helias was right. As much as she would love to remain there with her sisters basking in the love and pure joy of that perfect place, she could never do it. She would feel the pain of those under her protection, and she would have to act. The more her mind got spinning on the topic, the less capable she became of letting it lie.

"What would you do?" she finally blurted with her mouth instead of her mind this time.

Helias' warm smile somehow widened, "Exactly what I have always done, love all creatures regardless of the things they do."

"Some creatures don't deserve love," Cialia complained. "What about the gods? Do you see no fault in the things they do?"

"I see no fault in any of us creatures who are part of Coeptus," Helias finally spoke with her voice. It was a shame she used it so infrequently, as it gently vibrated the air like a song. "Unconditional love, Cialia, means there is no thing you—or any other creature on Ouloos—could do to change it. I love you, my dear, because you are exactly as you should be. I weep for you at times, of course, but not for anything you have done. I weep for you because of how those things you do affect you. I see in your eyes how much your task troubles you, and I admire your courage to face those challenges and never give up. It is one of the things I love most about you. You are a courageous champion, a hero to save all those on Ouloos who cannot save themselves."

"You say those sweet things," Cialia sighed, "but I hear accusations sprinkled among them."

"The only accusations you will find among your sisters are those you make against yourself. My words are true. Until you are able to quiet the fierce woman in you and learn to love all of Coeptus' creation for what it is, you will never truly be a Dragon."

Cialia's sigh was deep and a bit overly dramatic as she laid back against the soft sand. The sky above her—full of mighty, glorious Dragons swimming the currents of the air, red against the deep blue— was perfect as it always was. Everything was perfect. The warm air and gentle breeze carried the fragrances of flowers and ripe fruits all mingled with the rich, earthly smell of the greenery dancing delicately across it. All of that mixed with the magical scent of the Lake which didn't really smell like a lake at all. It smelled like power, primal and never-ending. If only she could stay there forever. If only she could forget her mission and leave those horrid creatures be. As hard as she might wish it could be so, that was something she could not do.

"Please stay with us, love," Lameah implored.

"She cannot, sweet sister," Helias almost sang. "She will remain among us for a time. She will replenish her spirit, drink in the perfect peace of our home, and she will dutifully charge off to kill the gods."

"You are right, my perfect love," Cialia looked in Lameah's massive eye as she replied to Helias.

"And we will love you for it," Lameah smiled.

"Despite all my flaws?" Cialia chuckled.

"In our eyes, you have no flaws," Helias corrected. "You are perfect as you are, and that is how we love you, exactly how you are."

CHAPTER 6
THE COMING STORM

The hall surrounding Daritus was no longer a massive, empty space surrounded by crumbling stone. It had been filled with furniture: massive tables decoratively carved and etched with images spinning yarns of Havenstahl's history, chairs for dignitaries of the great cities who would one day pack the hall to bargain and strategize with the king of the greatest city of men, and a great head table standing out above it all at the front of the room. Daritus still cared nothing of the great fish of Belscythia or the furious scarra of Gandystrint, but the great, wooden crests of those cities—along with all the other great cities Havenstahl could still count as friend—had been repaired to their former glory and painted in the vibrant colors they deserved.

Daritus stood before one of the lesser tables across from Kantiim and Spang, his two oldest friends and most trusted advisors. They all stared down at a map. Daritus grabbed a blue token which had been sitting on top of the castle and moved it to the coast of the Great Sea directly over a small dot with the word Castrine artfully written above it.

Kantiim brushed his graying hair back from his stony face and said, "Finally. My boots are tired of clicking upon these polished stones. They ache for the trail."

"I know they are, and I know they do," Daritus smiled back at his old friend. "The rebuilding is complete. The castle is safe once again. We can turn our eyes toward the lands which have been taken from us. Spang will accompany you and your men to Castrine. Ygraml will lead another half of what remains of our army against the invaders at Gorban's Sound. After you succeed, you will march south. Ygraml will march north. You will take back the entire coast from the invaders."

"I could kiss you right now," Kantiim rounded the table and shoved his elbow into Daritus' ribs as if embarrassed by his own comment.

"Succeed, and I'll kiss you back," the general chuckled.

"You can both keep your lips far away from mine," Spang interjected.

Kantiim laughed good and deep before replying, "Oh, I'm going to kiss you long and deep."

Spang rolled his eyes at Kantiim before mock whispering to Daritus, "Send me with Ygraml. I can't be stuck in a dark camp with this one."

All three of the gruff soldiers lost themselves to laughter. It echoed back of the walls and filled the great hall. The rich sound of happy men was a long missed song to Daritus' ears. It cast his mind back to easier times, laughing with these same two men at the pub or in the throne room in Druindahl. If only he could go back to that place at that time. Alas, the massive hall surrounding him would have to do. There weren't two other men alive he'd rather share the space or a laugh with.

Suddenly, Daritus stopped laughing and smiled at his two oldest chums. "How long has it been since we laughed together like this?" he asked.

"Probably not as long as this room has housed anything so boisterous," Kantiim replied amid the remnants of his laughter. "This room is like an old tomb. We've polished it up but failed to chase the ghosts of bygone days away."

"Ghosts or no," Spang chuckled, "it's been too long for both."

Before another word could be uttered by any of the three, Chagon and Tarantian burst through the massive, wooden door of the hall— these had also been restored to their former grandeur and then some— and raced up to Daritus. They clumsily bowed before him.

Fear danced across Daritus' eyes as Kantiim asked, "Is that you, Tarantian?"

Tarantian didn't look up as his hair, dirty from the trail, dangled in clumps before his face, and he replied, "It is, and the tale of how I come to be in this place instead of our glorious home at the top of the trees is a mighty sad one indeed."

Daritus' shock slowly subsided enough for him to ask, "Where is everyone else?"

Chagon adjusted his ridiculous chain mail cloak and blurted, "Grizzly mongs took to us on the trail," before his companion could answer.

Daritus set his jaw tight, growling more than stating, "Rise."

The two men did as instructed. Tarantian couldn't seem to pull his eyes up from the floor for fear of facing the furious glare of his general. Poor Chagon took the brunt of it. He had never served under a general and had no idea what it meant to feel one's wrath. Nor had he any idea how much worse it was to know the fiery anger flashing across those eyes was actually disappointment, even sorrow, in disguise.

After a few painfully quiet moments, it seemed Chagon could no longer take the silence or the general's horrible glare. He said, "Tarantian fought with honor. He stood tall against them vicious beasts. It weren't much, but I done what I could. I never seen no monsters like what attacked us, and…"

"How is it you managed to avoid a journey to the Lake when apparently no one else in your caravan can boast the same?" Daritus interrupted through the scowl which had taken up residence across his face.

"I sent three of the monsters to the Lake with our kin before they got the better of me," Tarantian finally piped up. "I would gladly trade places with any in that caravan if I could. Sadly, I was only knocked unconscious…"

"Aye and ripped open with infection coursing through his veins," Chagon interrupted, pausing only because Tarantian touched his arm and shook his head slightly.

"When you woke?" Kantiim asked, his expression just as tight as Daritus'.

"My head wasn't altogether too clear, dizziness had a firm hold of me, but I found no remaining souls to protect. Being all were apparently dead or had fled, it seemed prudent to make my way back here to alert you of the coming storm," the seasoned soldier allowed none of the emotion etched across his face into his tone as he gave his report.

Daritus' face moved as if his voice formed words, but none passed his lips. He wondered how many people died on the trail that day, or alongside it as they struggled through injury to find help. Of course, it was no fault of the grimy soldier before him who carried the soot of days on the trail without wash. It was the fault of mindless beasts from the snowy north who may as well have been myths before their existence was confirmed in his soldier's report. Where to lay the blame mattered little to the general as he failed to find words suitable to the moment.

"I would have done the same," Spang's voice finally cut through the deafening silence, "and you would too if you had any sense."

Relief washed over Tarantian's face as Daritus shifted his horrible gaze in his old friend's direction, "If I had any sense, I would have taken my wife and retired to a quiet villa on the eastern shores of the Sea of Sadness years ago."

"Nothing sad about that," Kantiim interjected with raised eyebrows and a smirk that sparked an awkward chuckle among him, Daritus, and Spang.

Chagon's shocked expression only had a moment to settle onto his face before his words poured forth with an equally shocked tone, "How is it ye can be laughing at the thought of so many dead?"

The misplaced chuckle ceased immediately as the three men thought about it. Kantiim finally answered, "Gods attacked this city, and a Dragon who looks like a common girl defended it with fire. My boots are soaked with the blood of my men mingled with the blood of beasts from across the Great Sea. It saturates the fields from here to the beach at Biggon's Bay."

"It isn't the dead who earn our laughter," Spang added, "It is the numbness in our hearts which prevents them from stopping it."

Daritus nodded his agreement as he looked Chagon over before asking, "And who is this brawny, brave, young lad who stands so tall for those passed on against three titans fresh from battle?"

Tarantian answered for his friend, "He is Chagon, formerly a hearty farmer who helped keep the good folk of Havenstahl well fed, back when there were still folk in this great city to feed. This young man is also the only reason I still grace the sweet face of Ouloos. If not for him and the ridiculous armor he wears, I would have long since swam the sweet waters of the Lake. Since losing his land to the fury of gods, he has proven a quick study with the blade he carries, and I will see him ride beneath the banner of Druindahl."

Daritus looked earnestly at the grimy soldier and asked, "Will you vouch for him? Would you walk into battle with this man to guard your back?"

"Above all others," Tarantian nodded.

"Then I will see it is so," he continued looking Chagon over, "We'll get you fitted with proper armor for a rider of Druindahl."

"If it's all the same, I would see him remain in that armor. It would be difficult to properly explain the importance of it, but we'd both like to see him keep the ridiculous thing," Tarantian's tone wasn't quite pleading but close.

Daritus shrugged and glanced over at Kantiim, "Do you suppose we can have this one fitted with something large enough to cover that mail in the proper colors?"

"I'll see it done," the old general replied with the slightest nod.

"Very well," Daritus smiled. "We'll see you properly suited up to defend this castle under my command. In the meantime, why don't the two of you get cleaned up and find yourselves a proper meal. The trail has been less than kind to you, and the news you bring promises very little time for rest."

"Indeed," Tarantian agreed, "that pack seems on a meandering path, but they are headed this way."

"Though I cannot understand what grizzly mongs are doing this far south, it does change our plans," Daritus shook his head before walking back over to his map and moving the blue token back over the castle. "How many in the pack?" he asked.

"Thousands," Tarantian replied quietly.

Before Daritus could offer anything else, the heavy doors of the massive room pounded open again. Tiegran and Bom followed close behind them. Both carried a good bit of grime from the trail on them. The former's dark locks remained luxurious despite the grime lilting them slightly, but his cheeks and red-trimmed, leather cuirass were deeply soiled with that same filth and failed to reflect a similar luster. The latter wore the traditional, drab tunic fitting a giant. It looked even less elegant than normal coated in mud and blood from the trail. Despite his condition, the giant's smile didn't dim in the least as he ducked slightly to avoid bumping his head on the jam of the grand doorway.

"A massive force of soldiers friendly to Havenstahl approaches from the southeast," Tiegran boomed, unable to contain his excitement. Good news came infrequently.

"According to the reports we've received, it is a combined force of at least one hundred thousand from the greatest cities of men," Bom added with equal vigor.

"Does this news give us cause to change our plans again?" Spang asked.

Daritus raised one eyebrow and shrugged before asking Tiegran, "How far off is this mighty force?"

"Maybe a moon," the young soldier replied.

"Maybe a bit more with the coming rains," Bom added.

"They'll be of no help to us against those beasts," Tarantian shook his head. "Those monsters can't be more than two weeks from our gates.

"What beasts?" Bom asked.

"Grizzly mongs," Daritus grimly replied.

"Horrible snow beasts from the north. They lack any kind of planning or logistics, but they swarm. It's as if all individuality flees and they become one, vicious creature," Kantiim added.

"It might be wise to draw all our forces back within the castle, pull up the bridge, and let them pass on through," Spang shrugged.

"Have you ever faced a grizzly mong?" Tarantian asked, the control he held over his tone sounded scarcely more than a thin veil.

"Indeed," Spang smiled as he stepped toward Tarantian, only stopping once they stood eye to eye, "a pack of ten, in fact. It was during my trial, my journey from ice to fire."

"You killed ten grizzly mongs by yourself?" the massive soldier scoffed.

Spang's smile widened as he replied, "I never said I killed them. I used my mind and wisely avoided them. I was unarmed and overmatched with nothing but a small scarra's hide to protect me against the bitter cold. The wise choice was to avoid the conflict. That is what I did, and it is what we should do now." He glanced toward Daritus as he finished the statement.

"If that were a choice we could make, it would be the wise one," Daritus nodded. "Unfortunately, I'm not at all comfortable with the idea of leaving the forest folk helpless in the wake of mindless beasts rampaging across the countryside and destroying everything in their wake. We will draw our forces back to the castle, but it won't be to hide."

"Grant me leave to make a diplomatic trip to Alhouim," Bom piped up. "If these beasts are half as devastating as they sound, we'll need all the help we can get. On top of that, if they make their way to this great city, my grandfather's stolen city could very well be their next destination. I will ask his assistance in turning the beasts away."

"Alhouim is dead," Daritus corrected. "That city is Maomnosett once again, reborn under the rule of your grandfather. If raising someone who hated men and the city of Havenstahl as much as your father is any indication of his feelings, he will never agree to help us."

"It's a fool's errand," Kantiim grimly added.

"I disagree," the young giant argued. "He has the city he wanted. Havenstahl was merely in the way of his goal. Now that his rump is where he believes it belongs, he has no reason to attack Havenstahl. He needn't know we intend to remove him from it once you take back the lands he's stolen from you."

The room grew suddenly quiet as the battle-worn general scanned the wooden crests mounted along the walls of the great room just below the ceiling. He absently scratched his beard as all eyes in the room scrutinized him. All the opinions had been stated, counsel given. Now the decision about what to do was his and his alone. A big part of him wanted to throw his arms up and let them figure it out for themselves. It wasn't his city, after all, and the one who should be defending it hadn't been seen since well before the battle at Biggon's Bay. Of course, he couldn't do that. All the eyes scrutinizing him as he tussled with these competing ideas looked to him for guidance. They had faith in him, trusted him to lead them through this storm.

"I do not like this one bit," he finally said. "What if he kills you?"

"It is a risk I am willing to take," the giant's tone oozed confidence. "However, I do not believe that is something my grandfather would do. As I stated, he already has the city he wants. I'm hoping this fact has mellowed his anger at me. On top of that, I will walk into his city under a white flag. As aloof as my grandfather may be, he still respects the meaning of that symbol. He may have belittling words of disgust for me and my betrayal of him, but I am still of the Maomnosett line, his line. That is the most important thing to him. Finally, I will ask Hountmytall Moy, the tallest of giants, and Lito-Bi, the fiercest trogmortem, to accompany me on my quest. I feel with them, and those under my grandfather's command who I can still count as friend, my life is in no danger."

Daritus considered this for several quiet moments before looking to Tiegran and asking, "Would you and Tarturan be willing to accompany our new friends on this perilous quest?"

"Indeed," the young soldier replied with perhaps a bit more eagerness than necessary, "we found many friends in that city before Ott took the throne from them. Aside from aiding in this mission, I'd like to take stock of their conditions."

"Will Tarturan say the same?" the general asked.

"There could be no doubt," Tiegran replied. "We've talked of sneaking off in the night to run a mission of our own to do the same. He will gladly march to that city."

Before Daritus could utter another sound, Chagon piped up, "Ye can count me in."

"But you're so fresh from the trail," Kantiim argued. "Are you sure you want to be getting back to it so quickly?"

"Up until just shy of a moon ago, I ain't seen nothing but me farm for most of me days," the new soldier shrugged, earning the slightest squeak from his ridiculous armor.

"You can count me in as well," Tarantian said. "I'll be guarding this one's back, and he mine."

"Very well," Daritus frowned. "Though I am not overly fond of this plan, there are a few truths I simply cannot ignore. Moshat has not been with us since we finished rebuilding the castle. Our forces have been decimated, and grizzly mongs are coming. The great force from the southeast will never make it in time to aid us in the defense of this great city, and we can use all the help we can get. It is worth the risk." He glanced around the room once more, making contact with each eye starting back at him, and said, "Make your preparations. You leave at dawn."

CHAPTER 7
BENEATH THE MOUNTAIN

The rock appeared oily and gray just outside the orange glow of torchlight. Bones littered the ground. Most looked like animals. Others appeared to be something the dwarves in Muljaak's small group preferred not to think about. How long had it been since any dwarves ventured this deep into the caves beneath Alhouim—or Maomnosett if you believe that imposter on the throne to be king? His rump wouldn't warm that seat for long if Muljaak had anything to say about it. Hopefully, the mighty men of Havenstahl would aid in taking it back from the fearsome giant.

The going had been slow. Though Alenaat's condition was improving, he still required frequent breaks and was unable to walk without assistance. Despite the two dwarves toting him about being more than able, Alenaat was a load to bear. The wounded dwarf's weak groan was a signal he needed to rest once again.

Lentaak and Chialdaan carried the young, injured dwarf along each with an arm draped across their shoulders. The groan prompted Lentaak to lean over and whisper to Chialdaan, "Set him against the wall here."

After unloading the burden, Chialdaan rubbed his shoulder and said, "How does such a scrawny thing carry so much weight?"

"Dead weight," Muljaak replied, his keen eyes scanning the darkness outside their small dome of light. Though slight, it offered a small sense of protection against whatever might be hiding just beyond its strength. After a few moments of quiet, he turned toward Lentaak and asked, "How well ye be knowing these caves?"

"More than a few summers have passed since I've had cause to use them, but they ain't changing from one moment to the next," the quietest dwarf in all of Alhouim replied.

"What about all these bones?" he asked grimly. "Have they always been littering these paths?"

"Aye," Chialdaan piped in, "I've been wondering that same thing. What other creatures might be hiding out in this dark with us?"

The sureness in Lentaak's expression faltered slightly as he replied, "I've been trying not to think too much about that."

Muljaak shook his head as a joyless smile crept onto his face, "Lots of noises besides the shuffling of our feet on these dusty rocks. Reminds me of tales told of that mountain what fell from the sky."

"Grindelhorn," Chialdaan spoke quietly.

"Aye, Grindelhorn," Muljaak agreed, "mighty mountain fallen from the heavens in the time before time, discovered by Grindel the nomad and mined by his descendants for generations until…"

"Aye, until," Lentaak quietly scoffed. "All them stories about what happened to the great clan of Grindel deep in the star what fell from the skies."

"Them mines ain't mined no more," Chialdaan interjected, "and ain't no dwarf I know brave enough to go find out why. Mining the ore in that place would be quite lucrative for any willing to risk it."

"Greed," Lentaak shook his head. "If anything did the clan of Grindel in, it was greed. Mining too deep in that mountain and toppling it from within."

Muljaak's face became graven, the shadows playing upon his features gave him a ghostly appearance. "That ain't at all what I heard," he said. "What I heard is they did dig too deep, but that ain't caused the great mountain to fall in on itself or nothing of the sort. They dug so deep they found other paths. Paths carved by other things. Things no tired dwarf wants to find in the darkness."

"Could it be the mighty Muljaak be afraid of the dark?" Lentaak offered a joyless chuckle.

Ignoring the jest, the mighty dwarf pressed on, "Afraid? Sure. I be very afraid, but it ain't the dark what scares me. What be hiding in that darkness, hiding so ye can't see it until it's too late, until them glistening fangs be piercing the tender parts of your throat and draining ye of your life's blood?"

"Grong's, I heard," Alenaat interrupted, his tone weak and gravelly, "but they ain't no grongs like what ye mighty dwarves faced in the battle of Maomnosett. These grongs have gone underground, digging and burrowing under mountains for ages upon ages. They eat up all the living things hiding in the soil until there ain't nothing else but their kin to be feasting on, and they do that."

"Cannibal grongs?" Lentaak's laughter echoed back off the cave's walls. "That be a fine yarn to spin round the campfire, but there ain't no truth to it."

"I heard them same tales," Chialdaan complained, "and more. Generations under ground have changed them. Their eyes can see in the darkness as good as we see with clear skies at midday. Their claws have grown longer as they dig and dig without the use of picks or tools. And their scales have smoothed so they can slither through the small spaces none of us could get through."

Muljaak nodded in agreement as Lentaak shook his head and waved the nonsense off.

Then the sound came. It was something none of them leaning against the cave wall in the dim, orange glow of the torchlight could ignore. It was a low growl at first, but it petered off until it was nothing more than quiet clicking, something more like a gear turning against a brake. It was nothing like a sound a living creature should make. Then the tentative footsteps of padded feet with claws scraping dusty rock mingled in with the clicking.

All three able-bodied dwarves jumped up at the same time. Muljaak and Chialdaan readied their axes while Lentaak held his torch out toward the sound providing as much light as the flickering thing was willing to give. The three stood tensely peering into darkness so pitch no shapes could be discerned within it. Nothing appeared to move within the void before them, but the sound remained.

Muljaak suddenly tensed up. A slight current tickled the hairs on his cheek. It was barely noticeable but carried the coppery smell of stale blood upon it. He turned toward the cave wall and shouted to Lentaak, "Turn that torch toward the wall over here. We are not alone."

As Lentaak obliged the command, Muljaak's eyes failed to believe what they clearly saw. The thing clinging to the wall at eye level with him did resemble a grong, but its body was too smooth and too dark. The armor plates which would adorn a normal grong's back from skull to tail were absent with nothing more than slight mounds in their place.

The thing's snout looked like any other grong if not a bit pointier, and the teeth within it seemed longer and sharper than a grong's should. The eyes though, they were the worst. They didn't look like grongs' eyes. They were massive black orbs glowing in the dim torch's glow, soaking up every bit of light available and reflecting it back. He froze as the beast coiled up its body and roared, launching itself toward his face.

Muljaak had seen enough battles that his limbs didn't require much guidance from his mind. Despite the fact that the suddenly useless thing keeping his cranium from collapsing on itself failed to provide any guidance, his body instinctively responded to the attack. The beast wasn't more than an inch into his jump before the big dwarf was pushing his friends aside with a stiff shoulder and swinging his axe toward its neck.

Those giant eyes grew even bigger as the mighty dwarf axe sliced through skin, meat, tendon, and bone. Muljaak's roar filled the small space as echoes of echoes bounced off the walls, and his victim's blood splashed all about his beard. "Ye can spin that tale around a fire if we make it out of this cave," he shouted toward Lentaak as the dead thing's body fell harmlessly against the floor.

The silence which followed was as deafening as it was brief. Deep growls mingled with screeching howls and filled the cave. There had to be hundreds of the grong-like creatures hiding in the darkness ready to descend upon the weary dwarves like madness on a lost traveler's mind.

Just as the sound of thousands of claws digging into rock joined the deafening chorus of growls and howls Muljaak shouted, "Run!"

Lentaak and Chialdaan heeded the command, gathering up Alenaat and charging as quickly into darkness as they could. Muljaak was hot on their heels, pushing them forward. The sounds grew louder as the cave shrunk around them.

"The walls be closing in on us," Chialdaan shouted.

"Aye," Lentaak breathlessly replied, "the path grows smaller ahead but opens up again after a time."

Muljaak suddenly realized they wouldn't make it. The beasts were gaining on his group too quickly, and, if the stories he'd heard were to be believed, those monsters would make it through the small spaces far more quickly than he and his chums could. He charged along for one hundred more steps and stopped. The cave around him had grown so small he could swing his axe from ceiling to floor and wall to wall. None would pass.

"What are ye doing?" Chialdaan shouted.

"Go," the mighty dwarf replied. "See them two safely to Havenstahl and return with a mighty force to take back our city from that bastard, Ott."

Chialdaan hesitated for a moment. Leaving a friend behind was nothing any solida wanted to do, but he couldn't argue with the wisdom of Muljaak's command. Lentaak would never get Alenaat out of there without his help, and someone needed to convince Havenstahl to make good on their debt to Alhouim. "We'll meet again at the Lake, old friend," he shouted.

"Ye keep your arse out of Lake for as long as ye can," Muljaak replied. Then he shouted into the darkness, "Come on, ye vile monsters. Bring your sorry carcasses to my hungry axe."

The torch nearly flickered out when the brute of a dwarf tossed it a few feet in front him—near enough to bathe his small battlefield in orange but far enough to avoid any glare. The vile creatures pursuing him had gained. Their throaty grunts and growls increased in volume as the horde approached. Muljaak couldn't see much past his torch burning on the dusty ground, but it was enough.

Suddenly, everything grew quiet. It was so quiet Muljaak could hear the sounds of his friends quietly grunting and complaining about the narrow passage Lentaak had described. Despite the grumbling, they sounded further off than the dutiful dwarf had expected they would be. That was all the better. Though he had the utmost confidence in his axe, those beasts would be swarming him at any moment.

Those eyes with their weird negative glow were the first things he saw. The beast was creeping slowly along the ceiling far more stealthily than any grong Muljaak had ever seen. These were obviously no dull creatures. They knew their environment well, and they knew how to use the darkness to their advantage. Thank the gods for the dim, orange light of his dying torch. Without it, that first beast might have snuck right up on him and ended his valiant last stand before it even had a chance to begin.

The cunning monster must have realized it had been spotted. It howled like a mountain scarra with her leg caught in trap as it lunged at Muljaak all fangs and claws.

This wasn't his first dance with a grong by far. Though the beast soaring through the stale air wasn't like any he'd seen before, it was a still a grong. A mere six inches separated razor sharp claws from the dwarf's face when he gritted his teeth and swung his axe. By the time the grizzly death bringer's momentum had ceased, the beast had been split from its snout all the way down to between its shoulder blades.

Muljaak snapped his blade hard to the right, slamming the twitching beast against the wall and removing his blade from bone in the process. The whimpering sound the thing made as it slid down the wall into a puddle of its own insides was a sweet song to his ears. His axe's appetite had been whet. Let the monsters come.

The stout dwarf stood strong as they came, gnashing their teeth as they climbed over each other to get to him. Every inch of cave wall was covered in them. Muljaak feverishly swung his axe. Limbs flew as bodies dropped from the ceiling, lunged from the walls, and leapt from the floor. Before long, the trampling horde had stomped out his failing torch and left no light for him to see the result of his macabre work. He didn't care. There were so many of them he didn't need to see what he was swinging at. Every stroke of his mighty axe connected with flesh and bone. It tore through meat and severed limbs.

The raging dwarf could barely sense he was in his own body by the time his axe became useless. There were too many, and they were just too close. He shoved the mighty axe forward into darkness, connecting with something that howled louder in response, and let the trusty, old friend fall to the floor. From that point on, it was all elbows, knees, and his stony forehead. Everything that touched him got one of the three until he felt the burn in his shoulder.

Muljaak couldn't see the beast that had sunk its fangs deep into him. That didn't matter. His rage was great enough as it was. He leaned his head over and bit the thing back. It was impossible to know exactly what part of his adversary was clamped within his jaws, but he bit down as hard as he could. The monster howled, released its grip, and the mighty dwarf was swinging elbows again.

Finally, he felt one of the slimy creatures slither past him along the wall. He grabbed hold of it with both hands and tried to pull it back. The effort was successful for the briefest of moments until the rest of the mob slammed into his back and pushed him further into the cave toward his fleeing friends.

Muljaak dug his heels in and tried to hold them back, but there were too many. His feet slid across the dusty ground. He kept swinging, pushing, and fighting for as long as he could. Then the claws and the fangs came. They slashed and they bit. He grew weaker with each swipe and each chomp. The cave had finally grown so narrow that none could get by him. This would truly be his last stand.

It didn't hurt as much as he thought it might when the fangs punctured the flesh of his throat. Perhaps it was the adrenaline, but he was certain a thorn that had wedged itself in the tender part of his foot as a young lad had been worse. What an odd thing to think about with a monster dangling from your neck and hoping to rip the soul from your body. He hadn't thought of that day in at least twenty summers. Yet, there was his foot as clear as the day it happened, that bloody mess staring back at him while he sat upon a stump viewing the carnage and listening to the harassment of his most bosom chums.

His leg was next. The fangs poked into his thigh. Something about the pressure of the beast's jaws made him feel his own pulse. That was an odd sensation. It probably should have hurt more when the monster violently shook its head and ripped the damn thing off.

It suddenly occurred to him how these vile creatures would get by him. With every piece of him they stole, he'd grow smaller. He probably wouldn't have laughed if there were anything he could do about it, but there wasn't. There were too many, and he was too tired. They would have all his limbs off and probably his head too before they were done. Then they would race through those small parts of the cave until they reached his friends. Hopefully, they had gotten enough of a lead. The thought seemed silly. These monsters were quick in the darkness. Then the world grew quiet, and Muljaak's thoughts ceased.

The path before Lentaak finally widened enough he and his small group could stand. After dragging Alenaat out of the narrowest passage any of the three had ever crawled through, he finally did just that. It seemed his eyes may have been playing tricks on him, but he could finally see light. His torch had died as his belly scraped the dusty floor of the cave, but now he could clearly see sunlight. It was dim, but it was there. Something about the passage must have changed. He hadn't been that way in quite some time, but he recalled enough of the last time he'd slunk along that very same passage he knew the light should still be a long way off. Perhaps the fear of being chased by those horrible creatures had his mind feeling as tricky as his eyes.

"Muljaak has fallen," Chialdaan said quietly as he worked his way out of the tight passage.

"How can you know that?" Lentaak asked.

"I just do," sadness coiled around the brief statement.

Lentaak had no time to respond. A moment after he felt Alenaat's body against the back of his legs, the ground beneath him had fled. He fell fast. It was difficult to tell how quickly he slid down the steep embankment as the dim speck of light in the distance wasn't enough to offer any visual cues to his rate of descent. It didn't matter much. He probably wouldn't be able to gauge his speed if he were leaping off a mountain beneath a blazing sun. He was falling much too quickly, and that was all the info he needed to let his terror roar. And roar it did.

"Lentaak?" the raspy tone of Chialdaan's voice had all the characteristics of a shout, but it sounded far too quiet for anything that might have boomed from that dwarf's mouth.

The plummeting dwarf was far too busy screaming to offer any kind of response. Even if his wild cries had left any room in his wide opened mouth for any other sounds to pour out, his mind couldn't put together a cognizant thought. Translating any idea that may have occurred to him was an even greater impossibility.

It felt like a wall when he hit the still water. He sunk beneath the surface so quickly, the idea he had fallen onto the cave floor didn't even have time to settle in. Luckily, the one thing which did sink in was the idea to stop screaming. An open mouth while sinking fast into dark water was a good way to drown.

As disorienting as it was to dip down into the drink, he kept enough of his wits to swim in the direction he'd come. He must have sunk at least three times his own height. He was a strong swimmer, by dwarf standards, and it took a few long moments to break the surface. Once he had, and his adrenaline had a chance to cool off after falling, it occurred to him just how cold it was in the small cave pond he vigorously bobbed about in.

His breath quickened as his limbs churned feverishly to keep his head above the shallow waves. "I'm here," he finally called out into the darkness.

"What happened?" Chialdaan replied, his voice sounded far off.

The question seemed silly after all the screaming and splashing he'd done, but the dark had been disorienting enough before he found himself bobbing in frigid water. There was no time for arguing, so he didn't. "The ground what used be there ain't no more," he shouted instead. "There be a steep cliff. I ain't getting back up there."

"As well ye shouldn't," Chialdaan hollered back. "Them beasts be coming fast. Back up."

Lentaak couldn't see Alenaat's falling form, but the sound of his scream was undeniable. The scruffy dwarf's voice was high-pitched and squeaky enough when he wasn't hollering out in fear. The sound the poor sap made while plummeting through darkness was downright hard on the ears. A moment after that horrible sound began, Chialdaan's roar joined it in a chorus of terror that lasted until two big splashes ended the song.

"Help me grab this one," a breathless Chialdaan called out in the darkness.

Lentaak obliged, moving toward the sound and looping his arm under Alenaat's armpit. "Swim toward the light," he shouted.

The going was slow. Dwarves aren't the greatest swimmers and tugging along an injured oaf ruined any speed adrenaline could have gained them. However, the dim light in the distance grew closer with each stroke. The quietest dwarf in all of Alhouim almost found cause for relief until he heard the growls.

"They be hot on our heels," Chialdaan shouted.

The dwarves pumped their arms and legs faster amid the echoes of screeching howls. Then there was a splash, and another. There were so many, it sounded like an avalanche crashing into the Great Sea. The beasts had not given up the chase.

Finally, Lentaak's hand slapped against wet rock. The light ahead was still pretty far off, but he could faintly make out the ground before him. After helping Chialdaan drag Alenaat out of the drink, he slowly got his bearings back. That light was the hidden cave entrance at the base of the mountain he was looking for, but it used to be at the end of a long and winding path. At some point, that floor must have crumbled into the dark cavern surrounding them. Perhaps it had been the great quake on Maelich's day two summers prior. The mountaintop had trembled slightly that day. With all the drinking and dancing and merriment going on, they had all assumed it was the mighty thunder of thousands of happy dwarf feet pounding into the dirt in celebration. Maybe it had been the mountain's innards crumbling beneath them.

"Move," Chialdaan's voice snapped Lentaak out of his brief bout of reminiscence. The cause really wasn't important anyway. The fact they were close to escaping the darkness was the real story. At least in the light they could turn on their pursuers and put up a fight.

The light grew larger as the sounds of the monsters chasing them grew louder. It was a lot of splashing, growling, and howling at first, but it wasn't long before the grinding sound of claws scraping against stone began mingling with the rest.

Lentaak pumped his legs as hard as he could while dragging Alenaat along. Though he knew Chialdaan to be stronger and faster, he did his best to match the brute's pace. The glorious sun was just a few hundred feet before him. The thought got his churning legs moving even faster. He could see the glorious green of the vines craftily planted to hide the entrance from any who didn't know it was there glowing with the wonderful sunlight just beyond them. A smile managed to slip onto his face just before he missed a step and tumbled to the rocky floor beneath him.

Moving as fast as they were, Lentaak's momentum carried all three of the fleeing dwarves to the floor. It was probably just the terror amplified by the horde gaining ground on them, but it seemed their growls and howls and shouts grew even louder as they all scrambled back to their feet.

"Damn your clumsy feet," Chialdaan grumbled. "Ain't ye got the surest step of any dwarf who ever lived?"

Lentaak ignored the jibe but agreed with the sentiment. His emotions were raging like a young dwarf in the throes of passion pressing his lips against his lover's for the first time. Though a passionate kiss was a million miles from his current situation, he had about as much control of his emotions in that moment as a young lover would.

The sounds of thick and sharpened claws scraping against rock muddy with soot and water from drenched dwarves echoed in the massive cavern cavorting with the growls and shouts of mindless beasts. Lentaak thought his heart might pound right out of his chest as he and his chums tumbled back to the rough ground a mere ten feet from the freedom hidden by those glowing vines.

"Damn my stupid feet," Chialdaan hollered at the darkness.

Alenaat just groaned something low and defeated.

Lentaak had barely considered getting back to his feet when he felt it. It only scraped the sole of his boot, but there could be no mistake about what it was. The thought of those black claws reaching out for him in the darkness flashed through his mind as he kicked both his legs and howled as if he'd been stabbed in the gut. "Move," he finally shouted.

The terrified dwarf gave up on the idea of gaining his feet opting instead to crawl across the slippery ground dragging Alenaat behind him. Apparently, Chialdaan had the same idea. Whether it was sheer terror or the fact their wet boots were no longer trying to navigate slimy, wet rock, they seemed to make better time on the ground than they had while running. The horrible sounds so close they had his eardrums pounding served to quicken his pace even more.

Those glorious vines were right before him. Lentaak stretched out his hand and grabbed hold of one, pulling himself toward the exit and the safety of the sunlight it failed to completely hide. Just as he thought his small group would make it through that glowing portal to freedom, Alenaat grew heavier. The poor waif howled in pain.

"They've got hold of him," Chialdaan screamed.

"Pull, damn it," Lentaak shouted back at him.

Lentaak watched in horror as Chialdaan failed to heed his command. Instead, the brute launched himself over Alenaat and into the beast who had grabbed a hold of the scrawny dwarf's feet. That would be their end. Chialdaan would battle until all the life had left him, and then the gruesome beasts would move onto to him and Alenaat. No one would ever hear of the rescue or the bravery of any of the stout dwarves who laid down their lives for the failed cause.

"Go," Chialdaan shouted after battering the beast with his fists.

Shock that Chialdaan was barking orders at him rather than bleeding out in the filtered sunlight nearly froze him in place, but Lentaak heeded the command. He pulled with all his might and dragged Alenaat through the vines and into the magnificent sunlight. He only allowed himself the briefest moment of relief as he pulled his injured friend far enough away from the hidden cave entrance that he could offer at least a bit of protection. He couldn't leave Chialdaan behind. Though the beastly brute was probably already dead, he couldn't live with himself if he failed to confirm that.

Three short steps were all he made back toward those vines when Chialdaan flew out from them with one of the slimy beasts pounding into his chest. The three fell to the ground, all of them rolling several feet before any of them could right themselves.

Chialdaan was the first to make it back to his feet. His scowl was covered in gore that saturated his beard and dripped onto his grimy tunic from three deep gashes on his cheek. The wound didn't slow him down in the least as his right fist swung wild at the beast who had started screaming as soon as the sun's rays hit its wet skin.

Lentaak jumped up and dragged the confused dwarf away from the sizzling monster he had just punched. The creature's form quickly began melting as it writhed in smoky pain.

"The myths be true," Lentaak couldn't hide his shock as he watched the sun burn the poor creature to death.

Screams from behind him dragged his attention away from the smoking monster. A few snouts poked about the vines here and there, but only one other cave grong tried challenging the sun, and that one met a similar end to the one Chialdaan had punched.

After a few moments of howling and screaming, both the monsters were nothing more than smoky piles of goo and ash. A few moments after that, curious snouts stopped poking through the vines, and all the grunting, growling, and howling stopped completely.

Then it was quiet.

It seemed a long time had passed before Chialdaan touched his cheek, hissed at the pain, and lost himself in laughter. "I ain't thought I'd see the light of day again, and here I stand."

"Aye," Lentaak laughed back at the brute. "Let's get our sorry carcasses across Galgooth and get the two of you to Havenstahl and the healing hand of Hagen."

CHAPTER 8
SAND AND SKY

The sun blazed bright above the cracked, dry ground beneath Perrin's feet. She knew it was some kind of trick. The flat ground she stood upon, sweating behind her sword, only persisted for roughly twenty feet in any direction. It wasn't quite a perfect circle, but it was close. Beyond that small bit of order, chaos reigned. Were they stars, planets, comets maybe? Perhaps, but the shapes were all wrong and the colors impossible. They raced across various hues in various saturations amid an inconsistent sky. If it were sky at all. The difference between ground and sky was impossible to discern in the queer place without a clear delineation between the two in the horizon.

Her opponent stood before her in a relaxed stance wearing a confident smirk beneath his smoldering eyes and purposely careless hair. It would be nice to knock the look off his smug face. Unfortunately, they had been training all morning, and Dirk had proven to be an exceptional swordsman. Of course, it could be that her skill hadn't grown as much as Glord would have her believe. None of the men in her group would ever let on, but she was pretty sure they went easy on her during training. This warrior from the city with no name in the land of chaos afforded her no such luxury.

"You move like a warrior who's been training for years," Dirk surprised her with the compliment.

"Don't mock," she complained before dragging her forearm across her forehead in a failed attempt at clearing away the sweat or the drenched hair plastered to it.

"I wouldn't dare," he seemed genuinely offended by the claim. "I have been training with this sword since I was a lad. What's more, defending my home from the creatures who haunt this wonderful place has been my only job. According to your own proclamations, which are very self-deprecating—believe me, my queen, if I ever hear anyone, anywhere speak of you in the same fashion you speak of yourself, I will strike that fool down where he stands—you are very young to the warrior's way."

"I appreciate the compliment," she blushed, "but I am no one's queen."

"Whether you like it or not, you are queen of the greatest city of men," Dirk countered as he flicked a lazy forehand toward her face.

She parried the attack and countered with a quick backhand and a thrust that had him on his heels. "A title bestowed only because my husband is the king. I am no leader," she grunted while continuing her assault.

He spun around her attack and put her on the defensive as he continued to disagree, "Again, you belittle yourself. After all you've done, do you really see yourself as this mouse you describe? When I encountered your small group with my riders at my back, you were the one rallying those men who followed you to the place that is the ultimate terror for anyone who hails from your side of the Lake. They followed you because you are a natural leader."

"I am a mother who is terrified about what might be happening to her son right now," she shook her head. "That is all I am. Nothing more," she finished with a thrust toward his midsection.

"In this place you can be anything," he smiled wide as a circle of ground raised up to shoot him over the attack and launched him into a flip over her head, "but you are far more than what you think of yourself."

Perrin's eyes were wide as she spun toward him just in time to block a slash at her face. "How?" was all she could muster.

Dirk simply smiled, dipped his head slightly to the left, and raised his arms out wide. A moment later, the ground beneath her feet bucked wildly and sent her careening into those arms. Her momentum carried the two of them onto the cracked dirt beneath them which somehow softened as they crashed upon it.

They were both laughing as Perrin lifted her head off his chest and noticed the fierce amber color of his eyes. Her cheeks flushed again as she averted her gaze, unable to look at the hunger lingering behind his for too long.

"Well, aren't the two of you, cozy?" Ycharaz's accusing tone snatched the warmth away from the brief embrace.

"We were training," Perrin stammered as she struggled back to her feet.

"Training? To do what, my queen, tickle the back of his throat with your tongue?" he asked with a joyless chuckle.

"Someone sees you as more than his fearless leader," Dirk's smile faded as he glared at Ycharaz for a few moments before adding, "I was teaching her how to use the environment to her benefit in battle. Lessons are always more impactful when you don't realize you're being taught anything."

"Interesting battle stance," Ycharaz scowled, "cuddled closely into your adversary's chest. Care to show me the technique?"

Coated in a thick sheen of sweat, and as comfortable as one might expect, Perrin quickly grew tired of both the exchange and Ycharaz's accusatory tone. "Enough," she finally groaned, "if our brief time in this place has taught me anything, it is that we must move and act as a tight unit not a group of prideful individuals driven by emotion. Dirk has left his home to guide us on our journey and teach us to navigate this foreign environment. We should appreciate rather than condemn the effort."

The crestfallen soldier's deep bow to one knee was as mocking as his tone when he replied, "Your will, my queen."

Perrin sighed as she shook her head, failing to trick herself into thinking Ycharaz's feelings about what he had witnessed were far off target. Dirk had an odd charisma about him, and he had orchestrated events perfectly to put her in a position where emotions could easily overcome logic and common sense. The more the competing ideas tussled in her head, the more agitated she became with both men standing before her. Neither of them had any right to question her outside of strategy or tactical maneuvers, and, even then, they were nothing more than advisors.

She suddenly grew equally agitated with herself. Dirk was correct when he suggested she was the leader of this group. If she expected these men to follow her, she had to be someone worthy of following. Would she follow herself if walking in their boots? It was a question she couldn't answer. Were they following her into peril because she inspired them to some greater purpose or because they felt a duty to protect her? Did they still see her as a damsel requiring strong men to save her? Could she see herself as anything more? She wanted to, but a small part of her yearned for that time when things were so simple. She could never be the person she was then, but the blissful ignorance of the world outside her window that damsel enjoyed did have its pleasing qualities. In those days that seemed so long ago, her entire life had been dedicated to making the man she loved happy. As easy as it was, she despised that weak thing who would serve at a man's whim and hide behind his shield of protection. For all the pain those soulless monsters who ripped away her joy when they came to steal her child had caused her, they did grant her one blessing. They gave her purpose, a reason to do something. Despite that faint longing for those bygone days, she would never go back there and trap herself within those walls even if she could. She could never be happy in that place again.

"My queen?" Ycharaz's voice finally dragged her away from thoughts better left unexplored while attacking the trail.

"Forgive me. My mind was far from this place," she replied. After composing herself, she continued, "Training is done. Where are the rest of the men?"

"Making camp," he replied. "Hard to say whether it will still be that when we wake."

All in the group had ceased using terms like morning, day, or evening as the words carried no meaning in the lands beyond the Lake, the place where the maps don't go. If time existed there, it had no control of anything.

"We can help them finish the work," Perrin replied.

"I will give us some cover," Dirk smiled. "Before we left my home, Antopy had been teaching us about trees. They sound wonderful. I can't promise how long they'll last or what they'll become, but they should shade us from any light long enough to find slumber."

"I would like to see what trees from your imagination would look like," Antopy's voice arrived a moment before she appeared next to Dirk, stepping out from behind a starry sky as if it were a wall, unbroken until she appeared with her light brown locks drifting about the soft skin of her face like a crown.

Perrin's tone betrayed how startled she was by the queen's sudden appearance, "I thought you wouldn't be joining us on this journey."

"I will not," Antopy smiled, "but I allow my mind to remain open and see much. Despite the negative impact your lesson had on your valiant soldier's fragile emotions, it was valuable. I felt it worthwhile to pay you a visit and explain Dirk's ability to control his surroundings in greater detail. It is a skill you should learn. You plan to defeat these lands and battle a power beyond your comprehension. A girl with a sword poses very little threat to anything in this unpredictable place, much less a great and powerful god."

The obvious slight had her feeling small and foolish as she shrugged and replied, "I am that, I suppose, just a girl with a sword, and I see the folly you so clearly point out. No one has painted it so clearly for me before. Seeing it doesn't change what I must do, or my belief that I can. I believe I will hold my son in my arms again. What I can't imagine is controlling anything like Dirk did in that moment. I don't even know where to begin."

"You will never do anything you don't believe you can do," the queen of a place with no name in the land where the maps don't go smiled wider, "but imagine what is possible when nothing is impossible. They called it magic before the act was forbidden in the lands from which you hail—bending the laws of nature to your will and disturbing the perfect order so cherished in those parts."

"Well, I can't do magic," Perrin frowned. "I am barely adequate at swinging this sword around."

Antopy's smile faded as her voice softened, "Try something for me." She pointed to a swirling purple spot in the sky and continued, "Think of a memory, something that brought you joy, and want it. It has to be something meaningful, impactful."

Perrin's brows dipped toward her nose as she scoffed, "Dirk summoned a circle of dry ground to fight upon. How meaningful or impactful could dry dirt be to anyone?"

Antopy laughed and replied, "Dirk has been training to manifest his desires since he was a young boy. Like any other skill, it is improved by practice. You must first learn what it feels like to allow your wants to find you. Once you know this, you can search for it. The search becomes easier with each journey until the act seems like magic to the untrained."

Perrin's eyes narrowed. As impossible as it seemed, she had witnessed Dirk toy with their surroundings and make the world around him do exactly what he wanted. The first thing that popped into her head was Geillan, then her husband. Both seemed impossible, but they were the two things in the world that brought her the greatest moments of joy in her life. She wanted nothing more than to have her family together. It was something she had never experienced in her brief time as a mother. Now both were hidden, one kidnapped and the other run away. If that queen or witch or whatever she was were to be believed, she'd have to focus on one of them. Maelich was her true love, even after breaking her heart by fleeing his duties for the company of a corpse, but ever since she'd heard his first, helpless cry, Geillan ruled her heart. She focused on him.

She suddenly remembered that dark and horrible day when Kallum's priests came calling. They weren't Kallum's priests at all. She'd thought as much at the time, but Antopy had corrected her when first they'd met. Ijilv commanded those vile, dead things to steal her love, her brand-new baby boy. The halls of the castle at Havenstahl always had coolness about them, but on that day the hallway outside her chamber had been downright cold. A chill shot through her as she recalled it. Geillan's tiny body had shook so violently as he screamed terrified and agitated in her arms. The helpless feeling that had so consumed her as she failed to calm him in that moment returned like a gaping hole from her throat to her gut. She felt so small and useless. There was nothing she could do to calm him. Then the flame came. Though she stood next to Antopy on a wild and ever-changing landscape, that same hallway at Havenstahl surrounded her. She felt the same shock at the realization her sweet babe had the same power as his father. It flared up and licked her face, Dragon's Fire. The pain she felt in that moment was worse than anything she'd ever felt. It burned so hot it almost felt cold, colder than anything she could imagine. She dropped him to the hard bricks, and his flames grew. He laid there on the cold floor screaming and blazing in a raging ball of flame.

Everything else melted away. The only thing that remained was her baby boy flaming and screaming as she stared down at him. His tiny body convulsed as flames surrounded him and licked up toward the sky. She yearned for him. She wanted to ignore the flames and pluck him up into her arms to soothe him, but she heard that voice. In that moment, it didn't matter which of those bastards it had been, Kallum or Ijilv. Which of them spoke the words meant very little. What mattered was the vile thing had called her precious babe his son. Rage burned in her. She wanted to punch and stab and choke the wicked god.

Suddenly, she felt real heat. Flames licked up past her face. Her trousers were burning. The idea to drop to the ground and roll until the flames subsided flashed through her mind before she was on the ground with Ycharaz above her frantically patting the flames down. "My queen," he shouted at her.

Then the flame was gone. It fled as quickly as it had come. "I'm fine," an odd joy tiptoed about her voice as she realized what those painful flames meant.

"Your mind has opened," Antopy smiled as her words validated Perrin's thought. "Your love for Geillan took you back to that awful place, and you manifested that flame. Odd," she added with a cocked brow, "I expected a happier memory."

Sadness settled in to dampen her joy as she replied, "There was precious little time to make any before those monsters came. His flame is really all I have."

"And that memory helped you create the same. Think about that," despite the sweetness in Antopy's tone there was just a hint of scolding swimming about in it. "That is the lesson. Keep yearning. Keep trying. Keep practicing. Nothing is beyond your abilities."

Then she was gone again as quickly as she had come, that witch or queen or whatever she was. Perrin gave the quick disappearance little thought as her mind shifted quickly to the lesson. Antopy had given her a gift before departing, and she would hold tightly to it. The path she took to conjure those flames was etched on her mind like an open door waiting for her to step through again and again.

CHAPTER 9
THE EDGE OF CHAOS

The sky—if it could be called as much—spiraled and swirled. It stretched and twisted into impossible contortions of equally impossible colors. No constants existed in the mayhem. Colors blazed brightly before dimming to near imperceptible levels only to change completely and blaze in a different hue even brighter than before. Shapes were inconsistent. Smooth edges became rough and ragged only to round out once again. Celestial bodies impossible to name or identify followed no apparent predefined paths, zigging and zagging and colliding with one another. These indefinable things grew and shrunk as quickly as their colors faded and blazed.

Moshat stood at the edge of a crumbling landscape which shifted as rapidly as the colors it bled into, the edges between each growing and receding as if in constant battle with one another. He was a perfect, glowing contradiction of the madness surrounding him. His white beard hung straight and tidy all the way to his waist, glowing brighter than a thousand suns. His hair and robe glowed with equal brilliance. He gripped his staff tighter, all his will focused on convincing himself he was unafraid. Despite the effort, the faintest hint of terror coiled tightly around the base of his spine.

His brother, Kaldumahn, stood beside him, equally brilliant against the chaotic scene. The presence of his brother—the god known, feared, and worshipped as the great, silver lion who stalks the skies— did little to quell his slight twinge of fear.

"Why have you brought here, Moshat?" the god's voice was deep and mighty, a thing both horrible and glorious. "When you failed to meet me at our temple as we had discussed prior to venturing off to rally the various tribes of men who will strengthen our vigor with the weight of their love and adoration, I had no idea it was to saunter off to this place that made you feel so," Kaldumahn paused as if straining to recall the exact word, "sick, I believe you said."

Moshat didn't need to see the smug look upon his brother's face to recognize the jibe. He loved throwing those barbs, obviously thinking they made him sound clever. There wasn't anything clever about the great silver lion. If only he could allow himself to fully commit to his charades. Maybe then he could come up with something that truly stung. He was too worried about ensuring his sarcasm was fully understood. Any veil the simple creature might employ to disguise his intention was drawn back or laid bare to eliminate any potential misunderstanding of his true intention.

"What I felt when I told you that is precisely what men describe as feeling ill or sick," Moshat refused to play along, "but we haven't the time to discuss that topic again."

"It is just as well. You are horribly outmatched in our debates." Kaldumahn laughed longer than necessary, obviously a last-ditch effort to spark an argument. After letting the laugh simmer into a low chuckle, he finally gave up and asked, "Fine, brother, why then have you brought me to this horrible place where the order we love is so unwelcome and the tower we failed to find the last time we stood on this very spot remains as absent as it was then?"

"Because it is there, right before us at the edge of time where it has stood since the beginning of time," he smirked as he finally turned his head toward his brother to see the smug look replaced by something twisted and confused.

"You have lost your mind," Kaldumahn finally blurted.

"On the contrary," Moshat chuckled at his befuddled companion, "you have failed to use yours to its full capacity. You see, when last we stood on this spot, we were rash, confused, possibly a bit afraid of our brother and that loose Dragon. We had no plan. Once we had one— full credit to you for that—I had time to reflect on the time we spent here looking for that missing thing."

"Please speak plainly, brother," the silver lion sighed. "Though I do not *feel sick* as you described it, I have no desire to look upon this hideous scenery any longer than necessary. Not to mention, that loose

Dragon will soon enough return to the hunt."

Kaldumahn's frustration delighted Moshat. His brother loved games when he was the master of the board. He was far less fond of them when someone else had a stronger command of the rules. Moshat finally had the upper hand. If only he had more time to toy with his brother.

After a few gratifying moments watching Kaldumahn squirm, Moshat finally replied, "You are not looking at it correctly."

Recognition sprawled across Kaldumahn's face as he gasped, "Of course. Why did I fail to see it? We are not bound to this dimension, trapped in this plane like some simple, physical beings. We are free to roam in the negative spaces, split time, and dance among the shadows sidling in between the elements."

"Indeed, brother," Moshat pounded his staff into faded, purple dirt that splashed like water. "Look again."

There it was, suddenly stretching up into the chaos above them, a cyclopean tower constructed of massive bricks, black and oily. Scanning from its base to its crown, Moshat recalled the first time he had seen the structure so long ago. It hadn't changed a bit. Perfect blocks fit precisely together to form a structure taller than anything else ever made by men. Of course, neither he nor any of his brothers knew the architect or builders who constructed the thing, but it had to be men. As beautifully precise as the thing was, no god would ever concoct something so crude.

"He is with us," Kaldumahn's booming voice broke the silence.

His eyes followed his brother's gaze up the archaic tower and confirmed the same. Ijilv—the architect of the war at Havenstahl who tricked even wise Brerto into believing he was the scattered god, Kallum—stood tall between two massive stone spires that crowned the structure like horns and smiled down at them.

"He sees us," Kaldumahn trembled.

Locked in Ijilv's gaze, Moshat was unable to respond. He could feel his brother's presence stomping around in his mind. His staff glowed brighter as he pushed back against the intruder. The sick realization of how strong his brother had grown was apparent in the smile that spread wide across Ijilv's face.

"I will rule you all," Moshat recognized Ijilv's voice, but the god's lips hadn't moved. The voice was in his head.

He pushed harder. All his will, all his might, and all his rage focused on that snaky smile casually resting between the horns of a mighty tower. By the time he felt Kaldumahn's fingers interlock with his own and drag him away, his cheeks trembled with effort and spittle had formed in the corners of his mouth.

The world went completely black for a moment. In the next, it was completely white. This pattern repeated several times and several more before Moshat slammed his eyes shut. The momentum of travel was obvious, but every time he opened his eyes all he saw was complete black or complete white until finally the travel ceased. When he opened his eyes again, he was seated upon his throne safely within the stronghold he shared with Kaldumahn.

"He knows," Moshat mumbled.

"Indeed," Kaldumahn agreed before asking, "What did he do to you?"

"Do?" he thought about it for a moment before adding, "Nothing. He was just there."

Kaldumahn looked up at the smooth stone of the domed ceiling high above them and asked, "What was he looking for in your thoughts?"

"He wasn't looking for anything," Moshat scoffed. "He just wanted to show me his power. He knows none of us considered him equal. He was alone, haunting a tower of men at the edge of oblivion. Now I wonder if Cialia is strong enough to defeat him. Perhaps the dragon is not the horror we should be concerned with."

"He is far stronger than we could have possibly imagined, but don't fool yourself into thinking him her equal," Kaldumahn shook his head. "She will burn him to dust and scatter him to the wind when their paths finally meet."

"What about the dragon he stole from Havenstahl?" the question hung heavy above their heads.

"Could he harness that power?" the idea seemed impossible, but the power Moshat felt from him while locked in his horrible gaze was like nothing he'd ever experienced. It was raw and primal, fierce even. It felt older than time or space and broader than the cosmos.

The silence grew louder as neither had anything else to say. Then something stumbled out of the crushing quiet. It was an idea, a stretch, of course, but something that just might work. Perhaps the great hawk in all his hubris had actually shown them the way with his efforts to terrorize them.

CHAPTER 10
THE RAMPAGING HORDE

Weeks had passed marching across dry, cracked land before it begrudgingly began giving way to wetter and more fertile stuff. Vegetation grew thick along the banks of the river Maelich and his Shaiwah had followed through the desert. That wasn't anything new. What was new was how far from the water that vegetation began growing as they progressed. And the variety. Instead of nothing but a long line of berry bushes, they came upon small trees and flowers and even fruits growing wild. At first, these new wonders seemed like out of place aliens in a foreign world, brief disruptions in the cracked dryness baking around them. However, as they stormed along, those lonely plants became unbroken, like wild gardens until they gradually gave way to a proper forest, and a wet one at that. Rains become a frequent occurrence. The showers never lasted very long, but it wasn't uncommon for Maelich's group to be soaked by three to four a day. At first, the rains were a welcome companion, washing away the dust and the heat to which they'd grown so accustomed. After a while, a day of dryness would have been a luxury.

Despite the soaking rains, the forest provided many benefits to the Shaiwah. The first was the sun. It no longer proved adversary. Small pools and even proper lakes became frequent landmarks on their path keeping their waterskins full. The lush canopy above provided so much protection, the Shaiwah even washed the thick coating of dye they covered their skin in to protect themselves from the blazing sun that ruled the skies above the cracked land they called home. Their skin was surprisingly pale considering the harsh environment they lived in, almost gray with a ghostly, blue hue remaining from years of berry juice leeching in. Of course, none of the skin exposed after washing away the thick dye from the berries that grow wild in the dry shrubs around the Shaiwah's home had ever seen the sun. As far as Maelich could tell, even babies were coated in the mixture.

He recalled the first pool they encountered. Ding leapt up from beneath the water smiling and scrubbing at his arms. It was the first time he had seen true joy in the young Shaiwahnian's eyes outside of the first time they'd met. That same joy glinted in all the Shaiwah's eyes in that moment of recognition when they believed Maelich was the savior promised them. The glint had steadily dimmed since that day. It was as if their belief in him waned as quickly as his while they trekked toward a land they believed was stolen from them while he believed less and less that it even existed, much less belonging to the people he led.

Four villages had fallen to the mighty Shaiwah since the beginning of their campaign. Maelich wouldn't have called them mighty during training. However, after watching them decimate village after village, it was hard to deny they were just that. They had only suffered two casualties, and one of them was an accident. A young warrior, Horp, grew too excited while chasing down a large, hairy man from one of the villages they destroyed. So eager to prove himself a mighty soldier, he failed to notice a large stone. It tripped him, and his head slammed unceremoniously down onto a thick stick impaling him through his right eye. Ding finished the big, hairy man off with vengeance, as if it had been his fault Horp ended his own life. The fury in Ding's eyes as he cut that man down hurt Maelich to his very soul. There was something so heartless and cold about it. He wondered if the innocence that had glinted behind the young Shaiwahnian's eyes would ever return or if the unforgiving rage that took its place had chased it away forever.

The Shaiwah's confidence grew with each victory until they were soaring. They had become an unrelenting force that believed nothing could stop them or stand in the way of their goal. A pit grew in Maelich's belly in direct proportion to his Shaiwah's ability to defeat and utterly destroy their supposed enemies. It was like a sickness sprawling about his gut until he felt full and queasy as he watched untrained, innocent, peaceful villagers decimated by his mighty warriors. Ymitoth had called him a conquering king after the first battle. Haunting a foreign forest while seemingly innocent folk are cut down for no other reason than existing as remnants of an alleged conquering army that had stolen the Shaiwah's land didn't leave him feeling like any kind of king. Though the mighty force following him were conquerors, he grew less and less convinced that was anything close to what he wanted to be. How long could he pretend to be this thing he'd become, a mighty king ruling over a callous band of marauders? All the innocence he had seen in those eyes looking at him to lead them to the land promised them by Maulom had been erased, replaced by bloody, unsatisfied vengeance thirsty for power. It seemed that was how all men fell, slowly devolving into heartless, violent creatures devoid of even the slightest hint of compassion or empathy until something equally vile finally ends their journey toward whatever goal. It seemed so senseless.

The stump beneath Maelich's rump wasn't a terribly comfortable throne as he gazed out into the lush greenery sprawling before him still wet from recent rains. Despite the discomfort of his seat, it would be a perfect place from which to rule. If only he could convince the Shaiwah they didn't need to occupy a city none of them had ever seen, that this wonderful place so full of life and nourishment could be their home providing them everything they would ever need. Of course, he had tried. None of them would hear it. The story had been written, and it was his job to fulfill his destiny and deliver them theirs.

Ymitoth sauntered over to disturb Maelich's melancholy. It was a welcome distraction. Despite the blood splattered and dried onto his cuirass, gauntlets, and cloak, he looked fresher than one should after so many battles. Maelich grinned as the wind grabbed hold of the old soldier's bronze hair. Somehow, the gray streaks in that glorious mane only made him look the hero all the more in the dim light of the forest. Those black, dead eyes didn't even bother Maelich anymore. He could barely recall the time when those empty things had troubled him so.

"Ymitoth," he smiled wider at his mentor as he motioned toward a large, flat boulder beside the stump he sat upon, "please join me."

"Ye've been more and more distracted the further along on this journey we get, lad," Ymitoth's voice dragged Maelich further from his lamentations.

"I have," he agreed. "Does this feel like victory to you?"

"Aye," the old soldier nodded, "These eyes have seen many a

battlefield in their day, and this is what victory looks like." He paused long enough to get Maelich to look at him and added, "That is, aside from the downturned corners of your mug there. Most times, in fact, all times I've seen, victory comes with wide smiles, laughs, and maybe a jig or two danced in honor of the occasion. Ye look like one in mourning."

"I am that," Maelich decided. "I mourn the Shaiwah's lost innocence; I mourn the lost lives of innocents falsely sold to me as vicious killers who would destroy my people; and I mourn the loss of my soul as I guide my brutal warriors against untrained townsfolk."

Ymitoth shook his head and kicked a pebble toward a small brook running alongside them, "These ain't new feelings ye're having, and ye know I ain't agreeing with ye on this one. Adversaries be adversaries. If a man be standing in the way of your destiny, ye move that man or cut him down."

Maelich grimaced at his father's words. It was mostly because he knew they were correct. That was the warrior's way. That had been his life for as long as he could remember. All he ever needed was a mission and to be pointed in the right direction. In all his years, he had never gone around an obstacle. He went through.

Maelich was about to respond with more evidence of why the path they were on was the wrong path when he was distracted by the deep growl of an angry scrod. The poor thing had obviously escaped being a victim of the Shaiwah. His fur was matted and covered in blood that appeared not his own. As impossible as it seemed, Maelich's heart sunk even further. Would it stop at his boots or bleed into the ground until his soul completely died? How long had the loyal beast remained to protect his family before realizing the meat he was protecting no longer carried the souls of the people he loved? His eyes grew warm as the poor animal triggered thoughts about all the senseless loss.

Ymitoth would have something cheeky to say about the tears, but Maelich let them come as he stooped down and held his hand out to the tentative animal. "Shh, boy," his voice cracked a bit as he did his best to sound soothing. "It's okay, laddie. No one will hurt you."

Ymitoth drew his sword. Maelich frowned at the sound as he glanced up at him. Still, it was a prudent thought. If the scrod attacked a quick kill would minimize the damage he took. Hopefully, the old soldier would just stand there with his sword held high and unchallenged, and Maelich could win the scared animal over.

The beast approached tentatively as the hair along its spine from the base of its skull to its tail slowly smoothed out. At the same time, that tail slowly began wagging. After a few wary steps, the scrod was scrutinizing Maelich's outstretched hand with its snout. A few moments later, the animal was licking Maelich's face and getting rough scratches behind its head.

Maelich smiled up at Ymitoth as the grizzled soldier stowed his blade. "See, there is no need to take any more life from this forest."

Something suddenly occurred to Maelich. Where had Mountain gone? He was with them when they arrived at the Shaiwah's cave, but he couldn't remember the last time he'd seen the loyal animal. He glanced over at Ymitoth and asked, "Where is Mountain?"

"He ran off only days after we arrived at that cave," Ymitoth shrugged.

"Why don't I remember that?" Maelich searched his mind but found nothing.

"Ain't no idea. He ran off chasing one of them scaly things, the, um…" he paused.

"Chukwoka," Maelich assisted.

"Aye, chuka…whatever, anyhow. That beast chased after one of them things. Ye called after him, but ye know he'd been a wild one, too much time free in the forest with that bastard, Braggon," Ymitoth nodded as he spoke, recollecting the events. "Ye searched every day for a good week, but never found him."

It all came rushing back. How had he forgotten? They had grown so close on the trail, a boy and his dog. How could he forget that bond? The memories failed to make him feel any better about it. They merely added to the black melancholy eating at his soul.

CHAPTER 11
BICKERING BROTHERS

Brerto rested his head against wet brick, oozing moisture as if it were sweating. He glanced over at his brother, Kallum, who was chained beside him with his chin resting on his chest. The blazing white hair which crowned the god's head and matched his own perfectly looked a dirty and dingy gray. He bowed his own head enough to catch a glimpse of the shabby business dangling from his own scalp. It was difficult to get a good look at it, but it appeared at least as dingy as his brother's. How had Ijilv done it? How long had that treacherous bastard been planning the apparent coup against all his brothers?

Glancing around the cell offered little solace. He didn't actually feel cold, but the twisted, wet stones haphazardly piled on top of one another to resemble something like walls made him feel the starkest chill just the same. The idea made little sense. If Ijilv were to be believed, Cialia had scattered him, burning him up with the power of Dragon's flame. If that were true, he no longer existed as anything more than a ghost inside Ijilv's head. Even if his brother was lying and his true form leaned against wet brick in a lonely cell, he still shouldn't feel cold.

The longer he spent haunting the place, the more difficult it became to deny the veracity of Ijilv's words. He remembered the feeling. She was inside of him, pushing, forcing her way deeper into his consciousness. Despite all his power, he couldn't hold her back. She was relentless. Then the pain came. It was something he had never experienced. Pain was something a god could not feel. At least, he had never believed it possible. It was as if she ignited every cell in his body simultaneously and each burned from the inside out. Of course, he knew the form he occupied in the physical was no more physical than the form he found himself in just then, chained in an imaginary cell somewhere deep in his brother's mind, but he had also studied physical things enough to understand what an accurate comparison it was. How she did it was a mystery, but she burned him to dust.

The more he thought about it, the more plausible Ijilv's taunts and proclamations became. He suddenly felt alone. Kallum was quite possibly the last being in any plane of reality he cared to spend time with, but he was someone to talk to, something to pass the time.

"Wake up, brother," he spoke softly, his voice sounding strange in his own ears echoing off the wet stone surrounding him. Ijilv hadn't missed a detail while concocting his illusion.

Kallum didn't budge.

A wicked smile slithered across Brerto's face as he shook the chains bound to his wrist and fastened to the stone above his head and shouted, "Kallum, great eagle, god among gods, awake!"

Nothing.

It suddenly occurred to him that his brother wasn't feigning sleep at all. He was off somewhere. How long had he been chained in this horrid place? Obviously, long enough to find a way out, even if it were only with his mind. "Where are you off to, brother?"

"He was watching me," Ijilv's booming voice filled the small cell as Kallum's eyes snapped open.

"You didn't expect me to be with you on top of the tower," Kallum chuckled through an evil grin.

"How?" Brerto asked. "How did you figure out a way to cast your gaze from this place?"

Ijilv waved the idea off before Kallum could respond, "The great eagle hasn't solved any great puzzle. You both are welcomed to see all I see. All that is required from you is desire. Once you have overcome your ire, your feelings of betrayal, and your humiliation at being bested by me, I want you to rule by my side, all of us brothers together with our champion."

"Lies," Kallum's chuckle faded with his smile. "Admit I solved the puzzle of this prison you've locked us in."

"You've never solved a puzzle in your entire existence. Once you learned the worship and adoration of sentient creatures fueled your power, you ceased seeking any further knowledge," Brerto chuckled before roaring with laughter.

Ijilv raised his eyebrows and shrugged before agreeing, "He is right, you know. For all the power you accumulated terrifying the poor souls of Ouloos into worshipping you, you know very little about the nature of things."

Kallum's expression lacked the humor his brothers shared at his expense. "I will destroy you both. You will kneel before my glory."

Ijilv's roaring laughter abruptly ceased as he looked at Kallum and soberly said, "You have no power here, because there are no creatures to fear you. All your threats are as lifeless as the last leaf blown from a dormant tree by a furious, autumn wind being chased by winter's first blizzard. Save your ego some bruising and stop making them."

"At least I never cowered at the edge of existence, hiding, withering away in a tower no one else could see," Kallum scoffed before allowing a smile to slip onto his face. "But they can now. Our beloved brothers, those treacherous fools, have defeated your illusion, solved one of your curious riddles just as I have. Yet, you failed to move against them. You simply stood and watched them like a creeping voyeur, terrified to engage but unable to look away."

"You're a fool if you believe that," Brerto chimed in, "Well, you're a fool either way, but our fair brother has obviously been planning this for a long, long time. He has manipulated all of us in his game, and he is currently manipulating our brothers. As always, they will play their roles unable to veer from their painfully predictable paths."

Kallum rattled his chains violently as he shook his head, "Nonsense. You grant him too much glory. He has never engaged, never risked anything for any cause. He is nothing more than a coward hiding away as I've said."

Sheer delight danced across Ijilv's smile as he asked, "What would you have done, brother, most powerful of all the gods?"

"Something rash and foolish no doubt," Brerto laughed.

Kallum's voice shrunk to nearly a growl, "I would have destroyed the great lion and his useless companion. I would have bathed them in my glory and cast them into oblivion."

"To what end?" Ijilv prodded as his smile grew wider.

The bound and furious god's expression mellowed as he gazed off far past the crude walls surrounding him. After a few moments of unsettling quiet, he finally replied, "To rule, of course. To rule all. All of you, my brothers, were only ever an obstacle to my goals, syphoning my power away, diverting my people from the truth of my glory."

"That is precisely why the lad of the Lake destroyed you," Brerto's tone lost the chiding quality it had carried moments prior. "Your narrow-minded focus allowed you to rise above the rest of us in strength, but it blinded you to everything else. That fact made you an easy foil."

"Brerto is quite wise," Ijilv conceded. "There is so much more to this universe than you could possibly understand. I have stood at the edge of oblivion and gazed off into the horror that exists beyond. It is terrible and terrifying, but, once you manage to control your fear while beholding it, I tell you, there is beauty. Layered in that beauty is truth. You were born from the Lake as all things including myself, but not exactly the way you believe. I could explain it to you, but even if you were able to comprehend you would never believe. It is enough for you to know that our brothers are playing their parts perfectly. They found this place precisely as I had planned. Mind you, I had expected them to find it far sooner, but the threat of destruction by Dragon's flame had them as frightened as it should. It is a dangerous game we play. However, right at this moment they are hatching a plan to fight Cialia and discovering this hidden tower reminded them of something they had forgotten. Finding this tower allowed them to believe they could defeat the Dragon. If not for this simple act, they would not have even tried, instead hiding away in their stronghold casting spells to attempt keeping her at bay."

"I won't pretend to understand your goals, but I believe you," Brerto nodded.

Kallum remained unconvinced, "You are no better than any of us. Ruling is all you care about. Your only plan was to hide away while the rest of us destroyed ourselves leaving you with no one to compete with you for the glory of being the one true god. It seems you will succeed in that goal."

Ijilv's smile widened as he crouched down before Kallum and gently held his brother's cheeks in his hands. As he gazed into the god's horrible eyes, he felt a love so pure. He wouldn't voice the feeling of course. The sentiment wouldn't be believed, but he did truly love all his brothers. Despite their bickering and warring against each other, they all were exactly what they needed to be.

CHAPTER 12
BAIT

Leisha slumped upon her throne, a chair unremarkable compared to any other seat in the room, precisely how she wanted it when she levied her first command as queen of Druindahl so many years ago. The gaudy thing they had presented her with was destroyed, replaced by the simple chair that held her weight as she worried over what might be happening in Havenstahl.

As she stared down at her wrinkled, peach gown it occurred to her how shabby and unkempt she'd become wasting away in a throne room few found cause to visit. There was too much to do rebuilding an army her vengeful daughter had destroyed with her flame. She'd almost given up after that. It was difficult to resolve the idea in her own mind that she had birthed a thing so powerful it could destroy any living creature, or even a god. It seemed as soon as she had—pulling herself up and resolving to be the light her people needed to guide them through the darkness—a god came calling with another purpose. This one seemed devious. The dingy, wilting hair dangling about her downturned head was a testament to how heavy the idea was as it weighed on her mind. Things like bathing or primping seemed so much less important than considering if your god had enlisted you in laying a trap for your daughter. Regardless how mighty that titan had become, Cialia was still the baby she cradled in her arms so many years ago and nursed in the dim light of the very room surrounding her just then. It seemed a lifetime ago, and yet, it seemed like just the other day. Time could be strange like that.

The low groan of the heavy, wooden doors opposite her throne—so perfect in their construction and beautiful with meticulous carvings of Dragons leaping forth from their faces—reminded her she needed to have the hinges oiled or replaced. The horrible sound they made was unbecoming of the perfect objects they were. There were undoubtedly more things she was leaving undone as she slumped and idly fretted over things outside of her control. Despite her desire to loudly proclaim in her own mind that she would stand and tend to those things left undone while she wasted away in the lonely, empty room, she couldn't bring herself to do it. The weight was too great. It pushed her deeper into her chair and pressed her chin deeper into her chest.

A sharp clicking of boots on polished tile followed the door's grumbling. The sure and dutiful cadence left no doubt who owned the purposeful gait. It was Boringas storming in as perfect as always. She didn't have to look up to know the boots earning the loud clicks echoing off the walls were polished and buffed to a glossy, black sheen. She didn't need to see how the tight, black trousers tucked into those perfectly kept boots flexed with each of those damnably confident strides. There could be no doubt the leather of his brown cloak would be equally buffed and shining, and the blood red sash fastened at his left shoulder and draping to his right hip would be perfectly pressed and tidy. She didn't need to see his perfect hair to know the top of those luxurious locks were pulled back into a ponytail while the rest bounced gracefully about his shoulders. She didn't need to see any of those things, but she looked up anyway. Hopefully, he had news about Cialia or Daritus or Havenstahl or something more than just his tidy appearance and disapproving frown to offer her.

"My queen," the loyal soldier's voice boomed amid the loud clicking of his polished boots. Even the man's voice sounded clean.

"Sweet Boringas," the smile she gave him as she raised her eyes to meet his was painfully fake and took great effort, "please tell me you come bearing heartening news."

Boringas bowed deep to one knee and replied, "I have news."

She didn't like the sound of that, nor the way his tone dipped as the words drifted from his mouth. She had asked for a very specific kind of news, good news, something to grant her the smallest amount of solace while her entire family was off battling monsters, their own demons, or waging war against the gods. It was such a helpless feeling to remain trapped in her throne room still terrified by a visit from that vengeful god who'd come calling to promise an eternity of horror should she fail in her mission to dissuade her beautiful daughter, her Dragon, from exacting flaming vengeance against him and the gods.

She sat quietly for a few moments wrangling all the troubling thoughts stomping about her mind until Boringas finally asked, "Would you like a report?"

The sigh she offered carried more meaning than her words could ever hope as she replied, "Forgive me, Boringas. Yes, please share what news you have, good or bad."

Boringas' joyless, half-hearted smile offered as much comfort as his lack of adding a qualifier to news had as he proceeded, "We have received no word about Cialia or her whereabouts. The last report we have is the one you received directly from the mighty Kaldumahn himself. As far as we know, she is still locked in battle with Brerto."

"I know she still lives," Leisha interrupted. "Whether she remains locked in battle with the horrible thing or has cast him to oblivion, I would have felt it had she failed. Both my children have died before, and I felt it when they did. I felt their pain. I would know. She must still live."

"Indeed," Boringas agreed though his eyes lacked the confidence the word portrayed. He awkwardly cleared his throat and continued, "The force Kaldumahn described, drawn from all the great cities of men, continues on their march toward Havenstahl, and, with the help of Moshat, that greatest city of men has been rebuilt."

"That is more heartening news," Leisha's smile gained the slightest bit of authenticity.

"Alhouim has fallen," Boringas' smile faded.

"Damn it, Boringas. All the bad then all the good," her form slumped as she asked, "How?"

"Reinforcements have arrived from across the Great Sea, and Doentaat perished," he sighed long and deep. "He had been lost in the woods. They found him, but injuries he sustained proved too great for the meager healing supplies available on the trail. The loss sent Bindaar into a rage. He marched on the beach at Biggon's Bay, and his force was decimated. Maomnosett Ott marched into the dwarf city and took it without incident. Maomnosett has been reborn, rising up from the ashes of Alhouim."

"Reinforcements?" Leisha latched onto that one word and turned it over in her mind as a pit filled with terror and despair grew deep in her gut. "They must be planning another attack on Havenstahl, on my husband. Can we send assistance?"

"Only at the risk of losing the small bit of protection we've managed to rebuild here," he shook his head. "Our ranks continue to grow, and the skill of our recruits continues to improve. However, the force protecting this city and the Dragons is a faint shadow of what it once was. I hate to say this to you, but if Havenstahl falls and those horrible monsters from across the Great Sea turn their attention toward the Lake, we are the last line of defense. I love Daritus like a father, but we are unable to assist him in his campaign."

"Damn your logic," she snapped, though she knew he was correct. Her husband would say the same. She would too if not for the overwhelming doubt stomping all over her resolve. She let her forehead drop into her hand as she asked another question for which she didn't really want an answer, "What about the pack of grizzly mongs my caravan encountered on the trail?"

"And the one which followed it," he somberly added. "At least most of the members of yours survived."

The pain she felt at all the loss welled up in one tear. It teetered on her eyelid for a moment before cascading down her flushed cheek, "Does the meandering path of those monsters continue toward our fair city?"

"If only," Boringas shook his head. "Our troops may be green, but they are well prepared to protect our fair city from those mindless beasts. Sadly, their current trajectory will land them in Havenstahl within..."

"And the mighty soldiers of all the greatest cities of men will rid Ouloos of the horrid monsters," Kaldumahn's voice—the voice of a god, at once both terrible and beautiful—was undeniable as it reverberated off the shiny prang walls and filled the room.

Leisha fell to her knees from her chair as Boringas quickly did the same, both prostrating themselves before the glory of the god who had suddenly appeared from nowhere. Many words, thoughts, and ideas echoed within Leisha's mind, but none of them proved mighty enough to conquer her fear and reach her lips.

"Rise," the god finally commanded, lowering his voice to something slightly less terrifying. "We have much to do and precious little time for pleasantries."

His words were reassuring, even his tone to some extent, but she recalled the last time the god's words carried her to a level of comfort where she spoke frankly to him. The sound he made, that deafening roar so deep it shook the very foundations of her fair city along with her insides and intertwined itself among a high-pitched scream that left her ears ringing. The chorus of terror mingling together and crying out in between those two extremes had made death seem a blessing. She felt compelled to heed the command but refused to let her guard down.

She warily raised her head and respectfully asked, "Mighty silver lion, god of gods, precious Kaldumahn, what would you have us do?"

Despite his eyes—seemingly devoid of color while swirling with all colors imaginable in equal saturation, an incomprehensible contradiction—continuing to be as beautiful and terrifying to behold as ever, the rest of his countenance appeared relaxed, aloof, perhaps even approachable as he smiled and replied, "I would have you both rise as I commanded. Then we can speak plainly about things which need to be done."

Both Leisha and Boringas did as instructed, but neither was bold enough to look directly at the god. Looking upon a god was more than a mind could bear. Leisha recalled the first time Kaldumahn had come to her. It was in a dream, but it was the most real experience of her entire life. He was there with her in her subconscious, and he was at least as glorious and terrifying as he appeared standing before her just then. When she had awoken from that dream, the joy, pain, and horror all remained. She couldn't remember how long those feelings stayed with her, but she did remember confronting those feelings. Were they physical things she actually felt or a psychological effect of knowing she had been that close to a god? In the end it didn't really matter. She had neither the time nor the energy to explore the thought.

Kaldumahn's perfect, white hair, beard, and robe all glowed with all the glory Leisha remembered. Despite refusing to look directly at him, the light gushing forth from his majestic form was still blinding. After wrestling with her fear for a few quiet moments more, she finally asked, "What should we do?"

"Very good," he replied. "The first thing you must do is listen. Fair Boringas here has provided an accurate accounting of things he can know at this point. However, there is much of which he is unaware. For instance, your mighty daughter, your Dragon, has defeated the great and terrible Brerto atop his mountain. She defeated his illusion and scattered him to the wind." He paused long enough to allow a response. When it became increasingly apparent neither in the room with him were feeling bold enough to reply, he continued, "Weary after her battle, she has journeyed to the Lake to reflect and commune with her sisters. She poured everything into overcoming Brerto's illusion, and her resolve has been tested almost to the point of breaking. However, I expect her to be ready to continue her campaign any day now."

Careful to contain her excitement for fear of offending the god, Leisha replied quietly, "That is heartening news. Do you know where she will go next?"

"She will be looking for me, and she will sense my power," he replied as flatly as his mighty voice would allow. "I expect she will find her way here, and that is exactly what I am planning."

New fear, different than the fear she felt for herself standing before the mighty Kaldumahn who could reduce her insides to goo with the sound of his voice, fraternized with a sudden twinge of anger. This new fear and the anger accompanying it—which she desperately tried to hide from her beautiful and terrifying guest—were born of a mother's love and her desire to protect her children no matter the odds, no matter the cost. Her voice was scarcely more than a whisper as she timidly asked, "Are you setting a trap for my daughter in her own city?"

Kaldumahn chuckled as he asked, "Is there any force greater than a mother's love? You would do anything, no matter how fruitless, to protect your beloved children. Despite the fact they are the most powerful beings in all creation, you are still compelled to stand before any danger they may encounter, and that is precisely why you are my chosen. Rest easy. You need not fear my response to you being exactly what I need you to be. This is no trap. I am counting on you to persuade your mighty daughter to consider her goal fulfilled. She has removed the evil from this world and can turn her attention to showing Ouloos a new path, one filled with love and understanding amongst all creatures, a true paradise earned by her great effort."

Something about his tone didn't sit right with Leisha, but she dared not challenge him. Instead, she asked, "Where will you go, and where will you be when she arrives?"

"I love the forest," he smiled. "I shall wander among the grandeur of these glorious trees until she arrives. I will sense her presence. Power recognizes power above all else. She will come to you first. You will convince her of the things I have said, and I will come with my brother, the great and mighty Moshat to offer our guidance in the building of her new world."

"As you wish," Leisha dropped back to her knees, bowing before the god as if in prayer. "Though I am unworthy of your grace, you honor me with the peaceful bliss of your presence and the greatest of gifts, a command from your perfect lips."

"You are worthy," the god replied, "mother of gods, my chosen, do not fail me."

Leisha remained there prostrate on the floor afraid to move, think, or say anything else. After a bright flash that made the world look red to her closed eyelids, the room was silent. The only sound she could hear was the sound of her own breathing mixed in with the short, rapid breaths of Boringas.

Finally, Boringas piped up, "He has gone, my queen."

"I know," she quietly replied into her folded hands without looking up.

"I don't believe him," the dutiful soldier said quietly.

Leisha leapt to her feet and covered the short distance between them in a blink, closing her general's mouth with her hand as she implored him, "Never say anything like that out loud again. Never even think such things. The gods know and see all. He would destroy you, maybe our entire fair city, for less. Whatever you need to do to cast those ideas from your mind, do it, and never let thoughts like that return to your head again."

She held his mouth shut like that for a few moments, her wide eyes imploring him to heed her command. When her expression finally relaxed and she removed her hand, he replied flatly, "Your will, my queen."

Beneath Leisha's great city in the trees and deep in the Forgotten Forest, Kaldumahn strolled among the towering trees allowing the scents and sounds of the forest to relax him. It had been far too long since he'd walked among the calm serenity of nature. Even before he and Moshat had hidden themselves away in their fortress, he found fewer and fewer reasons to venture out and experience things.

Surrounded by the scents of decaying leaves and fragrant shrubs, and the glorious symphony of birds singing amongst the highest branches of the canopy, he decided if everything went as planned, he would spend his days enjoying everything in Coeptus' creation. He would never again hide himself away detached from everything.

"Will the queen of Druindahl play her role?" Moshat suddenly appeared beside his brother.

"Indeed," Kaldumahn smiled, "but not because I successfully persuaded her to our cause. She is terrified."

"Good," Moshat finally smiled back. "Fear is a wonderful motivator. Hopefully, the fear you've instilled in her festers deep in her gut and keeps her on the correct path."

"It will," Kaldumahn assured him. "When Cialia comes home to her fair city in the trees, her mother will do her best to convince her that we are not her enemies. She will fail, and I will attack."

"And I will guard your back," Moshat's smile widened. "It is a good plan, brother. This will work. Though her power far exceeds our own, she's had no training on how to properly wield it, and she knows very little about the nature of this world."

CHAPTER 13

BETRAYED BY BLOOD

The trail up Mount Elbahor toward Maomnosett—that great, historic city of dwarves now twice stolen from them by giants of that line—was still soft from rains as the group from Havenstahl marched along it. Despite weeks of working together to rebuild a broken city and find lost and injured soldiers, the cohort remained two smaller groups rather than one cohesive unit. Maomnosett Bom had given up his armor in favor of a ruffled, white shirt underneath a comfortably soft cloak in the blue of Havenstahl, a gift from the incomparable tailors of that glorious city. He walked beside Lito-Bi, the finest trogmortem soldier in Ouloos' history. The fierce trogmortem had declined the offer of comfortable new threads and still sported the blood-stained pauldrons and leather trousers he had worn at the battle of Fort Maomnosett. Bom knew his good friend thought he was a bit soft for accepting the fine clothing, but it seemed the type of gesture that would help the people of Havenstahl feel more comfortable with his small group and more accepting of them.

Hountmytall Moy, the tallest living giant, wore similar clothing to Bom. The latter wondered at how many lourng had lost their coats to spin enough thread to weave such a massive cloak. Bom flashed a sad smile at the towering creature. He'd never seen him so clean. The giant had even had his hair tidied up by the most renowned barber in Havenstahl. He should have been standing tall and marching proud. Instead, he trudged along, bent like the sky was a heavy burden with the corners of his mouth turned down in what Bom thought might have been the saddest frown he had ever seen. He hoped this mission would help find a quick end to the war, a truce, and hopefully a quick path back home where all the giants and trogmortem who had made the journey across the Great Sea could cast genuine smiles on their own lands once again.

Bom shot a similarly sad smile back at the four men in the group who trailed behind them, all transplants from Druindahl except for Chagon. The fact the men walked separately from him and his two companions filled him with a far deeper sadness than what his painfully forced smile showed. There were a few men from Havenstahl and a few members of his group of giants and trogmortem who had been working hard to foster something that felt like kinship between the two groups, but it had proven a tough hill to climb. Most of the individuals involved in the effort were on the trail with him, and they still felt like separate groups working toward a common goal rather than a team marching under the same banner. Perhaps that would never change, but he held out hope it might.

As Bom's group crested a hill, the Sacred Pine stretched toward the sky before them. Twice as tall as any other tree on the mountain, it stood like a sentinel, mighty against the elements and patiently waiting for a challenge to its post.

"That tree," Bom looked back over his shoulder at the group of men behind him, "is that the tallest tree in all the land on this side of the Great Sea?"

"Near enough," Tarturan began, the musical quality of his voice bearing a stark contrast to his appearance. At just a hair over seven feet tall and thickly muscled under his gaudy armor, the man was near a giant himself. As he brushed back his wavy, dark locks and gazed up the length of the great tree he added, "We have trees even older and taller back home in my forest. I hope to see them again someday."

"There be trees in that Forgotten Forest even taller than that pine up ahead?" Chagon gasped, his heavy mail cloak creaking awkwardly beneath his new, leather tunic. As proud as he was about the blood, red sash draped across his left shoulder and circling beneath his right armpit to rise up his back—the mark of a rider of Druindahl—Bom didn't have the heart to tell him he looked like a young lad wearing his father's shirt.

Tarantian laughed at his new chum as he concurred with his old chum, "Indeed there are. When this war is finished, I will take you there so you can see the city for which you ride, and the forest in which it dwells, in all its grandeur."

"I would like to see that too," Bom added.

"You would be welcomed as my guest if ever you saw fit to make that journey," Tarantian smiled back. "I'd be happy to have you."

"I want to go home," Moy chimed in, his tone as bent and withering as his posture.

Despite Moy's depressed bearing, and the trogmortem's massive size, Lito-Bi had to stretch nearly as high as his arm could reach to pat the enormous giant between his shoulder blades, "We all do, and we will as soon as the war has ended. Except maybe, Bom here. He might just travel off to lands unknown to see trees of incredible stature with our new friends."

"Is that what you will do, Bom?" Tarantian asked. "Will you accept the invitation and accompany me to the most magnificent forest imaginable?"

Joy finally filled out Bom's smile as he replied, "There is nothing I want more than to go home, but your invitation fills my heart with promise. I just might allow myself a moment of respite to accompany you to your home. If it is half as majestic as what you describe, I don't see how I could live with myself if I missed it."

As the group neared the base of the giant pine, the mechanism fastened to it—and used to stretch dwarves to the point of their joints popping, holding them in place until the sun, the elements, and starvation ended their time in the physical—glinted in the sunlight. All of them on the trail knew the stories of how Maomnosett Ahm had used the contraption to terrorize the dwarves of Alhouim and keep them dutifully toiling away in the mines until Maelich had come to relieve that monster of his head and free the city from his rule. However, none of them could fully comprehend the psychological effect the torturous thing had on the dwarves of that city. Nor could they fathom the sheer defeat of having the thing re-installed after tearing it down so many summers past.

"What a horrible thing that is," Bom commented. The joy his voice had gained while musing about a journey with newly won friends fled as a hint of disgust slipped in to take its place.

"Your kin did that," Tiegran smoothed back his messy, black hair before quickening his step to walk beside the giant and remind him of his heritage. Despite being the smallest in the entire group, the young soldier had no qualms about battling against giants or any of the nightmares from across the Great Sea.

"A fact that sickens me to my core," Bom replied somberly.

Moy looked down at Tiegran and added, "And the reason we are here. All of us who came to Havenstahl under this very white flag I hold high above my head left our people because we don't believe in what they are doing. I stand before you ashamed of things my kin have done."

Bom smiled up at his massive friend, "Indeed, old friend, we will do all we can to heal those old wounds and see the dwarves of this place free to rule themselves once again whether that be through diplomacy or force."

Two trogmortem stepped out from behind the Sacred Pine, each larger and broader than Lito-Bi. Both were armed with twin lingads—curved blades with handles jutting three quarters of the way down their lengths that were held against the forearms and wielded with a punching motion—and the traditional armor of trogmortem warriors which consisted only of spiked pauldrons that were more for instilling fear in the hearts of enemies than affording any form of protection from attack.

Lito-Bi recognized both his former pupils. "Elquin-Ti and Gayon-Ja, you still wield those archaic toys?"

Gayon-Ja spat on the ground before replying, "I'll carve you up in a heartbeat with these beauties."

"I trained the both of you to fight with the true weapons of any real trogmortem," Lito-Bi growled through a grin just wide enough to expose his fangs. "I didn't teach you to bring toys to any battle," the sun glinted off his blackened claws as he flexed his fingers and added, "swing those useless things at me, and I'll give you another lesson."

Moy gently placed his hand on the trogmortem's shoulder as he spoke to the two accosting them, "We march under a white flag. There will be no carving with blades or claws."

"Your king, Chi-Ta, would honor the white flag, as would my grandfather," Bom added. "Will you do the same? Though we do not wish to spill your blood, I intend to stand before Ott, and you are horribly outmatched."

"You're all traitors," Elquin-Ti grunted. "We will present you to the king, but you must leave your weapons behind."

"All of you are armed," Tarantian complained.

Tarturan touched his old friend's forearm and continued the argument as diplomatically as possible, "As Lito-Bi has accurately stated, the most effective trogmortem weapons are their claws and teeth. Giants are the same, armed even while unarmed. We men, we lack these natural weapons the rest of you boast. It is unfair to strip us of the only instruments granting us anything close to equality with you."

"You are not equal with us even with your weapons," Gayon-Ja laughed, "but they will remain behind if you desire an audience with our king."

Bom turned toward the men in his group and said, "You are right to fear the intentions of these two, or anyone else under my grandfather's command. The four of you can remain here while the three of us stand before him."

"Ain't a chance of that," Chagon's eyes narrowed as he scowled at the two trogmortem blocking their path. "I ain't been a soldier as long as the rest of ye, but I learned one thing on the trail with Tarantian. Be they alive, ye leave none of your kin behind."

"Chagon is right," Tarantian added. "The three of you may hail from lands far across the Great Sea, but all of you are kin now. We accepted this mission, and we will see it through."

Bom simply smiled and nodded at his new friends.

The two trogmortem guards wore menacing grins as they watched the men in the group relieve themselves of their weapons. All four men wore equally friendly expressions as they scowled back at their adversaries. Bom remained tense. The uneasy calm between the riders of Druindahl and the two trogmortem acting on behalf of the usurper from across the Great Sea was painfully thin. A quick move from either side might very well be seen by the other as an act of aggression. Luckily, all both sides did was sneer at each other.

The walk from the Sacred Pine was quiet. Despite all the posturing and threatening Elquin-Ti and Gayon-Ja had done beneath the rich, green needles of the Sacred Pine, both wore expressions saturated more with fear than hubris or aggression. The streets which were bustling only a moon prior were void of life and lined on both sides by quiet shops with boarded up windows. No dwarves stood gossiping or challenging each other to feats of strength or even sharing pints whilst pontificating on the state of this or that.

A brightly painted sign creaked in the breeze on chains that probably should have been replaced five summers ago. The image—a happy dwarf clicking his heels as ale splashed out of the mug he held—brought a smile to Tarturan's face. The massive soldier turned to Tiegran and said, "I've many a fond memory of that place, and probably many more forgotten, tipping back ales with our dwarf friends to celebrate Maelich's day. Shame the place is so quiet."

"I've never been," the young soldier sighed. "I was far too young back when Maelich slayed the giant and haven't made a dwarf friend I felt close enough to make the trek."

"You don't know what you're missing," Tarantian smiled fondly at the grand building. "Though I don't remember many of the details, I recall more than a few summers when the celebration of that day lasted several, never-ending food and drink. Say what you want about dwarves, but they know how to celebrate."

"It sounds wonderful," Bom interjected, feeling a bit detached from the men in his group. Then he added, loud enough for their guides to hear, "After we've chased the usurper off his throne and banished him from the city, I'd like to join you for a celebration just like you've described."

Elquin-Ti looked back and offered a sneer but had no additional comments to add until the slight incline they walked leveled off and the palace Ahm had built so many summers prior stretched up toward the sky before them. It was surrounded by a massive wall of brick and mortar reinforced with glimmering prang that stretched one thousand feet from east to west and rose 50 feet from dirt to sky. The main gate, as massive as it was, seemed small to all but the men in the group. At fifteen feet, it was just a hair higher than the top of Lito-Bi's head when standing completely straight.

Surprised by how oddly small the gate would be for most giants, Moy looked down at Bom and asked, "Wasn't your uncle fifteen feet tall?"

"Thereabout," Bom nodded.

"That gate looks no taller than that," the massive giant complained. At better than twenty feet tall, he'd have to crouch mightily to get through it. "Why would he build an entrance so small?" he finally asked.

"If you believe the stories," Tarantian piped up, "these walls were built after his palace which resides inside to present a stronghold for his solidas to protect it. Seems a bit silly now. Until Maelich came calling for the giant's head, Maomnosett Ahm never had anything to fear from men."

"What are solidas?" Bom asked.

"They were Ahm's dwarf soldiers," Tarantian replied.

"They were a force to be reckoned with," Tarturan added. "Your grandfather's forces witnessed that firsthand during the battle at Fort Maomnosett."

"Indeed," Lito-Bi acknowledged. "What the stout dwarves of Alhouim lack in stature, they more than make up for in spirit."

"My father and his father both fell to their mighty axes," Moy added in a somber tone.

Elquin-Ti finally broke his silence as he glanced back and spat, "Traitor."

"To my kind and my kin, I probably am that," Moy's form deflated further as the ghost of a tear he hadn't the energy nor the emotion left to muster haunted a space just below the rim of his eyelid, "but I can no longer support Ott nor his evil campaign."

The temperament of the group shifted as they entered Ott's courtyard. The two trogmortem guiding the visitors from Havenstahl changed from something close to fear to something closer to hubris. Meanwhile, the sure confidence of the group of men, giants, and trogmortem they led lost its edge. The wide expanse stretching from the south gate to Ott's recently acquired palace teemed with grongs, trogmortem, and a handful of giants.

The courtyard terminated at the grand stairway leading up to the massive palace. At its top sat the mighty and terrible Ott. Even Moy who bettered the newly anointed King of Maomnosett by more than two feet in height felt a slight shiver at the slight of the beast of a giant perched upon his dead son's throne. Scarred from recent battles, the monster appeared more terrifying than he ever had before. His bored expression somehow made it worse. He had nothing to fear from the small group of emissaries from Havenstahl and absolutely no concerns about any repercussions that might arise from anything he decided to do to them.

Gayon-Ja gave Lito-Bi a grin and asked, "Care to have that dance now, old friend? The numbers no longer favor you."

"We did not come for a fight," Bom's tone remained calm and direct as his eyes remained on his grandfather.

"Wise choice," Elquin-Ti chuckled as he pointed at Bom. "You, come with us. The rest of you best not move."

"We are all to stand here in the damp dirt under a blazing sun?" Moy complained. "I would think the great and mighty Ott would receive us as guests."

"The lot of you are lucky to be alive," Gayon-Ja shrugged. "You can stand there or take your traitorous carcasses back to Havenstahl to lick the boots of the men you serve."

Lito-Bi growled quietly at the slight but kept his tongue. Further debate seemed useless, and his hosts were enjoying his group's frustration far too much.

Bom looked back at his friends, mustered the most genuine smile he could, and said, "I will present our case to my grandfather. Please remember we are guests here and show our hosts no aggression."

The two trogmortem guided Bom toward Ott's throne. Leading him like a prisoner, each held one of his wrists. The young giant could feel their eyes scanning him, searching for weakness. He refused to give them the satisfaction. Despite the fear gripping his gut like a stony fist, he managed to keep his eyes on Ott and a friendly smile upon his face. The closer they got to the spot where his mighty grandfather would listen to him or pass judgement against him, the more foolish the idea seemed. He had felt so confident about it when he made the recommendation to Daritus. As his captors stopped him ten feet in front of the stairway leading up to Ott's throne, that confidence had completely fled.

"My traitorous bastard of a grandson has returned to me, one of the many failures in my line," the mighty king of Maomnosett seemed aloof as he examined his claw-like fingernails.

Bom dug deep to muster enough will to keep his fear from showing on his face as he replied, "I am this thing you describe, dear grandfather. I have given you no reason to feel pride as you grace me with your glorious gaze. However, I pray you listen to my words."

The great and terrible Ott finally looked his grandson in the eyes as he feigned interest in what the young giant had to say, "Give me these all-important words, grandson. Enlighten me with your wisdom. Impress me with your wit. Give me one, small reason to be proud of any creature wandering about with my blood coursing through their veins. Prove to me you are more worthy than your uncle, or your father, or anything those foul weaklings spawned. If you cannot do that, then convince me why any utterance from your foul lips should stain my eardrums."

"Mighty Maomnosett Ott, king of this great city, and ruler of the dwarves who inhabit this place, a vicious threat darkens your door," Bom began, stopping only when Ott had cut him off.

"Havenstahl?" Ott's hearty laugh filled the courtyard earning chuckles from all but the small contingent from the city he mocked. "The men of that city pose as much of a threat as they ever have, precisely zero."

"No, grandfather," Bom continued calmly once the mighty giant stopped laughing, "the threat I describe does not hail from any city of men. The beasts I speak of hail from the frigid north, far beyond habitable lands or any place a reasonable man might travel. They are violent, horrible, and near mindless monsters that destroy everything in their wake."

Genuine interest bled into Ott's expression as he leaned forward in his chair and replied, "Go on. These creatures you describe sound like something I must consider."

The fear gripping Bom's spine eased, if only slightly, as he proceeded with more confidence, "Grizzly mongs, thousands of them. As massive as any trogmortem and at least as terrible. Though not completely mindless, they make no distinction between one creature and another. Meat is meat, and their hunger seems never ending. The men of Havenstahl will battle these beasts. If they are successful and turn the horde away, this will be their next destination."

Ott quickly stood from his throne like the time for action was upon them. "You were wise to bring news of this threat to my ears. Perhaps you are not quite the failure I expected. Now, I understand. You seek an alliance with Maomnosett to turn away this threat, also wise. Together, the great cities of Maomnosett and Havenstahl could never be defeated by any force no matter the size or make up."

Bom swelled with pride as his grandfather walked down the steps toward him. He could scarcely believe his plan had worked. When he had first given voice to it, he hoped it might. However, deep in his gut, he knew it never would. Yet, here was the great and mighty Ott bounding toward him with pride dripping from his smile.

When Ott finally reached Bom, he towered over him. Despite that, there was no fear. For the first time in his life, Bom felt truly accepted by his grandfather. He forgot all the times the massive giant had referred to him as slight or not a true giant, or any of the other insults he'd endured growing up so much smaller than all his kin. For the first time in his life, he almost felt loved by someone with whom he shared blood besides his mother.

"I will heed your advice, grandson, pride of my line," Ott nearly gushed. "Kneel before me, pledge your life to me, and I will agree to the alliance you seek."

Bom failed to hold back his tears as he knelt before the mighty Ott, fiercest of giants, and his grandfather. "Thank you," was all he could muster without breaking down completely.

Ott stroked his grandson's hair as he smiled down upon him. However, it wasn't joy turning the corners of his lips up so. As he stood there feigning pride, his other hand slipped to the small of his back to fetch his dagger from its scabbard. No one else in attendance noticed the gesture until the vile king of Maomnosett quietly slipped the blade into his own blood just behind his left shoulder blade.

More tears flooded over Bom's eyes as he felt the cold betrayal slip through his flesh. The pain of that betrayal was far worse than the feeling of the blade slowly slicing through his meat and arteries. The maniacally pleased look in his grandfather's eyes only made it worse. He'd been a fool to believe that bastard, or any other giant, would ever see him as anything more than a failure. No one would ever speak his name or sing songs in his honor. He'd be forgotten like a pile of excrement once it's been cleaned from the bottom of a boot. That was his last thought as he collapsed onto the dirt, and his soul slipped from his body to make its journey to the Lake.

Every dwarf, every giant, every trogmortem, every grong, and every man standing in the courtyard in the blistering sun who witnessed the horrible betrayal gasped in unison. A chilling silence followed. Each wide eye on each of the faces of the group from Havenstahl glanced fearfully around the courtyard, waiting for the soldiers in Ott's army to attack and give them a similar fate. Nobody moved. All eyes remained trained at the raging giant, covered in his own grandson's blood with wild eyes and a disgustingly satisfied smile.

Moy was the first to respond. "No," he shouted, as he charged toward Bom's falling form.

The tallest living giant made three steps before Ott's only living son drove his shoulder into Moy's chest and toppled the giant to the ground. "He's mine," Ohm shouted.

Ott had swiped a handful of Bom's blood off his cheek and begun licking his fingers by the time Ohm reached him. The sight only served to fuel his rage. No matter what Bom had done, he was still blood. He was still Ohm's nephew. It didn't matter how short or slight he was. It didn't matter that he had left to broker peace with the men of Havenstahl. That was all politics, and Ohm cared little for politics. All that mattered to him in that moment as he watched his father reveling in the spilled blood of his kin, was the treacherous way in which he had exacted his revenge. He hadn't challenged the slight giant to a fair fight. He acted as an assassin, a coward. There was no honor in it.

Ott's smile only widened further as he yanked his blade out of Bom's shoulder and awaited his son's assault. "Come to me," he shouted as Ohm leapt toward him.

When Ohm's shoulder pounded into Ott's gut, the momentum carried them all the way back to the staircase. The furious son grabbed hold of his father's hair and pounded his fist into the bastard's face. "Vile coward! How could you betray your own kin?" the words came out as grunts through his clenched teeth.

Ohm had only managed to hit his father three times before the very same blade that had killed his nephew moments prior was racing toward his gut. That blade never found its mark. Ohm wasn't the only one in the clearing that day who felt betrayed by his king's behavior. Moh, Moy's brother grabbed hold of Ott's wrist to stop the killing blow before it could connect. A moment later, Moy grabbed Ott's other wrist and held him fast while Ohm continued to pummel him amid a stream of vile curses and accusations.

The assault continued until Ohm had grown weary of pounding on his father's head. "How could you?" he asked, nearly breathless. "How could you betray your own kin in cold blood? You are a coward. Any respect I've ever held for you has fled with my nephew's spirit."

A few teeth were missing from Ott's bloody smile as he looked back at his son with malice and insanity, "You're a traitor, just like he was." He raised his voice and shouted, "Seize him."

No one in the courtyard moved to aid their failing king, but Oyg, Ohm's son responded loudly from the crowd, "My father's words are true. You are a coward. You are no king. You deserve no respect or admiration from any creature." Then he raised his voice and added, "To all the giants who can hear my voice, I call for a traitor's death for the pathetic worm, Maomnosett Ott. He has proven himself a coward, and a pitiful excuse for a giant. Who is with me?"

"Second," more than one voice shouted out from the crowd simultaneously.

"Traitor's death," more voices responded.

Ohm grabbed hold of his father's hair and maintained it as he spoke the judgement, "You are no king. You are no titan. You have betrayed your blood. Ouloos will be better without the filth you are to soil her precious ground. I sentence you to death."

The rest of the group from Havenstahl stood back and watched as Ohm, their new friend Moy, and the rest of the giants gave Ott, King Maomnosett, a traitor's death. He was hit, bit, and kicked by every giant in the place until he was finally dragged to his feet to hear the last words he would ever hear.

"The Lake will have your soul, and the sand will have your blood," Ohm pulled his father's face close to his own as he growled his words through tightly clenched teeth.

As those last words left Ohm's mouth, he kept his firm hold on Ott's hair and grabbed his chin with his other hand. At the same time, the brothers Moy and Moh pulled the king's arms away from each other. Ohm's sons, Oyg and Oyt each had a hold of one of their grandfather legs, and they pulled them apart with equal vigor.

When the great and mighty Ott was finally ripped apart, his cries were not pitiable. He died exactly as he had lived, raging, angry, and unwavering. There were no words saturated among the horrible sounds which poured from his trembling lips. His eyes carried a damning enough message on their own.

The rest of the group from Havenstahl grew increasingly agitated as the rest of the crowd in the courtyard writhed in a mixture of rage and excitement. Chagon nudged Lito-Bi with his elbow and asked, "Should we be running right now?"

"Do not move, and do not make a sound," the trogmortem replied. "We would never make the gate."

"If it's a fight, we fight until life has left us," Tarturan whispered.

"Pray it is not that," Lito-Bi whispered back.

Ohm's entire form trembled as he held his father's head aloft before the slowly calming crowd gathered before him in the courtyard. "This is my father," he said with disgust. "He may have been an honorable giant in days long past, but this thing I hold before you is not that. This vile creature deserved no love, no adoration, and no fealty from any of you who stand before me. I will take his throne and be a better king than he ever was."

There was no argument staining any of the eyes staring back at him and the grizzly trophy he held aloft before him. Only one in the crowd gave voice to any of the various competing emotions swirling about the mass gathered there. "Will you fight the beasts of the north with us, old friend?" Moy asked.

Ohm dropped his father's head to the dirt unceremoniously as he turned toward the tallest living giant and shook his head. "I will not. My new city has nothing to fear from any beast," Ohm replied, his tone matter of fact before turning toward the crowd and adding. "However, any of you are free to join these fools in their quest to aid Havenstahl in this mission."

"I am with you," Moh, Moy's brother answered the call with great vigor in his voice.

"Father, will you hold me in contempt if I join our friends in this mission?" Oyt, Ohm's youngest son asked.

"I love you, my son," Ohm smiled, "and I am proud to call you that before all who can hear me. Succeed in your mission and return to me with stories of your glory."

Oyt's brother, Oyg added, "I will not join you on this quest, brother. I will remain here to help father rebuild, but I will hold you in my heart."

While the giants discussed among themselves who else would depart to assist the cohort from Havenstahl and who would remain, Gayon-Ja approached Lito-Bi and the men from Havenstahl. None of the menace his countenance had carried up to that point remained as he said, "Lito-Bi, mightiest of my kind, forgive the callous way I treated you upon your arrival in this place. All your kin will support you on your mission to aid the men of Havenstahl. We are with you, brother."

As the men in the group watched the exchange, Tiegran nudged Tarturan and whispered, "So, no fight?"

Tarturan smiled down at his young, ambitious friend and asked, "Are you disappointed?"

Tiegran's expression was answer enough. He was hoping for a battle to the death against the nightmares from across the Great Sea.

Tarantian chuckled and said, "We need to do something about this one. He's apt to start a war with our new allies."

Chagon shook his head, "Ye keep that fire. We'll be needing it when them beasts come calling.

CHAPTER 14

THE ENEMY REARS HIS HEAD

The sky above the Lake was perfect as always with no clouds to mar its incomparable beauty. Glorious Dragons, mighty and beautiful in their perfection, swam the warm currents and sang their glorious songs. Beneath all that magnificence, Cialia sat cross-legged in the warm sand. Though her body was there at the edge of the Lake, the source of all life and connection to Coeptus, her mind was far away.

Lameah laid beside her. Her massive, scaled head inches from Cialia's lap. "Where are you off to now, sweet sister?" the Dragon asked with love dripping from her voice.

"She is physically with us," Helias, the Great Mother, Queen of all Dragons replied with just as much love in her voice, "but her mind is elsewhere. She searches for her enemies, those who would destroy the creatures she protects. You know that is her way, my love."

"It is my way," Cialia's eyes snapped open, as she replied. "You know this."

"I know," Lameah replied with the same sweetness her precious voice always carried. "I only wish it weren't so. I only wish you would grant yourself one small bit of the peace you seek for those you protect. Forget the gods and their wiles. Stay with your sisters."

Cialia's expression hardened slightly as she replied, "Three gods remain to torment this place, and three gods must pay for all the horror they have authored against those very creatures you describe. There can be no peace in this place until that happens."

"And you are the judge who will speak their sentences, as well as

95

the executioner who will carry them out," Helias smiled down at them.

"Again, you speak sweetly as you accuse," Cialia sighed. "It sounds as if you pass judgement against me."

"As I have told you time and again, sweet sister, the only judgements you will find in this place will come from within your own mind," Helias' voice sounded like a smile.

"Fine, I accuse myself," Cialia almost grunted. She knew her sisters' words were true. What she couldn't understand was the fact neither of them seemed to understand the importance of what she was doing. All the gods were vile. How could they not see it?

"A lack of understanding is not the problem, love," as always, Helias knew exactly what was going on in Cialia's head. "You battle against. That is your way. Dragons allow. I hope against hope someday you will join us. Until then, we will love you with all our hearts and patiently await the day you find yourself completely one with us, a true Dragon, not just a woman wielding the power of Dragon's fire."

Cialia shook her head and prepared to respond with more contrary ideas when something grabbed a tight hold of her attention. It was more a feeling than anything tangible or definable. It felt like power, ancient and primal, and it felt like it didn't belong.

"There it is," Helias' sweet voice chimed like a bell. "Your next victim calls out with a challenge to your strength."

"Kaldumahn is in my home," Cialia failed to hide her anger from her sisters who had never felt a similar emotion for themselves. "That vile creature exposes himself in a place I hold so dear. If that is not a challenge, I cannot imagine something that would be."

"Of course, it is a challenge," though her smile never faded, Lameah did lose a tear at the meaning behind the words she spoke.

"Indeed," Helias agreed. "He knows you will sense his power in that place you hold so dear, and he knows you will attack him there."

"It is a trap, sweet sister," Lameah let the tears flow.

Cialia set her jaw tight as she stood and said, "He is a fool to lay a challenge against me. This will be the last mistake that vile creature will ever make. I must go and face him, but I promise to return to you again when my duties are completed."

"We will wait for you, love," Helias smiled through tears equal to Lameah's.

CHAPTER 15

THE CONQUEROR SLEEPS

Complete darkness was followed by brilliant, uninterrupted light in frequencies faster than any eye could possibly track. No dark could ever hope to be as absent of light as the dark moments, and no light could ever hope to be as free from shadow as the moments of total light. Though the two conditions alternated, both seemed to exist as constants running alongside one another rather than each replacing the other. Within these two constants sat the four obelisks in the circular room at the top of Ijilv's tower. Hovering in between those four obelisks Geillan slept. Less than a summer had passed since Ijilv sent his dead-eyed men, his borrowed terrors from Kallum sprung from the darkest depths of man's nightmares, to kidnap the young man as a newborn babe. Yet, the sleeping form hovering there appeared to be a young man of at least twenty summers.

Ijilv was there with Maelich's stolen heir, the sleeping Dragon, watching his prize, his purloined and adopted son as he slumbered, growing faster than any creature had ever before or ever would again. The young man was as perfect as a man could be. His long, golden hair floated around his head like a crown as his flawless skin wrapped tightly around immaculately structured bones in perfect symmetry.

The great hawk, Ijilv, the hidden god who haunted the tower at the edge of time since Kallum's favorite had perished and left the place empty, gently dragged his fingernail along Geillan's perfect cheek. His gaze filled with genuine love as he beheld the perfect creature. No man could ever be as beautiful or as perfect as the being sleeping before him.

"You are pathetic," Kallum's voice echoed in Ijilv's head.

Brerto's voice followed, "Has a god ever loved any creature as much as you love this thing you coddle so? What has this useless being done to earn your adoration?"

The most genuine smile Ijilv had ever mustered raised the corners of his mouth and even his eyes as he replied, "This is the son of the Dragon. Maelich, the twin, spawned this perfect thing to be what he could never be, a conquering king. Witness a man with the power of Dragon's Fire capable of bringing all Ouloos to heel. For everything either of you, or any of us gods for that matter, ever believed ourselves to be, our power is but a shadow of this young man's strength. Brerto, great white tiger, you were defeated by Cialia's Flame. She is but a kitten compared to the might of my son."

"He is not your son, you fool," Kallum laughed. "You are as delusional as you are pathetic."

"Our brother has a point," Brerto conceded. "Reality does not seem a friend to you right now. I can feel this young man's power, but I am not convinced you have the strength to control this beast you have corralled."

"Nothing I can say to you will convince you," Ijilv's smile didn't waver in the least as his tone became as earnest as it had ever been, "but you must know my plan was laid long before either of you were even ideas. I have seen the time before time. I have solved all the riddles and cracked all the codes. Once my will is done, all will be revealed to you, and you can revel in your brother's glory, standing by my side as the gods you should have been from the beginning. I will teach you to fulfill your true potential, brothers. That is why you are here with me now. We will be as one." Then he turned all his attention to the sleeping young man before him and whispered in his ear, "Soon you will wake, my son, and this world will be yours."

By the time Ijilv's fingernail reached Geillan's jawline, the room at the top of the tower, the obelisks surrounding Geillan's sleeping form, and even the eternal dark and eternal light evaporated. They gave way to a blue sky glowing in glorious sunshine. Fluffy clouds lazed along slowly in a calm and comforting breeze. Geillan was there, awake and sitting on a large, flat boulder in front of a peaceful lake. He held a fishing pole in his hand. Its line was in the nearly still water, calmly swaying in the ripples of light waves gently lapping against a sandy shore.

Ijilv stood behind the young fisherman. Brerto and Kallum stood with him, surprised to be freed from their bonds. The three watched in silence as something beneath the surface tugged at Geillan's line.

The proud god leaned back toward Brerto and whispered, "He will catch this one, watch."

"You fool," Kallum scoffed as he failed at trying to walk away.

"I have freed you from your bonds, brother," Ijilv smiled, "but you must know they were as imaginary as the beauty surrounding you now. The fact you no longer really exist is still a concept beyond your grasp."

Sadness sparkled in Brerto's eyes as he conceded as much, "He speaks truth. I did not want to believe it, but he has managed to imprison us in his mind, victims of his will."

Geillan noticed the commotion behind just has he was wrangling a magnificent fish onto shore. It was good sized, at least ten pounds. Silver scales flashed with hints of blue in the bright sunlight. He turned and said, "Father, I have missed you. Look at this one. She is a beauty."

"Quite magnificent indeed," Ijilv gushed as any proud father would.

Kallum had had enough of the pointless charade. He shook his head at Geillan and said, "You must know this is not..." His lips suddenly froze, and no further words would come out.

Anger flashed in Ijilv's eyes as he glanced first at Brerto and then at Kallum. "I tried to be gracious, grant you a short reprieve from your sentences, but you spit upon my efforts. I will not have you spew your filth before my son. It is time for you to go back to the room I made for you."

Geillan had barely opened his mouth to speak again when his father's two companions vanished. Shock echoed in his eyes as he asked, "Who were those men?"

"Fools," Ijilv smiled. "They are of no consequence."

"Then why did you bring them here? You told me this place had to remain secret so that wicked wench could never find me. What if they tell her where I am?" his expression melted from shock to fear.

"Come here, son," his smile widened as he waved his hands to invite Geillan into his embrace. He hugged him tight as he continued, "They would not dare tell her anything about you or this place. They are your uncles, but, as I said, they are fools. I foolishly thought you might benefit from meeting them, hearing a perspective different than my own. Obviously, I was wrong. Perhaps we will try again someday."

"I have uncles?" he smiled at the idea.

"Four of them, in fact," Ijilv nodded.

Confusion spread across Geillan's face as he tilted his head to side and asked, "Why have you never mentioned them to me?"

"They are all beneath you," he said as he held the young man out to arm's length. "Forget about that now. We have much to discuss. Have you been training?"

Geillan rolled his eyes, "Of course, I have."

"Show me," Ijilv waved his hand toward the blue sky above a bank of pines with rich, healthy needles, a deeper green than any tree in the waking world.

Geillan leaned his head back, closed his eyes, and raised his arms out to his sides. Flames immediately began swirling around his hands, two circles growing in size until each was roughly three feet in diameter. Once the swirling flames stabilized, his eyes snapped open glowing the same red as his flames. He waved his right hand in an arc over his head and across his body until it had completed a full circle that ended where it had begun. At the same moment, a streak of flames shot across the sky above the pines following the same path as his hand. He repeated the gesture with his left hand. Once both hands were back in their original positions, two massive circles of red flame spun quickly above the forest.

"And then?" Ijilv asked.

As soon as the words left Ijilv's mouth, Geillan forcefully dropped his hands to his sides. At the exact same moment, both circles of flame above the forest crashed down into the pines. There were no flames licking up toward the sky as they consumed trees. The effect was more immediate than that. One moment there were hundreds of lush trees full of life, and the next moment there was a pile of ash where those trees once stood.

"Impressive," Ijilv commended him. "Your movements are dazzling." Then he pointed toward another bank of trees and said, "Now, show me the same without any theatrics."

Geillan's frustration bled through a bit as he rolled his eyes, "But you said wielding Dragon's Fire was art. Should art not be at least artistic in its application?"

"When the moment calls for artistic presentation, yes, indeed it should. However, not every adversary will grant you the time necessary to dazzle them with theatrics. There will be times when you must strike without mercy or warning because that is what your opponent will do to you if given the chance. My son, my love, I do not ever want you to give any adversary that chance. It would break me," Ijilv coached.

As soon as the last word left Ijilv's mouth, the trees he had pointed to erupted in an explosion that shook the ground and echoed across the lake. The report was so loud it caused him to jump earning a wide smile from his pupil.

"Better?" Geillan asked, confidence oozing from his smile.

"Much," Ijilv smiled back, pouring every ounce of resolve he had into not allowing even a hint of fear to glimmer in his eyes. "You are almost ready. That is good. We have very little time. Your mother is coming. She will be here soon."

Geillan absently kicked at a tuft of grass as he asked, "Why does she want to kill us?"

"I told you. She is a witch. She wants your power. I saw it in her eyes the moment the midwife placed you in her arms. She told me as much later that evening as you slept, a beautiful cherub in your basket, the moonlight playing off your cheeks. I was so overcome with joy as I looked down upon you," Ijilv paused as a faraway look drifted behind his eyes. After a few carefully calculated moments, he shook his head and added, "Imagine my shock as she told me her plan to sacrifice you at the Lake of Dragons."

A tear teetered at the edge of Geillan's eyelid threatening to moisten his cheek as he asked, "So, she never loved me?"

"Oh, my son," Ijilv again pulled Geillan into his embrace and held him tight. "She never loved anything but power. I am so sorry. It should not have to be you, but I fear she is far too powerful for me. You are the only creature alive who can stop her. That is why she searches. For as long as you live, there is a creature powerful enough to destroy her and save this world from her wickedness. You must defeat her."

"I will, father," he pulled away and looked earnestly into Ijilv's eyes. "I will never let her hurt you."

Ijilv sniffled and wiped away a fake tear as he smiled at the boy and said, "I know, son. Now, come and show me this glorious fish you have caught."

CHAPTER 16

THE DESTROYER

The forest floor smelled fresh beneath the canopy. A light breeze carried the perfume of wildflowers and berries in the glowing light of sunrays filtered by leaves wet from fresh rains. The delicate scent mingled with the earthy odors of shrubs and the soft dirt of the trail. Cialia materialized on the ancient path about a mile from the city she missed so and drew a deep breath in through her nose. She could have arrived directly in her old room in her hidden city high up in the trees, but then she would have missed the opportunity to enjoy the peace of her forest. A bird flitted from branch to branch in a small fir tree and tweeted as if in agreement.

Of course, there was urgency to her mission, but the god had not moved since she sensed him. Her sisters had probably been right about it being a trap. That was fine with her. There was no need to rush the hunt so long as her quarry believed he was the hunter, and she was the prey. Being underestimated wasn't anything new to her. Kaldumahn would learn what folly it was just as the rest of them had.

It seemed the journey had been too short as she rounded a thick, healthy oak and the wide clearing beneath her fair city in the trees sprawled before her. A few hundred men dressed like soldiers and clad in the blood red of Druindahl trained. All but the one barking orders seemed far too young and far too small to protect anything or march off to any battle. There may have been a few others who looked game for warfare, but not nearly enough.

"Cialia," Leisha's voice pulled her away from her assessment of the green force masquerading as riders of Druindahl.

"Mother," Cialia smiled as a sudden gust shook through her golden curls and sent ripples through her white gown.

The two women embraced. Cialia pulled away before Leisha was ready to let go. Had she not, the hug may have lingered beyond eternity. Relief wrapped itself up in the embrace, all twisted around the longing a mother carries whenever her children are away from her.

Cialia's smile widened as she toyed with one lock of her mother's hair that had gone completely white and said, "It suits you."

"It suits me?" Leisha blushed. "The white hair of an old woman suits me?"

"You are as beautiful as ever, mother. The forest air suits you," she smiled. Then her eyes raised a bit as she added, "It is not age that shocked a streak of white in your golden hair. Fear did that. He came to see you. Did he threaten you? The gods always threaten. Did he command you to bring me before him? What torture has he promised if you fail?"

"Your mother isn't the only one who is beautiful as ever," Boringas's deep voice sliced through the slight tension that had settled in between the two women.

Cialia rolled her eyes as she turned to embrace him, "Boringas, my dearest friend. Though I appreciate the compliment, you know I have never cared about such things. Grab us some swords, and you can compliment me on my technique."

Boringas offered a joyless chuckle as he said, "I would love nothing more than to be bested by the greatest sword in the history of Druindahl, but, as always, you haven't come to see me or even your mother. As always, the powerful and mighty Cialia is moved by great purpose."

"Yes, of course," her smile faded. "I am a hollow thing without feeling or emotion, an unyielding soldier blind to all but the mission before me."

"That is not what I meant," his smile fled as quickly as hers had.

"But it is true," she snapped. "You would have me sit with you and chat, reminisce about days gone by. We could sip wine, and you could once again profess your undying love for me, tell me to forget the trail, forget who I am or what I want so I can be your dutiful wife. I would love nothing more than to be that person who could settle for such things, but I am not."

"If only you were," Leisha sighed.

"Yes, mother," Cialia laughed, "If only I would demure and accept Boringas' hand, he could shelter me from the wiles of this world. Then you could rest easy knowing I had a hearty rider of Druindahl to protect me and put babies in me while my true love lies waiting for boots to trod upon her once again."

"I said none of those things," Boringas complained.

"No, you did not, but those are your feelings," her form seemed to deflate as she sighed. "I have told you before, sweet Boringas, I do love you. You are a good man, probably the best man I have ever known. Any woman would be lucky to have you, and you deserve someone who feels that way, someone who can give you that. I am whole, complete. I need nothing from anyone, and I have nothing of myself to give. I would never do that to you."

A slight frown crept onto his face as he pressed on, "And I have no say in what is done to me? A lifetime of sorrow would be worth even the most fleeting of moments if for in that brief amount of time I could believe you felt for me what I have always felt for you. Would it be so bad to sit beside me, to help me protect this city you profess to love so much?"

"It would do me well to have at least one member of my family by my side," Leisha chimed in. "And no, my desire to see your hand intertwined with fair Boringas' hand is not because I think you need the protection or guidance of any man. But where is your joy, dear daughter? Will you never take even one moment for yourself?"

"I have had enough of this fruitless debate," Cialia sighed. "Where is he?"

"Kaldumahn is a friend to Druindahl," Leisha dodged the question. "If you refuse to remain here among your people to protect them, you cannot take him from us."

"Your mother is right," Boringas added. "I could tell by the way you looked upon our weakened defenses that you realize how desperately we need the help."

"No god is a friend to anyone but themselves. As long as you serve their purpose, you will remain in their good graces. Once that changes, you will be cast aside like refuse."

Leisha cast a nervous look toward Boringas who only shrugged and shook his head. They both knew Cialia well enough to know nothing they said would sway her. Kaldumahn probably knew as much as well.

That idea tangled itself around Leisha's nerves enough to raise the hairs on the back of her neck. The god knew they would fail. That could only mean he believed he could defeat her. The bright flash that filled the forest meant she wouldn't have to wait long to find out if her worries were well founded.

By the time the light from the flash had dimmed enough that shapes could once again be discerned amid the light, all in the forest but Cialia cowered on their knees with faces buried in the dirt. She turned to face the god. He looked like nothing more than an old man leaning on his staff to her, a stark contrast to when he first allowed her to look upon him in all his glory. All the awe she felt in that moment so many years prior was gone, replaced by vengeful contempt.

She expected a command to kneel. Instead, he smiled and said, "Fair Cialia, protector and champion of all the creatures of Ouloos. We are all in your debt. You have destroyed the evil in this world and given us a chance to build something new and beautiful in its place."

Cialia's expression grew stern as she replied, "Evil still exists in this place."

"You have grown quite powerful, young Cialia, but you still have much to learn. The power you command is great and terrible. As you have grown comfortable wielding that great power, you have grown even more rigid in your ways. You assign evil to things without considering intent. I can help you see things for what they truly are, help you understand how something perceived as evil by one is actually crucial to another. At the same time, I can help you control your great power and use it to do so much more than simply destroy the things you do not like in this world," despite the condescension saturated in his words, he managed to keep even the slightest note of it out of his tone.

A laugh died at the back of her throat before it could be born into the world as she maintained her cool expression. "Yet another who would counsel me on the error of my ways. You are a vile thing, a corrupter of righteous souls who cares only of your own agenda. There is nothing I can learn from you. I know of your works and the evil you have authored against all creatures of Ouloos. I have judged you, Kaldumahn, great silver lion who stalks the skies, and I have sentenced you to oblivion," her tone remained as cool and aloof as it had begun while she accused the god.

The fear she expected to see on Kaldumahn's face as she made clear her intentions was absent. The fact was unsettling. Despite all his hubris and false bravado, Brerto's expression reflected pure terror once he realized she had defeated him. The great lion showed nothing of the sort. The expression on his face echoed something closer to satisfaction. His lack of fear, or ability to hide it, meant very little to Cialia. He would have the briefest of moments to reflect on his evil ways before she scattered him to the wind and rendered him unable to ever harm another creature on Ouloos again.

Cialia's eyes grew a fiery red as she focused her intent on his awareness. Gods are different than men or dwarves or giants, or any other living creature for that matter. Even when dancing in the physical, they don't inhabit physical bodies. Neither are they completely spiritual. They are something else. When scanning a man, Cialia could step right into their mind and feel their thoughts. The gods were aware on so many different levels, it was like exploring a labyrinth. Fortunately, it was a journey she had made before.

Kaldumahn's black eyes swirled with all colors at once as he pushed back against Cialia's will. Those beautiful and horrible incomprehensible things that were so terrible to behold would sicken anyone else in the forest that day, but Cialia remained unmoved. The gods wielded no terror horrifying enough to turn her away. She pressed deeper into his being with her mind, stretching, reaching out to invade every bit of his psyche.

She was almost there, so close she let the flame come. Invisible to any but her it slithered along her awareness and into Kaldumahn. In moments she would release her control on it and scatter the god to bits. Then something changed.

Kaldumahn's staff grew brighter as his hair and gown glowed with equal brilliance. It seemed a trick at first, but somehow the resistance Cialia felt grew stronger. She hadn't felt that from Brerto. Perhaps the great tiger had been unprepared when she battled him atop Mount Alharin, or perhaps the great lion was just that much more powerful. Whatever the reason, she strengthened her resolve and pushed harder.

As she pressed, probing deeper into the labyrinth, it suddenly occurred to her that she and Kaldumahn were not the only great and terrible forces in the forest that day. Moshat had to be there somewhere, but she couldn't feel him. He was blocking her somehow. She suddenly realized she could not defeat the great lion while the mighty bear was distracting her. She pulled the flame back into herself before allowing it to swirl about her arms.

Leisha's voice sounded far away as she cried out, "Cialia, no!"

Turning back was not an option. The god had committed an eternity of sin against Ouloos. She had judged him, and the sentence must be carried out. She thrust her arms toward the god and released her flame. In that very moment, she felt a mighty tug on her will. It seemed only in her mind, but it was strong enough to physically pull her body back and yank her arms toward the sky. The canopy above was immediately engulfed in flames.

Cialia caught the briefest glimpse of Moshat as he slipped out of the air next to Kaldumahn and whisked his brother away. Both gods were gone, and Cialia was left with red in her eyes and rage in her heart. She closed those terrible eyes and focused on Kaldumahn. Enough of her essence remained with him that she was able to follow them, splitting through time and dimension. She stepped into the scenery and was gone.

Leisha watched her daughter, her Dragon, her champion blink out of existence in pursuit of her prey. Then she looked up to the canopy as terror gripped her soul. Her perfect city in the trees would burn, the victim of a vengeful power who had completely lost all sense of mercy consumed by justice and vengeance.

Something even more horrifying than the loss of her home occurred to her as she stared up at the terror above. "The children!" she shouted to Boringas as she finally found the will to rise from the ground.

"Come," the dutiful soldier answered, fully prepared to charge into the fire and save all he could.

The heroic gesture was dashed against the soft ground by a charging horse as a voice from deeper in the forest shouted, "Make way. The horses have escaped the corral."

Leisha gave only the briefest glance to Boringas as his body crashed against the ground. She hoped he wasn't dead. She couldn't spare a moment to check his condition as the city burned. The only things she could focus on in that moment were the children. They would all be with dear, sweet Daleen learning how to make their ways through the great journey of life. As much as the dear, old soul loved those children, she was ill equipped to save anyone from anything. She could barely walk herself anymore. Leisha had to do something.

Bodies ran this way and that in the periphery. Some tried to wrangle horses. Some helped usher folks away from the flames. Others ran for water to help fight the flames raging above their heads. Leisha barely noticed any of it as she raced toward the carriage that would take her up to the blazing canopy.

As the cart carried her soundlessly toward the terror, the heat seized her. It was like nothing she'd ever felt. Her skin was instantly clammy and coated in a thick sheen of sweat. She should have run. She should have turned that cart around and ran toward safety, away from her daughter's horrible flame. But she could never do that. All the heroes of her city were saving all they could. The children had no one to save them but her. Once the cart reached the canopy, she charged onto what was left of a walkway tormented by roaring flames and into a blazing furnace of Dragon's Fire.

CHAPTER 17
EMPTINESS

The world seemed like a gray smudge, devoid of color or detail. Two banks of trees roughly six feet apart from one another stretched up further than trees should before branches from either side reached out toward each other to form a canopy far above Maelich's head. The two opposing lines of trees stretched off together into the unremarkable distance. It seemed a proper trail except for the fact it never appeared to dip, raise, or bend in either direction. Thick fog covered everything making it impossible to discern if this space that had all the markings of a trail actually was that. It was as gray and muddy as everything else.

Maelich didn't worry very long over deciding whether the space he walked along between the two banks of trees was a trail or something else. He had been there enough times to know he would never know. It occurred to him in that moment that he didn't really care all that much. There were no surprises, nothing to discover. The first time, even the next, and perhaps a few times after, the place seemed wonderful and worthy of deep exploration. By now, he'd spent enough time in the place it had all but lost any luster or mystery it had once held for him.

As he walked straight through the thick flog blanketing everything, he barely noticed the way it swirled as his body passed through it. That seemed almost odd enough to wonder about, but not quite. Though the fog swirled more like a liquid than some gas or vapor in the stale, forest air, he couldn't feel it at all. It took little contemplation to decide nothing felt like anything in that place because he wasn't really there.

Knowing he was in a dream removed any possibility for wonder. The only things he wondered about in that moment were how the black horse would present herself and how long he'd have to wander before she did.

"Help me, Maelich," the voice called out as if in response to his thought.

Hearing a plea for help carried on a voice with such urgency in such obvious distress would normally spark Maelich to action, but he was tired of the game. The last time she had come to him in a dream, she spoke plainly enough. Everything she had said prior to that seemed to be tied up in some kind of riddle, but she had just appeared that time. She didn't beckon like some twisted game of call and seek. Instead of charging off toward the sound, he shouted, "What do you want from me? I know this isn't real. Why not just show yourself instead of toying with me?"

"Help me, Maelich," the voice cried out louder with more urgency.

"I will not," he decided quietly, wondering if she heard the reply. The thought brought the slightest smile to his lips. He finally had something to wonder about. If nothing else made sense in this place, would the volume of his voice matter regardless the distance it had to travel? Was there actually any distance to cover?

"Help me, Maelich," there it was again, even louder.

"I would rather not," he said quietly again. "Why is it always me who has to help? Maybe I need help. Who will help me?"

Despite his frustration with the black horse and the games she played, there was a small part of him that wanted to search for a break in the tree and charge after the voice. He decided he wouldn't do that. At least, he hoped he wouldn't. In fact, he probably would. "No, no, no," he whispered as he sat down upon the ground and crossed his legs. "I'm not going anywhere." Then he raised his voice and hollered at the trees, "I am going to sit here until you show yourself to me or I wake."

"Help me, Maelich," the stubborn voice cried again.

Maelich shook his head. He wasn't sure for whom he'd made the gesture. Was it just to convince himself that he wasn't going to do what he had said he wouldn't do? He didn't know, and he wasn't sure how much he cared right at that moment. He had just noticed that his entire body was beneath the gray, swirling fog. It covered him up to his nose in fact. It didn't smell like anything, but nothing really did in that place.

"Help me, Maelich," the voice was louder yet again.

He ignored it. Instead of leaping to his feet and charging toward whatever danger might exist beyond the trees, he plunged his head completely beneath the fog. It was just more gray, dingy and unremarkable. He wondered how long he could stay there submerged under imaginary fog that looked like nothing at all. It wouldn't be very long. Whether it was duty, curiosity, or some other damnable thing entirely, he had to know what the black horse wanted to show him. He stood back up and looked toward the trees in the direction the voice had come.

"Help me, Maelich," the voice shouted this time.

He shrugged as he walked toward the trees looking for a way through. There wasn't one. He pressed his hands against the smooth bark of one of them. It didn't feel like much. He could tell he was touching something, but it didn't feel like a tree or stone or even dirt. Moving his hands around the trunk didn't help. Something stopped his progress halfway around the tree. It didn't feel like anything was there to stop his fingers from probing deeper, but he could move them no further.

"Where are you?" he shouted at the trees.

The answer wasn't helpful. "Help me, Maelich," the voice hollered louder again.

A break suddenly opened in the trees directly before him, and he was no longer on a trail. It didn't make any sense. It all happened so quickly, but a perfect circle of the same trees that a moment prior had been a never-ending trail suddenly surrounded him. It seemed impossible. Yet, there he was standing at the edge of it. The black horse was there near the center. She stood just beyond a stone altar, artfully etched with symbols Maelich didn't recognize. There was a body on the altar. It was too far away to make out any details about the figure in the gray, but the delicate gown it wore suggested the still shape was female.

"Once again, you invade my dreams to show me death," Maelich complained quietly. Then he shrugged and asked, "That doesn't look like another dwarf. Who is it this time?"

"Come closer," despite the oddity of it, the black horse's smile seemed genuine enough. "See for yourself. Some things cannot be told to us. They must be experienced."

"I would rather not look at dead things I do not recognize and feel emotions that seem unfounded when considered against that lack of recognition," he shook his head.

"But you must, Maelich," she argued. "There will come a time when you remember things you have forgotten. They will not come slowly. You will not have adequate time to process them. They will be like a flood. I do come to you bearing nothing but death but believe me when I say I do this to help you. Without closure you will drown in that flood. You will break."

A brief chuckle saturated with frustration slipped past Maelich's lips as he asked, "How do I gain closure looking at a dead thing I do not recognize?"

The black horse's smile remained as genuine as it had been as she replied, "You will know when you know. And when you do, you will be happy you have these memories to which to cling."

He sighed long and deep. Though he was fairly certain the black horse was wrong, and the body laid out on that slab would be meaningless to him, he had to look. He had to test his theory. He kept his eyes trained on the fog as he approached. When he finally raised his head and saw the woman's face, he knew he was wrong.

In that same moment, a light from somewhere up in the canopy shown down on her. Little specks glowed within it. Perhaps it was dust, but the tiny, swirling particles seemed to glow from within rather than reflecting the bright light in which they swam. Maybe they were fairies, or some other fantastical creatures existing in the myths of men. None of that mattered to Maelich as he looked upon the soft, beautiful face lying before him. Her pale skin was flawless and surrounded by golden curls that splashed like waves around it. Her eyes were closed, but somehow, he knew they were deep, brown, and enchanting.

"Leisha," he muttered as an odd heat in his chest and behind his eyes heralded the coming tears. They came like a flood as his legs went slack beneath him and he collapsed onto the corpse's chest. "How do I know you?" he sobbed.

The emptiness he felt in that moment seemed a contradiction. It was too full of feeling. As he clung to the body wailing, he felt so many things that had weight and mass. There was a longing, a yearning for something he knew he needed but couldn't define. A heavy sense of loss festered in his gut and mingled with regret. Though he had no idea what this thing was that he had left undone, there was no denying it. It was too heavy, weighing him down as it loomed above him. All of it was wrapped in sadness so deep and dark no light could ever hope to chase it away. Yet, as much as all of it was, he felt empty just the same.

"Why does this hurt so bad?" he finally raised his head up off Leisha's chest and asked. "I do not know this woman."

"Like you said, her name is Leisha, and you do know her," the black horse lost her smile and seemed genuinely sad as she replied.

He buried his face back into Leisha's chest as he cried, "How do I know her, and why do I not know that? It is not fair that I must feel this pain without knowing why." A bit of anger slipped in to cavort with the emptiness as he raised his head back up to the black horse and spat, "You are a witch, a vile thing who takes joy in causing others pain. Does it please you to see me so broken? What have I done to deserve this?"

"I am no witch, Maelich, and I do not wish to cause you pain. This is necessary. You must feel these things, and it is my duty to guide you there. If it could be any other way, I would make it so," she replied gently.

Maelich had more to say, more venom to spew at the vile thing who invaded his dreams and caused him such pain, but she was gone. As he flopped down to the ground and slipped beneath the fog, he realized the dead woman, Leisha, was gone too. He curled up in a fetal position and cried. He released all his pain, longing, emptiness, and rage out as he wept helplessly in a forest he knew really wasn't there.

When he woke a moment later in a forest that was different than the one he had just left, the tears, and emotions that had forced them from his eyes, remained. He was awake, safe from the terrors of his subconscious. Yet, the pain remained. The waking world offered him no respite. It seemed so unfair to feel these things without the reason behind them. It was like trying to battle a foe who wasn't there.

A deep sigh helped slow the stream of tears cascading down his cheeks, but it did very little to lessen the pain. That raged like a burning fire while seeming as empty as the blackest cavern in the deepest pit. He stood and leaned against a tree. As he wiped his eyes, it occurred to him that the tree he leaned against actually felt like a tree. It had rough bark broken up by ridges like a tiny mountain range covering it from top to bottom. That was something. Somehow, being able to feel something physical helped distract him from the terrors slithering around his mind. His tears finally ceased.

Morning had yet to break, but he could barely see the first glow of the sun threatening the eastern horizon filtered through the trees. It wasn't near enough light to see anything, but the glow from the prior night's cooking fires helped a bit.

The rest of the camp remained asleep. That was good. He hadn't realized it until just then, but he was leaving them. The revelation saddened him, but they didn't really need him anymore. If he were honest with himself, he knew he had become a hindrance to their mission. He no longer believed in it, if he ever had, and they had proven more than capable of carrying it out on their own. He had trained them to be efficient killers, and they were that. Ymitoth could guide them to their goal. He believed in the mission. Right in that moment, Maelich had no idea what he believed in anymore. He just knew he had to get away from it.

He grabbed enough supplies for a few days in the forest. He wouldn't need much. There were plenty of rivers and ponds cutting through the thick vegetation, and game was plentiful. On top of that, many of the trees offered sweet things to eat that grew right from them. He didn't know where his path would lead, but he intended to see it to it to its end.

Maelich had almost made it out of the camp unnoticed when he heard the quiet gruffness of Ymitoth's voice, "Where ye off to, lad?"

"I do not know," Maelich whispered without turning back toward his mentor. "Will you try to stop me or talk me out of leaving?"

"Ain't much sense in that," he whispered back. "A man's got to head in whatever direction his heart be leading him. Ye'll be needing to see that journey through. Go quietly. I'll take care of the Shaiwah."

"Thank you," Maelich whispered as he walked away.

CHAPTER 18
BORN AGAIN

Waiting is hard for anyone. It's worse for a hardened soldier who knows the enemy is at the gates. That's how it was for Kantiim as he slouched in a simple wooden chair he'd propped against the wall beneath the great crest of Belscythia. The brightly painted relief on the thing looked strange as he leaned his head back to look up at it. The great fish leaping from the water looked more like some strange, wingless bird diving down from a wavy sky. It had only been a few days since they'd received word that a pack of wild grizzly mongs worked their way toward Havenstahl on a meandering path, but it felt like weeks had passed.

Daritus and Spang stood over a map the former had sprawled across the table. It was the same damn map he'd been staring at since the invaders had arrived in Biggon's Bay. They would spend hours staring over the thing, strategizing and moving tokens from here to there and there to here. Kantiim had grown tired of it. Nothing was happening anywhere. They hadn't received word from Bom or any in his group, there had been no further word about the grizzly mongs' progress, and there had been no further reports about the massive force from all the great cities of men.

"Nothing has happened for days," he finally said. "How can the two of you have anything else to talk about over that damned map?"

Spang glanced over at Kantiim before raising his eyebrows and shifting his gaze across the table to Daritus. When Daritus failed to respond, he said, "He has a point, general. That blue token you just moved back over the castle is right back where it started when we began, and it made the same four moves yesterday that it made today. Perhaps we should give this map a rest. Maybe grab a pint and some grub to pass the time?"

Daritus sighed and ran his hand slowly through his normally luxurious, brown waves that had grown limp and dirty after days of neglect. "I fear I'm losing my mind trapped within these walls," he finally said. "The truth of it is, I am not certain what we should do next."

Kantiim suddenly jumped up and said, "Then stop worrying over things we cannot possibly change and let us go out to do something. We can leave Ygraml in charge of the forces here at the castle. He is one of my finest generals. The men respect him. Then the three of us can take one hundred men and challenge that pack of wild beasts from the north."

"We would be no match even with one thousand men," Spang sighed.

"Spang is correct," Daritus agreed. "It would be unwise to execute a bad plan simply to defeat the boredom we all feel."

"I know this," Kantiim replied a bit louder than he intended, as he began pacing. After a few moments he changed course, "What about the coastal towns? Before we learned of that pack, you were going to send Spang and I to Castrine. With the three of us, a good plan, and one hundred men, we could easily take that town back from those bastards from across the Great Sea."

Something sparkled in Daritus's eyes as he said, "The idea is not without merit. The hills around Castrine would be perfect for launching an attack against the town."

"And it is our responsibility to defend them," Kantiim quickly agreed. "We have been failing horribly at that."

Daritus looked over at Spang who simply shrugged and nodded.

"Then it is settled," Daritus raised his arms out to his sides. "We leave at dawn."

True joy spread across Kantiim's face at the prospect of doing something more than sitting and waiting for the next tragic report. That joy was so complete, the sound of the heavy doors to the great room opening did nothing to dampen it. He didn't care who followed them in or what report they brought. He would be marching in the morn.

Hagen's bent form followed those heavy doors into the room. He seemed no more than a whisper from the Lake as he shuffled across the polished stone toward them. His blue robe dragged on the floor behind him as if it had grown two sizes. The old man seemed to shrink with each passing day.

"Fair Daritus," Hagen's voice was hoarse and feeble. "I bring word."

"From Moshat?" Daritus asked quickly without glancing up at the old healer.

"Sadly, no. He has not been with us since the castle was restored," Hagen replied. "However, I do have heartening news. Thousands more have returned home, and I was able to steal many more souls from the Lake than I had hoped."

When Daritus finally turned his gaze to the old healer, he was shocked with what he saw. Hagen was old when he had met him so many summers prior, but the creature leaning heavily on a staff and hobbling toward him looked like a corpse. "Hagen?" he finally asked before grabbing a chair and rushing over to him. "Here, old friend. Sit, please."

Hagen waved him off as he said, "Do not fret over me. I am not ready for the Lake just yet. Based on the looks on all your faces, I do not look quite as healthy as I feel."

"Forgive us fools," Spang blurted. "Healing is hard work, and none of us understand the toils."

"On that we can agree," the old healer shot a warm smile at Spang before turning his attention back to Daritus. "I am weary, old friend, but I am fine."

"You are a horrible liar, brother," Antopy's voice rang out next to Daritus a moment before she stood beside him, her simple gray frock fluttering as if a breeze blew through the massive room though no such current pushed any air around. Long, light brown waves fluttered and danced about her shoulders and chest in the same imaginary wind.

Her sudden appearance jolted the brave general so, he nearly stumbled out of his boots. By the time he righted himself, his sword was drawn and leveled at the new intruder. "Witch," he shouted.

"Such a foul thing to say to a guest," Antopy feigned shock. "I prefer student of the mysteries of Coeptus."

Kantiim had also drawn his sword by the time he added, "Whatever that was you just did sure smells like witchcraft or some kind of magic to me."

"Magic," her voice earned a dramatic note as her eyes flashed blue, and lightning sprawled chaotically just beneath the high stone ceiling of the room. "There is no such thing as magic. There is only understanding of the universe and your unique place in it." Her smile never dimmed in the slightest as she looked toward Hagen and asked, "Will you not introduce me to your friends, brother?"

"I do not know you," Hagen shook his head. "Nor do I know if you are a witch as my friends suspect, but I must tell you, antics like that are bound to have you labeled a witch in these parts."

"You claim to be Hagen's sister?" Daritus' tone was more fitting for an interrogation than a simple question to a guest. "How is that possible? He is well beyond ninety summers, and you could barely have seen your thirtieth."

Antopy pretended to swoon at the comment, giving Daritus a wink and allowing the slightest blush to color her cheeks as she replied, "Though I appreciate the compliment from such a strong and just soldier, I assure you that your old friend has seen hundreds of summers, and I am his elder. Do you believe the disrespect he has shown me?"

Hagen's old eyes, suddenly sparkled with youth and recognition. "Antopy? Could it really be you?" he asked. "It seemed…well, I thought… What are you doing in this place? You said you would never venture across that forbidden forest of lost souls to the lands of maps and men."

"And I had never the intention," she smiled. "Unfortunately, it seems you have forgotten much bound by the rules of gods and men, and they need you to remember."

The recognition that had sparkled so briefly in the old healer's eyes faded as quickly as it had come as he shook his head, "I am what I have always been, a healer, a servant of Havenstahl."

"It might be best if you quickly come to the point of your visit, witch, or whatever you are," Daritus interjected. "Despite his age, Hagen has one of the sharpest minds I have ever known. If he knew you, he would know."

"I do, I suppose," Hagen seemed suddenly distracted. "She must be Antopy, but these things she says I should know, well, I simply do not."

Antopy rolled her eyes as she took one of Hagen's gnarled hands in her own and said, "It was fear that blocked these things from your conscious mind, brother. When a god levied his command of no more magic, you believed him. This despite the fact you knew very well that the things he considered magic were nothing more than knowledge."

"No, no," Hagen shook his head with more vigor, "there is no such thing as magic. Things must be how they must be. We must have order."

"You love the order Kallum promised. No, commanded. That is what drew you to that place, but it is not what destroyed your spirit, that child who lived within you constantly seeking knowledge ready to be filled with truth, whatever form it came in. That died after you stormed across that cracked and desolate façade that faker had painted across my lands—the place where the maps don't go as your kind would have it—and battled that titan. Do you remember his name? Of course, you would not, could not having blocked it all to protect yourself from the fear you felt. You were outmatched, barely survived. Let me help you remember, dear brother. His name was Merkhal.

The sparkle of recognition was back in Hagen's eyes. With it came an expression of fear none in the room had ever seen on the old healer's face. He fell in a heap and shook like poison tore through his innards.

Daritus charged toward his shaking form, sliding across the smooth stone floor on his knees for the last few feet. Fear, bewilderment, and anger danced across his face in equal parts as he looked up at Antopy and shouted, "What have you done to him, witch? I command you to release him from this spell."

A moment later, Kantiim's blade was resting against her throat ready to slice it open and spill her blood on the polished stone. "You had best choose the next words that leave your lips wisely," he growled through clenched teeth. "They very well may be your last."

"Save your strength, mighty soldier," Antopy smiled. "You cannot kill me, for I am not really here. Well…I am in a way, but not really. Oh, never mind. I could explain it to you, but it would make little sense." She paused for a moment waiting for Kantiim to do something which would prove it to him. When he failed to execute a killing blow she added, "I am not your enemy. You need him, not the thing he has become, but the titan he once was. You cannot help him. I gave him a push in the direction he must travel, but the journey is his, and his alone."

"I believe her," Spang finally said. "I have seen many things in my day, and this is not the strangest."

Despite Antopy's proclamations and Spang's trust, Kantiim kept his blade firmly against her throat as Daritus worried over their fallen friend. That friend's convulsions grew stronger as inhuman sounds poured forth from his mouth which had locked wide open as if vomit would pour forth at any moment. Nothing did pour forth from that mouth, except for a bit of spittle, but he shook so violently that Daritus had to move back. His body twisted in ways that should be impossible for a young man still fit and ready for any challenge. As old as Hagen was, he should have broken in half.

Hagen's body continued to shake violently for several minutes as everyone in the room with him watched helplessly. Except for Antopy, she too watched, but she didn't feel the helplessness of her companions. She was certain of the outcome. She would never have ventured to Havenstahl if she wasn't. Despite all the years that had passed since he had left, he was still her brother. At one time, they had shared a bond stronger than anything she had felt since or probably ever would again. She knew he would remember. He had to.

The room filled with light. Not the dim glow of torches or candles, nor was it the blinding brilliance of a midday sun. The light filling the room was blue and crackling. The air hummed with energy as static charged up and down Hagen's form, lifting his shaking body from the ground, and arcing out to the ceiling, walls, and floor in bolts like lightning exploding in a stormy sky. Everyone in the room but Antopy dove to the floor and covered their heads.

And then it was done. When Daritus raised his head to see the twisted carnage that used to be one of the wisest men he had ever known, a young man stood wearing Hagen's cloak. "This is the darkest magic," he gasped with horror.

"There is no such thing as magic," the young man's voice sounded like Hagen's without the hoarse weariness it had recently earned. "Thank you, my dear sister. You have reminded me of so many things I have left to do in this world. Will you accompany me?"

"You know I will not," she smiled back at him. "That has never been my way. You know this will mean your end."

"I do," he smiled back.

"And you would have it no other way," she said as her body vanished. Her voice remained long enough to add, "I love you, brother. We will be one again in Coeptus soon."

"Hagen?" Daritus held the young man's face in his hands as disbelief washed over him. "How can this be?"

Both Kantiim and Spang wore slack jaws. Neither was able to muster anything which might be considered a cognizant thought.

"My sister is wise," the young man smiled, "far wiser than I ever was. She has never stopped learning and yearning to know more. I grew content. I felt safe, comfortable in my position. I knew what was expected of me, and I was more than happy to oblige. I had purpose. But that purpose I had found was never my true destiny. She was right. Fear can be an overwhelming adversary. I lost a battle to it many years ago. I will tell you the story someday. Today is not that day. Today, I will free the coastal towns and bring their people back to the safety of our fair city. Tomorrow will be a new day."

"Are you a witch?" Daritus had so many things he wanted to say, questions he wanted to ask, but that simple query was the only one that made it to his lips.

Hagen sighed, "You could think nothing else based on what you know of this world. Ask me again if we survive this. You are a righteous man, fair Daritus. I believe in time you could come to know things your mind in its current state would find impossible. I would love to teach you those things."

"How will you free our people?" Spang asked, finally able to find some words.

The young man smiled at him and said, "Magic."

Then he raised his arms wide and shouted in a voice both deep and powerful, "NGIR DU!"

Lightning flashed about the ceiling and the walls casting a blue glow as the hair of the other three men in the room rose with static. At the same moment, the same pale, blue light manifested in a swirling circle of energy. It expanded like it had depth, like it was a path to somewhere.

As Hagen stepped into the swirling mass, he looked over at Daritus and said, "I am bound for Castrine. Once I have freed the townsfolk there, I will send them here. Do not fret for their safety. I will make sure no terrors befall them on their journey. From there I will move south down the coast. I will free our people."

As soon as the young man who used to be Hagen turned away from Daritus, the swirling, blue tunnel vanished. The blue sparks of lightning ceased, and the hair of all three men still staring slack-jawed at the empty place where magic had just happened before their eyes fell back into place.

Kantiim was the first to break the suddenly still and silent air. "Have you ever?" he asked with shock wrapped tightly around his tone.

"No," Spang replied, his wide eyes still staring at the spot Hagen had just left.

Daritus' composure slowly returned as he finally replied, "I have killed a giant, stood before a god with sword drawn, but I have never witnessed anything like that which I have just seen. I thought I knew that man."

"He is the same man," Spang muttered. "He has only just remembered who that man is."

"What do we do now?" Kantiim turned toward Daritus and asked. "If that witch, or whatever he is, who is or used to be Hagen can truly free the coastal cities—"

"If what just happened is any indication, he can," Spang interrupted.

"True," Kantiim nodded toward him before finishing his statement. "What should we do?"

"We should drink," Daritus shrugged. "We'll let Hagen do whatever it is he does, and we will regroup with the light of a new day.

CHAPTER 19
MAGIC

The sky was clear that day, not a cloud to mar the blue perfection as far into the horizon as one could see. The town beneath that magnificent sky was far less majestic. Once a bustling seaport of well-kept huts, sturdy piers, and beautiful boats that were as pleasing to behold as they were sea-worthy, the place had become a ghost haunting the shore. The few huts which had survived the fires were nothing more than gutted, crumbling shells. Most of the one-hundred or so surviving townsfolk who weren't dragged away by the monsters from across the Great Sea for nefarious purposes were grimy with soot and chained together, tasked with cleaning the remaining fish they had left to feed the invaders.

Only five trogmortem remained with the captives in the city. All of them were beastly, nasty, and cruel. Their green eyes glowed when the light hit them just right, not like creamy jade or a sparkling emerald, but something ominous, the kind of eyes that startle you out of slumber while trapped within a night terror. They had rough, reddish skin that almost looked like hardened scales. Their builds were thin with wiry muscles, but they were still as wide across as two stout men, and more than twice as tall. Their bent postures kept their stony fists just off the dirt as they lumbered around threatening any of their prisoners who slowed even the slightest in their work with long, blackened claws and sharp fangs wet with saliva.

The biggest of them, Nalzin-Lo carried a massive whip with small metal shards fastened about its end. They jingled as he shook the thing and whistled loud when he cracked it. He was the first to notice the deep gray clouds forming atop the hill above the small fishing village. It was like a ball with rough edges swirling and expanding. Blue lightning arced within and around it occasionally striking out in zig zag patterns ten to twenty feet long.

"What do you make of that?" he yelled back to his kin.

"Strange looking storm right there on the ground," one answered back.

"Maybe the gods," another added. "Should we kneel."

"You saw the great tiger when he came to call on Ott in the great waste," Nalzin-Lo grunted back. "He didn't arrive riding lightning or floating in clouds. He was just there. No. Form up on me. If anything steps out of that mess, we'll rip it to shreds."

The swirling mass of clouds grew larger until it was a full fifty feet in diameter. Flashes of lightning came faster as the bolts traveled further and further out from the thing. Finally, a bolt arced out and blasted the trogmortem standing next to Nalzin-Lo. It blew a hole right through the nasty beast's chest and tossed him twenty feet through the air. The crack of thunder that accompanied the strike shook the ground and toppled the other four beasts right to the ashy sand.

"Stay down," Nalzin-Lo," shouted at his group.

Fear danced about the prostrate group as they watched the growing mass in horror. The lightning subsided slightly as the swirling clouds gained depth. Before long, it looked like a corridor expanding before them at the top of the hill, rather than a cloud growing just above the ground. When Hagen stepped out of the swirling tunnel, removed his hood, and shook out his healthy mane of light brown hair, those luxurious waves fell around a fresh face that could not have seen more than twenty-five summers.

Nalzin-Lo jumped to his feet, looked around at his brethren, and laughed, "He is a child." Then he looked back up at Hagen and commanded, "Best go back where you belong. There is nothing for you here."

"On the contrary," Hagen smiled flashing teeth as white as fresh snow, "I have come for those people you've been terrorizing, and I aim to see them free from beneath your heel. Leave now, and our quarrel can wait. Remain, and I crack the ground beneath your feet, burn you with lightning, and bury you beneath the waves where the fishes can pick your bones clean of your rotten flesh."

The threat only made the mighty trogmortem laugh harder. He nudged the warrior next to him and said, "We haven't the time for this. Kill the fool."

The grim trogmortem soldier heeded the command. He charged up the hill toward Hagen with murder in his eyes and a menacing war cry pouring forth from his lips.

Hagen didn't budge. His smile just widened as he raised his arms out to his sides and shouted in a voice as beautiful and terrible as a god's, "BARAQU!"

As soon as the command left Hagen's lips, three bolts of lightning from three different flashes in the sky all converged on the charging trogmortem. Thunder shook the ground as the massive beast exploded in a sloppy cloud of blood, meat, bone, and entrails.

He smiled at the remaining trogmortem and bellowed, "I warned you. I gave you ample time to free yourself from my vengeful gaze, and you have spat upon that gift. RIMANIS IM!"

Wind suddenly swirled around the three remaining trogmortem. Nalzin-Lo's eyes were wide with terror when his head slammed into one of his soldier's knees. Then something smashed into his elbow. He couldn't tell if it was a head, a foot, an elbow, or something else. The vicious wind spun so strong it dragged dirt up from the ground to color itself dingy brown as it stretched up into the sky, a hundred-foot whirlwind spinning faster and faster. Nalzin-Lo was nearly unconscious when the sensation of falling upward finally ceased. He just spun there, bouncing off his brothers, helpless and out of control.

"NAHU!" Hagen commanded.

The swirling wind immediately ceased, and the three trogmortem fell one-hundred feet to crash upon the merciless ground, smashing into bruised puddles of blood and vomit. Once the sound of rushing wind, bodies thudding dully against grassy sand, beasts crying and groaning, and bones cracking from the force of falling from great heights had ceased, Hagen turned his attention to the terrified townsfolk.

The grim menace that had twisted up Hagen's recently young face as he battered monsters with the elements smoothed into a friendly smile as he spread his arms wide and approached the chained and huddled mob. The sounds of dull sobs and heavy, chain links clinking and squeaking against one another as the frightened group hugged each other huddling as closely together as possible in fear of the next attack made it difficult for him to maintain the calm demeanor. If it were in his power, he would kill those monsters again and again. Thoughts like that were dangerous, but their crimes against his people had been great.

Thoughts of punishment suddenly swirled about in his mind. They were foreign. Much had changed in the past few hours—forgotten ideas and power well beyond any elixir he could concoct—but the idea of punishment wasn't one of them. It was new, fresh. He'd always been a man with a mind for learning and nurturing. Even the idea of using his remembered power to free his people wasn't born from a longing for revenge. After witnessing how cruel the beasts from across the Great Sea had been, and how callously they had treated his people, it was difficult not to embrace ideas like punishment and revenge.

The welcoming smile he had forced onto his face remained as he spoke soothingly, "Good people of Castrine, you have survived terrors no man should ever have to endure. You have lost many you love, your homes, your glorious ships, and even your way of life. You have spent your lives loving the Great Sea, showered in its glorious bounty, and now fear what comes out of it. There is much of that I cannot change. There is no power great enough to pull someone back from the Lake once that journey has been made, and the only thing that can heal this new fear is time. Havenstahl has failed you. I have failed you."

"Ye ain't failed nothing," a grimy, old woman popped her head up from the huddled mass. Her voice was rough with age, but strong. Her eyes, though gray from cataracts and partially obscured by messy, gray hair, sparkled with hope as she continued, "Them monsters did what they did. Ain't nothing can be done for what's been done. But what of us who remain. What do we do now?"

"SIKKURU PETU," Hagen boomed in response. Instantly, each cuff fastened to each wrist in the huddled mass popped open, and the chains binding the group clanged to the ground. Then he turned toward the hill behind him and shouted, "NGIR DU!"

The group of newly homeless refugees had just begun rising to their feet when bright flashes of blue lightning arced across the sky atop the hill. The crack of thunder that immediately followed drove them all back to the ground, prostrate and covering their heads.

"Please, good people of Castrine, you have nothing else to fear. I am here to help not harm you. In fact, I will see to it that no monsters from across the Great Sea will ever harm you again," his voice had gained an imploring note as he approached the brave woman who had spoken and touched her gently on the shoulder.

"Look there," he said, as he pointed toward the swirling mass of blue light that had formed atop the hill stretching into the horizon like a corridor. "You have nothing to fear. Despite the lights and clouds and sparks, that is nothing more than a doorway. You will walk through and find yourselves in the courtyard at Havenstahl. Walk up to the first person you see and tell them you need help. They will know what to do."

"How will they know?" the old woman asked. "We've got the look of grimy trail thieves."

"My voice will leave your lips when you speak, and they will understand," Hagen smiled down at her. "Now go. I promise you, once we've sent the monsters from across the Great Sea back to their homes, we will rebuild your village to its former glory. Your lives will return to normal."

The group obliged Hagen's command and trudged slowly up the hill. He watched as the able helped the injured until all had made it through. He waved his hand once the last had crossed the threshold, and the swirling mass shrunk out of existence. Then he turned his gaze south down the coast allowing the grim menace of his expression to chase his smile away.

CHAPTER 20
THE KING'S WIFE

The sky was a swirling kaleidoscope of colors, some common, others strange, and still others scarcely imaginable. No celestial bodies rested among the beautiful, chaotic mess, or at least they failed to stand out in all the blazing and glorious color. The ground beneath Perrin and Ycharaz as they lounged rapt in the magnificent show above them appeared to be actual ground for the first time in longer than either of them could remember. It was nearly the shade of dirt, and the structure they sat upon seemed like an actual boulder. A fine, milky, light purple dust-like powder was the only thing from preventing the area around them from looking just like a vast, dry desert.

"Were you jealous the other day?" Perrin asked, breaking a silence that had lived just long enough to become awkward.

"Was it day?" Ycharaz dodged the question. "It grows harder to gauge the passing of one into the next the deeper we travel into these incredible lands."

"Day, night, what difference does it make?" she smiled, more amused than annoyed by his game. "You failed to answer my question. Were you jealous? You certainly seemed so."

"That is a dangerous question," he scratched his head and stretched out. "On one hand, answering no might be a betrayal of my true feelings, perhaps even a lie to my queen. It has been a time since I studied any of the books of law bound up in the great halls of Havenstahl, but I fear that could be a crime worthy of death. On the other hand, you are the king's wife. Thoughts such as those you suggest could be considered equally dangerous, even more so. A mere thought from my king could reduce me to ash."

"Is that all I am, the king's wife?" she shook her head and gazed off into the rapidly swirling horizon. "That makes me sound like property, no more important than his sword or his boots."

"No," he touched her hand as his light brown eyes glistened with truth. "I was not finished. You are my queen. These things I feel are a betrayal of my king and your honor, but you are not wrong. I was jealous. I am jealous. I did not like the way you looked at him, nor the way he looked at you."

The shock he expected to see on her face as he made his confession was absent from her bright eyes as she pressed him further, "Of course. Will you tell me now how beautiful I am, how you cannot tear your eyes away from me? Would you reduce me to a thing to be coveted, or a naïve little girl who swoons at the sight of a strong man with a nice smile?"

Ycharaz's expression remained serious as he replied, "I would not, and I would never. I am certain you have seen your own reflection trapped within a looking glass. What you see gazing back at you is not you. I admire what lies beneath that face the world sees, as pleasing as it may be. Perhaps your eyes carry a hint of what hides inside, but it is not even them that keep me so entranced. You are fearless. Less than a summer ago you were a loyal, happy wife and soon to be mother safe within the mighty walls of your castle, and now you are a titan leading ragged, worn soldiers across a forbidden waste that has forever struck fear in the hearts of the mightiest of men. Yes, I was jealous as I watched the way your eyes sparkled as Dirk played his tricks, but not because your body pressed against his the way I wish it pressed against mine. No, it was because he could give you something I could not, something valuable, a lesson. You admired that gift, and I wished it was me who blessed you with it."

She scanned his face, looking for the crack, some hint he may be toying with her emotions or having a laugh at her expense. It never came. His eyes seemed to deepen as she stared into them. It looked like truth lying deep within, but could it be?

A loud howl distracted her from her search for some reality to all his words, as a bright red flash bled into something that resembled a spider web before being ripped to shreds by a violent wind. Added to all the heaviness surrounding them, the sound and light were too much. They both blushed and lost themselves to nervous laughter.

Ycharaz found his voice first and asked, "Is that what thunder sounds like in this queer place?"

Then she kissed him. Her lips were stiff, even tentative at first, but they slowly softened as he responded. Even as it was happening, she wasn't quite sure what drove her to do it. Maelich's face fluttered by like a flag flapping on a light breeze. Guilt suddenly filled her. Why? Why should she feel guilty for allowing the slightest hint of pleasure into a life that had become a weight to bear rather than something to cherish? He was the one who chose to leave her and sweet Geillan. She pushed the idea aside and pulled Ycharaz on top of her.

Passion had precious few moments to mount as the heat grew between them before Glord's shocked and angry voice chased them away, "By the Dragon's sweet tears, what on Ouloos do you think you're doing?"

Perrin covered her face in embarrassment as Ycharaz spun off of her and scrambled to his feet. By the time he was standing before his accuser, Glord's sword was drawn and pointed at his throat. His words were choppy and breathless as he held his hands up before him and said, "General, wait…"

The snarl on Glord's face was hint enough that he hadn't the patience for excuses when he growled, "Draw your sword, boy. You've been a sturdy soldier. Despite the betrayal, I'll give you a warrior's death."

"Glord, stand down," Perrin finally wrangled her shame and stuffed it deep enough into her gut to realize what was happening between her men.

One tear dribbled down his cheek and spittle flew from his mouth as he shouted back at her, "Don't!" Then he turned his wild gaze back to Ycharaz and repeated his command, "Draw your sword."

"I will not," Ycharaz held his hands out to his sides. "I would never raise my blade against one of my own."

It wasn't the blade slipping between his ribs and piercing his heart that caused the great pain in his chest or the tears that blurred his vision as Glord roared, "Then you can die a coward's death," into his ear. It was his betrayal that burned him so. Glord had been like a father to him. He was the first to notice him as a young recruit working against a training dummy and see something more in him. The true pain he felt in that moment as Glord's sword slipped all the way through his chest before popping through the skin on his back was emotional not physical. The fact the man he loved and respected more than any other man stood before him carrying out the ultimate sentence without a hint of love, compassion, or sorrow in his eyes while not even giving him a moment to argue his case was the true source of his pain. Nothing had ever hurt him so deeply. As consciousness slipped quickly away, he knew nothing else ever would.

"No," Perrin cried as her lips moved around other words that had no voice to propel them to any ears. She crawled over to Ycharaz's body and cradled him to her bosom after he slipped to the ground off Glord's blade. "How could you!" she shouted up at him.

A horrid mix of rage, sorrow, and guilt twisted up Glord's face as he looked down at Ycharaz's twitching body and cried, "He betrayed my king." Then he turned his raging eyes toward his queen and yelled, "You betrayed my king."

Though the guilt dripping from her eyes with her tears was as heavy a thing as she'd ever felt, she was done being accused. She stood up to her general and yelled back in his face, "Your king betrayed us all. Where is the Dragon? Where is our fair protector while his baby lies captive in some prison in this horrid place, and his generals kill their men in cold blood? Who will judge him for his crimes? Who can hold him accountable?"

The briefest hint of regret danced across Glord's face before it hardened once again. "You took a vow," he finally said.

"And he broke it," she snapped back.

His voice sunk to barely a whisper as he replied, "You broke my heart. You were supposed to be the best of us, the purest. I never had a daughter, but I loved you like that."

"That is not what love looks like," she screamed in his face while pointing down at Ycharaz whose body had finally stopped twitching, "and love should never come with demands. You didn't love me. You loved the idea of a person you thought I should be. I am not that. Kill me too, or flee from my sight, but you are not welcome by my side."

She fell back down upon Ycharaz's broken form, pulled him onto her lap, and cradled him like a babe. His brown eyes had grayed over. They stared lifeless at the swirling colors he had been admiring by her side only minutes prior. She held him close and wept into his torn chest.

Glord watched for a bit. The longer he did, the less justified he felt about what he had just done. The queen had been clear about her intentions. He was under her command. He broke his vow to her because she had broken her vow to his king. Who would hold him accountable? He glanced up at the same sky Ycharaz's dead eyes started into. This queer place wasn't his home. He didn't belong there. None of them did. As he looked at the twisted, foreign landscape around him, he decided he wasn't worthy of his queen's grace. He blasted a short, crisp whistle. A moment later, his horse charged up. It wasn't malice or anger that kept him from looking back as he mounted and rode off, it was guilt. He felt unworthy of her presence as he fled away in disgrace.

CHAPTER 21
THE GODS' KEEP

Kaldumahn and Moshat stood facing each other in their keep. Both shined with light glowing like a million suns. Kaldumahn's hair was perfect, straight, and silver. Moshat's was like a mass of living waves of perfect black streaked with perfect white. Both magnificent manes glowed with the same glorious light in equal brilliance to that which radiated from their impeccable, white robes. The elaborate and intricately designed Dragons perched atop their respective staffs blazed with equal brilliance as the two gods stood completely still with their eyes closed. Despite the impossible stillness of their forms, their mouths were anything but. Those moved feverishly over silent words as if the unheard proclamations they made were the most urgent statements ever uttered.

Behind the two silently chanting gods sat two perfect thrones, ornately carved from stone, and etched with shapes impossible for any man to create. Just beyond the two thrones, floated a massive circular crest. The image etched upon it—a mighty Dragon belching fire— glowed the same perfect white emanating from the gods in equal brilliance. Each intricate detail of the relief was perfectly clear despite the intense light the image poured forth.

As the two gods mouthed their silent proclamations, the Dragons perched atop the staffs they gripped glowed even brighter as if their brilliance might swallow up all other light in the circular room. These glowing images perched atop the immaculate, white staffs weren't real Dragons, but the details of their forms were so intricate and accurate in their execution that both looked as if they could leap to life at any moment. The Dragon on Kaldumahn's staff appeared triumphant with wings spread wide, while the Dragon on Moshat's crouched low and belched fire as if ready for battle.

Their lips ceased moving and their eyes—horrible yet glorious at the same time—snapped open as Kaldumahn whispered, "The destroyer approaches."

"Indeed. I have sensed her presence. She is near," Moshat agreed and then vanished, slipping just outside the spectrum of visible light, sliding in between dimensions, the void where nothing exists or can without first learning to see past the rules of physicality.

And then she was there. At first Cialia appeared as a cyclone, elements spinning around each other, groping and connecting. She slowly materialized— bits of her like dust swirling into a physical form—as she stepped toward Kaldumahn who now stood alone before two thrones. Her voice arrived before her face or lips, "I feel you pushing against me, trying to force me out of this place." Once she had fully regained her physical presence, she glanced around the perfectly smooth dome and added, "So this is how you've remained hidden from my awareness. I can feel the enchantments clinging to the walls. It was foolish to expose yourself to me."

As the final word left her mouth, a perfect circle of flame surrounded Kaldumahn. Just as the circle collapsed toward him, shrinking toward its center, he vanished in a flash of light even brighter than the glow of the crest behind him or the Dragon perched atop the staff in his hand.

Cialia focused her intention on the small bit of his essence she remained attached to and chased him with her will like a wild mountain scarra on the scent of a wounded lourng. Again, it was like racing through a labyrinth, twisting and turning, except these turns weren't just left and right. They went up and down and even upside down, sometimes swirling, other times rising and sinking rapidly like waves reaching multiple levels of twists and runs.

Then something hit her. Though her eyes remained wide, she didn't see anything physically strike her. However, the force that crashed violently into her belly felt like something with both weight and mass. Fire blasted forth from her in all directions, filling up the dome and challenging the bright, white light with a deep, red blaze. She caught the briefest glimpse of Moshat as he slipped into her reality and then back out again.

She regained her feet and drew her focus back within. A sudden urge to vomit swept through her gut where Moshat's invisible attack had landed. She calmed, pulled back within herself, and focused on breathing. The urge passed.

The ambush made it obvious that expecting a fair fight from any god was folly. The two gods had obviously concocted a plan which would allow them to avoid a direct confrontation with her. Instead, they would hide, splitting space and time to escape her rage, and only attack like cowards from behind. Her heart rate slowed with her breathing as her focus sharpened. She scanned the room with both her eyes and her mind waiting for the next attack. She didn't have to wait long.

Kaldumahn stood immediately before her when he blinked back into existence with a flash of light. His staff aimed directly at her head as if he might fire his power forth from the mighty Dragon perched atop it. Its blinding light was brighter than any light she had ever seen. She braced herself against the force of the attack, but it never came. Instead, a massive wave of energy crashed into her from behind. The powerful blast felt like a wall slamming into her back and pounding her to the stony ground. By the time she leapt back to her feet, red fire blazed in a circle around her, and both gods were gone again.

"Cowards," she spat.

Again, she drew her focus back within herself. Force alone would not defeat the two gods in their keep. They seemed stronger there. Somehow, she needed to unravel the mechanics behind their tricks, how they danced between dimensions and slipped from one to another. It seemed very similar to the way she split time when she traveled, but she didn't understand the power. In those times, she simply thought of where she wanted to be, and her body followed her will. She had never really thought about how the process worked. It just did. Perhaps what they were doing was similar.

She had barely decided to set her intention to the mighty crest hovering behind the two thrones when a great swirling wind whipped up around her and dragged her helpless into the air. Her body spun about wildly amid the circular current as it carried her up toward the ceiling before crashing her against the wall and dashing her back against the hard, stone floor.

Her eyes grew suddenly heavy as the room dipped and swayed

before her. Moshat was gone again as soon as she located him. She had barely regained her feet when Kaldumahn appeared before her and clenched his hand into a fist. Rage and satisfaction mingled together in an expression as horrible as his eyes as he gazed upon her and squeezed his fist so tightly his arm shook from the effort.

The pain in Cialia's chest was crushing and immediate. She could feel his fingers probing into her chest and gripping her heart. They mercilessly squeezed, crushing the muscle. The iron grip prevented it from beating. She fell back to the floor clutching her chest. It felt like a bull tubber sat upon her. She couldn't catch her breath. A brief, forceful cough fired blood past her lips to coat her chin and splatter the floor around her.

Her agony grew as she flopped about, her head growing fuzzier with each passing moment. Her focus waned. There was nothing but the pain. It filled her body and mind. She had to be stronger than it. This was her chance. Kaldumahn stood across the room. His consciousness was right there, dangling before her like a fat, ripe fruit just waiting to be plucked from a tree, but it was just out of reach. She latched onto that idea.

Her eyes clenched tight as she focused on that fruit. Ignoring the pain, she focused her intention on that flicker of awareness. Her flames slipped along the same path, reaching, groping, stretching toward their goal. It was so close, just out of reach. The squeezing pain in her chest exploded as the god battled back. Her head swam in a stormy sea of dizziness. She couldn't relent. It was just a little further. She was almost there. Let the flame go.

Then he was gone again as quickly as he had arrived, but so was the pain. She ignored the blood dripping from her chin and focused on her heart. It was bruised. She could feel it. Her ventricles and atria were crushed. She pressed her intention deep into the cells, willing them to heal themselves. Each individual cell had only begun to repair itself when pain erupted her head.

She glanced up to see Moshat in the center of the room, the maniacal look upon his face bathed in the glorious white light of his staff. His fingers arced out as if they gripped something while Cialia's brain ached in response. It was as if he were trying to physically break her mind crushing it beneath his might. She shifted her focus from healing her bruised heart to battling back against the god. Moshat may have the power to damage her brain, but he had no control over her mind. That power was one only she controlled. No god, nor man, nor any other being physical or spiritual could break her will or control her spirit. She pushed back harder against his efforts.

The wild sneer on Moshat's face slowly slipped from unbridled aggression to trepidation and finally to outright fear. Kaldumahn suddenly materialized next to him and gnarled up his hand in the same fashion. Both gods squeezed against Cialia's will with all their might. The glow of their staffs grew brighter and brighter as their efforts increased.

Cialia fought harder against their combined power, pushing, her will trudging toward their light. While she battled them with her mind, her heart continued to heal itself. Her face flushed with color as her blood flow returned. The dizziness fled, evaporating like morning fog chased away by the blazing sun. All her focus quickly returned as she resisted their might. Something snapped, a crack like thunder echoed off the perfect dome surrounding them as the light blazed even brighter for one brief moment. After that spec of time, the light was all that remained.

The three of them stood naked in perfect light with no beginning and no end. There were no discernable shapes in the light save the three of them. Cialia remained calm while fear danced about the faces of gods.

"What have you done?" Kaldumahn stammered.

"She has broken time," Moshat gasped.

"I have judged you, Kaldumahn, great silver lion who stalks the skies, and Moshat, mighty bear who lumbers about the north woods. You have failed in your roles as gods of the creatures of Ouloos. You have failed as guides to the bliss of Coeptus. I sentence you to oblivion," Cialia remained aloof as she cast her judgement.

Then the light dimmed enough that shapes could again be seen among the brilliance. The gods again held their staffs tight within their hands. All three of them were once again clad in their perfect, white robes. And then the gods were gone.

Cialia collapsed to the stone floor, exhausted. She thought about giving chase immediately, but quickly decided against it. They were prepared for her, and their plan had almost worked. She needed a moment to collect herself. She had grown so accustomed to being underestimated by the gods that she had underestimated them. The two of them were strong together. She needed to prepare before facing them again. She sat up, crossed her legs, and focused within herself as her breathing grew steady.

CHAPTER 22

REGRET AND DETERMINATION

Perrin cradled Ycharaz on her lap as she wept into his chest. His shirt was torn and bloody beneath her cheek. She had no idea how long she'd sat like that weeping over her broken soldier. The sky had changed several times, from the swirling colors she had admired with Ycharaz to something burnt and orange with hazy green streaks crisscrossing it to the odd, upside-down mountain range that sprawled out above her as she cried. No matter how she shuffled the events that led to her trusted general cutting down one of his most loyal soldiers, she could not deny the fact that much of the blame for the tragedy laid at her feet.

As she sat damning herself and wishing she could take the kiss back, something deep inside of her grew increasingly defiant. Barely a whisper at the back of her mind at first, it battled against the shouts of damnation echoing within her cranium. That whisper grew louder. She was the queen. The men who followed her beyond the Lake of Dragons to explore the place where the maps don't go served at her pleasure. Glord was wrong. He had no right to question her or her motives. The justification she felt as the idea grew was small consolation. Who had been wrong or right mattered very little with the result of her actions lying dead in her embrace. Ycharaz would remain dead either way.

She hadn't noticed the rest of her men ride up when Halogren's voice interrupted her tears. "My queen, what have you done?"

She'd grown used to his scars, but the scowl he wore when she looked up at him twisted and deepened them into something horrid and frightening. It seemed like a monster glowered over her as the pink ravines crisscrossing his flesh glowed in the odd light cast by the strange sky above.

Darg slurped heartily on his false teeth before adding, "The look on Glord's face as he charged past us was like nothing I've ever seen haunt his countenance."

"He was crying," Ganodin added. Whatever the fact may have meant to him failed to show through his thick beard and brows.

"In all my days, I cannot say I have ever seen that man cry," Jorgon tossed his blonde mane as his soft, brown eyes narrowed. "What could bring that titan to tears? What have you done?"

Perrin glanced from face to accusing face surrounding her, unable to find any words to describe the flood of emotions filling her just then. Part of her wanted to apologize to them for being a shabby excuse for a queen and a leader none should follow, but an equal part of her wanted to shout to any who could hear that she was the queen of Havenstahl. Her will was her own, and a queen's will towers above question or reproach. Even if she wasn't a queen, the idea any man would question her motives or judge her actions was something she could no longer accept. That meek girl who would do as she was told and acquiesce to any rules those men would place upon her had died or fled months ago. Whether it was the mission that killed her, or the trail, didn't matter. Right at that moment, the defiant part of her that wanted to shout proclamations of her own freedom to any who would listen sat beside another part of her that was wounded and didn't want to say anything. That bit just wanted to curl up in a ball and cry until the Lake called her home. She didn't do either of those things, nor did any of the words echoing in her mind make their way to her lips. Instead, she glanced back and forth among them through a blurry, tear-filled gaze.

Dirk finally broke the silence and shifted the accusations back at Perrin's accusers. "Is this not your queen sitting broken before you? Have you all not pledged your swords and lives to her? I have never visited the lands from which you hail, but if this is how noble men from those lands behave toward their queens, I have no desire to ever make any such journey. I may question my queen, but only after I have heard her words. Even then, those questions would be delivered without the judgement I hear dripping from all your accusations.

Shame on you."

Perrin had finally had enough. She wrangled her sadness, rage, and frustration enough that she could finally pull herself away from her fallen soldier. The look on her face grew stern as she stood and said, "Ycharaz and I found a moment of peace in this desolate place, and I kissed him. For receiving that kiss, Glord sentenced him to death. If you are unable to accept what I have done, you are free to go. I release you from your pledges to me. I accept responsibility for Ycharaz's death, and none of you feel greater pain than I at his demise. It is my fault. A fact that will haunt me until the end of my days. I am truly sorry for what I have done, but I can't change it. That is the last thing I will ever say out loud about it. You will need to accept that if you intend to remain in my service."

No words accompanied the intense looks from her men, so she continued, "Know this, you should feel free to question my judgement as a leader. I make mistakes, and I trust all of you to guide me to the correct answer when I do. But I will not be judged, not by you or any man. My life and my love are my own. Who I give them to is my decision and mine alone."

Ganodin was the first to renew his pledge. She watched in quiet relief as he dismounted his horse and walked purposefully toward her. She could have cried when he planted the base of his battle axe against the ground and knelt behind it. "I pledge my axe and my life to you, my queen," he said.

The others in the group quickly followed suit. They knelt behind their swords and made their pledges, the same pledges they had made when they agreed to escort her across foreign lands, so queer compared to any other place any of them had ever been. Though the words were the correct words conveying the correct messages, none of the faces staring up at her as those vows were spoken seemed to agree with their sentiment. Disappointment, frustration, and even anger swirled among those faces. It was difficult to fault them for feeling those things. She felt them all herself. Thankfully, the accusations she had seen in all their eyes when they first arrived to witness Ycharaz's corpse were absent. That was a start, and it was enough for her. She only hoped that over time the other emotions floating about their eyes would eventually flee as well.

The next words out of her mouth would have been something about building a pyre and preparing Ycharaz's body for ceremony. A warrior as dutiful and loyal as him deserved nothing less than a hero's funeral. However, those words died at that back of her throat as something pale and blue dashing across her periphery grabbed her full attention. The slight gasp that took the place of those perished words caused all the heads staring back at her to snap in the same direction as her slack-jawed gaze.

"It cannot be," shock stormed about her breathless proclamation.

Yellow eyes peered over a small mound of something that resembled broken, purple marble. They looked like dim lights gleaming from a pale, blue apparition until they blinked. The wild, white mass above those eyes looked like it could have been some form of odd bush all wild and unkempt. Perrin knew they weren't lights shining dully at her from beneath queer, colorless shrubbery. She remembered those yellow eyes and that wild, white hair.

"Is that tiny thing what has you so frightened, my queen?" Jorgon asked. "Say the word and I will see it off to the Lake."

"Wait a moment," Dirk intervened. "That is a palusculex. Damn."

Darg's tone dripped with interest as he interjected, "I've heard stories, but I have never seen one. If those stories are to be believed, we haven't anything to fear, tiny creatures, four feet tall at best."

"But quick, and obviously quite brazen to approach so closely to us," Halogren added.

"Are you afraid?" Jorgon smirked as he glanced toward Halogren. "I promise to be careful and give you no reason to shed tears for me."

Ganodin was the biggest of the bunch, and typically had the least to say, but he was by no means dense. He was the first to notice how violently Perrin trembled at the sight of this beast no one else in the group found the least bit frightening. "My queen?" he asked as he quickly approached her.

Darg suddenly shook his head realizing his folly. "That is the same manner of beast that stole your child right from your arms, ain't it?"

Perrin's words barely had a voice to propel them into the world, but everyone in her small group heard her when she said, "And they killed both my parents on that same day."

"Prepare yourselves," Dirk drew his sword. "I cannot speak about what happens on your side of the Lake, but in these lands, they travel in packs of at least twenty. They are fast, lethal, and expert at hiding from the eyes of men until they want to be seen."

As Perrin and the rest of her group stared at the wee thing

crouching behind the marble looking mound and failing miserably at hiding, the attack came. She couldn't recall having ever seen anything close to fear haunt Darg's features until that moment. Immediately after Dirk had laid down the command to his fellow soldiers, Darg had stiffened up. He almost seemed frozen as he slowly spun toward the group's rear. Those yellow eyes seemed even more terrifying racing behind vicious claws toward her man's face.

Shock choked out a command to attack before it made it past Perrin's throat. She knew a command to Darg to defend himself wouldn't have made a difference. Instincts would be in control with the danger so close. Still, it would have been something, maybe a jolt. Instead, she watched, helplessly locked on those horrible, yellow eyes. They were too wide and not tall enough, like long slits oozing dim light. The bony forehead rising from those grotesque eyes stretched too far toward the wild, white hair trailing behind it. Everything about the creature was too much. Its wide, flat nose seemed too big for its face, and its narrow mouth too small, right up until the latter stretched wide enough to fit the top of Darg's head into its mouth. The jagged fangs stretching from the thin, blue lips surrounding that mouth dripped with anticipation. They seemed eager to tear into tender flesh.

A dire helplessness stomped all about Perrin's mind as she willed Darg's limbs to move faster. His sword was in the same hand it had been when he renewed his commitment to her, but it wasn't moving quickly enough to defend the soft parts of his body from attack. The helplessness she felt quickly turned to mortifying dread as the look on Darg's face melted into shocked fear instead of hardening into stony resolve. It looked like he was moving through water. By the time the nasty, blue creature was close enough to attack, Darg's sword was aimed harmlessly out to his side. A brief gasp slipped past Perrin's lips when the beast latched on to her soldier's neck. She winced at the gurgling sound he made when he cried out, "Behind us," before dropping his sword and grabbing the beast with both hands.

Jorgon's hair whipping through the air in her periphery grabbed enough of Perrin's attention to realize all was not lost. Despite her flamboyant soldier's flair for the dramatic, the pretty warrior was an expert with edged weapons. His hair had barely settled into place behind him by the time a small throwing knife sliced the air between he and Darg. His movements were so calculated and quick, she hadn't noticed him slip the deadly weapon out of the leather sash he wore strapped across his chest diagonally from his left shoulder to the right side of his waist. A brief moment passed before the blade jutted out of the pale, blue monster's head.

The horrid creature didn't die. The wee beast's yellow eyes went wide with shock as their focus turned to Jorgon. It screeched a horrible sound that could almost have been a word if not so jumbled and lunged toward the fair-haired warrior. The distance seemed impossible considering the thing's small stature, but the trajectory of its jump would have ended right on Jorgon's face.

Perrin stood there frozen as if the very air around her was a series of chains holding her fast. Another command died in the back of her throat before crawling past her lips as little more than a weak groan. She hadn't been training long enough to depend on instincts to guide her. Battle still required all her focus and thought. Luckily, Jorgon's instincts seemed to be serving him well. He stood his ground with his head held high. The fact he hadn't bothered drawing his sword, or even another throwing knife, had her concerned, but the naked confidence oozing from his expression helped to ease it, if only slightly. The hint of fear that slithered down her spine as the beast's claws were nearly close enough to Jorgon's face to latch onto him fled as quickly as it came when his hand shot out like a brand fired from a tightly strung bow. That hand latched around the monster's neck and squeezed tight enough to make its yellow eyes bulge. Jorgon's other hand moved just as quickly to retrieve his blade from the thing's head. Perrin heaved a sigh of relief as soon as the light left the monster's eyes.

The world slowed for Perrin as she watched Jorgon triumphantly slam the dead palusculex to the ground at his feet before shifting her gaze back to Darg. The latter had fallen to one knee once free from the beast's grasp. Both his hands gripped a ragged gash in his throat and mostly failed at keeping a steady stream of blood from spurting forth with every beat of his heart. The blood came so fast. It had already soaked his shirt and was steadily dripping onto his boots. Perrin wasn't sure if it was a sense of duty, the damned instincts Glord had promised she had, or the resolve she saw chase a brief moment of panic from Darg's eyes, but her legs finally began moving.

She raced toward Darg as Jorgon, and the rest of her group, all did the same. By the time a wild pack of palusculex leapt up from behind the strange purple mound that had just begun morphing into something blue and squishy, Perrin and the rest of her group stood beside Darg ready to turn them away.

Despite how small the creatures were, the pack was terrifying as they raced across the changing landscape. There had to be thirty of the ferocious, little creatures. Though they looked like small men with limbs that were too long—they even wore pants, odd, checkered trousers—they didn't move like men. They loped using their long arms to propel them forward much faster than two legs could. They looked like a small stampede charging toward Perrin and her men.

Perrin stood directly beside Darg. She steadied him once when he nearly fell to his knees. Something kept him on his feet. Madness danced all about his eyes as he let go of his throat and grabbed for his sword. He had to know he was going to die, yet he stood beside her defiant against the Lake trying to call his soul from his body. The resolve in the simple act of standing up against the approaching hoard to protect his people filled her with hope. It strengthened her own resolve. She would stand against these monsters and cut them down despite the fear raging through her.

Perrin opened her mouth to call her men to charge, but Darg beat her to the punch. He was obviously trying to shout when he said, "Men, attack." Most of the air must have escaped through the ragged gash in his throat, because it sounded like barely more than a whisper.

"Men, attack," Perrin repeated Darg's command. Her voice boomed like a proper general.

Her men responded. Her words still echoed in the sudden valley that had formed as odd peaks jutted up around them when all ten of Jorgon's throwing knifes were slicing the air toward the quickly approaching horde. Six of those landed killing blows.

Perrin held fast with her sword raised. The vicious faces growling back at her from the pack of monsters reminded her of her mother's death. That horrid day when two of the same manner of creature had come to steal her son. Her mother's face seemed to hover before her like a ghost as rage burned in her gut. She would kill them all. "Hold," she yelled.

Ganodin failed to heed her command. He charged out to meet the pack with his mighty battle axe swinging an immense arc before him. The massive death bringer sliced through the air until it finally cut into the tender flesh of two of those monsters. He sliced them in half at the waist before removing another's head on the back swing. One of the creatures managed to leap over the giant man's swinging blade and landed directly on his head. The monster clawed and bit at Ganodin's skull, but it seemed to get twisted up in the thick waves of his hair. The brutal satisfaction that swelled in Perrin's chest when Ganodin grabbed hold of the beast and crushed its tiny body in his massive fist felt foreign and wrong at first. The sight of Darg barely clinging to life and stumbling out to aid his friend chased the bit of trepidation away and steeled her resolve.

Though Darg stumbled forward slowly, his sword hand was true and sure. He took three of the monsters down before blood loss finally buckled his knees and drove him to the ground. He had sliced one through the throat, gashed another from throat to pelvis, and stabbed another through the heart before a fourth pounded into him with both feet and drove him the rest of the way to the ground. The thing's head was arcing off Perrin's sword by the time Darg's eyes grayed over, but she knew another member of her group was dead. The war cry that bellowed from her lips was something that might pour forth from a wounded scarra. It sounded like pain, hatred, sorrow, and loss all wrapped up into one desolate note. The painfully grotesque sound rallied her men all the more.

It seemed Darg's death affected everyone in her group as much as it had her. Halogren and Dirk ended up back-to-back, two masters of the blade elegantly dancing about their enemies and carving them up like artists sculpting macabre masterpieces. There were just too many of the diminutive creatures. One managed to get between Halogren's legs and trip him up while another lunged at his face all claws and gnashing teeth. The latter found it's mark and left four thin trails of gore down Halogren's cheek. He must not have felt it until the blood trickled down to his neck. Perrin recalled his story of how most of the nerves in his face had been severed when an exceptionally cruel pack of grongs had captured and tortured him. The grotesque smile peeking through the blood oozing down his face was horrifying. It made her even more happy to have him on her side as he slipped his blade through the temple of the monster clinging to his head. Dirk swung low and cleaned up the other one.

Despite being the least experienced fighter in her group, Perrin felt an odd tingle in her gut. It was some foreign sense of duty, a calling, some unnamable thing that made her feel she needed to protect the grizzled soldiers who had followed her into the odd lands they fought upon. It could have been death that cured her of the feeling. Luckily, the four claws that sailed past her face missed their mark. The instincts Glord had taught her about finally kicked in and drove her blade into the chest of the monster who had attacked her. Her movements were neither elegant nor overly efficient, but she managed to kill two more slashing with a forehand and then a backhand before Jorgon danced by slicing little, blue bodies in half as he went.

As flamboyant as Jorgon was with his hair and his throwing knives, he was anything but with his sword. His movements were quick and efficient. There were no wasted moves in his deadly waltz. Every twitch had a purpose. He carved his way through the mass of teeth and claws before working his way behind Perrin to guard her back. She battled on with increased vigor.

The palusculex's numbers dwindled enough for a glimmer of hope to take hold in a dark place at the back of Perrin's mind. Her men were expertly executing their craft while she held her own enough that she finally felt like she belonged on the same battlefield as these experts. Then a bright light flashed before her eyes. A dull and hollow sound followed right behind it. She didn't realize she'd been hit until pain erupted in the back of her skull. It seemed strange that she'd see the flash and hear the thud before feeling the club smash into her. It was a thought that would have to wait for another time as her knees buckled awkwardly beneath her and her grip on her sword loosened enough for the glimmering thing to crash to the suddenly hard ground. A moment later, she was lying next to her sword looking up at a quickly swirling sky. That sky was so inconsistent, it was difficult to determine if it was just the sky spiraling in its chaotic dance or dizziness from being clubbed. The sudden queasiness in her gut suggested the latter was probably the case.

Jorgon seemed to spin above her as he dodged and weaved among a group of grongs circling around them and swinging clubs at him. In between long blinks, she saw the one that got him. His eyes went wide when it struck him. She hoped he wasn't dead. Another long blink later, and those wide eyes were directly in front of hers. His cheeks trembled as his body twitched. She watched his eyes as long as she could stand while her blinks grew longer and slower. They never grayed over. Again, all she could do lying helpless on the ground beside him was hope he wasn't dead.

Her lids continued to grow heavier until she just couldn't open them anymore. Thoughts of leaving her body there so far from her home and making her final journey to the Lake were a faint whisper as the sounds of clubs pounding against flesh and men yelling grabbed a firm hold of all her attention. She thought it was Ganodin's voice she heard crying out before consciousness fled. Hopefully, her mission hadn't killed them all.

CHAPTER 23
HOPE

The great hall at Havenstahl was quiet except for the random chuckling of three half-drunk fools. Of course, none of the titans in that room were truly fools but give even the most brilliant man enough ale and his mind won't shine with quite the same luster. That is where Daritus, Spang, and Kantiim had found themselves sitting in that great, empty hall and waiting. Daritus' map had been tossed to the floor with its painted tokens scattered about the stone, and all three men slouched on simple chairs tipping back tin pints of some exceptionally bitter stuff they'd foraged from the cellar. In the absence of anything to do, they had taken to drinking and trading yarns of things they had done.

"And there he was, the fool," Spang slurred a bit as he chuckled, "the greatest general in all the land, the mighty Daritus, half lame from besting the mightiest of giants in one-on-one combat and not at all fit for battle standing before a god with his sword raised."

Kantiim laughed so hard he nearly fell out of his chair amid the echoes of his revelry. "What on Ouloos were you thinking?" he asked correcting his chair before it fell out from under him.

"Had I been thinking, I don't suppose I would have been standing there," Daritus replied laughing just as hard.

"Of course, he wasn't thinking," Spang continued. "The mighty Brerto, the great white tiger, twenty feet at the shoulder when standing on all fours is looming above him, and here he is aiming his sword at that monster's heart."

Daritus abruptly stopped laughing as an earnest look spread across his face. "I was going to kill him," he said without a bit of fog in his voice.

"You were going to get swallowed by a god and slowly digested," Kantiim laughed and slapped his knee. This time he failed at correcting his balance. His chair tipped and spilled him onto the floor. All three of the men laughed even harder.

Once the laugh petered off to low chuckling, Daritus changed the subject. "What about you?" he asked Kantiim. "Do you remember the first time we met?"

"You shut your filthy gob, you old scrod," Kantiim laughed again as he righted his chair and refilled his cup from a big jug the men were sharing.

Spang chuckled, "No, you shut your gob. This is one of my favorites."

Daritus' smile nearly ran out of face to spread across as his eyes sparkled with nostalgia, "It was a small village far to the north of my fair city, Druindahl but still under her protection. I was a green recruit at the time. That was well before my sweet wife came to that same city as a refugee of those dead-eyed men and the gods who ruled them— tale for a different time. Faroman, the great beast of the south bay, was my general. That man was a force of nature."

"He was no man," Spang interrupted. "He was the spirit of war."

"If war had a soul," Daritus agreed before continuing. "We had received word of a rogue pack of mercenaries terrorizing the north words, pillaging, sacking villages, and robbing travelers on the main road to the north. The riders of Druindahl were dispatched to bring these vile scrods to heel."

Kantiim squinted up his face and mocked, his lips moving around soundless words until he finally gave them voice, "And then you came to Oak's Bend, a small logging village in the north…"

Daritus interrupted, "Where the nights are long, the days are short, the work is hard, and the spirits flow freely at Karragan's Crutch."

"There was many a morning I woke on the dirty floor of that dingy place with no recollection of how I got there," Spang laughed. "Karragan, may the Lake bless his soul, he'd never grant you no extra comfort, but he'd never turn you out to the trail in any condition other than ready to tread upon it."

Daritus raised his glass as if to toast the idea, and said, "Indeed, that is another story for another time. This story is about Karragan's bar keep. He was a lazy oaf by all accounts I've ever heard."

"You best watch that tongue," Kantiim mock threatened his general and oldest friend. "I know that good arm of yours ain't near as good as the one that giant lamed, and I have both of mine."

"Fair point," Daritus took no offense as he dove back into his story. "Forty hardened mercenaries stood at the edge of town ready to steal all they could from the good folks of Oak's Bend and tear that quiet little place to the ground when one hundred of Druindahl's finest rumbled into that quiet town, and what did we find? What great force stood before that heartless pack of marauders?"

Both Spang and Kantiim knew Daritus wasn't looking for an answer to his question. The cagey, old general was merely pausing for effect, so they both remained quiet. Neither cared that any suspense was wasted because, not only had both lived through the event, but it had also been told to them at least a hundred times by the very same narrator. They let their old friend have his moment. They even leaned in closer for the big finale.

"This man," Daritus' smile somehow found more face to widen across, "well, a shadow of him anyway, stood alone, protecting his village with nothing but a dingy mop in his hand, and a soiled apron tied about his waist. He was too small back then, didn't hold the mop like he'd ever held a weapon, but what I saw in his eyes was something like I had never seen before. Those were the eyes of a titan. If that man had even a hint of fear in his heart that day, you would never know it."

"If only that were true," Kantiim laughed again. "I nearly shat myself."

"But you stood your ground," Daritus quickly replied. "That is the mark of a true hero in my eyes, and that is why I would stand beside you against any foe, damn the odds."

"Here, here," Spang agreed with a raised glass. "That is precisely what Faroman saw standing there, a hero standing up for his kin against impossible odds."

The laughter faded slowly as the three men rifled through old memories in their minds and sipped at their cups. Old loves, battles of days gone by, and pranks among friends while out to trail. The three men had spent more summers together than some soldiers ever live. Most who've witnessed real battle would agree that escaping death was the mark of a true warrior, not those who hide, but those who lead. They become generals, commanders, leaders among men. The three men sharing pints and stories in that big empty room were all those things.

They may have sat there well into the evening, perhaps even until the light of a new day, had the door not pounded open ahead of the sound of purposeful steps echoing off the walls of the big, empty room. There was an urgency to those steps, and there were too many of them in such random cadence that anything less than an emergency seemed unlikely.

Daritus turned toward the door to see who owned such urgent strides. The two men weren't a surprise, except maybe their appearance. None of the men in his command looked ready for maneuvers parading around the courtyard in honor of the king, but both Tiegran and Tarturan were covered in enough mud and blood they looked like they could just as easily be part of a trail as treading upon it. The three dwarves with the two riders of Druindahl, whose sashes looked more brown than red, were in even worse shape. The entire group looked beaten and downtrodden.

The three dwarves in the group weren't all that surprising to Daritus either, except it seemed two were missing. He had received reports of four dwarves planning a mission to rescue a fifth. The beaten one, barely clinging to life, was Alenaat. There was no mistaking that one. He'd only met the dwarf once during a celebration of Maelich's day and recalled thinking at the time that he'd never met a meeker dwarf. The thing dangling between the two dwarves holding him up was even thinner and gaunter in his dirty cheeks than the drunken creature he'd met that day.

He recognized the two holding Alenaat up as well, Lentaak and Chialdaan. Neither looked much better than their beaten chum. Both looked like they'd been chewed slowly by a giant, digested for days, and shat out upon the trail to fester in the sun. They'd obviously had a rough go of it, but where were their two companions who'd begun the journey with them?

Daritus almost asked after the whereabouts of Muljaak and Glaadrian when Tiegran interrupted the thought. "Bom has fallen. Your concerns about his grandfather were not unfounded."

The young soldier's words were sobering. "How is it you survived?" Daritus asked.

"Ott is dead," Tarturan replied.

The look haunting Daritus' countenance would be fitting for one who'd just tasted something horribly sour as he asked, "You battled the beasts from across the Great Sea? How many have you lost?"

"We battled no one, and we lost no one," Tarturan shook his head.

"His own kin ripped him to shreds," Tiegran added.

Tarturan shook his head as he continued, "I will not pretend to fully understand giant customs, but he betrayed his own blood. Bom knelt before him, and Ott killed him in cold blood like a coward. The rest of the giants there would not stand for the betrayal. Ott's own son led the charge. Then they let us leave. Our ranks now swell with hundreds of trogmortem and a score of giants."

"Yet me kin remain prisoners," Lentaak piped up. He had kept quiet while the men gave their report, but he had urgent business to present. He couldn't wait for the men of Havenstahl to contemplate the actions and customs of foreign invaders.

Daritus shifted his gaze to the frustrated dwarf and his companions and asked, "They let the three of you leave?" Then he shifted his gaze to Alenaat and added, "He looks like he's had a go of it. Does he require immediate care?"

"He be in far better shape than what we found him in," Lentaak snapped. "That bastard, Ott had him chained up to the Sacred Pine, a breath from the Lake he was. His soul ain't leaving his body no time soon, dragon blossom and fairy weed. Some rest is all he'll be needing now."

"Hagen would be proud," Daritus smiled.

Chialdaan looked around and asked, "Where be that great healer? We might have stolen this one from the Lake, but he could use a once over by that man."

A confused look spread across Daritus' face as he replied, "Hagen is more than he seems. I am not quite sure what that means at this point, but he is not with us. No matter. We have healers in this city who can see to your friend."

"What about soldiers?" Lentaak asked. He pointed at Chialdaan and added, "Me and this one be planning to sneak back into Alhouim under the cover of night and free our kin. Havenstahl owes a mighty debt to Alhouim. I'd be seeing that debt paid with soldiers what can aid in the effort."

Kantiim walked over to Daritus and whispered in his ear, "We haven't the numbers to spare on what sounds like a lost cause."

Lentaak had been training his entire life to remain so quiet no normal ears could hear him. The feat would be impossible without a keen and well-trained sense of hearing. "Ye'd deny me request for repayment? Could it be the men of Havenstahl ain't nothing more than a pack of cowards? Do ye know how many of me kin fell at the battle of Fort Maomnosett protecting this gaudy castle or how many of me kin remain here in this place helping ye return it to its former glory?"

Kantiim bristled at the accusations, "You dare stand in my general's keep and accuse him?"

"Stand down, old friend," Daritus said quietly.

"He's not wrong," Spang added.

"Send me," Tiegran piped up.

"You can count me in as well," Tarturan added.

The room grew quiet as Daritus began pacing a short track, three steps this way and three steps back, while he quickly nodded his head. Any words that may have been waiting at the back of any of the throats in that room remained hidden from any ears as they let the general consider the news he'd just learned.

"How many men do you need?" he finally asked.

"I'd be liking to say ten thousand," Chialdaan snapped.

"Aye, I'd be liking to say the same," Lentaak added, "but we'll be sneaking in under the mountain, working our way up through them mines, and sticking to the shadows. Can ye spare a hundred men, good men, men who ain't afraid to face down them nightmares from across the Great Sea if they be finding us out?"

Daritus didn't hesitate, "Tarturan, put together this force. You will lead them. I leave you to decide who are the best men for the mission." Then he shifted his gaze back toward Lentaak and asked, "Your friend, he won't be joining you on this quest. You can take him to the infirmary. Hagen may not be with us, but his assistants will show the poor soul the utmost care."

Relief swept over the faces of Lentaak and Chialdaan, but the two men standing with them looked like they had more to say. "Well, why are you still standing about?" Daritus asked.

"We came upon one of Ygraml's scouts after finding these three along the River Galgooth. He was on his way here with heartening news. I sent him back to his general and vowed to bring his message to your ears," Tarturan replied.

Daritus shrugged and said, "Well, let's have it then. What is this wonderful news?"

"The beasts from the north head back in that direction, back to their snowy homes," Tiegran blurted.

Tarturan shot a soft elbow into his young friend's ribs as he added, "Indeed. It seems the grizzly mongs have lost whatever cause they had to journey to our great city. They are on a direct path back to their homes."

Daritus shot a look at Kantiim who replied, "I will take one thousand men, one hundred horses, and all the trogmortem and giants who now fill our ranks, and we will aid Hagen in taking back the coastal villages from the invaders."

"One thousand men and one hundred horses?" Lentaak hissed.

"Would you like them to aid you in your campaign?" Daritus asked over raised eyebrows.

Chialdaan sighed deep before piping in, "They won't be doing us no good. We ain't marching on the front gate, and that ain't near enough to take back our castle."

Defeat clouded Lentaak's eyes as he agreed, "As much as I'd be liking to storm the gates of our castle and show them bastards a real battle, them ain't the kind of numbers we'd need."

"Very well, you all know what to do. See it is done," Daritus drained his pint and then glanced over to Tarturan and added, "The farmhand, Chagon. He will not be among the men you choose for your mission. Send him and Tarantian to follow that horde of beasts and make sure they remain on a straight path to their homes."

"Your will, my lord," Tarturan bowed as if honored by the charge.

"I am no lord," Daritus grumbled. "Will everyone please stop bowing to me?"

CHAPTER 24

DISTRACTED

Brerto examined the wet, crumbling brick of the cell he shared with Kallum. The thick, rusty chains which had held the two in place were gone, but neither could move from their respective spots against the wall. It had taken him some time to accept his new reality, but he had. Both he and his brother were trapped within Ijilv's mind and no longer in control of their own wills. Time had never been of great import to him. What does an eternal being care about time? It's an abstract concept really, nothing more than a method of tracking the orderly movements of planets and stars to provide some linear measurement of the quick journey from birth to growth to death for creatures who experience such things. Suddenly, however, time seemed like the most important thing to him. How long had he been in this place, trapped within his brother, and how much longer did he have?

"How do you suppose he did it?" Kallum's tired, gravelly voice was a sad mockery of its former glory.

"How did whom do what?" Brerto feigned disinterest, but the truth was he desired an answer to the question at least as much as his brother.

"Must you?" Kallum complained. "You know precisely of what I speak. How did he trap us here, within him? How did he know things would happen just as they did?"

Brerto scratched absently at his dingy, gray hair that had once been luxurious and brilliant white. He knew it wasn't hair at all. In fact, no physical action he took was actually happening. He wasn't even there at all in the physical sense. Still, he answered, "That is the mystery. I never thought him so ambitious. Yet here we are."

"Soon to be joined by our brothers if he is to be believed," Kallum quickly added.

"Indeed, and after all we have seen, it is difficult to discount the veracity of any utterance from his perfect, damnable mouth."

"Everything we have ever done has been meaningless," Kallum sighed.

"Not at all," Ijilv suddenly appeared before his brothers glowing bright white and glimmering in all his glory. "Each action you have taken—no matter how seemingly small or insignificant—has been crucial to propelling us to this very moment and all the moments which shall come after."

Brerto shook his head and sighed, "And you the great conductor orchestrating it all from the shadows at the back of the stage. Is that what you would have us believe? You have won, brother. I am uncertain how, but I can no longer argue with the reality of it all. However, what I cannot do is believe you were able to influence us in our actions. You have proven wiser than I and stronger than Kallum. That much I will admit."

"You used the twins against us," Kallum added. "The minds of men are fragile and easy to manipulate, and you manipulated them."

"Of course," a devious smile snaked across Ijilv's face, "but only after I had manipulated you."

"I spoke the prophecy of the Lad of the Lake, and Kaldumahn spoke his false prophecy. Had you not interfered, I would have destroyed that prideful boy and turned my gaze to his sister," Kallum scoffed.

"Had you succeeded, Maelich would have destroyed Helias, and Ouloos would have been destroyed with her," Ijilv shook his head. "You are a fool if you still believe anything else. She was the last thing holding the portal to Coeptus open. Cut off from that, Ouloos would have withered and died. And I only interfered in your battle with Maelich because you seemed to have gained the upper hand. In any event, none of that matters. I am the one who whispered your prophecy into your ear and Kaldumahn's into his."

"Impossible," Brerto humphed. "I would have sensed your essence in our brothers' words. Each of us have an undeniable signature which remains with all that we create." He thought for a moment about it before looking over to Kallum and adding, "It had never occurred to me until just now, but those words belonged to neither of you."

Ijilv was suddenly aware. Of what he wasn't precisely certain. The prophecy he whispered to Kallum in bygone days were not his words. It was too late to lie, his expression had already betrayed him, "No, those were not my words, but I did whisper them into Kallum's ears."

"If not Kallum's words and not yours, then to whom did those fateful commands belong?" Brerto asked.

"I do not know," Ijilv blurted before his thoughts could catch up with his mouth.

Then something tugged his attention away from the conversation. It was a feeling, something like a hunch but with more definition. "As much as I enjoy our fruitless debates, I have much to do."

"Could it be the wise Ijilv is not as clever as he thinks?" Kallum chuckled.

"Perhaps," he flashed a condescending smile. "Though I owe you no explanations, I will indulge. The great snow beasts from the north have lost their way and turned back toward their frigid homes. The mighty men from all the great cities of men need an enemy, and Havenstahl must remain under siege." And then he was gone.

"I still cannot believe he has accomplished hiding out in his tower at the edge of time and reason completely detached from everything," Brerto sighed at the empty space where his brother had just stood.

"You had hoped to do as much from atop your great mountain," Kallum shrugged.

"Yes," he agreed, "but I failed. I am not convinced he will."

"You admire him," a bit of surprise slipped into Kallum's expression.

The idea sickened him to his core, but he couldn't deny it. "I do," he finally agreed.

Ijilv materialized in a small, dark cell far beneath the tower. The walls were the same black, cyclopean stones that made up the rest of the massive structure. There was a stairway winding down and down, deep into land beneath the tower that would grant access to the small, forgotten room for any who could find the entrance, but Ijilv had no use for it. He simply decided he wanted to be there, and he was.

He required no flint or flame to bring to life the torches lining the walls of the room. He simply desired light, and there was. Once that blazing, glorious light had chased all but the most ambitious shadows from the hidden places in the room, the three came into view. They stood in a triangle with their heads bowed beneath their hoods.

Kallum thought he was so clever when he first brought them to life from the ashes of his failed magician. Another thing Ijilv had whispered into his brother's ear. The great magician, Merkhal's soul may have made its journey to the Lake, but his countenance could still strike fear into the hearts of men. No man or creature would recognize the long dead magician in the three, exact duplicates of one another, but their black, dead eyes and wild, snarling natures would have equal effect.

No words were necessary to bring the leader of the three to life. He raised his head and drew back his hood. His hair and beard were wild, orange snarls, and his eyes were black and dead like two obsidian orbs. Ijilv controlled their every thought and deed, each one with him. What they saw, he saw, and what he willed, they did. Ijilv closed his eyes and sent them to the forest northeast of Mount Elbahor.

CHAPTER 25
DEEPER INTO DARKNESS

The foliage seemed to thicken with each step down the soggy trail if it could still be considered that. The deeper into the forest Ymitoth and the Shaiwah traveled, the narrower the thing got. At least the thick vegetation provided some cover from the seemingly everlasting rains that rarely ceased to pour forth from sprawling skies hidden from view above the canopy.

Ymitoth carefully chose his steps as he pushed or cut thick vines and leaves that were long and pointy out of his way. He led the Shaiwah on a meandering path winding around trees, that were bare up to their balmy crowns, and thick shrubs. Though the canopy protected the group from the intense rays of the sun, the air was still damp and hot. At times, it seemed steam rose off the wet leaves. As miserable as the cracked lands where the Shaiwah had settled were, Ymitoth was finding it difficult to see the wet forest as much of an improvement.

Ding followed close on Ymitoth's heels. As the journey unfolded, he'd become somewhat of a shadow for the grizzled, old soldier, always close on his tail. "Days no Tahnka," Ding commented as he looked about the canopy with his mentor.

"Aye," Ymitoth agreed.

As Ding had suggested, it had been days since the last village they had encountered, if it could be called a village at all. It wasn't much more than a handful of small huts with thatched roofs. The inhabitants had been more ferocious in their defense of their homes than any of the other villages they'd overtaken up to that point, but they suffered from the same lack of training. They certainly didn't fit Maulom's description of a furious fighting force.

As if summoned by Ymitoth's doubt, Maulom approached from farther up the trail. His close-cropped, perfect white hair and beard were as impeccable as his gleaming white suit. The man strolled as if he were walking down a wide trail without a care in the world, not troubled at all by the same vegetation Ymitoth was hacking through with his sword, dulling the damn thing with each swing.

"Look how far you have come. Where is Maelich?" Maulom boomed, his arms spread as wide as his smile.

"I thought ye might be knowing something about where that one got himself off to," Ymitoth stopped and shrugged. Then he added, "As far as how far we've come or how close our destination, I ain't an idea about either one."

The impeccably dressed man seemed suddenly troubled, "When was the last time you saw Maelich?"

"Two days," Ding interrupted with irritation in his voice. "We sleep, Maelich there. We wake, Maelich no there."

"You let him leave," his smile faded completely.

"It ain't me place to be keeping no man from whatever path his boots wish to tread," Ymitoth shrugged again.

Maulom's eyes narrowed as he looked Ymitoth over. "What goes on behind those black, dead eyes?"

"Ye know more about me eyes than I do. Ain't no looking glasses be hanging from any of these trees," Ymitoth's tone conveyed his disinterest. "As far as what be going on behind them, the mission. Though I don't seem to be having a very good go at it, I'll be leading these good folks to their homes in Maelich's stead."

Ding smiled wide as he patted Ymitoth between the shoulder blades, "Ymitoth good. He lead. Maelich no good. He leave us."

"It would seem so," Maulom stroked his beard as his mind wandered. "As always, Ding, you prove far wiser than most men would give you credit. I will find Maelich. I have my ways."

"And what about us?" Ymitoth asked. "We ain't seen a village in days, and them ones we did didn't seem like one people. These be disconnected tribes. We ain't seen no mighty fighting force like the Tahnka you described."

Maulom smiled as he shook his head, "A skeptical mind is an asset to any military commander. That is why you are perfect for this task.

Take heart in knowing you are on the correct path. You will find a city like nothing you have ever seen, more magnificent than even your precious Havenstahl. There you will find the Tahnka. They will test you and your Shaiwah like you haven't been tested before. You will be outnumbered, and there is strong magic in their weapons. However, you have trained your men to be fierce, each of them worth ten men. You will help them take back their city, and Maelich will return to rule as their king. I will see to that."

CHAPTER 26
THE CALLING

Sadness is a strange thing, sometimes difficult to define. It comes wrapped with so many other things that, though different and unique, have blurry enough edges mingling in with it they are hard to identify as separate entities. Loss was one of those. The sadness stomping all about Maelich's mind was caused by loss and a longing to understand why. Two days trudging aimlessly through a dense, wet forest did nothing to ease the feeling. Everything was dark, and there were few distractions to pull him out of his own mind. Perhaps he should have stayed with the Shaiwah. No. They had been flying so high, and he would have only dragged them down from the great heights their victories had earned them.

Things didn't change much from one moment to the next as deep in the forest as he was. A small brook would bar his way, and he would find a way over it. Oftentimes, the effort required was nothing more than a well-timed hop in the stride of slow jog. Other times, the crossings took a bit more ingenuity, but never anything more than hacking off a vine to throw across a low branch or pushing over a dead tree to serve as a makeshift bridge. The forest seemed never-ending in its bounty. None of it proved challenging enough to distract him from the emotions blackening his soul.

He had no idea of his destination, but he knew he was going somewhere. Buried deep within the loss he felt something cavorted with the sadness, fighting to be heard among the emptiness. It shouted a hollow sound, like a small voice drowned out by rumbling thunder.

It was faint and far away, but he could hear it. Like the black horse who invaded his dreams to speak riddles and show him dead things he knew but couldn't know, this voice called to him, drawing him toward this mysterious destination. Despite this lack of knowing, with each step he knew he grew closer to his goal.

He stopped at a brook and wiped his brow. As wet as his sleeve was from the damp air, the effort did very little to pull any of the sweat from his glistening forehead. Everything was moist. He grabbed his waterskin and emptied it. Seldom do things happen with such perfect timing in the forest. The thought kept his attention for as long as it took him to refill the skin.

As he crouched there next to the fast-moving water of the narrow brook contemplating the synchronicity of an empty waterskin at precisely the same moment when a means to refill it appeared, he suddenly felt vulnerable. There were no mysteries for him in any forest. He had spent too much time exploring, adventuring, and hunting. Every sound had a reason, and he knew them all. It wasn't an out of place sound that had him spooked. It was a feeling. Like the sadness or the odd pull toward some unknown destination, something tugged at his awareness. Something that was there but somehow wasn't at the same time.

A horrible screech pulled his attention away from that unknown something chasing around his mind. The sound would have been terrifying had he not known the manner of creature capable of making such an unsettling sound. It was a horny witch, a large, nocturnal bird of prey that—despite all the myths about them being actual witches capable of enchanting men and feeding on their souls—desired only to hunt and feast on rodents scurrying about the forest floor. The startling sound wasn't the confident cry of a beast racing from the canopy to dive on its prey. This was a cry of distress.

It took Maelich a moment to locate the source of the sound after corking his waterskin. A quick scan of the canopy proved fruitless. Even if there was enough light to discern shapes among the shadows, horny witches were expert at blending into their environments to avoid being noticed by prey until it was too late. Though up was the natural place to look for a bird, the sound hadn't come from above. Then he found it. The bird cried again the moment he saw it. The animal was in distress. It had somehow gotten its wing twisted up in a bramble across the brook, and it thrashed about wildly.

Maelich hopped across the brook and warily approached. The thing had fierce, amber eyes that seemed to plead. Directly above that were the tufts of feathers that resembled horns and earned the first half of the animal's name. They weren't actually horns, of course, but they helped feed the myths about these birds having magical capabilities. They were just birds, and forest folk were terribly superstitious.

Fear of the beast morphing into a beautiful enchantress and casting a spell to turn him into a newt, or some other slimy creature wasn't what slowed his stride and added caution to his steps. The bird was massive. From head to tail, the thing was as large as a big man's torso, and it had a wingspan of at least twenty-five feet. Its talons were designed to hold prey still while its mighty, hooked beak tore into flesh. Maelich wanted to free the creature, but he didn't want to earn a deep gash in his arm to remember the effort.

"Shh, shh, shh, you're okay," he whispered as he held his arms out to his sides in as unthreatening a posture as he could muster.

The thing squawked something threatening and snapped at Maelich with its beak. The quick strike startled him enough he almost lost his feet. He took a deep breath and chuckled. It was too late to turn back. He couldn't if he tried. It wasn't in his nature to turn his back on any creature in distress, no matter how hard the thing tried to hurt him.

He dropped his pack and rifled through it for a moment before finding a canvas sack he used to keep dried meat when he was lucky enough to have any. It had been a time since he was quite so fortunate, and the bag was empty. He took a wide berth around a tree and snuck up behind the bramble. It wouldn't be an easy move, but if he proved quick enough, he could get the bag over the bird's head. The fabric was thick enough to protect him from that razor sharp beak.

He was quick, but the bird was a bit quicker. It wasn't a deep gash, but the tip of its beak nicked Maelich's wrist enough to earn a slight trickle of blood and a grimace from the attempted hero. "Damn," he shouted as he wrangled the sack and tied it off around the base of the thing's neck.

It took a few moments of violent thrashing about before the thing calmed down enough that Maelich could gently massage its belly. A few more moments of that, and the thing stopped moving almost completely. It just trembled as Maelich cooed quietly next to the sack.

"Okay," Maelich was breathless. "I know you can't understand my words, but I'm going to help you."

The bird calmed enough that Maelich was able to gather an accurate assessment of the situation. The wing was tangled up pretty good in the bramble. He couldn't just grab his dagger and hack away at it. The mission would require care and precision. He examined the mess for a few moments following each individual twig, branch, and vine, and then he found it. A thick vine wrapped around all the thin bits pulling everything tightly together. Had the animal not panicked, it would probably be freely soaring among the highest branches of the canopy.

Maelich drew his dagger and then a deep breath. He wrapped his left arm around the trembling animal, held it close, and said, "Give me one moment, and I'll have you free from these bonds."

He wasn't foolish enough to believe the bird would sit still long enough for him to remove the bag from its head once the wing was free. He'd have to move quickly. Once that wing was free and it started flapping wildly about, he'd have to yank that sack of the thing's head and get out of the way quick. Hopefully, the terrified animal wouldn't turn on him and attack. It was a chance he'd have to take.

He heard the growl at the exact moment he slashed at the vine. It wasn't the sound of any animal he knew. Scarra, lowland or mountain, had a deep, menacing growl. A scrod's growl was much the same. Amatilazo screamed more than growled, but when they did it was a distinct sound easily differentiated from any other sound in the forest. This growl was different than any of those. It was so much deeper. It would take a massive throat to make a sound like that.

Maelich had no time to trouble over the growl as his strike was true. As soon as his blade finished slicing through the vine, the horny witch's wing was free and flapping. He grabbed hold of the sack and fell backward away from the thrashing animal. It flapped once before the jaws of a beast like nothing Maelich had ever seen closed on it.

It happened so quickly he hadn't gotten a good look at the monster. It was massive, twice the size of a mountain scarra. Perhaps it was shock, but as the thing lunged over him it seemed to stretch the length of two tall men from shoulder to tail. It was difficult to tell in the darkness, but the thing's belly appeared to be white fur. The rest of it was orange or yellow and covered in black spots. That was all he could make out of the quick flash that ripped the bird out of his grasp.

Animals eating other animals is a part of nature. That didn't matter to Maelich just then. He felt a connection to the bird he'd just saved. That animal was his damsel in this dark wood, and a soulless beast was crunching its bones to dust while he lay helplessly on the forest floor.

The sound he made as he leapt to his feet sounded foreign to his ears. Maybe it wasn't only the bird's demise troubling him just then. Maybe it was all the sadness and loss and longing and other things he couldn't give names to swirling together with his desire to do something, to have control of something, to know something.

The blood on the thing's snout looked like black tar in the dim light, but its eyes glinted like yellow fire. Its pointy ears pinned straight back as its massive jaws opened wide to expose three-inch fangs, and it growled that deep, horrible sound again. It crouched low. Maelich knew the pounce was coming. His sword would be useless, so he didn't draw it. Instead, he gripped the dagger in his hand and waited for the attack.

He didn't have to wait long. The thing covered the distance between them in a heartbeat. Maelich crumbled as it came, but it wasn't fear that drove him to his back. His head would have easily fit into the beast's massive jaws, and that would have been his end. If his head wasn't there, the monster couldn't bite it. Instead, it snapped at air, and Maelich's dagger slipped between its ribs.

It roared. The sound dripped with rage, fear, and pain. Maelich wasn't sure if beasts could feel emotions. If the sound the thing made were any indication, they did. It took three steps toward the brook and collapsed.

It wasn't the most flavorful meat Maelich had ever tasted but it was far more flavorful than chukwoka. As he ate the beast, he killed more for revenge than sustenance, it occurred to him how strange was his anger. That same bird would have killed scores more living things had the creature not killed it. It wasn't any different than the beast eating the bird or Maelich eating the beast. It made no sense, but the act somehow felt like justice.

CHAPTER 27

FOOD

The room was fuzzy at first, no discernable shapes just a blurry orange hue interrupted by long blinks. Perrin's head ached. That was the worst of it. As her mind started firing more quickly other pains jumped out. Those were dull and unremarkable, soreness in places one would expect to be sore after any sort of skirmish. The pain in her head was formidable. It stood out among the rest.

Stiffness in her shoulders was probably the next in severity of the parts of her body which ailed her just then. She tried to stretch her arms out. The effort was a failure. She was tied fast to a girthy stick. It had to be the trunk of a good-sized tree the way her arms and legs stretched around it without encircling it completely. One end must have been leaning against the wall. Her backside was higher than her head, and that was pointed at the floor.

"Keep still," Dirk whispered from behind, or below her.

She couldn't heed the warning and looked up toward the sound, or down the way she was facing. The movement attracted unwanted attention. Her hands stung instantly. She didn't see what struck her, but it felt like leather.

"Girl awake," a gravelly voice growled to her left.

"She will be next," a deep voice boomed from across the room.

Perrin kept her head as still as possible as she scanned her surroundings with only her eyes. Her fingers still throbbed. It didn't make any sense to invite more torture if she could avoid it. She will be next sounded ominous. She needed to find the rest of her men.

168

The room surrounding her was chipping clay, probably white once or gray but stained from ages of neglect. A handful of torches scattered about the room cast an orange glow on everything. Thick wood slats that were probably windowsills at one time were as splintered and worn as the slats of wood covering the holes where glass might offer a view outside the place. There wasn't any art or decoration in the room, nor were there any useful looking tools aside from an axe and a handful of long knives. There was one table she could see. Three grongs lounged around it. Perrin didn't have much experience with grongs or the way they showed emotion, but these looked bored, waiting for something to happen.

Bile raced up the back of her throat when she spotted an abused leather chest plate on the floor. It was torn up pretty good and coated in blood that appeared too fresh to be old stains. Despite its current state, she knew it was Glord's. She managed to keep the meager contents of her gut from spilling out onto the floor, but the tears that welled up in her eyes ignored her brain's commands. They leaked freely down the sides of her temples like little rivers rushing toward the edge of a cliff to cascade into tiny waterfalls. "That is Glord's breastplate," she whispered a bit too loud and earned another stinging whack on her fingers.

"That is the queen of Havenstahl you are treating so callously," Halogren's voice sounded deeper and carried more authority than she'd ever heard it. "You would do well to release her, beg her forgiveness, and pray she decides not to return with ten thousand riders to trample your bodies to pulp."

The command earned laughter from the grongs at the table and a great bellow from that deep voice across the room. She'd yet to see the owner of that voice, but he sounded monstrous. "Your queen will rot in my gut until I dump her behind my hut," the voice chuckled.

Then a sharp pain blazed on Perrin's calf. She'd only ever been bit by an animal once, and that is precisely what it felt like. Though she did her best to keep from crying out, she failed. It was more than just the pain. She didn't see it coming, and it shocked her. Her slight yelp earned more laughter from the grongs in the room and probably the palusculex too. It was one of those little, blue monsters who had bit her. The thing smiled at her with bloody fangs when she caught eyes with it. Then a chorus of high-pitched voices started chattering. It was a horrible sound. She imagined that was the sound the vile creatures made when they laughed. Rage boiled in her gut at the idea the same type of vile creatures who killed her parents and helped to steal her precious son stood laughing at her, reveling in her pain.

"As my faithful soldier has plainly told you, I am the rightful queen of Havenstahl, ruler of the mightiest army in all of Ouloos, and I will rain fire and pain upon this horrid place. I will not grant you quick deaths. Every pain you cause me, or my men will be repaid one hundred-fold. You will suffer for this callous treatment and horrid hospitality," despite the vulnerability in Perrin's slightly cracking voice, the veins about her face swelled and spittle flew from her mouth as she raged.

The roaring laughter of that mighty voice whose owner she could not see filled the hut. The booming footsteps which followed it seemed just as loud. They shook the walls and the large pole she was tied to. It also shook the table the grongs lounged around and caused the knives to clink together. All those sounds mixed with the chattering laughter of palusculex and the gruff grunting of grongs spun together in a symphony of terror that slightly chilled Perrin's boiling rage. It wasn't quite enough to chase the defiant look from her face, but it did cast a bright light on the emptiness of her threats. There would be no fire or pain raining on anything at her command if she died in the awful place.

The thing's face was massive when it crouched down to her level. At first, she thought it was looking at her but quickly realized it couldn't. There were scars around its eyes. One of them looked like nothing more than ragged flesh, lumpy and poorly healed. The other looked gray and dead. His breath smelled like stale blood and rotten flesh. His yellow fangs looked dull and barely useful. His bulbous nose was misshapen. A long gash from one of his nostrils all the way up to the dead looking gray eye hung wide open and vibrated slightly every time he breathed.

"You're a trogmortem," Dirk said with a bit of confusion in his voice.

The grizzled monster reached out with a clawed hand and cradled Perrin's head gently as she tensed up. Then he said, "Highness, allow me to introduce myself. I am Shacolin. I never cared much for kings or queens or any one's rule for that matter, but you can consider me king of this hut. I expect the same courtesy you would grant any of your contemporaries when visiting my kingdom."

"Get away from my queen," Halogren shouted with all the authority his voice had when he'd made his first threat.

Shacolin stood and walked past Halogren to the body tied above him on the pole. The whole thing moved when he gave it a nudge. "Damn," he muttered. "This one is dead."

The pole shook violently as he yanked the body from it and tossed it onto the floor. Twenty palusculex swarmed it as soon as it hit the ground. Some of them bit and tore chunks of it off. Others gnawed different parts. Still others ripped into bits of flesh with their claws and tore them away before chomping on them like random hunks of meat.

It was Ganodin. Perrin caught sight of his eyes. They were gray and dead and stared right at her, wide like two ghostly moons. It was probably her imagination, but those dead eyes seemed to accuse her. It was her fault after all. Helias had told her all her men would die on this journey. Ycharaz was dead, Darg was dead, Glord was dead, Ganodin was dead, and it was all her fault. More threats raced up from her gut to the back of her throat, but Halogren's came faster.

"Cut me loose, you vile thing, and prove to me you're not a coward like your kin," he roared. "I cut down scores of your kind from across the Great Sea, and I'll see you off to the Lake just the same. Loose my bonds, you pathetic, broken creature."

Perrin strained her neck to see around her bound arm. She immediately wished she hadn't. Shacolin chuckled as he felt around for Halogren's face. The poor man was helpless as the trogmortem's jagged claw stuck into his eye and plucked it out. The slurping sounds Shacolin made as he popped the little morsel in his mouth mixed with Halogren's pained scream was more than she could take.

"Release my men now, or you needn't worry about the mighty armies of Havenstahl trampling this horrid pit. I will kill you myself," her scream was low and throaty, almost a growl. It sounded like she believed the threat, though thoughts of surviving fled quickly away.

Shacolin smiled wide in her direction as he felt around Halogren's face again and plucked out his other eye. He made the same satisfied slurping sounds when he popped that one in his mouth, "The eyes of men are a small but tasty treat. It would be a shame to boil them away."

The pole shook again. As much as she didn't want to look, Perrin strained her neck again to see. She had to witness the brutality to let it feed her rage. Her uncertainty fled. She wasn't sure how she would do it, but she would kill the disgusting creature.

Halogren's screams finally abated. His voice cracked as he

threatened, "If you could see my face, you would know nothing you could do to me could break my spirit. I will escape these bonds, free my queen, and destroy..."

A quick rap to Halogren's head ended the inspired rant as Shacolin ripped the soldier from the pole and tossed his body out of Perrin's sight. She didn't need to see the torture to know the horrible trogmortem was boiling her faithful soldier. The loud splash followed by screams no soldier who had experienced the horrors Halogren had would ever make if not enduring the most pitiable of suffering. Shacolin was boiling him alive. She could hear his struggles.

"Get down," another voice shouted. It was followed by a dull thud.

The moment Halogren's screaming ceased, Perrin knew he was dead. The rage boiling in her gut was a thousand times hotter than the cauldron Shacolin had callously tossed one of her men into. Bound to that pole, she could only imagine the look on his scarred face, the fear and agony that must have twisted his features so. Could those images be any worse than the sounds he made as his soul was literally cooked from his body. A stream of damning curses sat just behind her teeth waiting for her to gain enough control that her voice would sound powerful rather than wild and fearful.

Before she could launch the verbal assault, Dirk spoke up, "I know who are, beast. Shacolin is not your name. You may not be it anymore, but you were once Remel-Kinc. You are no honorable trogmortem. You were cast out by your kin, a worm sniveling at the boot of a great wizard. Defending that cruel monster is how you lost your eyes. Remind me, how old was the fair maiden who bested you on the battlefield?"

If Shacolin cared at all about his former honor, he didn't show it as he chuckled, "Remel-Kinc was a fool. I have no regrets. I am quite happy here. As far as I can see, this place is a paradise."

"Fifteen summers," Dirk kept pressing, "a wee, young lass of fifteen summers stole your sight with her blades, pathetic. Did she also rip your teeth out? Is that why you need to boil men before you can eat them?"

"You've a sharp tongue on you," Shacolin grunted as he took a step toward Dirk.

Dirk lowered his voice and whispered to Perrin, "This hut is unnatural in this place. It takes a great deal of focus to maintain order in these chaotic lands. Perhaps threats and brute force are not our best bets for survival."

Perrin took the hint. She closed her eyes and focused her energy within. This place beyond the Lake was bound by no rules, constantly shifting and evolving. She focused on the lesson Dirk had given her during sword training. She had to move quickly. Dirk had the big trogmortem distracted. She focused on her bonds. The heavy, oily chains weren't any more real than anything else in the hut. All of it had been conjured from the broken mind of an aging beast. Despite Shacolin's lumbering steps, she calmed herself, shuffling her rage to the periphery of her awareness, and allowing her breathing to grow steady. If only the things wrapped around her wrists and ankles were flower petals instead of chains.

Shacolin was right next to her when she fell from the pole she'd been bound to and landed on the hard floor surrounded by light violet flowers streaked with white. The sound she made when she hit the floor got his attention. That would buy Dirk some time to focus his attention on freeing himself and anyone else who remained alive.

She looked up at the massive beast. His lumpy nose sniffed deeply, dragging in mucus that refused to separate from the crust lining his nostrils. He cocked his head to the side, listening for sounds that might give her location away. She remained completely still, scanning the room for a weapon to use against the monster looming above her.

"Your sword, my queen," Dirk shouted, pulling Shacolin's attention away from her as he tossed the thing to her.

The blade felt good in her hand as she wasted no time. She slashed at his shins as Dirk's blade stabbed toward his heart. At the same moment, Jorgon flew over the top of her and tackled a grong who was sneaking up to brain her with his club. She heaved a brief sigh of relief. It wasn't so much for the rescue but the fact that Jorgon still lived.

The trogmortem's hide was tough. Dirk's blade didn't puncture near deep enough to cause any serious damage. The monster looming above Perrin just laughed as his head dropped as if he were looking down at the sword poking out of his droopy pectoral and swatted Dirk with a backhand. Dirk had been correct. With a pack of palusculex leaping around the room and the handful of grongs there to help the old trogmortem, brute force would never win the day. She pulled within herself again. She thought it would be just perfect if the floor bucked violently in that moment.

The floor did just that and more, quaking violently, it rolled and shifted, knocking grongs down. The walls of the place vibrated just as violently as the floor. Perrin rolled toward Shacolin. He was so off balance when she connected with his ankles, she toppled him completely. As soon as the monster crashed to the floor, she jumped on his chest, retrieved Dirk's blade, and tossed it toward him. Then she saw Halogren.

The inky black cauldron bucked and swayed above a roaring flame. The brew within bubbled and boiled, and Halogren's corpse had gotten stuck by its armpit with one arm hanging over the side. His face had always been challenging to behold—he'd been horribly disfigured during an imprisonment with a pack of exceptionally cruel grongs— but now it was cooked through. He looked like meat staring with no eyes at nothing, his face twisted in a grotesque look of sheer agony.

She had become so drawn into the horrible sight that she didn't see Shacolin's fist racing toward her face to bash her against the floor. A moment before that stony fist struck her, Dirk pounded into her. They both rolled until they slammed into a violently shaking wall.

"We must go now, my queen," Dirk shouted.

"Jorgon, on me," she shouted toward the fair-haired titan.

There was no fear on Jorgon's face as he stood between Perrin and Dirk, and the beasts who would attempt to bar their path. "It has been an honor serving you, my queen. This is where my journey ends. Dirk, see our queen safely to our destination, or I will avoid the Lake and haunt you for eternity."

Perrin was frozen there for a moment as she watched the last of the brave men who accepted her challenge to accompany her across these terrible and horrifying lands slit a grong across his throat before taking another grong's club to his cranium. The next swing of his blade was wild. It didn't hit anything as his knees buckled, and he stumbled like a drunk. The palusculex who latched onto his neck with jagged, little fangs smiled at her past the gore. She made one step toward her failing soldier before Dirk grabbed hold of her collar and dragged her through a hole in the wall.

The world around her was a blur after that. The sky did the things it did. Sometimes looking like sky except random, like a mob of stars in a battle royal rather than an orderly procession of heavenly bodies making their predetermined paths across the sky, and others looking like a sea, vast fields of golden grain, or other things that had no viable description in the lands from which she hailed. It all bled by like the colors of a painting left out in heavy rains.

By the time Dirk called their horses to halt, Shacolin, the grongs, and even those vicious, nasty palusculex seemed like distant memories, things that happened long ago, faded like a garment left too long in the blazing sun. Ganodin's gray, dead eyes were immediate, as if they still stared at her from the chaotic sky. Halogren's black, empty sockets yawning from within the cooked meat of his face were the same. Even Jorgon's soft, brown eyes seemed to accuse her from the darkness, his handsome jaw marred by gore from his torn throat sloshed about by a gruesome beast. All those horrible images were as fresh as if they were happening right at that moment. Would they haunt her until the Lake called her home? As she stared into chaotic darkness, she decided she deserved it if they did. Helias had warned that all who accompanied her would perish on this journey. She should have made the trip alone.

CHAPTER 28
OLD FRIEND

There was no wind on the hill that day. The grass appeared well kept. It seemed impossible. The field stretched out for as far as Maelich could see in any direction. As he glanced about looking for an end to it somewhere, he realized he could see neither the top nor the bottom of the hill. It seemed to stretch on forever above him and below at forty-five-degree angles in both directions. Even more puzzling was its deep green hue. It appeared lush and healthy, but the ground was so dry there couldn't have been rain for days. There could be absolutely no moisture in the soil sprouting the greenest grass he'd ever seen.

He had a sudden urge to be somewhere else. There was no particular destination in his mind. He just wanted to be anywhere other than sitting on the impossibly green hill. After a brief, internal debate, he decided up was the best direction to move. By the time he rose and turned toward the top of the hill, or at least up since he couldn't really see where the top of it was if it had one, the hill was gone and the grass along with it. The land surrounding him had become flat and dry like the cracked land where he first met the Shaiwah, but it was different than that somehow. It was dry and cracked, but it looked gray like something had charred it black and faded over time. He could see a tree in the distance. It was crooked and bent. It had no leaves and appeared just as gray as the land surrounding it.

He glanced all about the strange landscape. There were no other landmarks besides that lonely, charred tree. By the time his eyes made it back to the thing, he heard a bark. It was a familiar tone. It sounded just like Mountain. As the thought processed in his mind, the beast came into view.

It was Mountain bounding toward him with his tail wagging and his tongue hanging out of his mouth. It felt like a tear perched on his eyelid. It had been so long since he'd felt anything close to joy, the emotion was just too much to contain. However, when he went to wipe dampness from his cheek, there wasn't any. It was as dry as the scorched land surrounding him.

There was precious little time to consider the odd lack of moisture on his face before the big scrod leapt toward him and pounded into his chest toppling them both to the ground. The laugh that bellowed from his throat as the two of them rolled across the dusty ground sounded like pure joy to his own ears. He couldn't remember the last time he'd laughed.

"Who's a good boy?" he gushed as he scratched behind the scrod's ear and earned some sloppy kisses on his cheek from the animal's slobbering tongue. "How did you find me?"

"You're not really here," his joy slowly faded as the realization settled in. Mountain hadn't found him. Neither of them were really anywhere. It was just another dream, an illusion, a fanciful hope for something different than what his life had become as he journeyed toward some unknown destination without any clue of his goal.

As if on cue, Maulom's voice cut through the sounds of Mountain's panting and Maelich's dying laughter, "He is not. You failed him like you failed the Shaiwah."

Maelich closed his eyes and shook his head. When he opened them, Mountain was gone and so was the scorched dirt that had surrounded him. It had been replaced by wet brick. He pulled himself up against a fountain. The splashing water was loud. It sounded like a waterfall or rushing rapids. He glanced up at the statue at its center. It looked like the great fish of Belscythia and spewed water forth from its open mouth. The pool surrounding the great statue seemed too small to house the mammoth fish, and the walls too short to contain it. Water gushed to more walls of the same brick beneath his feet. They were so tall he couldn't see the tops of them, and they formed a perfect square around him and the fountain.

He stood up and found himself face to face with the white horse. Though they stood in water up to his knees, his boots didn't feel wet. His voice didn't sound right in his own ears when he finally addressed the horse. "Maulom, it has been a time since you've come to invade my dreams. Why not speak to me in the waking world?"

"Where are you, Maelich?" the horse asked.

He suddenly recalled the first time Maulom had come to him in his dreams speaking in riddles and hinting at things but not saying anything useful. It was fun to be on the other side of such an exchange. "I am standing in a courtyard in front of a fountain with walls too short to contain the great spray of water from the massive statue of a mighty fish contained within it that is surrounded by four walls whose tops are so high they cannot be seen," he smiled as he described his surroundings in as much detail as he could.

The white horse shook his head, "Do not toy with me, Maelich. Where on Ouloos does your head rest at this very moment?"

"How could I know?" Maelich's smile widened. "You invaded my dreams, you charged me with a journey you claimed I had to make, and you convinced me to lead a foreign, untrained people across unforgiving lands to take back a city you claim was stolen from them long before any of them ever lived. I am in a forest. That is all I know."

Maelich blinked. It was an average blink, no longer or shorter than any other time his eyelids involuntarily closed to moisten his eyeballs. Yet, when they opened again the courtyard was gone. The fountain, water, and bricks were all gone with it. The glistening bricks of the impossibly tall walls had been replaced by wooden slats, and the blue sky above by a roof of wooden timbers. He was seated on a simple wooden bench with his back to an equally simple wooden table. The white horse still stood before him, but there was a bar behind him. The thing looked like it had at one time sported a glossy sheen, but it had dulled over time. The place looked like a pub save the fact there were no people chatting, laughing, and sharing pints.

"You are a fool," the white horse grunted.

"I suppose," he said as he thought about it. "It probably was foolish to heed the command of a talking horse who posed unanswerable riddles and I only knew from my dreams. I am a fool just as you say."

"I did not speak to you in riddles then, and I have no riddles for you now," the horse complained with a frown. "You must go back to the Shaiwah. Your scrod probably died slowly, starving in unforgiving lands while he cooked under the equally unforgiving sun. That is your fault. Do not sentence the Shaiwah to a similar fate. They need you, Maelich. You are their king."

The oddity of a horse frowning was lost on Maelich as he felt a sudden twinge of sadness, "They don't need me. You said yourself, I couldn't even take care of a scrod. He probably is dead. Ymitoth is a better leader than I ever could be. He should lead them. Besides, I'm drawn toward something else. I don't know what it is, but it pulls at me. I can't fight the urge. I don't know where it is, but it is the only place I know to go."

"Oh, he did lead them," the white horse said as he raised his eyebrows. "He led them right to the city that was stolen from them so many summers past, and right into a trap. Those who remain are prisoners of the Tahnka. You must go now and rescue them."

"I am unsure if I believe you, Maulom. Even if I did, I am certain I could do none of the things you have commanded," Maelich shook his head as he stood. "Do not haunt my dreams again. You are unwelcomed here."

The white horse opened his mouth to speak but vanished before he could.

Maelich continued speaking to the spot where the horse had been standing, "I hope you are lying. I may never know one way or the other, but I know I cannot find them, at least not now. There is something I must do. I don't know what it is, but I know I'm heading in the right direction."

CHAPTER 29
JUDGEMENT

Cialia sat in total darkness. All light beneath the stone dome had ceased when Kaldumahn and Moshat had fled. That was fine with her. She needed a moment to recharge and reflect before racing back into battle against the wily gods. She'd been far too brash in her assaults against them, and all of them had been far better prepared than she expected. It made little sense to rush. She had eternity to speak and execute their sentences.

"Why not come home for a bit?" Helias' voice chimed in her head. "Let the Lake recharge your spirit."

"Not yet," she replied with her mind. "They had a plan to draw me out and attack me. Now that I have engaged with them, they will not stop until I am dead, or they have been scattered to the wind. The gods have no honor. There is no vile thing they will not do to hurt me. I must destroy them to protect the innocent creatures of Ouloos."

"You are correct, sweet sister," sadness dripped from Helias' tone. "They will hurt those you care for in order to hurt you."

"They will," Cialia remained in her mind as she spoke plainly. "I cannot let them. I must be prepared."

Then she felt it, the power. It was almost a smell, the kind that soaks into your sinuses so deep it has flavor. It was strength, ancient, primal, and unforgiving. It smelled like gods. She knew they were taunting her. It would be unwise to take the bait and follow that scent, but intention was layered within the odor. Kaldumahn and Moshat planned to kill all the giants and grongs inhabiting Maomnosett, that ancient and proud dwarf city that had once again fallen to the rule of the proud giants of the Maomnosett clan.

As unwise a choice as it might have been, it really wasn't a choice at all. She could still feel Helias' sadness saturating the air around her as she focused her intent on the courtyard in front of the palace at Maomnosett. She could see neither Moshat, the great bear, nor his brother, Kaldumahn, the great silver lion who stalks the sky, but she could sense them both. They were hiding, but they were there among the giants, grongs, and dwarves milling about.

As she focused more intently on that place, her body became lighter. It was a gradual shift as her awareness drifted slowly from the physical to a spiritual realm. She knew that wasn't really what she was doing, but it was the best way she could understand it for herself. She thought of it as dancing in the spiritual or splitting time. It was neither of those. She didn't fully understand it, but she was learning quickly. There are an infinite number of dimensions existing along the same lines of reality literally right next to each other. The only effort required to shift from one to another was knowing you could. That was the part she struggled with. The gods seemed expert at dancing between dimensions, hiding just outside the realm of visible light in whatever plane of reality she occupied at any given moment. She needed to learn to see them all at once to take that protection away from them. The lesson would have to wait. She had gods to kill.

Time means little once you've grown beyond it. One million summers all happen in the same instant. That was how it felt as Cialia gave up her physicality in the darkness beneath a stone dome and materialized in the courtyard before the palace at Maomnosett. Fear colored all the faces in the courtyard as all stopped to behold the fair-haired Dragon who didn't resemble a Dragon at all. Despite the fact it wasn't a massive, red, scaled beast breathing fire before them, she knew they all understood the power hiding beneath her delicate form.

Maomnosett Ohm, the recently crowned king of the dwarf city was as burdened by pride as all the mighty giants who came before him. He hid the fear she sensed wildly coursing through his veins as he addressed her. "State your name and business with house Maomnosett," he said with false disinterest sprinkled in his tone.

"You know my name," Cialia's voice echoed with authority all about the courtyard, "and you have nothing to fear from me. You are under my protection as are all creatures of Ouloos. There are gods among you, gods you do not worship. I am here to destroy them as I have destroyed the gods you do worship."

The giant king remained aloof as he began, "I am Ohm of house Maomnosett. There is no force on Ouloos I fear, and no…"

Ohm's words melted away as the grand palace behind him exploded in a cloud of flying bricks and debris. The force toppled the giant from his throne and down the steps that led up to it from the courtyard. He rolled until he lay before Cialia looking up at Moshat, the mighty bear who stalks the north woods, standing on his back legs where a palace had been. His expression dripped with the fear he had desperately been trying to hide.

The mighty bear's roar shook the walls surrounding the courtyard and the mountain beneath them. His fur glowed perfect, white light as his eyes swirled with all colors in equal saturation. His frothy mouth dripped as if he hungered for the flesh of giants. That mouth easily sat fifty feet above the crumbled brick and stone about his feet as he slashed at the air with his mighty claws.

The great and terrible Ohm trembled at Cialia's feet, but she remained unmoved as flames swirled tightly around her forearms and she spoke her judgement against the god, "Moshat, mighty bear who stalks the north woods, you have failed those who worship you. You have failed Ouloos. The city of Maomnosett is under my protection as are all living things on Ouloos. You have no power here. I have judged you. Your sentence is to burn in Dragon's fire."

She suddenly sensed Kaldumahn's presence behind her. He had been hiding outside of her awareness. She expected the attack and spun immediately to face him. His staff and entire body were all aglow as she released her flame.

Two fire balls gobbled up the still air of the courtyard, but he was too fast. He vanished as quickly as he had come. When he appeared again, he was beside her. By the time she called the flame again he had already slammed his staff into the mountaintop.

The concussion of the blast shook the ground and knocked her to the dirt beneath her. She didn't remain there long, but the tricky god was gone again by the time she leapt back to her feet. She slowly scanned the courtyard, waiting for the god to reappear and launch his next attack. Moshat continued to roar behind her, but he stood his ground.

Then she smelled something different. It stood out among the primal scent of gods. It smelled like old stone piled up in a dead forge. Molten rock leached up from beneath her feet and wrapped tightly around her. It would have burned her flesh had she not called her flame to protect her, a thin layer between her and the precious pord from the mines beneath the mountain. It hardened immediately, trapping her arms at her sides and dropping her to her knees with its weight.

"Maomnosett Ohm," Moshat, the mighty bear shouted in a voice both beautiful and terrible, "you are a false king. Your gods are dead, and you have no protection."

Despite his trembling form, Ohm stood tall before the god, defiant to the end, "Giants bow before no being. We know no gods."

The great bear crashed down on the giant, crushing his bones and pulverizing his flesh into the packed dirt of the courtyard. A blazing white blast erupted from his mighty paws when they connected with the ground obliterating the giant and sending cracks deep into the mountain.

The mountain heaved beneath Cialia. Elbahor would crumble to dust. She reached deep into the caverns beneath the mountain with her will and focused on all the souls toiling away. She touched them all with her awareness and shouted, "Run. Run as fast as you can. Leave this place."

She felt their fear. These were the beings she was there to save from callous gods, and she had failed them. She pushed against the god's will with her own. Every shred of her intention focused on keeping the mountain from collapsing and crushing the faithful dwarves working in the mines, chipping ore away from rock. None of them deserved to die beneath the tons of rock that would pulverize them to dust, and she wouldn't let them.

Then she sensed something else. A small group of dwarves and men skirting beneath the mine along hidden and forgotten passages. They were going the wrong way. She scanned their thoughts. A dwarf named Lentaak was among them, leading them. Rage and hate and anger coursed through his veins, but it wasn't revenge he was after. It was freedom, freedom for his kin.

"I know you can feel the mountain quaking around you. Turn back," Cialia spoke to his mind.

"Ain't no chance of that," she sensed his reply. "We'll be saving our kin or dying along with them."

The sentiment was frustrating. Dwarves and men were no different than giants or trogmortem, or even grongs. They were all driven by pride or honor or some other foolish ideal that meant very little to the souls they left behind once duty claimed them for the Lake. Still, as foolish as the gesture may have been, she couldn't just let them die. The idea strengthened her resolve. She pushed even harder against the god's will. Her flame flared up spinning wildly about her and melted away the rock that had hardened around her. Within moments, molten rock smoked about her feet as a ball of flame surrounded her. It slowly but steadily expanded as her effort intensified.

The bear refused to break. She could feel his will pushing back against hers. He kept his paws planted firmly on the ground pressing, pushing, and focusing all his intention on toppling the mountain. White light flared. His paws blazed like a burning star while that same perfect light shone brightly from the cracks running all along the ground.

Then Kaldumahn returned and slammed his blazing staff into the ground. It burned just as brilliantly with the same perfect light. She could feel his will just as strongly as Moshat's. They both pushed into the mountain trying with all their might to crack it beneath their combined will.

Cialia pushed back against them even harder. Her flame flared, a perfect blazing ball of fire slowly growing beyond her control. She was barely aware of the commotion in the courtyard as giants, grongs, and a handful of dwarves bound together with chains fumbled about trying to escape the heat of her judgement, but their fear was at the front of her consciousness. It oozed from them. She had never seen a giant cry, but she could taste the salt from Oyg's tears as thoughts of those he'd leave behind dominated his mind.

It was too much. How could she control the flame while focused on her adversaries? She shifted some of her attention to containing the fire blazing wildly around her. She had to, at least long enough to let the frightened souls escape through the southern gate. At the same time, she pushed even harder against the two gods. They were relentless.

Suddenly, the courtyard was gone. A swirling corridor of flame stretched before her. Moshat was at the end of it. Not as the bear, but in his godly form. He gripped his staff as it blazed with bright light. He pointed at her with his other hand as his lips moved around soundless words.

Another corridor of flame stretched out behind her. Kaldumahn stood at the end of it with his staff glowing in the same fashion, his lips speaking the same silent curses, and his eyes swirled like madness with all colors at once.

As the two gods battered her with their will, ghostly faces haunted both corridors. There had to be thousands of them, ethereal and floating in the dark space between the flames. Their eyes flashed with fear. Their thoughts echoed like shouts down a canyon. They were the reason she could not fail. The mountain would not crumble. She would stop it.

Her soul was exhausted, but she pressed even harder against their will. Pushing in each direction, her body expanded toward both the gods she battled. Though one sat before her and the other behind, she faced them both. Each was betrayed by the slightest hint of fear marring their perfect and horrible eyes as the fire in her own eyes accused and threatened them with punishments both horrid and unimaginable.

CHAPTER 30
THE SWARM

Grizzly mongs are pack animals. Men without a mind for intense study and observation see them as mindless beasts fueled only by hunger. This is true to some extent. However, these mindless beasts have a deep social structure which differs greatly from other pack animals like scarra. Both lowland and mountain scarra form packs. These packs are typically between ten and forty members, and they are violently protective of their respective territories. Grizzly mongs are not. Instead of attacking rival packs who wander into their territory, these great snow beasts from the north adopt the new members and expand.

This behavior seems unsustainable. It would be in the lands where men dwell, farm, and compete with beasts for meat. The only competition for food grizzly mongs have in the lands where they dwell comes in the form of the creatures they hunt. Every beast in those snowy and forbidding lands is an apex predator. Any of those could be the hunter seeking fresh, grizzly mong meat as easily as they could be the victim of those same vicious beasts. There is power in numbers, and, in most cases that far north, numbers are the difference between the hunters and the hunted. Since ranging from their snowy homes, the pack of thousands which had been terrorizing the road from Havenstahl to Druindahl was not finding enough to sustain itself. There simply wasn't enough food as far south as they were. They were hungry. Hunger was the one thing which could affect their behavior.

A small herd of fallon caught the pack's attention on their slow journey back to the snowy north. It wasn't near enough to satisfy the pack's hunger, a little better than one hundred at best. This was a new problem for them, and it all but destroyed the intricate social workings of the pack.

It began as a swarm. Fallon are fast and expert at avoiding predators. However, occupying different lands than grizzly mongs, they have no experience with these cunning beasts. The grizzly mongs circled around the herd, nipping and swatting, corralling them into a clearing before descending on them like flood waters over a broken dam.

Fallon grunted, snorted, and stomped. They were useless warnings, as the herd had no place to flee. They were surrounded by vicious and hungry grizzly mongs. It took moments for the pack to decimate the herd. Once life had been stolen from all the fallon in the clearing, the swarm devolved into an orgy of consumption. White fangs tore into flesh, picking bones clean and staining white fur pink with blood. Before long, there weren't more than scraps left on any of the carcasses, and the orgy devolved further into a rabble of beasts, none bearing any loyalty to another. There was only hunger. Beast battled beast for the tiniest morsel as the sun's light faded from the sky.

Then fire battled back the encroaching darkness. A line of torches blazed to life at the northern edge of the clearing. The dead-eyed men stepped from shadow into the orange glow. Their dirty, brown robes looked auburn in the firelight. All three removed their hoods in unison. Their wild, orange hair and nappy beards seemed to burn like flame on their heads and faces in the flickering light. Their black, dead eyes reflected the light and appeared to burn just the same. All three were identical to each other like each was a copy one another.

The leader opened his mouth wider than a man's mouth should open. No words came out of the cavernous thing, just a sound like terror come to life. It was a layered thing. At the bottom a horrible rumble shook the ground. The middle was filled with laments like a chorus of men screaming out in pain. Sailing along the top of all that was a screech that could pierce eardrums.

The grizzly mongs cried out in pain as the horrible sounds swirled around the clearing. Some buried their faces against the ground and pawed at their ears. Others stomped about and shouted pitiable howls that were nearly drowned out by the awful chorus bellowing from the dead-eyed man.

One exceptionally brazen beast charged the group of three. Its claws tore into the dirt as it rushed toward them growling with vengeance. The thing stopped just before the leader and raised itself up on its back legs. In a flash, the dead-eyed man slashed out with a hand that looked like a man's save the stony claws protruding from its fingers. A look of confusion spread across the beast's face as its head cocked slightly to the side, and its insides dumped into a steamy pile in front of it. The poor creature fell to the ground in a heap. The other two dead-eyed men leapt onto the carcass and tore it to bits, filling the air with pieces of the dead thing.

The rest of the pack learned to fear those three immediately. They fled back to the south, racing as fast as they could from the terror of fire and claws.

The air smelled exceptionally fresh. The sun had just begun its slow dive toward the western horizon and remained high in a cloudless sky. The conditions weren't ideal for a hard charging ride up the trail. Luckily, a gusty, northerly wind carried with it enough of a chill to keep the air comfortable. If not for those refreshing gales, the horses pounding the dirt beneath Chagon and Tarantian would have given up an hour ago. As it was, they'd need to be watered soon.

Chagon wore a dopey grin as rivulets of sweat cascaded down his skin beneath his heavy, mail shirt. The sweat didn't bother him in the least. Charging down the trail with the red ribbons fastened to his horse flapping wildly behind him was the best place he'd ever been. He was a rider of Druindahl on a mission given by the mighty giant killer, Daritus, himself. Less than a summer prior, he'd been a simple farmer toiling away in the fields from sunup until sundown. Feeding the good people of Havenstahl was honest and fulfilling work, but nothing like being a soldier.

His grin widened as he glanced over at his trail mate, Tarantian. The man was a titan. They hadn't seen any real battle together, at least not against men, but the man oozed confidence. A soldier didn't earn that kind of swagger without having seen and done things that would make lesser men cry. Even the way he rode his horse as it charged down the trail seemed heroic. He was in complete control and afraid of nothing.

"I ain't never going back to no farm," he hollered at Tarantian over the thunder of horse's hooves pounding the trail.

Tarantian's hard face cracked into a warm smile as he looked over and replied, "You never could. Now that the trail has gotten a hold of you, you will long for it like a lover whenever your feet are not upon it."

Tarantian was correct. Chagon hadn't found the right words to describe what he felt before his friend gave voice to them. It was love, not the romantic kind of love that might swell in the breast and warm up the loins, but it was near enough. He had felt that longing during the brief time the two of them had stayed at the castle preparing for their first mission. He couldn't wait to get back to it.

As the trail raced by beneath their horses, they crossed the old wooden bridge over the river Galgooth and into the dwarven lands. Chagon hadn't traveled much or very far prior to leaving his farm on a doomed caravan to Druindahl, but he had traveled enough pitching his wares to know the border was just a hair more than meaningless. He'd met more than one group of riders from Havenstahl patrolling the area across the river. The dwarves of Alhouim didn't have much use for the land preferring to remain on their lucrative peak. They mined the great Mount Elbahor and traded their wares with the farmers of Havenstahl. The lands around that mighty mountain tended to get a bit wild. That's why none of the dwarves of Alhouim cared much when the mighty riders of Havenstahl patrolled it for them.

The great mountain loomed to the west as the trail skirted along its base between stone and forest. The sun had dipped far enough behind the great peak that the trail was covered in shadow. The shadows were expected, but something about the mountain wasn't right. Long, crooked lines of dazzling light gleamed from within and shined more brilliantly than the bright skies above.

"What do you suppose that might be?" Chagon asked.

Tarantian shook his head and replied, "I have never seen the like. Perhaps it is something that giant is up to. It is not our concern. We have been tasked with a mission. It is best to keep your eyes on the trail and our goal."

Keeping his eyes off the odd light blazing forth from the mountain wasn't easy for Chagon. In fact, it was all but impossible. "Is it moving?" he finally asked.

"I haven't looked," Tarantian's voice boomed over the rumble of horse hooves.

"It looks to be moving," he hollered back, "or, at least, trembling."

Tarantian finally looked over at the great peak. After a few moments, he voiced his agreement, "Yes, the mountain does appear to be rumbling. It would take great power to cause a mountain to quake in such a fashion. Whatever that great power might be is not our mission. Eyes on the trail."

Despite his best efforts to comply, the command was impossible to follow. Even as his horse pounded the trail carrying him ever further north and beyond the great peak, he couldn't stop looking back at it. The mountain itself was emitting light like the sun or the moon, or even a star. Every time he'd manage to drag his gaze away, he'd find his neck straining as his eyes slowly wandered back toward it.

The peak was a good deal behind them when Chagon picked the conversation back up, "Ye think it might be some folks need help back there?"

"Seems likely," Tarantian shrugged.

"Ain't it our charge to be helping folks in danger," the idea they would just ignore the potential peril of the dwarf city didn't sit well with him.

Tarantian tugged hard on his horse's reigns. Chagon followed suit a few more feet up the trail. After nudging his horse forward so the two were standing next to each other, he finally said, "We are sworn to protect all those in need. That is a truth. Right at this moment, there are thousands of folks in need who require our protection."

"Soldiers," Chagon complained, "men who have been trained to battle other men and monsters like them beasts we be following."

Tarantian sighed and scratched his head, "You have a lot in your head right now, and it isn't wrong. However, you are a soldier on a mission. Do you know why we train, why I launch the same repetitive attacks for you to defend and ask the same of you?"

"Like ye told me, ye mimic the attack patterns of our enemies so I ain't surprised in battle," he shrugged. "All that training might be helpful to them folks on the mountain."

"We train to develop instincts," the old soldier nodded. "When an enemy attacks you, you don't have to think about your response. You have seen it thousands of times before, and your body responds appropriately. On this mission, or any other, you must rely on your instincts not your mind."

His face twisted awkwardly as he digested the instruction, "So I should be wandering about like a mindless idiot with no thoughts in me head."

"That is not what I said," Tarantian sighed. "General Daritus gave us this mission because it is important. Imagine we charge back to Elbahor, conquer that mountain, ride into Maomnosett, and die from whatever power cracks and quakes that mountain."

"We might be saving some folks before the Lake be calling us home," he wasn't buying it.

"We very well might," Tarantian agreed with fake excitement in his voice as if Chagon had just given him a great aha. "So, in this scenario we both die heroic deaths, and our sacrifices save a few lives, or maybe even a few hundred. Meanwhile, those beasts turn around and head back toward Havenstahl, but they don't circle around Elzkahon and approach the south gate. No, they cross Galgooth and clamber up the side of that mountain and overrun the north gate. Those trained soldiers have no idea they are under assault until the city is overrun with vicious beasts, and thousands die. We need to make sure those beasts continue on to their homes. Their path has been a winding one, and we cannot be certain they won't turn back this way. If they do, we must guide them away from the northern pass to the south gate."

"They sent us off as bait?" Chagon's tone got away from him

Tarantian shook his head, "Guides. If they continue home, we spent some nice, quiet time on the trail. If they turn back toward Havenstahl, we'll lead them right to the south gate into the waiting arms of Havenstahl's mighty army."

"How will they know we be coming?" he squinted.

"Now you're using your mind for something useful," Tarantian smiled. "We aren't the only scouts about monitoring the movements of these monsters. Each has a different task."

Tarantian gave his horse a light kick to get him galloping again, so Chagon followed suit. He wasn't completely satisfied with the answers his new mentor had for him, but the words were beginning to make sense. He offered the mountain behind them one more strained look over his shoulder before deciding he'd let the argument go.

It couldn't have been more than half of a mile when Tarantian yanked hard on his horse's reigns again, touched his index finger to his lips, and pointed further up the trail. Then he guided his horse toward the edge of the trees along the trail. Chagon followed suit, though he wasn't quite clear on what they might be hiding from. He strained his eyes in the direction Tarantian pointed. The darkening sky was little help, but he was barely able to make out a rider charging on a hard gallop down the trail.

"It's difficult to make out who he might be riding for, but that is one of ours," Tarantian spoke frankly. "If his rate of travel is any indication, our mission is about to get quite a bit more exciting."

The rider was reining his horse to a hard stop beside them on the trail before Chagon could offer any form of reply. It was difficult to determine whether it was fear or determination weighing on the man's brow and turning the corners of his mouth down. He was clad in the blue of Havenstahl down to the ribbons streaming from his steed, but his dark waves suggested a rider of Druindahl.

"Duvel," Tarantian greeted the man fondly. "It has been some time. I heard it was you who blasted the great horn of Galgooth and called Alhouim to our aid before the battle at Fort Maomnosett."

"It was an honor," the faintest whisper of a smile tickled the corners of Duvel's mouth before fleeing in the face of duty. "As much as I'd enjoy reminiscing about the act, I haven't the time for idle chatter."

Chagon raised an eyebrow at the slight, but Tarantian didn't seem at all put off by it. Instead, the old soldier replied agreeably, "I feared as much. The pack moves back south?"

"I am to report directly to Daritus on the grizzly mongs' movements, and I have even more troubling news to share," he glanced back over his shoulder as if the pack were right on his tail. It was definitely fear Chagon decided when the man turned and finished, "I had never seen the dead-eyed men before. Even the stories told about how they broke into the castle and stole the prince from his mother's arms seemed like all the other myths I'd ever heard about them, but the three are the cause of the pack's return to our lands."

"What's that ye said?" Chagon blurted. "Them dead-eyed beasts be real."

"You had best get back to it. Take word to Havenstahl, and we'll make sure those beasts make their way to the south gate," Tarantian said to Duvel ignoring his trail mate. Then he asked, "How long do we have?"

"Two miles," Duvel replied. Then he drove his heels into his horse's flanks and yelled back over his shoulder, "Not quite as fast as your horses. Keep your eyes sharp on the trail."

Chagon was a bit put off that neither of the men he shared the trail with paid any attention to his question, but he held his tongue. He didn't know much about the three, but the stories he had heard painted a grim and horrible picture. They looked like men, but they weren't quite that. Something had stolen their souls long before Chagon was born. If they were menacing enough to frighten those massive and terrifying beasts, those pictures must be accurate.

He watched Tarantian stare north up the trail for a few minutes before breaking the silence. "So, we'll be heading back to Havenstahl then? We'd best get to it?"

"Not until those monsters are in sight," Tarantian shook his head. "Our horses can outrun them. We don't want to let them get too close, but we need to remain in their sight. We want them to chase us."

Grim unease settled into his gut as he continued, "What about them dead-eyed blokes that have them beasts all worked up?"

The soldier's expression didn't change a bit as he stared coldly up the trail and replied, "We hope our horses are faster."

It wasn't a satisfying response, but Chagon didn't expect he'd get anything better out of Tarantian just then. They had their mission. That was that, so he let it lie.

The sky continued to darken as they waited. It was probably in his head, but the light breeze gently rustling the leaves about seemed to pick up an icy chill. He pulled his cloak tighter around his neck. The squeaking of the mail beneath his shirt earned a sharp look from Tarantian. He must have been feeling just as tense about the idea of playing chase with a mob of massive beasts. That mail was constantly squeaking, and it had never earned any worse than a chuckle from him.

The idea that Tarantian might be feeling just as scared as he was waiting in the darkness for monsters chased away the last shred of confidence he'd been clinging to. Tarantian wasn't afraid of anything.

Chagon's mind hadn't made it too far down the path to mind numbing terror before Tarantian's gruff voice punched through the silence. "Shh," he commanded before adding, "the pack is near."

As soon as Tarantian stopped talking, Chagon heard the light grunting approaching from the north. "Should I be firing up a brand?" he asked.

"We'll have little success navigating this trail in darkness, and an equal amount getting them to follow us if they can't see us," Tarantian nodded.

Chagon heeded the command and grabbed one of three torches he had soaked and prepared for the journey. He hadn't had much time to train with his new mentor, but he always paid close attention to his lessons. Having the proper supplies ready for a mission was one of his first. He struck a flint, and the brand blazed to life.

As soon as the torch earned a healthy glow, the light grunts escalated to impatient growls and howls. Chagon hadn't noticed the sound of any footsteps prior to lighting the thing. The pack must have increased their pace. The ground rumbled with the sound of heavy, clawed paws digging into the hard trail.

"Go," Tarantian commanded, "half speed. Keep control of your horse. We can't afford to have them panicking when the pack gets close."

Chagon didn't look back. There was no sense in allowing himself to fall to panic before his horse could have cause to. He held up the torch, gave his horse a kick, and kept his eyes on the dark trail before him.

CHAPTER 31
ROCK AND FIRE

Cialia continued to grow, pressing and pushing with all her might and half her focus. The other half focused on the mountain itself. She held the rock together with her will. Each pebble, each grain of dirt split by the fury of the great bear pressed against itself by the strength of her intention. None would die beneath the mountain.

Her body had become flame as she expanded down each corridor toward the god pushing back against her at either end. Kaldumahn cracked first. The rage and determination twisting up his perfect countenance fled in the face of pure, unbridled fear. It oozed from him, and Cialia burned it up from her flame.

"You have lost," she spoke to his mind.

He smiled briefly before he vanished in a flash. His reply came a moment after he fled, "Foolish girl, you have no idea what terrors you have unleashed on those you claim to protect. Follow me and watch your good works come to pass."

She remained connected to him as he fled like a coward. A sense of victory filled her as she ate up his fear. The mighty Kaldumahn, great silver lion who stalks the sky faltered before the might of the great Dragon. The moment of satisfaction was brief as the god's flight ceased at the shores of Biggon's Bay. She saw him there smiling wide with his staff held aloft before him, glowing with all the power coursing through his perfect form.

He spoke no words, but the waters of the bay grew frothy with discontent. Hundreds upon hundreds of ships anchored in the bay populated by giants, trogmortem, and grongs. Any man from any of the great cities would count the frothy brew the bay had become crashing ship into ship and casting monsters from across the Great Sea into the drink a blessing. Perhaps a few moons prior, Cialia would have done the same. That was before she opened her eyes to the evil of gods.

Those poor souls cast into the breaking waves cried out to her mind. She could name them all. She could feel their fear and their pain. She could feel the burning in their lungs as their bodies cried out for air, and she could feel the effort of their minds as they failed at fighting it. Water filled lungs and choked the life from beings she swore to protect. The idea of justice faltered in the face of rage. Kaldumahn would die for his sins.

The mountain rumbled beneath her feet dragging her attention away from the churning waters of Biggon's Bay and the vile god who would indiscriminately take the lives of so many. The great bear hadn't given up the fight and had taken advantage of the distraction.

Cialia pulled her focus back to the mountaintop. She would deal with the silver lion in due time, but the bear would die atop the mountain that day. Her flames swirled madly about as she focused her will back on Moshat.

She regained enough control of herself that she believed she could release her flame at the god and keep the mountain intact when something distracted her. The mighty bear was not the only great power sharing the mountaintop with her. There was something else, a smell or a feeling. It was faint, hiding from her sight, but she sensed it there. It was enough to distract her to the point that her opponent recognized it.

Moshat pushed harder, bearing down on the mountain as he pushed back against her. She couldn't let him escape, not like Kaldumahn had. It was apparent there were no horrors they would not exact to defeat her. She had to stop him right at that moment.

Cialia latched onto Moshat's awareness and focused all her intention on it before releasing her flame. It blazed like a million suns as it slithered and sizzled from within her to within him. Her intention injected into each of his cells as she entered his will and exploded burning the great bear, mighty Moshat, to ash.

She collapsed to the ground sapped of all strength and barely clinging to consciousness. All her will focused into the mountain, but there wasn't enough left. The mountain quaked again more violently. She pressed harder, focusing all her intention on holding each piece together. It still wasn't enough. The mountain rumbled and shook even harder until it finally collapsed under its own weight.

All the voices cried out to her. They were damning accusations, as all their heroic intentions were crushed beneath tons of rock. She died a little with each soul that left its body to journey toward the Lake. She had succeeded in destroying the god but failed to protect the reason she needed to.

As she fell with the crumbling stone deep into the caverns beneath the mountain, she was barely aware of her flame encircling her, protecting her in a way she couldn't protect those she promised. She settled into a pocket of air surrounded by stone her flame had created for her just before consciousness fled.

Ijilv crept along the edges of reality just outside the spectrum of visible light watching Moshat, the mighty bear engaged in a battle of wills with Cialia, the great Dragon of Druindahl. A hint of disappointment tainted his smile as he lamented the limitations she imposed on herself. Of course, he needed her to be bound by those limitations, as sad as they were. He looked upon her like art, beautiful, perfect, and destructive. She could do anything, if only she believed it.

He suddenly felt naked, exposed like uncovered flesh to frigid air. He shivered. The idea forced a nervous chuckle past his lips. She felt him. The great Dragon of Druindahl knew he was there. She was learning. A large part of him was impressed at how quickly she was gaining control over her great power without ever having been trained to do so. An equally large part was terrified about what that must mean.

The fear fled quickly. Like a game of hide and go seek when the seeker is just around the corner from your hiding spot but turns to chase a different scent, she was just around the corner from him but couldn't see the edge of the wall to turn it. Soon, she would come for him, and she would destroy him with her glory. But that would not be on this day.

His brother exploded before him in blazing, glorious ash. The concussion of the blast was too impressive to allow fear any quarter. Glowing bits of light swirled and sparkled where his brother's beastly form had stood. His mouth expanded as the swirling colors in his eyes increased in speed. He sucked up all the shimmering bits, and his brother was his.

CHAPTER 32
THE WIZARD'S WAKE

There were ten proper villages or towns from north to south or south to north along the coast. Some were more populated than others. Some boasted artfully crafted architecture near worthy of a proper city and encroaching on high society, while others favored function over form. There were four north of Biggon's Bay. Castrine sat at the edge of the lands protected by Havenstahl and as far north as any man without a mind for adventure should dare. Angor's port wasn't more than a few miles south of there. A bit of a jaunt further south down the coast would place a traveler smack dab in the middle of Migdolah, named for the daughter of an eccentric duke who had convinced himself he was the king of Ouloos. The last town between Migdolah and Biggon's Bay was Ragdobahn. It was a haven for scoundrels of many stripes.

Kantiim opted not to bother with any of the northern towns. Instead, he led the force from Havenstahl straight west toward Biggon's Bay to the edge of the great waste before veering south toward the Fisher's Guild. It was one of the villages that favored function over form. It sat on the low cliffs twenty miles south of the bay and wasn't much to look at. When Kantiim's force rode through it, the place was flooded out and abandoned.

That was a surprise. It was no short distance from Castrine to the Fisher's Guild. Kantiim had expected to beat the man he had always known as the old healer there. Recent developments had proven that aged creature to be far more than anyone in Havenstahl realized, but he wasn't expecting what he'd found.

As he led the caravan of one thousand men—one hundred of those on horseback—hundreds of trogmortem, and no less than twenty giants down the coast, each town they passed told a similar story. Some were flooded, others burned out, still others looked like the ground had opened up and swallowed them whole, but in all of those instances they were completely abandoned except for one.

It was ten miles north of Gorban's Sound when the caravan came across an old herder leading eleven tubber that looked far too thin down the trail. "Hey there," Kantiim hailed the bent, old man whose tattered cloak appeared even older and more worn than him.

The man ignored the greeting.

"I said, hey there," Kantiim called out again. Despite the additional volume and authority he'd added to his voice, his greeting again went unanswered.

He gave his horse a nudge with both his heels to get next to this old man with gall enough to ignore a proper general of Havenstahl's army. Once he was beside the bent, old fool, he gave him a light pat on his balding head and said, "I am Kantiim, general of Havenstahl's army by way of Druindahl. Who might you be?"

The old man looked up at him cockeyed and confused and asked in a tone far louder than necessary considering their close quarters, "What's that ye said there, lad?"

Kantiim gave up on formalities and hollered back, "Where on Ouloos is everyone?"

The old man scratched his head as he shook it and replied, "He was a young wizard in a blue cloak, the blue of Havenstahl. That bloke called lightning from the sky and the very water from out of the Great Sea. Then he said some words I ain't had a clue what they meant, and may the gods strike me blind if the very ground didn't open and swallow me hut into the very rock me grandfather's grandfather built it upon."

"Where will you go?" Kantiim asked.

"I be headed for Gorban's Sound," the old man replied plainly. "They ought be having a warm cot for me old bones and some fresh oats for me herd."

Kantiim shook his head at the old man and said, "I don't expect you'll find any such thing in Gorban's Sound. All the villages along the coast have been burned, buried, or drowned. Guide your herd to the castle. You'll find help and a warm bed to rest your weary bones there."

"That be three days of hard travel for a bloke half me age," the old man grimaced. "I ain't the time nor energy for nothing like that."

"You'll find nothing but death if you continue on this path," Kantiim frowned as he fished a satchel of dry meat and a water skin out of his horse sack. "This should keep you out of the Lake for five days. You should make it to the castle by then."

The old man begrudgingly took the gift and changed course toward the castle, but he didn't do it without a good bit of grumbling.

Kantiim called the caravan back to march and continued further south. The coast remained as beautiful as ever in between the scarred and broken towns. The sun was diving quickly into the horizon beyond the deep, blue waters of the Great Sea. The sky in its wake was a canvas of colors, fiery red fading to orange and painting the handful of light clouds lazing about pink along their edges.

The sky up the trail was less appealing. Heavy gray clouds, nearly black, threatened furious storms. They seemed to billow, rolling and swirling like smoke from a raging fire. Lightning arced from one to the next and then to the ground lighting them up seconds before thunder rumbled up the trail.

Kantiim had nearly grown hypnotized by the swirling mass of storm clouds before him when Spang's voice snapped him out of it. "What do you make of that?" the last living member of the Dragon's Flame asked.

"We appear to be riding into quite a storm," he replied plainly.

"It looks unnatural," Spang commented.

"Perhaps we have finally caught up to the old healer," Kantiim's voice carried the slightest hint of trepidation. "Perhaps we should be afraid."

Kantiim waved his arm to get the caravan moving more quickly down the trail. He would have led the horses ahead of the foot soldiers, but the ominous clouds suggested keeping the force together might be the wiser choice. The men, trogmortem, and giants jogged while the horses trotted.

It wasn't long before the grizzled, old soldier thought about halting his troops and ordering them to run the other way. Hagen stood among the chaos with his arms outstretched. He shouted odd incantations and pointed at monsters from across the Great Sea as those formidable and terrifying beasts fled as fast as they could in any direction. Some raced down the sandy hillside toward the frothing shore while others fled toward the mainland. None of them found any solace from the storm.

Three grongs ran as fast as they could up the trail toward Kantiim and his men. He drew his sword but quickly realized he wouldn't need it. None of them had their clubs in their hands, and all of them wore wide, terrified eyes. The small group was no more than twenty feet from he and Spang when the black clouds above flashed brilliantly before emitting a sizzling bolt of lightning that arced out and vaporized them to smoldering chunks of burnt flesh.

A trogmortem racing toward the trees found a similar fate. The top half of the beast exploded while his legs remained standing, burnt or melted to the ground. Kantiim called his caravan to halt as his eyes fixated on the charred legs. Bile crept up the back of his throat, but he stopped short of vomiting in front of his troops. It wasn't so much the burned flesh. He'd graced enough battlefields and witnessed enough death in his day that there wasn't much a corpse could offer to make him feel squeamish. It was more the fact that these victims had no chance to fight back. When men or grongs, trogmortem, or even giants wage war against each other, they have a fighting chance to survive. It's fair, or at least fairer than death that creeps and sneaks before lashing out in a split second leaving no time to defend.

"I never thought I'd see something more terrifying than Dragon's flame," Spang gasped.

"Somehow this seems worse," Kantiim agreed.

The horror lasted only minutes, but it seemed to drag on for an eternity. Terrifying, monstrous beasts cried out in fear and agony as they fled in panic. None were spared from Hagen's fury.

As soon as the last creature expired, the storm ceased. Black clouds receded to make way for the glorious sunset painting the western sky. Aside from the small huts bearing the scars of lightning and a few small fires burning, nothing looked amiss.

The young man in the blue cloak walking up the trail toward them looked like a memory of Hagen. The wide smile that young face wore seemed out of place to Kantiim. In all the battlefields he'd survived, joy wasn't something he ever recalled feeling even in victory. Relief, of course, pride, maybe, but never anything that resembled happiness. No man Kantiim had ever met enjoyed taking life. It was duty. The look on the face approaching on the trail seemed far too comfortable with all the life that had just been erased.

"Hagen, old friend," Kantiim hailed the wizard, "you have freed the villages from the monsters who took them from the good folks who occupied them."

"Indeed," true joy dripped from the wizard's tone. "All the terrors not safe on their ships or haunting the top of Elbahor have expired. I have sent them back to the Lake."

Kantiim scratched his head as he searched for the perfect words to express what he was feeling about what he had just witnessed. When those perfect words didn't come, he proceeded as gently as he could, "I thought I knew you very well. It seems I was mistaken about that. There is much about you I don't understand. I wish not to earn your ire, but I must know how the devastation you wrought is worthy of that smile you wear."

"Where are the people you freed?" Spang blurted. "Did you kill them too?"

If Hagen were at all offended by either of the slights, he didn't let on. His smile never faded as he replied first to Spang and then to Kantiim, "They should be safe within the mighty walls of Havenstahl. I sent them there with instructions to take word to Daritus about the fate of their former captors. As for my smile, I do not relish in violence or destruction. Please do not mistake my joy for something so crude as that. I had forgotten much about who I am. My sister reminded me that I am not this old, broken healer you had come to know. I am a man who knows much about this world, and I have the power to protect our people from the nightmares across the Great Sea. You will not find me haunting the halls of the castle until the threat has been turned away. Perhaps after witnessing the destruction that has you so troubled, they will choose to leave peacefully. That would bring me true joy."

Many conflicting thoughts swirled around Kantiim's mind just then competing to make it to his lips. None proved victorious before a great crack of thunder grabbed the attention of every soul on the trail. The sound had come from Biggon's Bay. Black clouds swirled above it, flashing with lightning. Kantiim looked back to Hagen whose face had grown graven at the sight of those ominous clouds.

"That is not my work," the wizard said quietly.

"Who else has the power to bring lightning from the sky?" Kantiim hissed.

"It is Kaldumahn, the great, silver lion who stalks across the skies. He battles with Cialia, but she is not there. He is crashing the ships in the bay. It's a distraction," the slightest hint of shock slipped into Hagen's tone.

"Should we help them?" Spang piped up.

"Why?" Hagen asked. "I know much about our world and how to manipulate the rules, but I am no god. Kaldumahn could destroy me with a thought, and I would be unable to defend our city and her people." Then he looked like he was listening to a voice no one else could here before adding, "Havenstahl needs us. The grizzly mongs have turned back toward our fair city and the men waiting to defend her are horribly outmatched."

"How can you know that?" Kantiim asked. "If what you say is true, we'll never make it in time."

Hagen didn't respond. Instead, he stepped off the trail, raised his arms out wide, and shouted, "NGIR DU!"

Pale blue static suddenly swirled before him. It merged against itself and expanded until a circle of pale, blue light sparkled and spun like a wheel. It continued to grow like that until it stretched at least forty feet in diameter, and then it quickly gained depth. From the outside, it appeared to be nothing more than a large, spinning circle. However, when Kantiim peered inside, it looked like a long tunnel to somewhere.

"Follow me," Hagen commanded and stepped inside.

CHAPTER 33
THE FRENZY

Earthquakes were infrequent in the lands around Havenstahl, but both Chagon and Tarantian had experienced them at one point or another in their lives. None were so violent as the tremors beneath their horses as they raced down the trail past Mount Elbahor. The sky was dark east of the mountain, but there was still enough light for Tarantian to see the massive boulder fly over their heads.

"Race to Galgooth, lad," Tarantian shouted to Chagon as he dug his heels into his horse's flanks.

Chagon did the same. They had been keeping their speed in check to allow the pack of grizzly mongs to stay close enough to remain on the hunt, but that mountain was coming down. If they ended up pulverized beneath tons of rock, there would be nothing left of them to hunt. Their horses' hooves dug into the trail. It seemed the animals sensed the danger as much as their riders.

Once they made it to bridge, Tarantian hollered, "Stop here."

Both men turned to watch the mountain crumble. Streaks of bright light shined from cracks all about it. The ground around them shook violently as massive boulders bounced down its sides. A colossal fireball exploded on its peak blazing at least a mile up into the dark sky above. Then the mountain collapsed in on itself.

"By the gods," Chagon gasped.

"You mean, by the Dragon," Tarantian corrected, unable to believe what his eyes were showing him.

The crumbling mountain and falling rock whipped the pack of

grizzly mongs barreling down the trail into even more of a frenzy. They climbed over each other to escape the catastrophe. Not all were successful as immense chunks of broken rock barreled down the crumbling peak and slammed into small groups of them here and there, splattering them into the dirt or toppling them into the trees.

"Hold until they get close," Tarantian commanded. "We need them to follow us over this bridge."

Then he motioned toward the opposite shore and gave his horse a slight kick to get him on the other side of the bridge. Chagon followed close behind. The two stopped on the other side and waited.

The pack growled, snarled, and snapped as they charged down the trail, racing toward the bridge. Tarantian held his fist up next to his face signifying to Chagon to hold his position. The pack was less than one hundred feet from the opposite shore of Galgooth when he finally dropped his hand and yelled, "Move."

The race was on.

The final gasps of a glorious sunset dimmed in the western sky as torches blazed from the southern gate of Havenstahl all the way down into the valley. Daritus paced back and forth before three thousand ragged faces formed up in in columns one hundred across and thirty deep. He knew it was not enough to stop the terror Duvel had described racing to challenge them, but it was all he had. Most of those tired faces had just witnessed the last sunset they ever would, and he would lead them to that end.

It occurred to him as he looked upon those thin, ragged faces that had seen more in a short few months than many soldiers witnessed in an entire lifetime of service that he hadn't seen his wife in at least as long. She was safe in Druindahl. That was something. Hopefully, defending Havenstahl from the coming storm wouldn't prove to be his final stand, and he could see her again. By the gods, if that day came, he might never let go.

The faces staring back at him looked scared. They needed something from him, their broken general. If Kantiim or Spang were there, neither would have let him leave the great hall. In their absence, he needed to lead these men. He needed to give them words to lift them out of the darkness, to make them believe they could be more than they really were. He needed to make them believe they could stand tall against monsters.

The correct words were elusive as he paced before them, but he couldn't just pace back and forth in silence. As the ideas came together, he began with a question, "What is that behind you, glowing like a faint ghost in the fading light?"

There were no answers from the weary men looking back at him with fear in their eyes, so he continued, "That is Havenstahl, the greatest city of men. This city is not my home. Many of you share that in common with me. We followed a man here, a man with a promise. This was no ordinary man, but the lad of the Lake, a man who could wield the incomparable power of Dragon's flame. There is no greater power on Ouloos, and this man wields it as if it were a sword or spear. He is not with us on this night as monsters from the snowy north threaten our gate. You, all of you standing before me, you are the champions of this city. Maelich is not here to protect Havenstahl from these beasts, and you must do it in his stead. Who will stand with me?"

The response was unexpected. It was weak. Normally, when he stood before a group of soldiers riling them up for battle, the reply would be a loud and emphatic, "Hoy." What he actually got from the beaten bunch before him was little more than a murmur. It was disappointing, but he finally found a message he could latch onto.

"Is today the day you die?" he shouted the question at them.

There was no response aside from a surprised look here and there among the crowd. This whipped the wily general up even further. "I am your general, and I asked you a question. Do not keep me waiting," he shouted. "Is today the day you die?"

"No," the reply wasn't quite as emphatic as he hoped, but it was a response, nonetheless.

"I do not plan to die today," he began pacing with more vigor. "I need to know the men at my back have the same intention. If you plan to die today, you can march right back into the safety of our castle. Do you plan to die today? Let me know now. I will order that bridge down, so you can find your way to safety."

The crowd remained silent.

"None of you plan to die today?" Daritus asked again.

"No," there was a bit more volume in the response.

"I need to know you truly believe that," he shouted back at them. "These should not be empty words. You must believe the words you say. When I battled Maomnosett Bok, I believed I could defeat him. I believed I could kill a giant. He was my greatest opponent, but he is dead. I am not. I am just a man like all of you. These monsters we will face are powerful. They are terrifying. They do not need weapons. They are weapons. They will growl and snarl and snap. You must do the same. You must be the nightmares on this battlefield. You must growl and snarl and snap. The people of Havenstahl are depending on you to be more than just men. Are you more than just men?"

"Hoy," now there was volume. The response echoed down into the valley.

"Yes," Daritus shouted. "You are more than just men. You are titans. This battlefield belongs to you. Any man or beast who dare challenge you for the land you stand upon will know the fury of Havenstahl. These are not men standing before me. These are monsters."

"Hoy," they shouted back at him.

The echo of their shout had not yet perished in the valley below when Tarantian and Chagon rounded the bend, their horses' hooves kicking up dirt as they pounded hard against the trail. This was the moment of truth. If they had done their job, thousands of monsters would be right on their tails.

It only took moments to prove their success. The two men were halfway up the hill toward the force they would fight beside when the beasts rounded the bend. Thousands of shaggy, white monsters tore into the trail on all fours with claws ripping up the dirt. Their howls were deafening and terrifying. There were so many of them. They outnumbered the men on the hill by at least two to one.

Daritus wrangled his own fear and stuffed it deep into his gut as he shouted to his men, "Hold. There is your glory down in that valley. We will descend on them like terror on a young child's dreams."

As soon as Tarantian and Chagon were within shouting distance of the group, they veered off, dismounted, and waited to form up with the force that would charge down the hill toward the beastly invaders. Daritus drew his sword, took a deep breath, and gave the command, "Charge!"

Kantiim would have had him hang back somewhere in the middle of the formation, but Daritus had no intention of following his men into battle. He was the leader on that battlefield, and he intended to lead.

It took everything he had to keep up a reasonable pace and not be trampled by the men who—despite not being nearly as charged as he'd hoped to get them—raced toward the coming storm with reckless abandon. His hip and left knee cracked as he ran, but the effort seemed to loosen them up. They had grown as stiff as his shoulder on that side haunting the great hall at Havenstahl. He just hoped they didn't seize up before the two forces clashed halfway down the hill.

The horde charging up toward him was a truly terrifying thing to behold. Thousands of fierce, amber eyes seemed to glow in the dim torchlight running the length of either side of hill. Shaggy, white fur flowed behind the horde, flapping like the worn bits of tattered flags. The fangs were the worst. They were long and sharp, perfect for tearing up the flesh of men.

Daritus had planned to call his men to halt and plant their shields, but their enemies gobbled up the distance between them far quicker than he expected. Instead, he buried the fear battering his senses deep into his gut and shouted with all his might, "Now is your time! Send these beasts back to the Lake!"

The closest grizzly mong was no more than twenty feet from Daritus when the thing leapt high into the air. Instead of slashing at the beast, he called out a command, "Behind me," and dove beneath the monster as it sailed above him. As soon as he made it back to his feet, he spun and slashed with his blade. His cut sunk deep into the monster's flank and dragged across its spine while three of his men's spears skewered it from the front. The beast had yet to hit the dirt when he spun and slashed again.

The world slowed around him as he slipped into the horde. Beasts leapt over, past, and around him. He slashed at them when they were close enough. He dove beneath shaggy arms slashing claws at him as his blade cut into legs and arms and bellies and throats. He cut and hacked and killed, but the beasts just kept coming in a never-ending stream of shaggy death.

Then his knee tightened up. He had tried to crouch low under a wild, clawed backhand, but the stiff joint disagreed. He ended up bowing deep at the waist with his left leg stiff and straight. The bow wasn't deep enough to avoid the attack. It was only a glancing blow, but it had been delivered with such force it caught the top of his head and tossed him through the air like an empty sack caught up in a furious gale. Twenty feet of trampled grass sailed by beneath his flailing body before he crashed through the door of a small shop and landed on a dusty, wooden floor in a pile of splinters.

The shop was empty but spun around him like he'd had a few too many ales just the same. Everything looked purple and hazy in the darkness. A few deep breaths helped keep everything in his belly from spewing violently past his lips. A few more deep breaths helped the room stop spinning. He couldn't lay there all night while his men battled monsters. He rolled onto his belly and tried his legs. The left one stubbornly refused to hold his weight. He hadn't noticed the pain until the moment his weight bore down on that leg, but once he did it jumped to the front of his awareness. The damned thing was broken.

He should have stayed out of the fight to begin with, but that was never an option. With a broken leg, he'd be completely useless. Giving up wasn't an option either. He scanned the room and found his sword a few feet from him. It took several moments and quite a bit of effort, but he crawled across the dusty floor and gripped it in his good hand. Once armed and as dangerous as he would be for the rest of the battle, he crawled toward the broken door.

The terrors he witnessed from within the empty shop challenged his resolve. A young boy who could not have seen more than fifteen summers and had no business on a battlefield crumbled beneath the heavy fist of a furious, white beast roaring before him. The poor lad's sword was at his side when the monster's massive fangs closed on his neck, and his head was gone. Bile lurched up the back of Daritus' throat when the monster pushed the headless body down onto the ground and chomped into its torso. Daritus didn't even know the poor soul's name. He vowed in that moment that he would learn every name of every soldier defending the castle if he survived the night.

"No," he cried out to no one as tears flowed freely down his cheek like rivulets of salty sorrow eroding the grime. None of the men or monsters on the field heard his heartfelt command, but he made it again nonetheless as he choked out another, "No."

Then his eyes settled on the brave, young farmer so willing to serve who he'd only just met. It took a moment to recall the young man's name, Chagon. It swam through his head as if he were repeating an incantation. That fresh, young soldier with his ridiculous mail stood tall among the monsters rampaging up the hill and tearing through Havenstahl's finest, or at least the finest Havenstahl had to offer just then. He watched Chagon guard his good chum, Tarantian's back as that titan tore through the attacking beasts with the kind of vengeance that can only be personal.

The farmer proved his mettle that day as long, razor sharp claws raced toward his mentor's face. Tarantian never saw the attack coming. Lucky for him, Chagon did. The stout soldier stepped toward those racing claws and slashed with his sword. His aim was true, and the beast's arm arced into the orange glow of torchlight. The quick movement was enough to dump the helmet off the man's head pulling his mail hood back with it. A moment later, half of Chagon's face was in the armless monster's mouth.

Sadness, rage, and helplessness hammered Daritus' psyche each with equal vigor. If he could lay hands on that beast, he wouldn't need a sword. He'd rip that monster's limbs and head from its dirty, shaggy torso. All the emotions competing in his mind paled in comparison to the look he saw on Tarantian's face. Daritus knew the two had become like brothers in their short time together, and the young man's death was more than the gritty soldier could stand.

Five of the snow beasts died, skewered on the raging titan's blade, before he was pounded to the unforgiving dirt by an exceptionally vicious beast. The man kept punching the thing in its massive head until too many chunks of him had been torn off and he'd lost too much blood.

Daritus wailed as he laid there helpless while his men died before him. They were good men, loyal, honest, and true. Many of them had never held a sword in battle, and even more of the ones who had didn't hail from the city they had given their lives to protect. Where were the gods? What good was the worship the men of Havenstahl bestowed upon those absent creatures when mindless beasts could tear through them unchecked? It was a massacre.

Then something changed. He felt the hair on his neck raise as his scalp became tingly. There was a smell in the air like a coming storm. It wasn't the smell of rain. It was something different. The world suddenly lit up beneath a spiderweb of lightning.

Daritus dragged himself further out of the hut and looked down the hill toward the valley. He smiled through the tears as salvation marched out of a massive, swirling tunnel of blue light. Hagen led a group of seasoned warriors ready to battle the monsters rampaging up the hill toward Havenstahl.

It was difficult to determine whether it was the relief storming up from the valley, or the pain finally sapping the rest of his strength, but Daritus was suddenly weary. The world before him grew dim and then dark.

CHAPTER 34
THE EDGE OF THE WORLD

It was mesmerizing. A black canvas stretched to eternity splashed with a phantasmagoria of disparate visions that coalesced as often as they contradicted each other. Colors that should never happen in proximity to one another smashed together in explosions of light that hurt Perrin's eyes while colors that complemented each other perfectly swirled in such twisted perfection nothing could bring her greater joy. It hurt to look at, yet it was more beautiful than anything she had ever seen.

She stood at the precipice. It was like a cliff but not quite that. The edge continually crumbled beneath her feet, but something constantly renewed it like a never-ending cycle of life and death, a sunset followed by an immediate sunrise and then again and again. It was too much, but she had never felt such elation than that which raised the corners of her mouth further than they'd stretched in longer than she could remember.

She flashed that wide smile at Dirk expecting to see the same. The look on his face failed to reflect the sheer joy she felt in that moment. His eyes were wide and his mouth agape like he stood before a greater horror than he'd ever witnessed. "What terror do you find among this beauty?" she asked.

Dirk's voice was faint, barely a whisper, as he replied, "There is not beauty here only stark and twisted horror."

She couldn't believe his words. Antopy had sent him because of his desire to learn. It was all there before them, thought, knowledge, creation. It was a constant cycle of death and rebirth. It was humbling and terrifying, but awe inspiring at the same time. "That is truth before you," she shouted, "like no truth you have ever known or could ever know again. That is the only reality."

If he had heard her words, his expression failed to register the fact. It seemed he watched helplessly as someone slowly and methodically killed his mother. There was no joy or love in his expression only fear and sadness. It made no sense to Perrin. Most of her life had been spent protected by strong men and solid walls. Nothing was ever uncertain. Everything was always known. The randomness stretching before her was the exact opposite of that. The ground could crumble beneath her feet and cast her into the unknown, or a giant fish could swim out of the starry space and swallow her whole. Anything could happen, and she had no control of it. She could imagine nothing more thrilling. Giving herself up to the chaos was like escaping the confines of a dungeon and racing into the vast blue of a cloudless sky.

An unconscious laugh gushed from her lips. A fast tear followed it. Dirk leapt out into the madness swirling before them. She reached out for him, but he was swept up in it so fast she couldn't reach him. He circled back toward her as he slowly floated away. It looked more like stark insanity haunting his countenance than fear as his body swirled into the colors around him. His mouth opened and a sound came out, but it didn't sound like Dirk. Then he was gone.

Sadness crept around the edges of Perrin's joy as she watched her friend blend into the chaos like a scarra sniffing around the wires of a pig's pen unable to break the barrier. He made a choice, and it broke him. She had accepted so much blame for the fate of others lately but not Dirk's. He wanted the journey. Perhaps it was his destiny. Regardless the reason, he would have made it whether she had needed him or not. He found the knowledge he wanted. She hoped he was swirled up in it and learning as she watched the madness unfold.

Antopy suddenly stood beside her as youthful, gorgeous, and annoying as ever. "He is gone," she said plainly and without emotion.

"You don't care?" Perrin asked not terribly concerned if the queen of chaos from a false Havenstahl did or didn't.

"Of course, I care," Antopy smiled. "I love Dirk as I love all creatures."

"Loved," Perrin corrected.

"No, dear, love," Antopy corrected her back. "Dirk is not dead. He is eternal. I believe that is what he wanted. His soul will never journey to the Lake, but he will forever belong to the beauty before you."

"I don't believe he saw the beauty I see before me. He looked terrified," she replied, an odd smile still lingering upon her face.

"Beauty is sometimes terrifying," Antopy shrugged. "The fact makes it no less beautiful."

Perrin finally turned her head to look at the queen or witch or whatever Antopy was. A bit of sadness tarnished the smile that had taken up residence on her face as she said, "He was supposed to lead me to my goal. All my men died. Helias said they would. She warned me. She was correct. They are all dead. Then Dirk led me to the edge of Ouloos, the end of the place where the maps don't go, and I am no closer to my goal. I may as well jump into the chaos as he did."

"You've seen much recently," Antopy's voice was like a song, "but you still cling to rules which no longer apply. It is natural. That is how you were raised. You will never find your goal until you free yourself from those bonds and see things a different way."

"That makes very little sense," she complained. "I have two eyes, and they see things as they are."

"Then I suppose your journey is done, and you will stand here staring at this magnificence until the Lake calls you home or you dive into the madness to be one with it for eternity," Antopy shrugged. "Your journey is your own. No one can tell you where to go or how to be. I will tell you this. Once you figure out how to see past the imaginary rules you bind yourself with, it will be your end. Good luck, sweet girl. I hope you find some joy before that end."

Perrin had more words for Antopy, but she vanished as quickly as she had arrived. As smart as that woman sounded, she made little sense. There was nothing where she stood, certainly not the tallest tower ever built, taller than any structure ever built by men if the stories were to be believed.

The land around her was a mystery. Everything else she had seen since journeying beyond the Lake had been anything but consistent. She thought about that for a moment. It wasn't entirely true. Nothing had been consistent except in the places where someone exerted control over the chaos. Antopy had done it to create her mock Havenstahl, and Dirk had done it on a smaller scale when he trained her to control her surroundings. Even Shacolin, that blind and crazy trogmortem, had managed to control his surroundings despite his disability. She latched onto the idea and focused her intention on the cracked landscape sprawling to either side of her.

She gazed out at the chaos before her and concentrated with all her might. Her intention slithered about the swirling madness like a snake slithering about tall grass. She expected resistance, but there was none. Instead, it felt as if the insanity were inviting her in. It was almost as if a silent, imaginary voice whispered, "Join us."

"No," she said loudly at the black expanse sparkled with dazzling colors before her. "I have no time to play among your beauty despite my desire. I am here for a reason. You stand in the way of my destiny."

The air to her left vibrated. That wasn't quite right. It didn't vibrate, but it moved. It was strange, almost like a mirage. It was like when heat rises from the ground in the distance and looks like a vast pool of water, but it wasn't in the distance. It was right next to her.

She focused on the vibrating air. She pummeled it with her desire and invaded it with her intention. In her mind she pounded on a heavy, wooden door. When that didn't work, she kicked it. When the damn thing held fast, she pounded into it with her shoulder. Of course, this was all in her mind, but it worked. A tower slowly materialized in the shimmering air. It looked like a dream or a ghost.

She focused on the apparition. As her intention grew in intensity, the massive, stone structure solidified. It was as tall as the stories said or taller. It stretched up into the blackness as far as she could crane her neck and see. Massive, black stones piled on top of massive black stones, oozing like oily flesh fresh from training. There was a door at its base. She walked up to it and went inside.

CHAPTER 35
AN ASSEMBLY OF GODS

Nothing changed from one moment to the next in the small cell Brerto shared with his brother. Kallum remained beside him occasionally pontificating on this or that or asking the types of useless questions that can only end in fruitless debate. Sometimes boredom would get the best of him, and he would start the debate. He assumed it was probably the same for Kallum. What a sad waste they had become, two glorious gods with the power of the cosmos at their fingertips reduced to broken prisoners in a dreary, gray cell.

The cell was bland, perfect to help fuel the boredom. It never changed. The wet, crumbling bricks suggested water should be leaking from somewhere, but there was none. There was nothing that might prove interesting enough to distract from the horrid sameness of each moment in the awful place. He knew Ijilv wanted it that way to punish them. As much as his brother claimed to love him and the rest of their kin, the cell surrounding him suggested a different story. They were useful to Ijilv but not loved.

The silence became too much. He looked over at his brother who slouched with his head down and shaggy hair dangling about his chest feigning sleep and asked, "Do you believe he will succeed?"

Kallum lifted his head and rolled his eyes pretending to be annoyed, but Brerto knew it was a ruse. After a bit of poor acting, Kallum finally answered the question with another, "What is his goal?"

"Fair question," Brerto thought a bit but failed to come up with anything that made much sense. "Ruling all of Ouloos seems unlikely.

He never seemed as interested in gaining power through the worship of the simple creatures inhabiting that place. I would not believe anything he has said to us up to now, but he must have some goal. I suppose we can begin with his immediate goal of capturing all his brothers within his own mind. Do you think he can do it?"

"I have no doubt," Kallum quickly replied.

"How can you be so certain?" the quick reply suggested zero room for question in his brother's head.

Kallum shrugged, "We are here. For all their posturing and bold proclamations trumpeting their great power and grandeur, they have always been beneath us. He was able to capture us. He will capture them."

He shook his head, catching the dingy scraggle of hair hanging from it in the periphery of his vision. As much as he wanted to comment on their conditions and the conditions in which they were being kept, he decided to save those complaints for a different, fruitless conversation. Instead, he replied, "You have always underestimated them. I have battled them both, and they are in every way our equals."

"None of you are my equal," Kallum scoffed.

"So you think," Brerto's amusement flashed across his face in a brief smile, "yet here you sit trapped in this cell with me. We are ghosts haunting our brother's mind while those two you deem beneath us are free to rule in our stead. It is a mistake I will not make again."

"No mistake you make will ever matter again," Kallum smiled back at him. "We are no longer of any import."

Then the air changed. A light current brought the slightest chill. It was nearly imperceptible. If not for the stark sameness of everything from one moment to the next, Brerto wouldn't have noticed it at all. And there was more. It carried a scent. It was the first smell he'd noticed since failing to defeat Cialia atop his mountain paradise. That beautiful illusion boasted the most glorious smells. This scent wasn't like those at all. It was more of an odor, dingy and ancient, primal and powerful. It smelled like a god.

Just as he latched onto that idea, the air on the opposite side of his brother began to shimmer like ripples of water reflecting light, flashing and fading as the ridges of small waves caught it briefly before falling down into valleys. Then it sparkled. It was small at first, a tiny speck of twinkling light swirling amid the shimmering air. Kallum seemed startled by it, but Brerto knew it could mean only one thing.

A moment later, Moshat sat with them in the cell on the other side of Kallum. His countenance was as dingy and gray as theirs, and his robe and hair equally shabby. True elation lifted the corners of Brerto's mouth. He had no great love for any of his brothers, but Moshat's sudden appearance was something to break the monotony.

"Welcome home, brother," Brerto boomed as much as he could with his gravelly voice that was such a mockery of its former glory.

"The girl defeated you," Kallum added with a delighted chuckle. "She burned you to ash. Didn't she?"

"Where am I?" Moshat asked, his head darting wildly around the room. "What is this place?"

Brerto laughed and glanced around the cell before replying, "This beautiful dungeon is your home now, presumably for all eternity."

"Impossible," Moshat spat.

"Go ahead. Try to leave," Kallum laughed.

Despite the effort reflected on Moshat's face, he failed to move anything but his arms. It was a joyous sight. Brerto could barely contain himself, "Moshat, the great and mighty bear who lumbers about the north woods. You have no power in this place."

"I will destroy you both," Moshat's gravelly voice almost sounded like a growl.

"You will sit here with us until our captor has succeeded or failed in whatever grand design he has for Ouloos," Brerto shook his head.

Ijilv suddenly stood above the three bickering brothers, glorious in his glowing white robe and shimmering hair. The sight sickened Brerto. He couldn't decide if it was a deep, festering hatred or longing envy, or if one was the result of the other. Whichever might be true, he would have vomited on the floor at his brother's feet if he could.

"The great hawk, mighty Ijilv, guardian of the eastern skies, you again grace us with your presence," the disgusted tone of Brerto's voice bore a stark contrast to his words.

"Glorious I am," Ijilv smiled fondly at him. "Our small group has grown by one. Welcome, brother. You have arrived at the perfect time. I wish Kaldumahn were here with us to witness my son's glory. Sadly, he will miss it, but you, you can gaze upon his grandeur in rapt adoration."

"You are a treacherous bastard," Moshat grunted.

"And you are a fool," Kallum chided.

"A fool to believe our brother sought true peace for Ouloos, yes I was," Moshat replied soberly.

"He fooled us all," Brerto added. "As much as I would like to belittle you for belief in him and revel in your failure, you share it in common with us."

Ijilv finally interrupted, "Moshat, true peace for Ouloos is what I seek. Sadly, none of you had the desire to know things you could have known. This world festered under your rule and would have rotted like overripe fruit on the vine. I will help you learn those things in time. However, in this moment, my brothers, truest loves of my heart, we have very little time. The mother of the destroyer has arrived. I invite you to join me and witness the death of innocence."

Brerto's eyes squinted as he wondered what his brother was up to while that brother waved his arm toward the crumbling, wet brick across from the small cell he shared with his brothers. The spot Ijilv had waved at began to ripple like water, slowly at first, gradually gaining speed as it became a swirling whirlpool of gray. It stretched inward as the brick seemed to vanish in favor of a circular room. Geillan lay hovering between four obelisks flashing rapidly with the brightest of light. One moment the room was blazed in glorious white, nearly absent of shadow, and the next bathed in blackness with no essence of light remaining. The two opposite conditions shifted so rapidly, they seemed to exist in concurrence with one another.

Perrin suddenly appeared. The youthful innocence her face once possessed had been destroyed. The face of the woman standing there beside the sleeping, young man looked aged. It wasn't that her skin had lost its youthful tautness, or the gleaming blue of her eyes had dimmed in the least, nor had her blonde locks lost any of their luster. Experience weighed heavy on her brow as she gazed down at a young man she couldn't have recognized. Brerto wondered what might be going through her mind as she stood there caressing a cheek that must have appeared so foreign to her. If only Ijilv would give him leave to venture into the young woman's consciousness. What terrible delights might he find there?

The flashing lights were troubling, but Perrin remained focused on the young man hovering before her. It seemed impossible that this could be her sweet Geillan. He should still be a baby. Yet, as she slowly caressed the young man's cheek, she knew it to be true. He looked like his father.

Was it possible so much time had passed since she left Druindahl? There was no way. This had to be some kind of magic or trickery. The world beyond the Lake was so dissimilar than her home. Could time work so differently? She chased the idea for a moment before stomping it out. She hadn't aged any differently in this place. Perhaps it was Kallum. They were his priests who had stolen her baby from her after all.

"Your husband scattered the great eagle to the wind. Kallum did not steal your baby from you. I claimed him as my own. He is my son," Ijilv's voice echoed about the room not seeming to originate from any one point.

"My blood flows through his veins, and I have come to claim him back," Perrin shouted at the ceiling.

"You were brave to come here," Ijilv replied. "The decision surprised me. Poor Perrin, always hiding behind your knight. Yet here you are having conquered the chaotic lands beyond the Lake. I will reward your bravery and let you speak with my son."

The four obelisks surrounding Geillan suddenly ceased their flashing and the young man's eyes opened. He had her eyes. It was too much. Joy and sadness and feelings she had no words to describe swirled together and poured forth in great torrents from her eyes as she laid her head down on her son's chest. "My sweet babe," she sobbed.

"Mother," Geillan said quietly. He even sounded like his father.

"Rise, my son," Ijilv commanded.

Perrin stepped back as Geillan stood and approached her. His smile was like sweet relief as he gazed down upon her. It made no sense, but he had grown into a strong young man. Overwhelmed, she threw her arms around his neck and wept into his chest, "My sweet boy, how is it a man stands before me where a baby should lie?"

"You were foolish to come here, mother," his tone was cold and emotionless. "Father said you would."

Perrin stepped back and held onto his arms, "Your father is here? Did he find you? Where is he?"

"I am Geillan's father, and he knows why you have come," Ijilv's voice boomed about the room.

"No," she cried as she pulled him close. "He is not your father. I don't know what thing owns that voice, but I know his words are false. He is a liar. Come home with me to Havenstahl. We will find your true father. I will take you to meet your true family. You have so many people who love you."

"Father also said you would bring a smile full of lies for me," Geillan remained aloof as he loosely embraced her. "I won't let you hurt him. We will hide from you no longer."

She felt his embrace grow stronger as heat began in her belly. It was little more than slight discomfort at first, but it quickly grew into an unbearable pain like something was trying to rip out of her gut. She cried out as she recalled the day the dead-eyed men came to take him from her. He had blazed in a ball of flames that had kissed her cheek ever so slightly. The fact occurred to her just as flames leapt forth from her body.

"Why?" she screamed.

He didn't say another word to her. She saw one tear trickle down his cheek as the pain radiating out from her belly to the rest of her body continued to mount. That pain paled in comparison to the torment in her heart just then. She knew the man holding her was truly her baby, Geillan, stolen from her by dead-eyed bastards, heralds of a god her husband had destroyed, but, somehow, he wasn't that. She didn't know this man burning her body up from within. Fresh tears would have flowed in torrents down her blackening cheeks if the blazing heat of the flames consuming her wasn't evaporating them as soon as they came. This moment that should have marked her ultimate joy, a happy ending to an unhappy quest, was instead the lowest point in her entire life.

The world went black when the heat had boiled her eyes sufficiently to melt them out of her head. The sadness, emptiness, and loss gripping her heart had only a few moments after which to torture her before she was gone.

"He killed his own blood," Brerto gasped. "When he realizes what you have done, he will destroy you."

Ijilv ignored the comment and commanded, "Sleep, my son." As the words left Ijilv's lips, the obelisks settled back into their pattern of flashing, and the room returned to the two contrasting conditions of total dark and total light. Once the boy was once again hovering fast asleep between the four obelisks, he turned back toward his brothers and continued, "One day there may come a reckoning, but this is not that day."

"This is a dangerous game you play with a beast you barely control," Kallum added.

"Everything is going exactly as I have planned," Ijilv assured them. "The time is coming. My son will embody all that is evil in this world. When Maelich and Cialia come together to destroy him, Ouloos will be reborn. You will all rule by my side when their work is done."

CHAPTER 36
SADNESS

The sky above was crimson, but not the red of a glorious sunset. It looked more like blood. Maelich sat on still water. It was nearly so dark he couldn't see it, but he knew it was there. There was no boat beneath him, but somehow his trousers managed to remain dry.

A light flickered in the distance. It seemed like torchlight the way it danced in the darkness, but it wasn't the orange of a smoldering brand. It was a pale green. As he watched it, mesmerized by the chaotic rhythm of its movement, he had a sudden urge to stand beside it. He began rowing.

He had traveled a good one hundred feet across the water before realizing a boat now supported his weight above the water. It hadn't been there a moment prior. He was certain of that. Nor had he gripped the two oars he felt in his hands, and yet, there they were churning in the water and propelling him toward his goal.

He suddenly stood in the mouth of a cave. He didn't recall completing his journey across the water or docking the boat, but he must have done those things. The green light was gone. Nothing flickered. There was no noticeable source of light, yet he could see the cavern sprawling before him as clearly as if there were torches lining both sides of it. The entire place looked dim gray. There were no colors or shadows to suggest any depth. It seemed impossible the cavern sprawling around him could have completely smooth walls, but his perspective allowed no contrary proof.

As he walked through the unremarkable, gray space, bits of color began flashing about his periphery. They were brief, barely within view, and then gone as quickly as they had come. The first must have been yellow. It happened so fast he couldn't be completely certain of the color, but it seemed like yellow. Then there was orange, followed by purple, little flashes of light exploding just out sight. Though he failed to catch a good look at any of them, they cast momentary shadows about the wall exposing the cave's features for the briefest of moments.

His eyes chased around the dim gray searching for the mysterious lights and hoping to catch them before they vanished. Then he finally did. It was blue, but it wasn't a flash. It was more like a streak that began up near the cave's ceiling and darted further into the cave. It appeared so instantly and moved with such velocity he couldn't be certain his mind's interpretation of the details he witnessed within the blue light could be trusted, but he saw something in there. It appeared to sparkle, like dust floated about it catching and bending the light. Even stranger than that, a tiny person seemed to emit the light. It seemed as if the light oozed off the tiny form.

Maelich quickened his pace, hoping to catch up with the miniscule thing who created the small streak of blue in the dim gray of the cave. It was a silly idea. The tiny creature had moved so quickly there was no chance he would ever catch it even if he had a horse.

As if the thought of a horse were some sort of cue, the black horse stepped out of the nonexistent shadows and said, "Hello, Maelich."

"Not again," he sighed. "At least you aren't hiding in a fake forest crying for help you don't really need. What do you want?"

"You complain regularly about the scenery when we meet, but I have no control of that. You know we meet in your mind. I have no mastery over the scenes you show me," she replied.

"And what about the scenes you show me?" his tone carried a bit more sharpness than he felt in that moment. His anger at the black horse had subsided. At this point, he was just tired of the game.

A golden streak distracted him. This one was as clear as the blue one had been. It zipped past his face close enough he could make out the features of the tiny creature generating the light. It looked like a man. The figure was so small the idea seemed impossible. It couldn't have been any bigger than Maelich's pinky, but it did look like a man smiling at him as it sailed by his face. The tiny man had hair and skin the same color as the light oozing from him.

"What was that?" he nearly shouted.

"What was what?" the black horse asked.

"I know you saw it," Maelich complained. "What are those tiny creatures dashing about this place oozing sparkles and light?"

The black horse smiled, "Of course I saw that. I have seen many things in the few moments we've been speaking. That is a very non-specific term. How could I have known which of the things I've recently seen you meant by that?"

"Your games frustrate me, horse. Do you know what those tiny creatures are?" his tone remained saturated with frustration.

"They are the gidim, but you would probably call them fairies," the black horse seemed disinterested in his frustration.

"Fairies aren't real," Maelich shrugged.

"What is real?" the horse asked.

"Things I can see and touch are real," he replied bluntly.

"Are Dragons real?" Maelich could see where she was going, and he didn't like it.

"Everyone knows about Dragons," he replied.

"And everyone knows about fairies," the horse shrugged. "You have fairy weed and fairies' tears. If they weren't real, how would anyone know of them or the enchantments their dust can bestow to common things?"

Maelich sighed long and deep. He was tired of the debate and couldn't come up with any argument without an obvious and easy rebuttal, so he didn't try. Instead, he asked, "What have you come to show me?"

As soon as the words left Maelich's lips, the cavern vanished. He was in a circular room. Despite torches blazing at equal intervals along the walls, the place was the same dim gray the cavern had been. The black horse was there with him. She stood on the other side of an ornate alter that sat before him. The still corpse of a young woman lay upon it.

It was like a punch in the gut as he gazed upon her. The tears came immediately. He knew her name was Perrin, but he didn't know why knowing she was dead hurt so bad. He searched the darkest depths and corners of his mind but found nothing resembling a recollection of who this Perrin might be to him.

"Why do you do this to me?" he sobbed as he fell to his knees before the altar.

"It is not my desire to cause you pain, Maelich, but you will need it soon," the black horse remained damnably aloof as she said nothing useful.

"I need to understand why I feel these things for this person I do not know. Who is she to me? Did I love her?" he suddenly felt very alone. It wasn't like the solitude of the trail. He was used to that. It was often a welcome companion. This was loneliness, like dark dread creeping around the edges of an abyss waiting to suck up any life or joy to be had. "This is the foulest of torture. You are a vile thing."

"If you were ready to know these things, Maelich, you would know them," she said as she vanished. Her voice remained for a moment and added, "When you are ready, you will."

Maelich slumped there crying against the side of the cold stone for several minutes searching in vain for the reason behind all the pain he felt. Though he couldn't understand why it hurt so bad, he thought it made sense to say good-bye. If the black horse were to be believed, someday he would know. If this Perrin were important enough to earn these feelings from him, he would regret missing an opportunity for closure.

He stood and gazed upon the soft curves of her face. If only he could speak to her. Maybe her voice would spark some memory or some reason for the pain. Then her eyes snapped open, soft blue but red from crying. There didn't appear to be any love for him hiding within them.

"I blame you, Maelich," she spoke. "You did this to us."

The altar vanished and he collapsed to the hard floor. The room seemed to disintegrate around him as darkness cozied up. He was alone again with a fresh batch of tears to soak his cheeks. He cried, "I'm sorry," over and over again without truly understanding what he should be sorry for until darkness saved him from his tears and the pain forcing them from his eyes.

CHAPTER 37

BURIED BENEATH THE BAY

Consciousness was no friend to Cialia. As she lay curled up within a cocoon of flame protecting her from the tons upon tons of rock above her. She wished her flame hadn't saved her from the same fate to which she doomed so many. All the souls were gone, food for Coeptus, the continual cycle, but pieces of them remained. She could hear their voices shouting at her from the darkest depths of her consciousness. The songs they sung were macabre reminders of her failure. The god was dead. In that she had succeeded, but the cost was more than she could bear.

She thought about the flame swirling around her. She hadn't called it. It must have sprung from her subconscious mind, some kind of instinct. She could call it back and allow the rock to crush her to goo. That would be justice she deserved.

Something else called out from deep in her mind. Ijilv had been there on the mountaintop as she battled with the great bear. It was a strange thing. She knew of all the gods, but, somehow, she hadn't planned to speak any judgement against him. It was as if he'd found a way to hide from her awareness. The thought was frightening. If he was hiding from her, he must have a reason.

As much as she wished she could succumb to the voices crying out at her for justice, there were immediate threats she couldn't ignore. More voices cried out from Biggon's Bay where the great silver lion whipped up the waters into a frothy brew. Many of those voices belonged to souls who had yet to make their final journey to the Lake.

She couldn't turn her back on them. The day would come when she would face her own judgement, but this wasn't that day. On this day, she had more to do.

She focused her intention on the bay. Her flesh grew lighter as she evaporated into the air. A moment later, she materialized high above the waters of Biggon's Bay. Black clouds swirled as the wind whipped cyclones of water high into the sky while lightning arced across the gray mass and down to ships tossing about in the high waves. The cause of all the chaos appeared absent, but she knew he was there hiding just outside of her sight.

She took a deep breath and allowed her mind to see more than what her eyes would show. The shapes were troubling, impossible geometry, the building blocks of reality no human mind should ever have to endure. Cialia had no choice. She had to face them, decode the order, and travers the chaos to find the god hiding among the madness. The sentence she would speak against him required a deep connection. Her cells needed to know his cells. Her flame would invade every bit of his consciousness and break it apart to drift in oblivion for all eternity.

There he was. He didn't appear as the great silver lion who stalks the sky, but in his anthropomorphic form. He looked like any other man save the impossible glow of his white robes and perfect, white hair flashing light no human eye could behold without dying or at least slipping quickly into madness. The sight made her stomach lurch, but she couldn't look away. Her mind twisted and swayed as if she stood at the stern of one of those ships being violently tossed about the crashing waves beneath her.

She slowly gained control of it. The contents of her gut no longer threatened to spill past her lips. Then he looked at her. Those eyes were more unsettling than anything else about his countenance. Those black, dead things were anything but that. They had depth. Eternity swirled there in a torrent of every imaginable color—and even more a human mind couldn't hope to comprehend—twisting at impossible velocity. She was suddenly dizzy.

A voice cried out to her from one of the ships. It wasn't a verbal plea she heard with her ears but a prayer to a god who could no longer answer it. It was a giant making the plea, begging for respite from what appeared to be a natural disaster battering his ship. That one voice pleading for someone to stop the terror was the strength she needed. She steeled her resolve against the god.

"Cialia," Kaldumahn's voice boomed like a song sung by millions of perfect voices in impossible harmony, "the greatest cities of men lie in ruin while you trouble yourself with useless endeavors, depriving them of the protection you have promised and the gods who would do the same in your stead. You have failed them."

The accusations burned her to her soul. It was mostly because she could not refute them. She had failed. The men and dwarves crushed beneath Elbahor were victims of her failure. The souls drowning in the bay beneath her were the same. The thought only strengthened her resolve further. "No more souls will find the Lake because of you," she proclaimed to the god.

The words had barely left her lips when the sky above her opened. It wasn't rain that dowsed her into the drink. It was like a flood cresting the top of a broken dam. The force of it was so strong she was deep beneath the waters of Biggon's Bay before her downward momentum ceased. Bodies floated around her. Their wide, lifeless eyes accused her from faces twisted in terror.

In her head, the faceless voices of those poor souls shouted allegations. The god who had caused their demise earned none of their ire. It was her. She was the cause for the fear and pain they had to endure in their last moments. As the lifeless eyes and voiceless shouts battered her, she drifted slowly down and down into the depths.

No. It would be easy to give up. It would be easy to open her mouth and breath water into her lungs. She could end the accusations. She could end the pain of knowing all those souls ceased their time in the physical because of her, and she could end the feelings of sorrow for those they left behind. All those things would cease for her if she let go, but it wouldn't end for those still clinging to the physical. Those poor souls still needed a champion.

Flames swirled about her feet as she raised her arms out to her sides. Wave after wave crashed down upon her as she raced toward the surface of the water. She pushed against it, her flame propelling her ever faster. Each lifeless face she passed added to the urgency of her mission.

Cialia was a ball of blazing fire by the time she broke the surface of the water and soared up into the air to hover before Kaldumahn. The fear that flashed across his face said more than any words his perfect lips might utter as she invaded his mind. She pressed into his consciousness and gripped every shred of his awareness with her intention.

"Foolish child," he shouted, the perfect clarity of his voice faltered slightly.

"You have failed this world," she allowed none of the emotion coursing through her to slip into her tone as she judged him. "Your sentence is oblivion."

Just as she was about to release her flame and utterly obliterate the god, Ijilv's presence distracted her. She hadn't noticed him directly. She was too focused on Kaldumahn. It was his awareness that alerted her to the other god's presence.

"Treacherous bastard," Kaldumahn shouted. She knew the sentiment wasn't directed at her. It was the other god hiding above the bay and watching the horrible destruction below like a macabre voyeur who earned the great, silver lion's ire. He lashed out with one more condemnation before Cialia scattered him to the wind. "Vile betrayer," he cried, and Cialia released her flame.

The god exploded in a cloud of flame and ash. Relief swept over her. It was a brief respite as Ijilv's presence over the bay gained all her attention. She reached her consciousness out to his in hopes of learning something about his desires, but she hadn't the strength for it. She could almost hear his laughter as he casually blocked her efforts. She fell back toward the water, spent. The sky was clearing as she focused her intention on the Lake, those peaceful waters far from the dramas of men, and she was gone.

Ijilv soared high above Biggon's Bay as the great hawk watching his dear brother battle Cialia. It was just a matter of time. Despite the torture she put herself through, he knew none of his brothers had the strength to match her might. She would destroy the great, silver lion as she had the fierce tiger and the mighty bear.

Then it happened. He felt Kaldumahn's fear as Cialia gripped him with her will. She was an unrelenting force for which his fair brother had no answer. He was almost disappointed in himself at the joy he felt in that moment. He truly didn't harbor any ill will toward any of his brothers, but there was something undeniably satisfying in feeling their terror as they fell from their thrones toppled by a power greater than any of them could imagine.

He abandoned his animal form and materialized behind his perfect brother. "She will destroy you," he whispered in Kaldumahn's ear.

He knew Kaldumahn was too intent on battling Cialia to have energy enough to turn and look at him, but his reply was delightful. "Treacherous bastard," his brother shouted exposing his wounded ego.

Ijilv chuckled at the heartfelt cry as he whispered again in Kaldumahn's ear, "We will be together soon, my brother."

"Vile betrayer," Kaldumahn cried out a moment before he exploded into burning ash.

Ijilv's mouth expanded as he sucked up all the shimmering bits of his brother floating above Biggon's Bay. "The god is with me. We are one," he said as he consumed the last of them.

CHAPTER 38
THE FORGOTTEN ONE

Maelich woke in darkness. He blinked several times to give his eyes a chance to adjust, but there was no light to be had. A quick feel around on the ground surrounding him assured him he sat upon wet, lumpy rock. He thought about the cave he'd been in during his last dream when the black horse came to show him that dead, young woman who affected him so. He had no recollection of finding or entering a cave in the waking world. The last thing he remembered was camping in the forest and eating the beast he'd slain.

Reality seemed a tricky thing just then. The two horses toyed with him at every turn. He turned the idea around in his head a few times thinking back over everything that had happened since the white horse first came to visit him in his dreams. How much of it had been real?

The black horse's question jumped to the front of his mind. What is real? Sitting there in darkness he hadn't sought or remembered finding made the question seem more relevant than anything else he might ask himself. What is real? Was he dreaming or awake? It suddenly occurred to him that the air was cool. That was something. The air never felt like anything in the dreams those horses invaded. Perhaps that was a clue. It wasn't terribly helpful in the darkness. He had no idea where he was or where he was going.

As he sat contemplating how he'd gotten to this place he didn't recall travelling to, a light suddenly glowed in the distance to his right. It was dim, but it was there, pure white light slightly illuminating the slick walls of what had to be a cave. He knocked on the stony wall. It was wet. He could see depth in it. He had to be awake.

As he breathed in through his nose, he realized the air was musty. That was another clue. He thought for a moment about the dreams he'd had, and it occurred to him that he didn't remember any smells during any of those dreams. He had to be awake. This had to be reality and not some dream.

A few quiet moments passed before he decided that regardless of whether he was dreaming or awake, he couldn't just stand there forever. There was a light shining in the distance. That had to be something. He would explore the cave whether it was real or a dream and find the source of that light.

The path he followed twisted and turned alongside a small brook flowing toward the source of the dim light. As he listened to the sound of water flowing quickly beside him, it occurred to him how thirsty he was. He reached for his waterskin, but it wasn't there. A quick pat down assured him none of his supplies were with him. He didn't recall leaving them anywhere, but all he had were his clothes and his sword. Neither of those would help him satisfy his thirst.

He knelt next to the brook and gave it a sniff. The water smelled fine. He wasn't sure what he hoped to learn by sniffing it. Perhaps he was looking for a sulfuric odor. It didn't have that. It didn't really have any smell stronger than the musty odor of the cave surrounding him. He decided to give it a chance.

The water was cool, almost icy as he cupped his hands and dipped them into the drink. He gave the handful another sniff before slurping it into his mouth. It didn't taste any different than any other water he'd ever drunk. He waited a moment as if his body would alert him immediately if he'd consumed some bad water. Nothing happened, so he drank some more. Once his thirst was satisfied, he continued down the trail.

The light continued to grow brighter as he walked along. Life became apparent on the cave's walls. At first it looked like moss, but as he traveled along it thickened. It seemed impossible as no natural light could reach the plants growing along the cave, but the mossy substance slowly transitioned into vines which slowly transitioned into flowery plants. There were even fruits growing there. Maelich grabbed an apple off a proper tree without giving it much thought. The meat was sweet. It tasted like any apple he'd ever tried despite the fact It grew in a place nothing should grow.

As he absently chomped on the apple, a fairy raced by his face. This one left a pale orange trail as it sailed by. "Are you a fairy?" he asked a breath before the thing could vanish again.

It stopped, hovering there before him like a small, sparkling, orange speck. The response seemed to originate from within his own head rather than from the shimmering, orange shape, "I am gidim," it said.

"Isn't that the same thing?" Maelich asked

"You might say that," the voice replied, again more to his head than his ears.

"Do you have a name?" he asked.

"Do you mean the word my kin use to address me?" the voice asked.

"Yes," Maelich replied with the slightest chuckle. "That's what a name is."

"I am unfamiliar with that word, but if a name is what you say it is then my name is Jinky. You can address me that way if you'd like. If not, it won't make any difference to me," the voice replied.

"Hello, Jinky. I am Maelich. Do you know why I'm here?" he asked.

"Why would I know anything about you?" Jinky asked.

"I suppose you wouldn't know anything about me, but you may know if there is a good reason for anyone to venture to this place," Maelich shrugged. "I am on a journey but unsure of my destination. If I know what might be remarkable about this place, I might be able to reason why I'm here."

"Raya resides here. She is remarkable," Jinky replied. "And you're wrong to think I don't know about you. I knew your grandmother."

A purple, sparkling light suddenly appeared next to the orange light he now knew as Jinky. This one also spoke to his mind, but this one had a feminine voice. It said, "Do not listen to this fool. He knows nothing. He especially did not know your grandmother."

"You're a liar, Jana," Jinky snapped.

"Jana," Maelich latched onto the name. "Are you an honest soul? Do you know why I'm here?"

"Jinky won't tell you this. He's a trickster, but I will tell you. You are here for the same reason anyone would come to this place. You seek the wisdom of Raya," Jana replied solemnly.

Maelich was a bit dubious about the reply, "I don't know Raya. Why would I seek her?"

"I'm not a liar nor am I a trickster," Jinky interrupted. "Your grandmother was Kalia of Brickley's Bend."

"And you tried to convince her you were a troll," Jana's tone dripped with irritation.

"So, you did know my grandmother?" Maelich asked. "No one has ever spoken her name to me. I never met her, and I know nothing of her. Kalia of Brickley's Bend, was she a good person?"

"That is a name you should not know yet," Jana said. "Focus on your goal, Maelich."

"See," Jinky piped in, "I'm not a liar or a trickster."

"Shut up, Jinky," Jana snapped. Then she turned her attention back to Maelich and said, "You should continue on your path and speak with Raya. She will give you the answers you require."

Both lights vanished simultaneously. "Wait," Maelich called out. "I have more questions. Tell me more about Kalia of Brickley's Bend."

It was too late. They were gone. Hopefully, this Raya they spoke of would have some answers for him. He had so many questions, like who were the Tahnka? The Shaiwah had such deep fear and hatred for this people, but nothing Maelich had seen on their campaign suggested a people to be hated or feared. All the people they encountered seemed like nothing more than simple villagers. Beyond that, the fairies—or gidim, or whatever they were—appeared to know things about his heritage that no one else had ever shared with him. He hoped Raya could tell him something about the mysterious woman who was his grandmother that fairies knew about, but he didn't.

The questions swirling in his mind distracted him sufficiently from his journey that he barely noticed how the impossible greenery deep in the cave became a proper forest. As the light increased, the vegetation increased. The deeper into supposed darkness he traveled the more life abounded. Had he been less distracted, the impossibility of it all probably would have engaged all his attention. As it was, he may have been walking in total darkness.

He'd been paying so little attention to his surroundings, there was no way to know how long he'd been walking, but eventually he came to a wide clearing. There was a pond surrounded by trees and shrubs and flowers. The colors were vastly more vibrant than any forest or garden he'd ever seen. Oranges and purples, reds and blues, and hues of everything from not quite brown to bright pink. Vines wrapped themselves around all of it. There was no spot where he could see the stone of the cave's floor, walls, or ceiling that he knew had to be there beneath all the life covering them.

A woman sat upon a stone bench on the opposite shore of the pond from Maelich. The dark waves of her hair cascaded around a face wise with years but protective of its youthful beauty. Before Maelich could ask if she was the Raya the fairies had spoken of, she addressed him, "Welcome, Maelich. You have journeyed a great distance for answers. I fear you are not ready for some of them, but I will share with you what I can." Her voice was sweet nectar.

"I do have questions," his voice sounded inelegant to his ears compared to hers. "Can you tell me about my grandmother? Do you know of Kalia of Brickley's Bend?"

Her soft smile was like a dream as she demurred, "That is not the question to which you need an answer right now. Where are your people? Where are the Shaiwah? That is the question you should be asking."

"Ymitoth leads the Shaiwah," Maelich shook his head. "They don't need me."

"Maybe they do not," she smiled, "but you need them. The white horse gave you a journey, and you accepted it. You must finish that mission. You would not recall, but you have left many things undone. You must finish this."

A bit of agitation slipped into his voice as he replied, "The people they slaughter pose no threat. It makes no sense. These are not a violent people who would steal land from anyone. They live on the edge of existence taking only what they need."

"Stories are not always as accurate as we would like, but stories are all we have," the woman replied.

The reply was dissatisfying. "Are you Raya?" he asked.

"That is the name by which I am known," her smile was as sweet as ripe fruit.

"Those fairies said you would have answers for me," he complained.

"The gidim are free spirits full of love who care very little for the concerns of other creatures. They can be helpful when it suits them, but things suit them very infrequently. It is unwise to trust what you refer to as fairies. I do have answers, but you must learn to ask the correct questions," the sweetness of her tone never faltered in the slightest as she continued to withhold anything that may resemble an answer to any question he asked.

Maelich was about to press deeper into a conversation which seemed more and more fruitless when the greenery to his left began rustling. Instinct saw his sword into his hand well before his conscious mind thought to defend himself.

"You will have no cause to use any weapon in this place," Raya's words danced upon the sweet notes of her voice. "Not yet anyhow."

The creature that slipped between the vines and shrubs looked like a white horse without blemish, but it had a horn in the center of its head that made no sense on a horse. "What is that creature?" he gasped.

"No creature which exists in your world," Raya replied. "Here, she, along with her sisters and brothers, are known as unicorns."

Another slipped from the greenery along the wall, and then another. The first was deep black, and the next a pale blue. Both had a similar horn in the middle of their heads. It took Maelich a few moments to process what he was seeing. As he marveled at the amazing creatures who had begun drinking from the pond, he finally continued, "Have I left my world?"

"Not exactly," Raya sung her response. "This place exists within your world, but apart from it at the same time. Many summers past, someone proclaimed something which made it impossible for any of the creatures in this place to exist there any longer. They found me here. All who come in peace are welcomed in this place."

This Raya was at least as befuddling as the two horses. Maybe he was dreaming.

"You are not dreaming, Maelich," it seemed as if she could read his mind.

"How do you know my thoughts?" he stammered.

"The same way anyone else who desired could," she shrugged. "None of this is important. You have much to do. Ask me the question you need to ask me."

"It is not the question I want to ask you, but it is apparent you will grant me an answer to no alternative queries," he sighed. "Where are the Shaiwah?"

Before Raya could answer, the shrubbery along the edge of the pond rustled again. The sound grabbed Maelich's attention in time to see Maulom stroll out of the same dark spot where the unicorns appeared. His close-cropped, white hair and impeccable, white suit were as spotless as ever as he answered, "They languish in a dungeon in Eengurra. Like I told you the last time we spoke. You have failed them, Maelich."

"I don't believe I can trust you," Maelich said to him. Then he turned back toward Raya and asked, "Does this man speak the truth?"

"As much as he is able," Raya smiled. "Your people are in a cage of sorts."

"You must go now, Maelich," Maulom's tone was forceful at first. Then something about his expression changed. Maelich couldn't tell if it was fear, confusion, or close kin to one of those, but something troubled the man. His tone cracked when he turned toward Raya and stammered, "No, it cannot be. You are… I remember you, but I didn't. How are you here?"

Raya's smile remained as friendly and welcoming as it had been as she turned to Maulom and said, "Of course, you did not. I willed it so. Your presence here is somewhat surprising, but your desire to control Maelich made it almost inevitable."

"You knew he was coming," Maulom's tone tightened. "You were always conniving."

"The two of you speak of me as if I am not here," Maelich complained.

"Forgive me, Maelich. Maulom will beg you to leave immediately to free your people. You should heed his request. Go now," she smiled at Maelich. Then she turned her focus back to Maulom and said, "And you will wish to crawl back to your lord and tell him you found me. Perhaps he will smile upon you and help you find purpose in your existence."

"That is precisely what I will do," Maulom snapped. "Ijilv must know you exist. He must know you have hidden yourself from him, from us all."

"You will never rule this place," she smiled as he slipped back into the trees, "not by his side, in his stead, or otherwise. You will forget you found this place."

"I need answers," Maelich raised his voice. "You know Maulom. You know me. You know of the gods. You know why I am here. Why am I here?"

"The answers you seek are with your people in Eengurra," She smiled back at him. "Go to them and remember what you have forgotten."

CHAPTER 39
THE BROTHERS UNITED

It wasn't air Kaldumahn sucked into his mouth when he woke, but he drew the deep, dramatic breath in just the same. Wet, gray, crumbling brick surrounded him. There was nothing binding his limbs, but he couldn't move. "What is this?" he shouted.

Brerto's voice was the first to reach his ears a moment after he glanced up at his hated brother, "The great, silver lion who stalks the skies, welcome, brother. You are a prisoner with all your kin save Ijilv, the great conductor who orchestrated this monstrosity."

"You give him too much credit," Kallum complained from further down the line of prisoners.

He stretched to see past Brerto. Kallum was next, and Moshat beyond him. It seemed Brerto spoke the truth. All his brothers except Ijilv sat against wet, crumbling brick that felt like nothing against his back. They all looked dingy and gray, pale and shabby reflections of the glorious things they had once been.

"Ijilv has done this to us?" his tone mellowed despite his rage.

"We were all foolish and prideful," Brerto commented.

"The lot of you, maybe," his voice raised. "My plan would have seen us avoid a confrontation with that beast disguised as a young girl."

"If you had such a plan, why are you here with us?" Kallum laughed at him.

"I suppose I was a fool too, but only for trusting in my brother," he leaned out far enough to toss a disparaging look in Moshat's direction. "It was his foolish bravado that led to our mutual demise."

"You would have hidden away for eternity like a coward," Moshat spat back at him.

"At least I would have only had the misery of dealing with you," he grumbled. "Now I have to suffer the mighty eagle and the great, white tiger."

"Pitying yourself won't change anything," Brerto's tone was nonchalant. "It took me a bit to overcome it. You will too, in time."

He had more he would have liked to say, but it wouldn't amount to anything. Grumbling about the situation he'd found himself in wouldn't change anything and debating any topic with any of his brothers only ever served to frustrate him. Any of them could agree completely with a statement, and they would still argue an opposite point just to be contrary. Though it seemed he had plenty of time for fruitless arguments, he lacked the energy for it just then.

He sat there for more than a few moments staring at the barless cell he occupied with his brothers. It didn't take long for the boredom of silence to get the best of him. "It makes no sense," he finally grunted.

"What makes no sense?" Kallum asked. "The fact you intervened when I had the lad of the Lake trained by our brother and prepared to kill the last Dragon so we could wield the greatest power this world has ever known?"

"The twins wield that power," Brerto replied flatly. "We could have controlled Maelich. I do not believe Cialia would ever have submitted to our control."

"Had she ever found her flame," Moshat piped in.

"You agree with them now?" Kaldumahn was flabbergasted. He and Moshat had opposed Kallum and Brerto for centuries, frustrating each other's efforts at every turn.

"I am simply stating the obvious," Moshat shrugged. "Had we not intervened in their plan, Maelich would have destroyed Helias…"

"And Ouloos would have been completely cut off from Coeptus. This world would have withered and died," Brerto of all people chimed in.

"And you agree with me now?" Kaldumahn remained completely shocked by the exchange.

"I have had time to reflect," Brerto quietly replied. "Ijilv has shared things with us. It is nothing much, really, but enough that I could glean a bit of his perspective. He is far wiser and more powerful than any of us ever gave him credit."

"You are nothing more than a scrod looking for the next feet to sniff around," Kallum snarled. "You knelt before me when you thought I was the strongest of us, and now you wish to kneel before him. That is why you never would have ruled this place."

"All creatures can benefit from honest reflection," he couldn't believe he found himself coming to Brerto's defense on any topic, but he agreed with his hated foe. "You should try it some time."

"Forget all of that," Moshat finally intervened. "None of what has been matters right now. We have all betrayed one another at one point or another, and we have all found the same fate."

"And the same foe," his brother was onto something there.

"Indeed," Brerto added.

Kallum sighed long and deep before shaking his head and saying, "I have been here longer than the rest of you. I cannot say how much longer, as time is impossible to gauge in this place. Nothing ever changes. In all that time, my mind has only been on overpowering our captor and escaping this place. It is not possible. We are beaten, all of us."

Kaldumahn thought about this for a moment. The singularity of Kallum's statement was interesting. Ijilv had used their individual desire to rule all of Ouloos against them. Each of them felt alone in their efforts. It was as if each of them believed that at some point in some time somewhere, they would rule all. Even though he worked together toward similar goals with Moshat, and Kallum worked together toward similar goals with Brerto, each of them had their own agenda. Each of them was alone within their own minds. "What if we worked together against him?" he finally asked.

"What if we work together against whom?" Ijilv suddenly loomed above them wearing a devious grin.

Kaldumahn sneered up at him and spat, "You are the vilest of things. Never has a greater evil existed, and never again will another thing so foul be born into this place."

The foul wretch just smiled wider at him as he nearly purred his response, "I trust our brothers have enlightened you on the current state of things?"

"They have," if only he could transform into his beastly form and rip out his brother's throat. The great hawk would be no match for him. He would rumble across the sky and devour the pathetic bird.

"Excellent," somehow the snaky smile he wore grew even wider as he continued, "then you must realize you no longer have any will of your own, correct? You still feel it, of course. I am sorry for that. That desire will trouble you to the end. I would have preferred not to inflict such severe torture on my beloved brothers. I only sought to rule over you. Alas, it was unavoidable."

"And what is the end?" Kallum interrupted. "You have defeated us all."

Ijilv shook his head, "You all see me as this deceitful thing, prideful and desirous of glory and power. I am not that. Though I shared my plan with no one, I never deceived any of you. Kallum, you feel I betrayed you because I aided Maelich in your destruction. That could only be a betrayal if I had pledged my fealty to you. I made no such promise. Furthermore, the act itself would suggest any of us were greater than the rest, and that is simply not so."

Kaldumahn had heard enough of his brother's lies. "You betrayed Moshat and I," he fumed. "You aided us in our campaign against Kallum, and then manipulated Maelich and Cialia away from their destinies."

"No," Ijilv shook his head at him. "You believed I had chosen a side when I helped Maelich defeat our brother over the Forgotten Forest. I did not do that for you. I did that for Ouloos. You must realize by now that killing the last Dragon would have destroyed us all."

"And that much I agree with," he snapped back, "but then you turned Cialia against us while you hid away from her wrath."

"No, Kaldumahn. I assumed you would do that on your own, and you did not disappoint me," Ijilv shook his head again. "The problem all of you have is your desire to rule, to be worshipped. It is necessary, but it taints all your actions. None of you managed it well. All of you sought more. I recognized long ago that your desires would destroy balance and prevent Ouloos from ever being born."

"You make little sense when you rant," Kaldumahn had grown tired of Ijilv's pontifications. It was bad enough to be trapped in the small cell with his brothers. Being reminded of his failure only made it worse.

Ijilv obviously didn't care whether or not Kaldumahn wanted to hear his words, as he just kept going, "None of you have the patience to watch things long enough to truly understand why they are what they are. All of you hate the land east of the Lake but understanding how the two halves balance each other is the key to all knowledge. You have never stood at either edge of the world and stared out into the magnificence sprawling before you. Had any of you done this, none of my actions would be surprising to you."

"Blah, blah, blah," Kallum scoffed. "You say a lot of nothing."

If the jab troubled Ijilv at all, he didn't show it as he continued unfettered, "All of you believe this is the end, but I assure you we have yet to reach even the beginning. Ouloos will be cleansed of evil through the power of Dragon's flame, and she will be reborn."

Ijilv was gone as quickly as he had arrived. That was fine with Kaldumahn. Though he had used a lot of words, he hadn't said much while he stood before them. Whatever his plan was, he obviously had no interest in sharing it. The rest of his brothers continued to argue and debate. It was all garbled gibberish. He had lost. They all had lost.

The sand was warm beneath Cialia when she materialized next to the Lake. She rested her cheek upon it and wept. Tears streamed freely down her face soaking her hair and the sand beneath her. Sadly, they didn't carry away any of the pain she felt with them as they went. She closed her eyes tighter and reached over to dip her finger in the water.

It didn't feel like water. It was more like energy, vibrations, the light humming of vitality passing through in both directions. The souls of those she failed to save on both the mountain and in the bay were still arriving. All their experiences from all their lifetimes swirling with them to carry back to Coeptus. They were going home. Why did the idea make her so sad?

"That is a good question you ask yourself," Helias spoke to her mind. "Do you have an answer?"

"I do not," Cialia replied with her voice rather than her mind. "Perhaps because it is my fault."

"Fault," even in Cialia's mind, Helias' voice sounded like a song. "That is an unworthy concept akin to blame."

"Yes," Cialia finally lifted her head to gaze across the Lake at the mightiest of Dragons as she shouted, "it is my fault, and I am to blame for all the suffering and pain those poor souls endured in their last moments. I am a horrible creature unworthy of this place. How can you allow me to haunt your home?"

"That is a question you should not need to ask, but your weary soul needs an answer. Like all creatures, this place is your home. Even if you were not one of us and one with us, it would still be your home. This place does not belong to us Dragons. We are merely guides to draw the souls who are ready to make their final journey home," her voice remained sweet in Cialia's mind as she crafted words she didn't want to hear just then.

"And if all the souls I damned weren't ready to make that journey?" Cialia fired back.

"Who decides when a soul is?" the Dragon's refusal to allow Cialia's self-loathing was frustrating.

Cialia's soul just wept. She didn't have any answers, and she had no desire to think about it just then. The only thing she had was her sadness about what she had done. That poured forth in fresh torrents from her eyes as she laid her head back down on the sand.

While she lay there sobbing, streams of memories danced through her head. They were not her own. Some were happy. She saw big, rough hands clapping before her as she sang in a man's voice while watching a young girl dancing and smiling in a dingy, old hut. There were others in the room singing with her and clapping in rhythm while the young girl tapped in a bright, yellow dress decorated with pink bows. It was the celebration of her birth. She didn't know how she knew it, but she did.

A moment later, the hut was gone. That same girl was lying naked next to a fire in a clearing. Her small form was covered in blood. Those rough hands that had been happily clapping trembled before her. They were covered in blood too. She suddenly felt shame, loss, and regret but had no memories to shape the emotions into anything tangible. It seemed she had killed the poor girl lying before her who had once been so happy and full of life. Then the right hand reached toward the ground and gripped a handle. She felt her fingers wrap around it, but she couldn't see what it was she held. A moment later, a blade still coated with fresh blood glinted briefly in the firelight. A moment after that, she felt it drag across her throat and blood was pumping down her bare chest. Then darkness.

"Do not linger long in those memories, Cialia," Helias' voice was in her head again. "They are not yours, but the pain you gain from them will remain."

Cialia finally pulled herself out of the sand and knelt there. Her tears further dampened the wet sand she pulled up with her on her cheek as she asked, "Are you not at all affected by these vile things?"

"It is not my lot to judge," the Dragon replied. "I am merely a guide."

"And you love these creatures who do these vile things?" shock dripped from Cialia's tone.

"I love all creatures, Cialia. Dragons do not judge. I cannot say it any plainer than that," the Dragon's tone remained as frustratingly sweet as ever.

"I don't think I could ever be that," she shook her head. "I cannot love that man who could do those things."

"What did he do?" Helias asked.

"I can't know that, but she was naked and covered in blood," she snapped back.

"Perhaps he killed his own daughter," Helias smiled.

"It seems likely," the Dragon's casual dismissal of something so horrible helped to displace her sorrow with a slowly boiling rage.

"Or perhaps, someone else killed his daughter, and the blood on his hands was that of her assailant. Perhaps the loss of his daughter was what drove him to take his own life rather than guilt at taking her life," the idea seemed ridiculous, but she couldn't deny the possibility. It was frustrating, but Helias continued to make sense, "Every action any individual takes is the result of so many things. Every word spoken to them impacts the thing they become. Everything they witness shapes who they are. One act does not define an individual, and no action makes them unworthy of love if that love is unconditional. If you cannot feel those things for the creatures of this place, then you will never be a Dragon."

"If that is what I must do, I expect I never will ever be a Dragon," she felt so defeated. She had completed her goal. She had destroyed the gods she sought to scatter to the wind. Crying there in the sand didn't feel like victory.

"Perhaps not," Helias agreed, "but that is not the question you must answer right now. Is the work finished?"

She wished it was, but it wasn't, "No, there is another."

"Ijilv," the Dragon confirmed.

"I am not certain how he managed it, but he hid himself from me. Now that I've noticed his presence, it seems he's been with me on my entire campaign. He was there in the illusion Brerto had concocted for me. He helped me. I feel he's been whispering in my ear since the beginning," the thought had just occurred to her. "The thing I cannot understand is, what is his goal? He seems less vile than the rest, but he must be conniving. It feels like he used me, but to what end I cannot know. It cannot be good. I feel I must stop him, but I fear what that will mean. How many more innocent souls will suffer for my justice? Am I the real villain in this story?"

"Most of those are questions you must answer for yourself, except the last one. There are no villains. Evil is something the gods concocted to control the creatures of this world. All beings are driven by instinct. Some are troubled by reason. Those have been used and twisted by the gods in a scheme to earn worship," even describing concepts that seemed so troubling to Cialia, the Dragon's voice remained sweet.

A simple answer suddenly occurred to her. She could just let go. She could release her flame and allow it to consume her. She could end her suffering and the suffering of any who may have fallen victim to her wrath in the future. With a simple thought, she could remove a great and terrible power from existence.

"That is no answer," Helias' voice remained sweet but had earned a hint of authority. "Regardless of your inability to fully accept the meaning of it, you are a Dragon. You are asking many questions of yourself right now. I have one. Why have you done what you have done?"

"To protect the creatures of Ouloos from the vile whims of violent gods," fresh tears poured down Cialia's face as she cried.

"I know, my dear," the Dragon's voice sounded like a smile. "If you see yourself fit to judge any creature, the gods, or yourself, you must consider intent. How can you damn yourself for their deaths if your intent was to protect them? You failed in that for some of them. Others may find happier times ahead because of your actions. I do not see that as a crime worthy of death."

The Dragon's words were reasonable enough. Cialia wasn't certain she could accept them, but they were enough to keep her from releasing her flame against herself. She had much to ponder. As weary as her body was after battling gods, her mind was wearier. Sleep was a dear friend saving her from the thoughts swirling in her mind as she lay back down on the warm sand.

CHAPTER 41
EENGURRA

The path Maelich had taken out of the cavern where he met Raya wasn't quite a cave or tunnel. It seemed like he walked through an opening in the vines and shrubs along the wall and entered a dark corridor, but it wasn't really that. It didn't feel like he was walking. It was as if he moved without any conscious effort of his own. His body felt lighter too. It was almost as if he floated on the air rather than walking upon it. It was all very strange and lasted until the darkness fled in favor of a bright, blue sky.

There was no noticeable opening which would suggest a cave or hall of any kind. It seemed he had stepped right out of the scenery. There were trees with wide, balmy leaves, grass, and shrubs, but there didn't appear to be any caves or mounds of any kind. A river flowed beside him. It cut a meandering path through lush vegetation all the way to something he couldn't quite explain. It looked like a city, but the architecture was like nothing he had ever seen. The place was still a bit far off, but the buildings appeared to be constructed of bricks vastly different than the bricks used to erect any structures in any other city in the known world.

He knelt beside the river and cupped his hand for a drink. The water was cool and tasted fresh, untainted. Without his water skin, he drank down as much as he could before continuing toward the odd city.

His belly grumbled. The days had all been melting together for him, but he couldn't remember the last time he'd eaten anything besides the apple he'd found growing in the odd cavern Raya occupied. Many of the trees around him appeared to bear fruit. He grabbed something orange off one of the trees and bit into it. The skin was rough and sour, but the meat inside was tasty. He peeled the rest of the rind off and tore into it. It was sweet and satisfying. He plucked three more from the tree and leaned against it as he devoured them.

As he tore into the sweet fruit, it occurred to him there were no people about. A warring people would have guards posted along every pathway into their city. There was no one around. The odd thought was far less interesting than the fruit he devoured.

A bit of heartburn forced a belch past his lips once he finished his meal and stood to continue along the river. Some meat would have been nice, but as was the case on many journeys, he only had what the land chose to provide.

As he neared the city, the details of the buildings became more apparent. A massive wall surrounded all of it, but the buildings within were so tall, they scraped the sky from inside the barrier. The colossal structures no longer appeared to be constructed of any form of brick. Instead, they looked to be made of massive stones piled on top of one another. Perhaps giants resided there. He knew of no men who could cut stones that large so perfectly much less maneuver them into place on top of one another.

A man fishing at the edge of the river distracted him from the grandeur of the city. The rod he was using looked like nothing Maelich had ever scene. The spindle was a shiny silver color and it glinted in the sun. The man himself wore light fabric on his top that almost looked like a dress above his bare legs. His feet were clad in odd sandals that didn't appear useful for anything but fiddling around just before turning in for the night.

"Hey there," Maelich hailed the man with his arms out to his sides to show he meant no harm.

"Hello there," the man replied with a wide smile. He showed no concern about a stranger approaching. That was odd. The rod jerked as the man added, "Ooh. It feels like I've got a big one here," and then began tugging on the odd rod and reeling the thing in.

"I mean you no harm," Maelich continued to approach with his arms spread wide.

Though the man struggled with whatever he had hooked, his smile remained wide as he looked over his shoulder and replied, "Don't know why you would."

"What is this place?" Maelich asked, confused by the man's casual demeaner.

"The river?" the man seemed equally confused by the question. "The river is the Zag. Or did you mean the city? That is Eengurra, the greatest city of men."

"I suppose both," the whole encounter had Maelich feeling a bit off-kilter. The thought saddened him slightly. He had always fancied himself a friendly enough fellow. The idea he had become one who expected a fight out of any stranger he encountered was depressing.

"Quick," the man shouted, his voice strained with effort, "grab that net. Give me a hand with this if you would."

Maelich sprung to action. He grabbed the net. It was strange. The fabric used to weave the net was green. It seemed too light compared to its obvious strength when he gave it a tug. The metal was strange as well. The thing looked thick and sturdy, but the metal was light. It almost seemed hollow. Nevertheless, he grabbed the tool and splashed it into the water just as the great, silver fish was breaking the surface.

The fish was massive. It had to weigh at least twenty pounds. It thrashed about wildly. "There is no way this net will hold it," Maelich shouted.

"No, we've got her," the fisherman shook his head as he helped Maelich guide the fish to the ground. "She's a beauty."

Maelich watched as the man pulled the hook out of the massive fish's mouth. It wasn't a normal hook. In fact, it wasn't a singular hook at all. It was many hooks contained within a bright orange thing with green spots that looked itself like a small fish. That wasn't even the strangest thing. The strangest thing was when the man tossed the fish back into the river after holding it up and admiring it for a few moments.

"Why on Ouloos would you do that?" Maelich gasped. "You could have survived for days on that fish."

The man scratched his head and offered Maelich an odd smile, "I have plenty of food. I fish for sport. My wife and children are off to their studies, and I had a few quiet moments to myself. I like the quiet moments."

"Sport?" Maelich asked.

"You take no time for leisure?" the man's tone was incredulous.

Maelich thought for a moment before responding, "I cannot remember when I had time for any such pursuits."

"That is a shame, friend. These are the moments we get to know ourselves," the man smiled wide as he extended his hand. "They call me Adapa. You could call me that too."

Maelich gripped the man's forearm and said, "They call me Maelich. I am happy to meet you, Adapa. I feel I could learn much from you, but I fear time is not a friend to me right now."

Adapa chuckled, "I think I understand. Do you worry for your people?"

"You know of the Shaiwah?" Maelich's tone betrayed his shock.

"That explains the weapon you wear," Adapa smiled as he held out his hand and asked, "May I?"

"Of course," Maelich drew his sword and held the handle out to the odd fisherman.

Adapa's smile widened as he took the sword from Maelich and dropped his fishing rod. He looked awkward as he struggled with the weight of the massive blade through some techniques that betrayed his inexperience with edged weapons. "It's so heavy," he gasped. "Have you killed men with this thing?"

Maelich smiled at the man, "You're not a soldier?"

"No," Adapa laughed. "We don't have those here. I'm a scientist, a biologist if you want to be specific about things. Specificity is typically important to me. It may be less so to you."

"I don't know what either of those things are," Maelich frowned. "Do you grow things or kill things?"

"Neither. I study them," the man smiled.

The idea seemed silly. "To what end?" Maelich asked.

Adapa smiled wider and shrugged, "Well, to better understand the world in which we live and our place in it." His smile faded as he added, "A soldier's life probably allows very little time for study or idle contemplation."

Maelich thought for a moment. Though the man didn't seem to intentionally mock him, he did feel a bit mocked. However, as he turned the ideas over in his head, it became increasingly difficult to find fault with the man. He finally replied, "You are correct. I spend very little time on idle pursuits. There is always a mission, some goal to complete. The only thing I've ever really studied is an opponent, and that study was only to learn how to most effectively kill them."

Adapa finally handed Maelich's blade back to him and said, "My life seems strange to you. That much is obvious. Your life seems very foreign to me as well. However, you come seeking your people. You will have no need for that elegant blade. No one will accost you within the walls of my city. They will defend, mind you. We have ample and effective security. That blade would be useless against them, but you will remain safe if you come in peace."

"You don't want to keep my weapon to make sure I am unable to use it against you?" Maelich's brows dipped toward his nose as he accepted his blade back from the fisherman.

The man shrugged as he stowed his fishing gear and said, "I am no match for you without that weapon. There is very little I could do to stop you if you wanted to hurt me."

The man made sense. His casual demeanor in the face of potential doom suggested there wasn't much to fear in his city. The idea piqued Maelich's interest more than anything since meeting the odd fisherman. He had never been to a place where men suited for fighting weren't always ready to trade blades with any potential threat. That fact even more than the incredible architecture had him eager to walk along the roads of this place.

"Come," Adapa said, "I will take you to meet my queen."

Then the man loaded his gear onto a platform. It looked to be constructed of some form of metal, but it floated above the ground. It resembled a chariot in its shape, but it was larger than any chariot Maelich had ever seen. On top of that, it wasn't connected to any horses. There didn't appear to be any way to connect it to anything.

"Where are the wheels?" he asked.

"Carriages haven't had wheels since long before I was born," the look on Adapa's face made it clear how odd he found the question. "Why would we need wheels?"

"To roll your cart across the ground," Maelich's tone was matter of fact.

A look of recognition spread across Adapa's face as he replied, "Forgive me. We get very few visitors from the far reaches of Ouloos. You are unfamiliar with our technology. It would take more time than we have to give you a reasonable explanation which would make sense to you, so I'll keep it short. There is an element installed in the bottom of my chariot that is repelled by an element installed beneath the road. That same element is attracted to an element within my city. Together, they allow my cart to hover above the ground and even propel toward or away from my city."

Maelich's jaw was slack as he said, "That sounds like magic."

"There is no such thing," Adapa offered a friendly smile. "What you call magic, we know as science."

"What is science?" this Adapa character grew more intriguing by the moment. Though he spoke with the common tongue, he used so many words Maelich had never heard he may as well have been speaking a different language.

Adapa looked thoughtful for a moment and then said, "No explanation I give you will probably make much sense, but it is basically gaining understanding of what things are and why they are through observation, study, and experimentation. All magic has a reason. Science helps us understand the reason."

Maelich simply shrugged. Adapa had been correct. That explanation wasn't terribly helpful, but it was probably as close as he would get to understanding the odd man or his occupation.

"Come," Adapa waved for Maelich to join him on the platform. "I will take you to meet my queen. She may have answers that make more sense to you. If not, she can at least reunite you with your people."

Maelich helped Adapa load his gear onto the odd, floating platform, and the two men mounted the thing. The floor was silver in color, like metal. It had short walls constructed of the same material. That was odd. The entire thing looked like a very simple horse carriage, but he had never seen one made from any metal before. No smith he knew had the skill or equipment to concoct something so massive. Any carriage he had ever seen was made of wood. Of course, there would be the random embellishment, a house's sigil or something of that sort molded out of prang or some other precious ore, but never anything functional.

As odd as it was to be standing on a floating platform made of some foreign metal, it seemed there were stranger things to behold. There was a black space at the front of the thing adorned with a series of knobs and levers. It didn't appear they were intended to open anything. The black space was flat and shiny, but it didn't look like it could be opened. When Adapa smiled and turned one of the knobs, the entire thing lit up in glowing colors in all kinds of different shapes.

"Is that science?" Maelich gasped.

"Kind of," Adapa laughed. "This is technology. Science allows us to know things which help develop our technology. You'll want to hold onto something."

Then Adapa pulled what appeared to be two levers connected with a handle, and the cart rushed forward down the road. Maelich stumbled to the back of the cart before he was able to grab a firm hold of the side. The sudden motion had his gut tumbling as if he were falling from a great height. They moved faster than any horse carriage he'd ever been on, but there were no bumps. The ride was incredibly smooth.

As the cart raced above the road, Maelich slowly became more comfortable with the speed at which they traveled. He was even able to loosen his grip a bit and focus on the magnificent structures stretching up toward the sky from behind the great walls surrounding this strange place Adapa called Eengurra. All the structures were glossy black, shining in the bright sunlight.

"I have never seen stones like that," Maelich commented.

"Those aren't stones," Adapa replied. "The stones beneath are granite. They are massive and weigh several tons each, but the black material coating them is to capture energy from the sun. I helped develop it."

Maelich had so many questions. Nothing Adapa said made any sense. He started with, "What are tons?"

"A ton is a unit of measurement describing a thing's weight," Adapa replied. Then he looked Maelich up and down and added, "One ton would weigh about as much as ten men your size. The blocks used to construct these buildings are thousands of tons each."

"Thousands of ten men my size? How do you maneuver stones that heavy? Not even a giant could do anything with that," Maelich suddenly wondered if the man was making it all up. Perhaps this was some kind of ruse and Adapa was leading him into a trap.

Adapa's reply suggested there wasn't anything amazing about the things he was saying as he continued, "They are cut with lasers," he paused for a moment and added, "You probably have no idea what a laser is. Imagine if you could take the energy of the sun and focus it into the edge of a blade. That is kind of what a laser is." He paused again as if waiting for a response. When Maelich didn't offer one, Adapa continued, "Once cut, we use sound to maneuver these massive stones into place."

"Sound?" Maelich's tone dripped with incredulity. "Sounds can't move things."

"These aren't the kinds of sounds you can hear, mind you. In fact, if you could hear them, they would rupture your ear drums," Adapa replied nonchalantly.

Maelich's expression must have spoken volumes, as the man quickly added, "The sounds you hear are made up of waves that cause a membrane inside your ear to vibrate, and your brain processes those vibrations to understand them. Your ears can only process a small fraction of them. These waves can be very powerful. We have developed technology to harness them and use them to make the work of building far easier for us."

Maelich was finding it increasingly difficult to process the things Adapa told him. He could scarcely come up with the words to ask any more questions. These ideas were so completely foreign. It did sound like magic, incredible and awe inspiring, but this quiet, simple man presented the information in such a casual way it seemed commonplace. None of it was commonplace to Maelich.

As they merged into a line of similar carts heading into the city through a massive opening in the wall that had no gate passing a similar line of carts flowing in the opposite direction, Maelich finally found something else to ask. "Where is the gate? An invading force could storm right into your city. If you have no army, they could march right to your castle and take this place with very little force."

"That is precisely what your people did," Adapa chuckled. "They marched right through these streets and on to the temple of the hidden god."

"How many of your people did they kill?" Maelich's tone grew somber as he silently damned himself for leaving them, "And how many of my people died? What about their leader?"

"No people died. There was no fight. The people of this great city fled as your people marched through the streets right up to the temple like I said, and they were immediately subdued by our security forces," Adapa shrugged.

"My people have become fierce fighters," the things Adapa said about the lack of any kind of battle made about as much sense as building with sound. "How were they subdued without injury or death?"

"Our security force uses compliance pikes. Once your people made it to the temple, two of our guards removed their desire to fight, except the old one. He called himself Ymitoth. The pikes didn't seem to work on him, but he sheathed his sword and complied without incident. He said he had no more reason to fight." He must have noticed the shock on Maelich's face as he added, "It's kind of like telepathy. The compliance pikes send a signal into a person's mind by focusing and channeling the thoughts of the person wielding the stick."

"I don't know what telepathy is, but it sounds like these sticks allow you to control a man's mind," Maelich shook his head as he turned the idea over. "Is that more science? Controlling a man's mind sounds like the evilest magic."

The man shrugged as he replied, "I suppose it does when you put it like that. However, the alternative is bloody and horrible. Would you rather have your people beaten to death with sticks rather than calmly subdued?"

He wasn't sure. It was heartening to know none of the Shaiwah died in a battle they obviously could not have won. They had become fierce and experienced fighters while decimating villages on their campaign to this place, but their crude weapons would have been no match for Adapa's technology, science, and all the other words he used. Still, a man should control his own destiny to whatever end he finds.

Maelich continued troubling over ideas he could scarcely comprehend as the cart zoomed past shops and people wandering in and out as if they had no place to go. They all wore the same kind of loose fitting, light gowns Adapa wore. No one carried any weapons, and all the faces who turned to look at the odd foreigner racing by seemed carefree and happy. He wondered if they were all being controlled by these wicked sounding weapons, these compliance sticks his companion had described.

The cart turned a sharp corner around a fountain with a statue of a woman holding her hands up above her head and pouring water down from them. Maelich only had a moment to admire the thing as the temple stretched up toward the sky before him. The main building was pyramidal in shape and the same black as all the buildings around it, but it stretched further up into the bright, blue sky than any of them. A long promenade stretched from the front of it all the way to the main building. Massive obelisks coated in the same black substance lined either side of the walk. Lining either side of the obelisks were flowered shrubs and trees. Maelich gasped as he looked on the place. An entire city could fit inside the massive thing.

Adapa brought the cart to a stop in front of the promenade, turned to Maelich, and said, "Come. I will take you to meet the queen."

It still seemed strange there were no guards about, especially considering the sheer number of people who walked about the long open-aired hall. Some of them admired the plant life, stopping to smell flowers on their seeming journeys to nowhere. Others admired etchings on the massive obelisks. None of them seemed they had any place they needed to be or anything they needed to do.

As he watched folks wasting time looking at things, the etchings they admired grabbed his attention. They were difficult to notice when not looking directly at them, and they seemed to move as his perspective changed while he walked by them. One was a bird in flight. It seemed to hover above the surface it was etched into, and the wings seemed to flap as he walked by. He paused when he noticed and stepped back. The wings flapped in the other direction.

Adapa must have noticed how intrigued he was by the work as he commented, "They call that living art. It isn't all that complicated. There are multiple layers of the substance coating those obelisks. On each layer, a different though similar image is etched. I realize that coating looks very opaque, but when the light hits it right, the images show through. The way they craft it, you see a different image depending on your angle to the thing. That's why it appears to move as you walk by."

"That seems very time consuming," Maelich grunted.

"It is," Adapa agreed. "This city boasts many artists who spend all their time crafting pretty things for folks to admire."

"How do you feed all these people who have time for such idle pursuits?" it suddenly occurred to Maelich he had seen no source of food aside from the stuff growing wild on the trees since entering the city. There were no animals or farms, nothing growing, and no one tending anything.

"We have farms and fields of livestock outside the city walls. Everyone in Eengurra has a role to play. Folks who work the farms tend the farms, and folks who manage the livestock manage and slaughter the livestock. Everyone has what they need, and no one has more than anyone else," Adapa's tone suggested the things he said should have been obvious to Maelich.

"That doesn't seem completely fair," he noted.

"It seems completely logical to me," Adapa shrugged. "Some folks teach, some folks study, some build, some bake, some craft amazing visions for others to admire, and those," he pointed up the stairway to two men carrying long, golden sticks with large, clear, crystals at their tips, "protect the temple."

"Two men to protect this entire place?" the idea was ridiculous.

The man chuckled at the thought, "No, we have men monitoring things all about the city. You will never see them unless there is a reason you must. Two men just like those met and subdued your Shaiwah almost immediately after they entered the city. Had they not been so bent on fighting everyone they would have been welcomed in with open arms as I have welcomed you."

Maelich tensed when they walked by the two guards who didn't appear to pay him and Adapa any attention as they strolled through a wide opening with no doors into a cavernous room full of art and sculptures. Despite all Adapa's assurances, a small part of him expected the two men to attack with their compliance sticks. He wondered how he could even fight them if they could control his thoughts.

His tensions melted quickly away as the sheer size and opulence of the room overcame him. They walked upon glossy, white stone with streaks of black and gray cutting random patterns across it. Pedestals lined either side of the path. Each boasted some magnificent statue, pot, vase, or some other thing that didn't appear useful for anything but admiring. One piece caught his attention. It was a giant vase that could have been crafted of prang etched with intricate patterns that covered every inch of it except for the places where red, green, blue, and clear jewels had been encrusted. The most interesting thing about it was the likeness of a woman. It didn't appear to be painted onto the vase, but it had color. It was a perfect likeness of Raya, and it looked alive. Though she didn't move, it seemed as if she were watching him.

"You know of Raya?" Maelich asked as he admired the image.

"That name is unfamiliar to me. The likeness you're admiring is the forgotten one. The artist who rendered that was inspired. No one has ever actually seen the god. We just know of her," Adapa's smile remained as genuine as it had been though his words seemed false.

"But I met her in a cave full of life," Maelich complained. "I can't explain how I found her, but her name is Raya. She told me of this place and not much else. She must be your forgotten one."

"Sounds like a fanciful dream," the man chuckled. "What you describe sounds very much like other descriptions I have heard of the forgotten one meeting people in their dreams."

"I entertain many visitors in my dreams of late, but this was no dream. This was real," Maelich shook his head.

"As you say," Adapa replied. He seemed unconvinced but offered no further argument. Instead, he gestured toward the front of the room where a woman stood before an altar, "May I present Queen Eana, the first, the last, the eternal."

The woman wore the same light, loose fitting robes everyone else wore. Her hair was luxurious, dark curls that seemed intentionally careless. Her deep brown eyes peered brightly from bronze cheeks gently kissed by the sun.

"Are you Tiakwah? Are your people the Tahnka?" Maelich asked before introducing himself or offering any kind of pleasantries.

The queen's voice was as lovely and delicate as her countenance, "I know of no one who goes by either of those names, not a person nor a people. I am Eana, as Adapa has told you. This city has been here since the beginning of time, and I have always been its queen."

"The Shaiwah, my people, believe this was the land of their people hundreds of summers past when they were one with these people and called themselves the Ohna. The Ohna were ruled by a brother who loved peace and a sister who loved power and knowledge above all else. She found a cave where some being—perhaps your forgotten one—gave her the strength to overcome the lands and build a massive city, displacing nature and wildlife. You must admit this place matches that description rather well," Maelich didn't bother to hide his disbelief in her words.

Eana appeared unmoved. "That is an interesting story," she spoke calmly, "but it is not my story. Nor is it the story of this great city. There is no cave or great power hiding away in the bowels of Ouloos. The forgotten one speaks to our minds through ideas. Everything around is given to us through inspiration from the forgotten one." Then she stroked her chin and asked, "Who told you this story that prompted you to lead a savage people far from their home with ideas of taking my city for their own?"

"An impossible man named Maulom who first came to me as a white horse in a dream," Maelich sighed unsure if Eana could be trusted any more than Maulom.

"I am unfamiliar with that person. Is he trustworthy?" she asked.

"I am uncertain of anything," Maelich sighed again. "Are you? I have been told so many things by so many people. I don't know what to believe anymore. Most times I can't tell if I'm awake or dreaming.

The only thing I am certain of as I stand before you is the Shaiwah believe this is their home. They believe they belong here."

"And they are welcome to stay with us, as are you. All are welcome here. This can be their home," she smiled. "Or you can lead them out of here unmolested."

"If they are free to go, why have you imprisoned them?" Maelich squinted.

"They keep trying to hurt people," her smile remained as sweet as it had been. "You must understand we all have roles to play here. Protecting my people is my most important. I could not allow your Shaiwah to kill innocent folk going about their daily tasks."

"And you protect your people by controlling people's minds?" Maelich snorted.

"Yes, I suppose that is one way to describe it. We have no weapons here. There is never any need for violence. Suggestions are made by guards, and the crystals on our compliance pikes amplify those suggestions to speak directly with the receiver's conscious mind. It does not hurt them, but it is unwise to affect too much change on an individual's mind. We would never want to cause harm. That is the only reason they have been caged," Maelich searched her tone for any malice as she said the words, but he found none.

Maelich suddenly felt very small standing there in the cavernous temple surrounded by the magnificence of the impossible place. Too many ideas competed for his attention to focus on one singular thought. If only Ymitoth were there with him. He was wise in his own way. Perhaps he'd have some guidance about what to do. The thought of the Shaiwah overtaking Eengurra was silly at best. What would they even do with all the space? It would be lost on them. However, in his brief time with them he gleaned enough about who they were to know they would never consider integrating into this society. The idea that these were the people who stole the homes of their ancestors was such an important part of their identity, they could never abandon it.

"May I have leave to go to them?" he finally asked.

"You are free to visit them as often as you'd like," she nodded. "Will you be staying with us then?"

"I would prefer to be imprisoned with my people," he shook his head. "I am unsure if I can convince them to stay with you or leave with me, but they are my people. Their fate is intertwined with mine."

"Of course," she gestured, and two guards were suddenly standing beside him. He had no idea where they came from, but if Adapa could be trusted they would have been watching the entire time. "My guards will take you."

Adapa bowed slightly to Maelich and said, "I will take my leave and bid you farewell, friend. I do hope you find this destiny for which you search. I fear it may not be what you think it is, but I hope you find it just the same."

CHAPTER 42
GIVING UP

Daritus woke in his own chamber to dim candlelight. The last thing he remembered was Hagen—or at least the young wizard who used to be that old healer—leading a furious fighting force of men into battle against the very beasts he had failed to stop with the meager force who had remained in Havenstahl to protect the city. He had no idea how he'd made it back to the comfort of his bed or for how long he had slumbered. He hoped Hagen and the men had been successful in finishing off the snow beasts.

"Thank Coeptus you remain among the living," Boringas' deep voice startled him. "Hagen promised as much, but you have been asleep for nearly two days."

Daritus turned his head toward his old friend. The lighting in the room was less than spectacular just then, but he barely recognized the shaggy thing sitting beside him. Boringas was a tidy perfectionist. The man next to him was dirty and disheveled. It took a moment to process his former pupil's presence in Havenstahl. Once the thought occurred to him, he sat straight up in his bed and asked, "What are you doing here?"

"I come bearing disheartening news," the volume of Boringas' voice slowly dropped as he spoke the words until it was barely a hoarse whisper.

"Is Leisha with you?" though he asked the question, he was certain he didn't want the answer. Boringas would never leave his post unless duty required.

"She is not," the man's soft voice cracked as a tear trickled down his cheek.

Warmth began in Daritus' chest and moved quickly to a spot behind his eyes. Boringas was a seasoned soldier. It would take much to bring him to tears, and tears as quiet as those he shed sitting there in the candlelight had to be a memory of a greater flood. He knew the answer but asked the question anyway, "How is my wife?"

"She has made her journey to the Lake," Daritus heard the reply, but he failed to process the message. Those words spoken in that particular order about his love sounded like a message spoken in a foreign tongue. Before he could stop any more questions to which he didn't want answers from pouring forth from his stupid lips, they came, "How?"

Boringas paused. His body shook as he cried into his hand.

"How?" Daritus shouted this time. His voice had grown phlegmy and rough from the tears.

"It is difficult to find the words or even believe what I must tell you about the fires," the road-weary, emotional man trailed off into heavy sobs.

Daritus immediately knew the answer. That one word, fire, was the only clue he required, but he needed to hear it spoken plainly. To believe something so vile, so heinous, he needed confirmation. He needed Boringas to tell him that his daughter's duty was what killed his wife. He cleared his throat and spit phlegm on the floor as his face hardened and he said, "Find the words. I know it will be difficult for you to speak them to me, but I need to hear them. You need to tell me how my wife died and my city burned while under your care and protection."

"It was the gods," Boringas wept. "They came to Leisha. I saw Kaldumahn. He was glorious and horrible. My guts twisted and wanted to spill out onto the floor. They wanted us to convince Cialia she was wrong to seek their destruction. Leisha told Kaldumahn she wouldn't be swayed, but the gods had spoken. They waited. They knew she'd come. We tried to convince her, but she wouldn't hear it. She spoke her judgement against Kaldumahn, but it was a trap. When she released her flame Druindahl burned. We saved as many as we could. Your wife," the wailing man paused, overwhelmed by his sobs. When he continued, his voice was barely audible, "She was so brave. It was the children. She tried to save the children. The gods fled, Cialia chased them, and Leisha burned in Cialia's flame."

Daritus had more things he wanted to say, but no more words would come. Cialia's justice had taken everything from him. The city he loved, his wife, and his heart along with them. There was nothing left for him. Havenstahl was not his home. He'd been fighting to protect the place for more than six summers, and all because one of Leisha's children was the king there. He had promised to love them like his own, and he did. Cialia, he raised as if she were his own daughter, and Maelich he accepted when the baby who had been stolen returned to his mother as a man and king and Dragon. And they destroyed her.

The heavy door to the room slowly creaked open with Hagen's smiling face following closely behind it. Daritus paid him only enough attention to once again marvel at how young the old healer had become. That would remain an unsolved puzzle for him. There was no room in his heart for anything but his pain just then, if he had any heart left. If there were something more than just an empty cavern beneath his breast, it certainly would never feel love again.

"I see you're feeling better," Hagen boomed as he swept into the room with his blue robe flowing about him. He had always been so bent in his old age, but now he moved like a dancer.

"I feel nothing," his tone was a bit louder than he intended, but it fit his mood just fine. "I am a broken man. Giants and beasts broke my body, and gods and Dragons broke my heart and my spirit. There is nothing left for me in this land or any other. Leave me to die."

"Pity, I wish I had known your wishes before stealing you from the Lake," Hagen offered a friendly smile. "Your heart will heal, old friend. You will carry this hurt for the rest of your days, but your sweet wife would want you to go on. You know this, and I know this. As for your broken body, I have remembered many things about healing I had forgotten, and you can forget the things I told you after your battle with Maomnosett Bok. I healed you while you slept. Go ahead, try that shoulder."

"I don't care," a fresh batch of tears and snot poured forth. "You should have let me die."

"It is a thing I could not do," the young wizard's smile faded. "Take the time your heart needs to heal. I know it doesn't feel like it now, but it will over time. Rest assured, once it has the rest of your body will be ready for whatever your next adventure might be."

Daritus gained control of his tears again and continued in more measured tones, "Forgive me, Hagen. I know you deserve no blame for my pain. I just need time."

"I understand," Hagen smiled. "Luckily, Boringas arrived with a massive force from all the greatest cities of men. They have finally made it. They were too late to assist us with the grizzly mongs, but they are already getting to the work of planning an offensive against whatever forces remain."

"That is more heartening news," Daritus conceded.

"I was not finished," Hagen frowned. "I have some less heartening news. Would you like to hear it?"

"No, but tell me anyhow," his voice was barely more than a mumble.

"The man who leads this massive force is named Ymarhon. His father was a cousin to Ymitoth's father. He has a legitimate claim to the throne of Havenstahl. He has united the great cities and intends to execute that claim," Hagen's tone had grown somber as he presented the news.

"Good for him," Daritus spat. "I have no use for this place. My home was destroyed while I've been defending this foul city. He can have it. That throne was never mine to begin with."

Hagen raised his eyebrows and said, "What about Maelich's claim? You won't seek to defend it?"

"Maelich who?" a sad laugh erupted from Daritus' mouth as he said the words. "He abandoned his throne when he abandoned his people for a corpse. I have no love for that man or any care about whose rump warms his throne."

"I feel the same way," Hagen concurred. "The throne is empty, and Ymarhon has a claim to it. I intend to recognize him as the king of Havenstahl. He has expressed an interest in you remaining to lead his armies."

Daritus' laugh was long and spiteful before it ceased and he said, "I will go home and mourn my wife with my people, whomever of them remain. I'm not sure what I'll do after that."

"Kantiim suggested as much," Hagen's reply was quick and curt. "It saddens me to see you go. Ymarhon boasts a massive force of fierce fighting men, but he is sorely lacking in good leadership. All who have served with you intend to follow where you lead, even our new foreign allies."

"I am no leader," his voice grew choppy again as his tears returned with renewed vigor.

"But you are," Boringas interrupted with more force in his voice. "The men and giants and trogmortem who helped you defend this city see you as such, and they will follow no other man. Lead them to the city you once loved…"

"The things I loved about that city are gone," Daritus snapped back.

"Dulled but not gone," Boringas argued as the cadence of his words increased in speed equal to the immediacy of their message. "Her memory remains. The people who mourn her still love her. She remains on their minds and in their hearts. They need her. You must lead them in her absence. You must guide them out of this horrible darkness back into the light. We will celebrate her memory every day and cry at her loss each night before we find sleep."

A dry chuckle snuck past his tears as he replied, "It sounds like you honestly believe that heartfelt declaration. If you search your soul, I think you know it's a lie. There is no light for us to seek. There is only darkness forevermore."

"Enough," Hagen boomed interrupting the teary debate. "You will mourn the loss of your precious wife. We all will. But you will lead these men back to her city and rebuild it as your faithful general has suggested. Druindahl must be rebuilt. Men have turned their eyes from the destruction of Dragons, but men have short memories and are easily swayed. If ever another threat rises against our glorious guides to Coeptus, the mighty riders of Druindahl must be there to defend."

Daritus mulled all the words his two companions had spoken. None of it mattered much to him in that moment, but a small, logical voice from somewhere deep in the darkest corners of his mind suggested they might after he had sufficient time to mourn. He had no plans to toss himself from the window and make his own journey to the Lake. He'd have to do something as long he remained in the land of the living.

"I will lead what remains of the force who failed to protect Havenstahl to my fallen city," he finally said. "I make no further promises beyond that."

"That is enough for this moment," a smile finally made it to Boringas' face. "Your presence alone will lift the spirits of our people. Despite the pain we all feel, they have already begun to rebuild."

"Tomorrow, you can meet with Ymarhon," Hagen interjected. "He will do his best to persuade you to remain. It is obvious he will not succeed in his quest, but you must grant him at least a brief audience."

"I will leave with the sun," Daritus' tone grew nonchalant as if the idea were an afterthought. "I owe him nothing, and I have given more than my fair share to this city. Your voice will carry my answer to his ears in my stead."

Hagen shrugged, "Ymarhon will be greatly displeased, but in honor of our friendship and the horrible pain you struggle with I will do this thing you ask. I only ask in return that you give honest consideration to the throne of Druindahl once you are home with your people."

"That I can promise," he looked the old healer in the eyes as he nodded his agreement.

CHAPTER 43
THE AWAKENING

The journey out of Eengurra had been as awe inspiring and uneventful as the journey in with Adapa had been. The two guards who accompanied Maelich through the streets remained silent and aloof as they walked along with him, one on either side. No one they passed seemed to care. They were all absorbed in whatever distraction had their attention.

Maelich finally looked at the guard to his left and asked, "What is your name, soldier? You are carrying out my sentence to rot in a cell with my people. I should at least know your name."

The guard didn't look at him as he replied, "My name is not important to your story. When you recall this moment, you will remember only that I was a guard who led you to a cell."

It was difficult to argue the logic of the guard's reply, but Maelich tried anyway. "How could you know that?" he asked. "I remember many events since way back when I was but a lad that seem as if they happened only moments ago."

"But how can you confirm the authenticity of these memories?" the guard to his right asked.

"Because I lived them," Maelich shrugged. The answer seemed obvious.

"Despite our advanced technology and seemingly deep understanding of human thought, the mind is a tricky and ever-changing thing," the first guard contended. "Each time you recall an event and even the most minor detail changes that new detail becomes your reality."

The second guard picked up where the first one left off, "Without anyone to corroborate or challenge your story it can change over time until it nearly becomes a different story altogether."

"Is that how those sticks you carry work?" he nodded toward the second guard's compliance pike. "Do you destroy men's minds by changing the details."

"It is much more complicated than that," the first guard responded, "but not far off the mark. It is more than just the details. Men's minds are far more complex than other beasts. These tools do affect the details one recalls about an encounter with us, but they also impact emotions. Things like desire are very powerful. If I can convince you the thing or outcome you want is not what you want, you no longer desire it."

"I can't believe you don't see the evil in what you describe," Maelich shook his head. "Taking away a man's will is monstrous. Would you do that to me if I drew my sword?"

"Of course, we would," the second guard picked the conversation back up. "If you desired to injure us for any reason that desire would not be greater than our desire to not be injured. You see violence as part of your duty as a soldier. You think it is heroic. We disagree. Therefore, we would use these tools—sticks as you call them—to gently nudge you toward a different idea."

"No matter how you say it, it still sounds evil to me," Maelich shook his head again.

"As intriguing as this debate has been, it must come to an end. We have arrived," the first guard pointed to a massive though unremarkable building.

On first glance, it appeared very little thought had gone into the architecture of the place. It was just a very large square in the middle of a clearing. However, upon closer inspection it was obvious the thought behind the design was granted to function. The roof of the thing was the same shiny black as every other structure in Eengurra, but the walls all appeared to be mirrors. The small brook Maelich and the two guards had walked along since leaving the city flowed right into the place through what appeared to be a large grate made of light rather than any kind of metal.

"Why does the water flow into the place?" Maelich turned to his left and asked the guard who had refused to share his name.

"To water the vegetation inside," the guard shrugged. "It's quite pleasant within. The trees and shrubs and flowers surrounding us continue inside the structure."

"I thought it was a prison," Maelich scoffed. "I expected a cage or a dark dungeon full of cells with thick, oily, metallic bars."

"Their incarceration isn't meant as a punishment," the other guard piped up.

"Indeed," the first guard continued. "They have committed no crime. We are only keeping your friends confined to ensure they are unable to hurt anyone. Like Queen Eana told you, your people are free to go. They simply refuse to leave."

"They intended to commit what you would perceive as crimes against your people," Maelich's eyebrows raised as his lips dipped into a frown. "The goal was to take your city. They would have killed as many people as necessary."

"They would have," the first guard replied, "but we convinced them otherwise."

The path split left from the brook, the latter flowing in through the odd gate of light while the former followed along the mirrored wall of the building and around its edge before abruptly ending at a nondescript point halfway along the building. When they reached that point, the two guards turned toward the wall, and the first one said to Maelich, "Here we are."

Before Maelich could complain that the only place they had arrived was a point in the vast mirrored wall that looked identical to any other point on it, the reflection faded in a rectangular shape the size of a door, and he could see inside the place. He could see some of the Shaiwah within. None looked like they were in distress, but the faces they wore appeared agitated.

Ding was among the Shaiwah milling about. It was difficult to recognize the brazen young man who had become such a fierce warrior under Ymitoth's tutelage. He was clean. His hair was no longer matted as it had been back in their cave, and the thick blue dye he had coated his fair skin with to protect it from the sun's furious rays had been washed away. Maelich recognized his eyes though. The fire in the young man's soul oozed from those piercing, light brown eyes. Something deep behind them looked unfinished.

Suddenly, the two guards pounded their pikes into the ground, and the crystals at their tips began to glow. At that same moment, the agitation residing on every face Maelich could see within fled. In a few short moments, all those faces appeared calm and satisfied. The rectangular glass within the mirrored wall seemed to vanish.

"Go inside," the first guard commanded.

He wanted to knock the pike right out of the guard's hand, but they would just crawl into his mind as they had the Shaiwah. It wasn't a battle he could win with force, and he lacked the tools necessary to combat the power of the compliance sticks both guards wielded. "I'll go without incident," he finally said, "but I don't like what you do to people with those."

"They are unharmed," the second guard answered. "We merely offer them suggestions."

The lack of choice was a frustrating point he wanted to make, but the effort would be fruitless. They didn't see things the way he did, and he hadn't the time nor inclination to convince them. Acceptance and compliance were all they knew. The idea was minutely attractive, but it wasn't something to which he thought he could ever submit. A man's mind should be his own, his ideas unfettered by outside control.

As soon as Maelich entered the massive structure, the door-like opening closed behind him. He looked back at the guards, but it was obvious they could no longer see him. By the time he turned back toward the people within, Ding stood before him with rage flashing in his eyes.

"Why you leave?" the question sounded more like an accusation.

Maelich thought for a moment. He wasn't certain he knew the answer, but Ding would never accept that. The young warrior was so certain about his destiny there was little room for question. "I had too many questions about our mission to properly lead you. These questions were so numerous and troubling I was becoming a hindrance to the mission. Ymitoth was better suited to lead you," he paused to glance about the vast enclosure and finally asked, "Where is Ymitoth?" but Ding was gone. All the Shaiwah were gone.

A familiar voice provided the answer, "It is time, Maelich. I am uncertain if you are ready, but you must wake."

He recognized the black horse's voice, but her presence there didn't make any sense. "How are you here? I could not have dreamt all of that, the city, the queen, Adapa. Is this real? Am I dreaming?"

"Your mind is struggling against itself right now," she stepped out from behind a tree. "Your reality is your reality. The answers you seek lie at the end of this path." She turned and walked back into the trees.

As he watched her walk away, he decided he wasn't dreaming. There was no fog, and the things he touched made sense. That wasn't the case when the black horse invaded his dreams. Nothing felt real in any of their encounters. How she managed to manifest in the real world was a puzzle. He decided to follow.

The vegetation was thick along the path. The idea the building served as a prison seemed even sillier. It was a paradise. Food grew in abundance all about the place. There were animals everywhere. Birds flew among the highest branches, and small critters scurried about the dirt below. The air was comfortable and fragrant. Perhaps that was the trick. Make a prison a person will never want to leave.

The path ended at a clearing. The black horse stood next to a stone altar that resembled the ones she showed him in his dreams. Ymitoth laid upon the thing. "What are you up to, horse?" Maelich asked.

"I have no tricks," she replied. "I wish only to guide you to truth."

"And what truth is that?" he asked as annoyed as ever at her insistence that the games she played with him were anything less than tricks. "What do you suggest by showing me my father sleeping upon a stone slab?"

"This is not a dream, Maelich, and that is Ymitoth lying there," her voice cracked slightly as she replied. If she were playing games with him, it was a magnificent ruse. She even lost a tear as she spoke. "Come, see for yourself," she finally added.

Maelich approached the altar. Ymitoth looked to be sleeping, but his body lacked any movement to suggest he might be breathing. "Father?" Maelich quietly asked.

Ymitoth's eyes snapped open. They looked as black and dead as always. Maelich had grown so accustomed to their eerie appearance that he no longer found them startling to behold. He stared into the black things waiting for some words from his father or at least some sparkle of recognition, but there was none. "Say something," he finally said.

No words came, and Ymitoth's expression remained frozen.

Then Maelich saw something deep in the black, dead orbs staring lifelessly at him from his father's face. It was a quick flash, but he saw it. It was a small shape lying in his father's bed. It was a memory he knew, something forgotten. That idea stumbled around his consciousness. He didn't want to chase it around his mind, but he couldn't help it. It was there. He had to follow.

"Is this really my father?" his voice sounded strange to his ears as the question flopped from his mouth.

"You remember," the black horse said.

She was right. He didn't want it to be true, but it was. He did remember. His father was dead. The lifeless thing lying on the slab before him wasn't the man who raised him and taught him to be a man. It was just a lump of dead flesh he'd been controlling since that horrible day when Kallum's priests had taken him away. It all came back like a flood filling his head until it might burst and spray forth like a fountain.

Hagen had been there that day. The old healer did his best to soften the blow, but no one could have done anything to ease it. Ymitoth had been Maelich's only family through his childhood. He had no idea about his mother or his sister until he'd reached adulthood. Though he shared no blood with the man, they shared a bond nothing could break not even death.

He fell across his father's lifeless body and wailed. As he sobbed into the dead chest, he felt the body beneath him shrinking. He raised his head back up and looked again at his father's eyes. They no longer looked black and dead. They were gray and cloudy like any other corpse. The thing stiffened as he watched months of natural decay take the place of the healthy flesh he had used his power to reanimate.

He fell to the ground on his backside, dropped his head into his hands, and cried even harder. He felt dirty as he sobbed into his wet palms contemplating the thing he had done. His father had been such a righteous and honest man, and he turned him into a mindless beast just like Kallum's priests. "I don't deserve the power I have," he cried.

"Do not focus on the things you have done. They cannot be undone. Right now, you need to let yourself mourn," the black horse quietly replied.

It felt as if a dam had broken as more memories flooded in. Bindaar and Doentaat, those dwarves she had showed him who sparked recognition he couldn't explain danced through his mind skipping and clicking their heels as they splashed ale from tin pints. He remembered them. He remembered the first time they'd met when Bindaar was the faintest breath from death strapped to the Sacred Pine, and Doentaat was blaming himself for his best chum's fate. That was the same day he killed Maomnosett Ahm, and freed Alhouim from that cruel giant's rule. They saw him as a hero after that day and celebrated him every summer on the anniversary of the event. He felt he deserved their gratitude back then. He didn't feel like the person he'd become deserved anyone's gratitude anymore.

He chased deeper into the memory of those two dwarves until he'd grown beyond it. He stretched his awareness beyond the limits of his own mind and into Coeptus, that unknowable thing all can access but none can truly understand. He saw Doentaat die quietly in the forest surrounded by his kin. His body was battered from battles and his leg was off. Then he saw Bindaar crushed into the ground beneath a giant's massive fist. The axe the poor dwarf held before him to defend against the blow slammed through his body and into the dirt beneath him. They both died because of a battle that never should have occurred. He could have ended it before it had even begun if not lost within his own fantasy.

His mother's smile chased the horrid memories away but heralded even worse memories to come. The woman whose name he knew but didn't understand why, Leisha, was his mother. He remembered the first time they'd met, that moment when the lies he'd been told throughout his entire life lay bare before him in the glowing countenance of a beautiful queen. The homesick feeling that twisted his gut and weakened his knees in that moment returned as he sat beside the stone altar holding the decaying body of the man who had first told him that lie. Was anything real?

His mother was truly there, that much was obvious. All the faces the black horse had shown him were reflections of people he loved but couldn't recall. As much as his heart feared knowing any more about her demise, he couldn't help himself. He had to know. He pressed deeper into the memory, again stretching beyond it. Cialia had been there standing before gods and accusing them of things she saw as crimes. It was her flame that killed their mother. The strong, beautiful woman he had so little time to know and love had been burned to ash by his sister's twisted idea of justice.

That perfect soul—at least in his heart and his mind she was that— died as she lived, giving everything she had in protection of her people. He watched her race across burning walkways among flaming branches herding children to safety. She couldn't save them all, but she saved some. They would be her legacy, all that remained of a lifetime of service to others. He heard her cry out as the smoke and flame overcame her. Even as she drew her last breath, she tried to protect the children shielding them from the flame until she was nothing but ash floating on the currents high in the canopy of the Forgotten Forest.

It was too much. Had he the courage he might plunge his dagger into his own heart to end the suffering. The idea did little to ease his pain, but it did stay his hand. He deserved this pain. Had he been in Havenstahl when the beasts came calling, he could have ended them with a thought. Instead, he spent his time reliving days gone by with a shell who used to be the man he loved and respected above all else.

As he mulled the idea of the sentence he deserved, Perrin's face jumped into the forefront of his mind. He'd only seen twelve summers when they had met, and she was just into her fifth. Amatilazo had taken everyone who loved or cared for her away, and she had nothing left. He saw her as a sister then. When he returned from his training, he learned she didn't see him in the same way. The love they had found had been so pure, honest, and true. They should have lived out their days in happiness, loving each other and their baby who he'd never got to meet. That was his fault too.

Geillan, the name jumped into his awareness. His son had been born while he was away. He suddenly felt sorry for himself. Snot blasted from his nostrils as a fresh batch of tears poured forth from his eyes and he shouted, "You don't deserve anyone's sorrow, not even your own."

The brief moment of pity he felt for himself made him feel dirty, small, and weak. He was a pathetic excuse of a man leaving everyone he cared for alone. He watched his wife's adventure play out in his mind as the dead-eyed men took everything from her, and she embarked on a journey that would end in her death at the hands of their child. None of it should have happened.

The black horse's voice cracked as she quietly said, "You are finally awake, Maelich. My work here is done."

He damned himself until sleep finally came to overpower him and save him from the horrible things he had done and left undone.

The End

ABOUT THE AUTHOR

E. Michael Mettille is the author of Kill the Dragon (Lake of Dragons Book 1), Kallum's Fury (Lake of Dragons Book 2), Kill the Gods (Lake of Dragons Book 3), and Hell and the Hunger (as Mike Reynolds). He has also written numerous short stories and poems. Mike has spent the last twenty years in direct marketing, print, and communication. He is fascinated by history, belief systems, the human condition and how all of those things work together to define who we are as a people. The world is a wonder and, based on the history of us, it is a wonder we have a world left to wonder about. Mike lives in Milwaukee, WI with his wife, Shelia, and their two dogs, Ziggy Stardust and Lady Stardust.